Escape . . .

Sometimes a boy's  his bicycle.

For most people, rain is an inconvenient common-place. For Rafe and Snowy, it is the center of existence.

Nothing changed after First Contact. Nothing, that is, except art.

Imagine . . .

The life of a brigand is reshaped by Crusader hands.

The Bwotik offered us peace, but it was a peace with no assurances, no commerce, a peace that protected their secrets. In other words, a peace we couldn't accept.

The creature lying in the field was dark, deadly and the only treasure they'd ever possessed.

Suppose . . .

A sword and its wielder break the most honorable of traditions.

Virtual reality had created a generation who knew no murder, no violent crime, no human contact. Or had it?

No chains could hold the King of the Escapologists—not even the shackles of death.

Dream . . .

A dog and his boy walk the long road to high orbit, to get back to the Gardens.

How far would Annie go to create the perfect love?

Wonder . . .

A nation had gone from rags to riches practically overnight, but its newfound wealth has pitted culture against culture and a man against his past.

Sometimes, even gods can't just walk away.

When you live at the edge of a flat world, it's hard not to wonder what's on the beneath side.

What has been said about the
L. RON HUBBARD
PRESENTS
WRITERS OF THE FUTURE
ANTHOLOGIES

"This has become a major tributary to the new blood in fantastic fiction."

GREGORY BENFORD

"From cutting-edge high tech to evocative fantasy, this book's got it all—it's lots of fun and I love the chance to see what tomorrow's stars are doing today."

TIM POWERS

"I recommend the Writers of the Future Contest at every writers' workshop I participate in."

FREDERIK POHL

". . . an exceedingly solid collection, including SF, fantasy and horror . . ."

CHICAGO SUN TIMES

"A first-rate collection of stories and illustrations."

BOOKLIST

"L. Ron Hubbard's Writers of the Future Contest and the *Writers of the Future* anthology represent not only the premiere showcase for beginning writers in the field of speculative fiction, but also a wonderful teaching tool for aspiring authors."

JOHN L. FLYNN, PH. D.
PROFESSOR OF ENGLISH & MODERN LANGUAGES
TOWSON UNIVERSITY, MARYLAND

"The untapped talents of new writers continue to astonish me and every *Writers of the Future* volume provides a wellspring of the greatest energy put forth by the ambitious writers of tomorrow."

KEVIN J. ANDERSON

"This contest has changed the face of science fiction."

DEAN WESLEY SMITH
EDITOR OF *STRANGE NEW WORLDS*

"Some of the best SF of the future comes from Writers of the Future and you can find it in this book."

DAVID HARTWELL

"Not only is the writing excellent . . . it is also extremely varied. There's a lot of hot new talent in it."

LOCUS MAGAZINE

"As always, this is the premiere volume in the field to showcase new writers and artists. You can't go wrong here."

BARYON

"This contest has found some of the best new writers of the last decade."

KRISTINE KATHRYN RUSCH
AUTHOR & EDITOR

"Once again, Writers of the Future provides some of the most imaginative and thought-provoking speculative fiction."

PARSEC MAGAZINE

L. RON HUBBARD

PRESENTS

WRITERS

OF THE

FUTURE

VOLUME
XIX

L. RON HUBBARD

PRESENTS

WRITERS

OF THE

FUTURE

VOLUME
XIX

The Year's 14 Best Tales from the
Writers of the Future®
International Writing Program
Illustrated by the Winners in the
Illustrators of the Future®
International Illustration Program

With Essays on Writing and Art by
L. Ron Hubbard • Will Eisner
Sean Williams

Edited by Algis Budrys

Galaxy Press, L.L.C.

Suspense: © 2003 L. Ron Hubbard Library
Introduction : © 2003 Algis Budrys
Numbers: © 2003 Joel Best
Trust is a Child: © 2003 Matthew Candelaria
A Boy and His Bicycle: © 2003 Carl Frederick
A Few Days North of Vienna: © 2003 Brandon Butler
A Ship That Bends: © 2003 Luc Reid
Bury My Heart at the Garrick: © 2003 Steve Savile
A Silky Touch to No Man: © 2003 Robert J Defendi
To The Illustrators of the Future: © 2003 Will Eisner
Dark Harvest: © 2003 Geoffrey Girard
From All the Work Which He Had Made . . . : © 2003 Michael Churchman
Beautiful Singer: © 2003 Steve Bein
Gossamer: © 2003 Ken Liu
Ten Years After: © 2003 Sean Williams
Walking Rain: © 2003 Ian Keane
Blood and Horses: © 2003 Myke Cole
Into the Gardens of Sweet Night: © 2003 Jay Lake
The Year in the Contests: © 2003 Algis Budrys

Illustration on page 13 © 2003 Mike Lawrence
Illustration on page 55 © 2003 Nina Ollikainen
Illustration on page 71 © 2003 Jared Barber
Illustration on page 98 © 2003 Staci Goddard
Illustration on page 163 © 2003 Mike Lawrence
Illustration on page 196 © 2003 Vance Kelly
Illustration on page 270 © 2003 Youa Vang
Illustration on page 291 © 2003 Jared Barber
Illustration on page 315 © 2003 Adrian Barbu
Illustration on page 342 © 2003 James C. Trujillo
Illustration on page 393 © 2003 Nina Ollikainen
Illustration on page 445 © 2003 Daniel Willis
Illustration on page 470 © 2003 Britt Spencer
Illustration on page 538 © 2003 Asuka Komai

Cover Artwork: *The Galleon* © 1973 Frank Frazetta

ISBN: 1-59212-165-9

Library of Congress Control Number: 2003109436
First Edition Paperback 10 9 8 7 6 5 4 3 2 1
Printed in the United States of America

CONTENTS

INTRODUCTION

Written by
Algis Budrys

This is the nineteenth in the annual series of anthologies called *L. Ron Hubbard Presents Writers of the Future*. Putting it another way, it has been nineteen years since we met in a side room of Chasen's Hollywood restaurant to celebrate the conclusion of the first year of L. Ron Hubbard's Writers of the Future Contest.

It seems barely credible now. We had twelve writers—among them Leonard Carpenter, Karen Joy Fowler, Nina Kiriki Hoffman, Dean Wesley Smith, Mary Frances Zambreno and David Zindell, none of whom were household names at all.

And we had judges and friends—Ray Bradbury, Robert Silverberg, Theodore Sturgeon, Jack Williamson, Roger Zelazny and A. E. van Vogt, who, no question, clearly were household names.

In the book, Robert Silverberg, who also contributed an essay on a writer's beginnings, began by saying "What a wonderful idea—one of science fiction's all-time giants opening the way for a new generation of exciting talent! For these brilliant stories, and the careers that will grow from them, we all stand indebted to L. Ron Hubbard."

What he referred to is best summed up by quoting LRH's introduction to that first volume.

A culture is as rich and as capable of surviving as it has imaginative artists. The artist is looked upon to start things. The artist injects the spirit of life into a culture. And through his creative endeavors, the writer works continually to give tomorrow a new form.

In these modern times, there are many communication lines for works of art. Because a few works of art can be shown so easily to so many, there may even be fewer artists. The competition is very keen and even dagger sharp.

It is with this in mind that I initiated a means for new and budding writers to have a chance for their creative efforts to be seen and acknowledged.

LRH has offered an unprecedented opportunity to beginning writers; substantial prize money, nationwide publicity, and each year's anthology of the winning stories. And as of now, we have over 250 published winning stories, each representing a new career. As evidence are the thousands of subsequent short stories and novels published by the winners of the Writers of the Future Contest.

In addition, a few years after the Writers' Contest, we began L. Ron Hubbard's Illustrators of the Future Contest, bringing the same opportunity to creative people who expressed themselves in that manner. With twelve winners each year, we thus far have published over one hundred new illustrators appearing in these pages.

Each year, we host workshops for the winning writers and illustrators, holding them in various locales such as Taos, New Mexico, The George Washington University, the Library of Congress, California's Pepperdine University, Sag Harbor on Long Island, and, as of a few years ago, in the L. Ron Hubbard Library in Hollywood. In the years since that beginning, other aspects of L. Ron Hubbard's vision have revealed themselves. Chief among them is that at the end of each year we select the top story and the illustration from among the quarterly winners and award two additional prizes of four thousand dollars each. (To find out more about these in detail, turn to the back of this book and read the complete rules for both Contests.) But there have been other changes, among them the fact that the first seventeen volumes of this book were issued by Bridge Publications but now the publisher is Galaxy Press in Hollywood, California. Galaxy has become the publisher of L. Ron Hubbard's fiction, so it made excellent sense to move the book over.

So, "What is new?" the faithful reader might ask, a question which leads directly to the introduction of *this* anthology.

In this volume, we're delighted to present an article on "Suspense" by L. Ron Hubbard, an essay on illustration by Will Eisner and "Ten Years After," a testimonial of success by former Writers' Contest winner and *New York Times* best-selling author, Sean Williams.

Frank Frazetta artwork is certainly not new to the *L. Ron Hubbard Presents Writers of the Future* anthology series. *This* cover, however, *is* new and is entitled "The Galleon."

Within the pages of this anthology are fourteen short stories and novelettes written by aspiring writers newly discovered through the 2002 Writers of the Future Contest. These previously unpublished stories are as fresh and individualistic as the imaginations of the writers from which they were conceived and written.

A new crop of illustrators, having successfully competed and won in the 2002 Illustrators of the Future Contest, have rendered the illustrations for each story in the anthology. These illustrations, based on the artist's interpretation of the writer's words and utilizing the artist's skills, are all new.

We now look to the past introductions to the *L. Ron Hubbard Presents Writers of the Future* anthologies and well recall when we introduced such other "new writers" as Jo Beverley, Nancy Farmer, James Alan Gardner, Robert Reed, K.D. Wentworth and Sean Williams, and such "new illustrators" as Sergey Poyarkov and Shaun Tan. Stellar careers one and all, all discovered by their respective contest, and all first published in the anthology.

We have no doubt *these* newly presented writers and illustrators will move forward to achieve their professional publishing aspirations as have those in whose footsteps they follow.

Having said this, we introduce the rising new stars in the ever-emerging Writers—and Illustrators—of the Future galaxy of stars.

NUMBERS

Written by
Joel Best

Illustrated by
Mike Lawrence

About the Author

Joel Best has sold stories to a variety of publications, including his Finalist story of last year, "Prague 47," to Writers of the Future Volume XVIII. His success continued this year with winning a top spot in the Writers of the Future Contest and the subsequent sale to this anthology.

Joel has lived all over the United States and currently resides in upstate New York with his wife, Debra, and son, Noah. He would like to thank the former for her steadfast support and the latter for (finally) sleeping through the night.

About the Illustrator

Mike Lawrence has always been in love with art and grew up drawing. He studied fine art at the University of Oregon where he discovered woodcuts and printmaking two years ago. Mike recently graduated with a bachelor of fine arts in printmaking.

Although he started out studying painting in college, Mike found printmaking more compatible with his dream to be an artist and illustrator, a fact that shines through in the following illustration.

Patrick ran away, but Annie kept a copy of the equations that created him in a brass locket around her neck. They provided diversion as she calculated puppies and kittens for clients or drank tea on the balcony as the airships sailed by. Her apartment building lay on a major transport line whose ships had names like $\int ¥X$ and $\sqrt{s}G(s)$ etched into their bows.

She would take out the tiny sheet of paper, carefully smooth the creases, and scan the many lines of numbers while attempting to locate the error in her math. The equations contained incredible complexity. So many hours of computation. She never meant to write womanizing into her lover. Devotion was the goal; not a man who gave his heart to anything in a skirt.

Mistakes happened. Creative mathematics was anything but an exact science.

Eventually she threw the locket away. It proved too strong a reminder of that last dreadful conversation with Patrick.

"Every time you fall into someone else's bed a piece of me dies."

"Those other women mean nothing."

"They do to me."

"I can't help myself. You made me this way. If I could change ..."

He stopped coming home and, so angry her hands shook, Annie wrote 2-3-5-7 on the apartment's front door. This sequence of primes was antithetical to his equations, just in case he crawled back to her, which he hadn't, not really. It was in a phone call a year later that he said, "Meet me at our favorite place."

Annie was putting the finishing touches on a gray Persian kitten when the phone rang. Half the day writing equations for fussy Mr. Doohan. He'd been waiting a week for his pet. Kept calling her, wanting to know *when*. Her rent came due soon, she needed the money, the last thing she needed was to forfeit this order. She'd picked up, heard Patrick's voice, and something sharp grabbed at her middle. Damn. She crumpled the paper with its web of numbers and the Persian, barely formed on the worktable, evaporated.

Hissing into the phone, "What possible reason could I have for wanting to see you?"

"We're in love."

"Not anymore." But hanging up and staring at her hands only worked for an hour. Annie gave in and went to their special spot from the old days, the little coffeehouse on a hill, cozy and dark and quiet as an attic. She hadn't been here in ages. Part of why she and Patrick used to love this spot was the messed-up lighting. The illumination equations on the ceiling were so stained with nicotine that customers, chairs, tables, even the fish tank in the corner carried a yellow tint. The result was an illusion of age. Yellow was the color of old paper, of history.

He sat in the back, dressed exactly as she'd last seen him. Jeans, a ragged denim jacket, filthy sneakers covered with ballpoint-penned eights. Eight was Patrick's favorite number. Tip it on one side and you have infinity. Beautiful. Mathematically elegant.

He looked up at her. In one hand, an oversized mug of coffee, black. In the other, a cigarette flavored with whimsical equations. Patrick exhaled a tiny clipper ship that sailed an unseen sea over their heads and said, "Please take me back."

"What about the dancer?"

"You know about her?"

Annie sat down and fanned away the ship as it tacked toward her face. Patrick's addiction to tobacco was another flaw of integers. God.

"You hear stories."

"Ruby and I only lasted two weeks."

"She meant nothing, of course."

"Only you matter to me."

Patrick ground out the cigarette and immediately lit another. A cloud of hazy butterflies materialized.

"Seven other women followed her."

Making eight. Naturally.

"Why are you telling me this?" Annie asked.

"Because you deserve to know the truth. Because I miss you and want to come back to you."

She thought about that for a time.

"Maybe . . . I could make some additions to your equations."

She hated saying the words. How could this end up any way but badly?

"I'm begging," Patrick said.

She gave a nod, still worried, but so full of hope in spite of herself that she felt as buoyant as helium.

● ● ●

Daddy drank equation wine while painting, a bubbling vintage that smelled of fresh earth and set young Annie's thoughts adrift. She would breathe its aroma and watch him at the easel. His huge hands, the charcoal outlines, the first brushstrokes of color. Daddy's landscapes were so vivid she imagined stepping into the canvas and losing herself in cadmium meadows and rose madder forests.

Sometimes Daddy drank too much. He'd smile over the rim of his glass. "Wine lets me dream," he'd say. "Your heart's desire always begins with a dream, darling." He moved away when Annie was almost seven. Daddy came to her room in the night before the morning when Mother told her he wouldn't be back, ever. Annie knew something was wrong. Daddy's clothes were wet and steaming. He'd been out in the rain. He sat beside her and said, "None of the bad things have anything to do with you. Don't forget that." Annie didn't know what to think. What bad things? Daddy sat so quietly. She held her favorite doll, Missy Pretty-Bow. The room was dark. She'd never been afraid of the dark. With shadows you could make pictures of anything you wanted.

Daddy bent over her and she felt the warmth of his tears on her cheek. He walked into the hall and down the stairs. She heard the front door open and close, then nothing but steady drumming on the roof, and she counted *one two three four,* closing her eyes and waiting for the dream that would bring Daddy back.

• • •

The weather broke down again. In theory, meteorological mathematicians equated an appropriate ratio of fair versus foul, but Annie forever seemed caught in an unexpected rain. She hated rain. No good ever arrived with a storm.

She led Patrick from the coffee shop. The wind had teeth. Raindrops as big as her thumbnail. They stung upon impact. She imagined running nude through the street and being pummeled to death. There was a happy thought.

Jot down a coincidence equation, throw the paper to the air. She waited. Half a minute passed. A cab swung around the corner, splashed through a puddle, and jerked to a halt in front of the shop.

"I forgot how handy it is to have you around," Patrick said with a shy smile.

Annie's chest ached.

This is a mistake.

I don't care.

"Come on," she said, dashing to the curb.

●●●

As a child, she lived next to an aging mathematician. Old Gus, who smelled, when the breeze was right, of hair tonic and pee. Who scratched numbers in a bare spot in the grass of his front lawn. Annie hid in the hedgerow and watched one bright afternoon. She was fivegoingonsix. Her father wouldn't be leaving for another year. Six was an important birthday. Annie couldn't wait for six, to be almost an adult. Her parents said never go into that strange man's yard, not to get a lost ball, not for any reason.

Gus wrote more numbers in the dirt and peered at the sky.

"Come, dammit."

She felt a little thrill. Damn. Everyone knew that was a bad word. Gus paced back and forth, muttering damndamndamn. Annie held her breath and waited for him to turn to stone.

A small blue cloud appeared high above. A speck, a dot, a little blob that resolved into a whirlwind of fist-sized birds the color of the ocean. Gus held wide his arms and the birds swirled around him singing so very beautifully that Annie felt large.

The ocean blue birds found homes in the trees, the bushes, on the roof of Gus's house. Peeling paint house. Leaning walls house. They smoothed their feathers and he did a little dance.

When Daddy went away, abandoning his easel and family, Annie thought a great deal about the blue birds. Gus made them with numbers. Gus loved the birds. She loved Daddy. Daddy was gone. With numbers you could make things you loved. These facts strung together, one two three. She knew how to add. Even babies could do that.

Numbers granted power.

Her mind whirled with the implications.

•••

The cab's engine equations were bootleg and out of alignment. The vehicle coughed and coasted to a halt. "Sorry," the driver said, scribbling frantically. Shooting blind, Annie thought, but he must have stumbled onto the correct series of computations because the cab finally lurched into gear and rattled the rest of the way to her apartment.

She took Patrick upstairs, first erasing 2-3-5-7 from the door so he could go inside with her. She made tea, had him take off his jacket and T-shirt. Patrick's upper torso was a mass of equations. Annie remembered calculating the placement of every integer. It wasn't that long ago since she gave this man form and substance. She'd used blue ink. Blue was a good color, her favorite since childhood. The equations started at his navel and spread upward like cobwebs.

"Will there be any pain?" he asked, when she brought out her mathematician's pen.

"I doubt it."

"I'm a little afraid."

"Just relax." Annie started near the sternum, just below his heart, and made the first few revisions to Patrick's love and loyalty. Of paramount concern would be the bolstering of his strength of will, his sense of fidelity.

"I feel strange."

"You'll be fine."

Additions here and here, alter this equation, an inversion of that one. Patrick's original numbers were

Illustrated by Mike Lawrence

already insanely convoluted. Annie had to work slowly. Mathematicians usually didn't alter a finished project for good reason. Once everything was computed and in place, it didn't take much shifting around to throw it all into complete disarray.

Suddenly he clung to her, overloaded and balanced on the knife's edge of shutdown.

"Something . . . wrong."

She'd done too much.

"*Annie.*"

"I'll fix it." Close to panic, she took a delicate razor from her box of tools and used its silver metal smile to slice away the equations she'd just written. Numbers flaked away like dirty snow caught on the bit of breeze that crept in through the crack in her bedroom window.

Patrick relaxed and rested easily in her arms.

Now Annie knew. She couldn't change his math. That option simply was not open to her.

"Please, please stay with me this time," she whispered, holding him like a child.

In the morning she woke alone. Again.

• • •

The only time she drank equation wine Annie dreamed of an ideal man who loved her with his flawless heart and shared with her a perfect life. The dream washed over her as she sat by a lake. Mother had moved them to the country. Annie liked the lake and often lost herself in thought by the water.

"What should I call you?" she asked the man from her wine dream.

"That's up to you."

"I've always liked Patrick."

"Then Patrick it is."

Annie had sneaked the wine from the chest where her mother kept all of Daddy's things. She was eleven.

No, fifteen. Eighteen. Twenty-four. Forty. Seventy-nine. All of these and none; equation wine played strange tricks with one's sense of time. Eternity rolled into a ball. All moments merged into one. Simultaneity became law.

She reached for Patrick. He pulled away and turned to mist. Annie called and called for him, and when her head cleared she was eleven again, only eleven.

•••

After Patrick ran away for the second time, Annie spent more time in the studio calculating for her growing list of clients. Six months passed, she stayed busy. Pets were big business these days. Lots of wealthy men and women out there with fond childhood memories of a beloved tabby or cocker spaniel. Dogs and cats were extinct. According to popular myth, they succumbed to a mathematician's error. The reality of the situation would probably never be known, but precedent existed. Take the ibis, the dodo, the passenger pigeon.

A perky beagle pup had been giving her trouble. Annie drank mint tea and tweaked calculations. Numbers swam in her vision. No, not right. Change. Recalculate. More tea. This project was such a potboiler; a living bauble for a rich woman!

Eventually the creative juices flowed more evenly. The math unfolded properly, the beagle took shape. By evening it sat on the worktable eyeing her with unabashed adoration. Annie didn't much like dogs. Canine intelligence largely depended upon an owner's wishful thinking. Most dogs had roughly the same brain power as a footstool.

The beagle started yapping. She temporarily deleted its vocal equations and locked the beast in the bathroom. Now time stretched for her. So much easier when there was work to be done. Remove the focus of a project awaiting completion and every second dragged. Annie drank her tea by the window. A soft rain smeared the glass. Rain, always rain. She pulled the shades and turned down the lights. That helped, except that now she talked to herself: Mathematicians carried on many solitary conversations. Blame the numbers forever humming in their minds, eroding the borders between subconscious and conscious.

She spoke of Patrick. What else?

"Of course the additional equations were too much for him, what did I expect?"

"You had to try."

"It was a selfish act."

"He needed improvement."

"But I almost killed him."

Lightning flared and the room turned white for an instant. She imagined him standing by the bookshelf. Pure imagination, of course.

"I want him back."

The part of her responsible for the other half of the dialogue laughed.

"Be careful what you wish for, dear."

● ● ●

College was hard work. Annie spent most of her days alone. Not much time for friends. She wore a shell that very few could breach. For a short brief time there was a dark-eyed woman, Melissa, who belonged to a variety of underground organizations. Melissa represented mystery. She didn't live on campus. Annie had no idea where she went at night. They'd meet for beer and music at one of the local bars. Without fail, Melissa would spend most of the evening sitting in a dark corner, eyes nervously looking all around.

"I am going to equate the ideal man," Annie once

said after too much beer. "He'll be tall and strong. He'll love me passionately. Together we'll . . ."

She faltered. Her cheeks grew warm. These thoughts were too personal to share.

In time Annie drifted away from Melissa. Her studies consumed every moment. Numbers. They were a life unto themselves. They were enough.

Senior year and a letter from Mother arrived. It was the first time Annie had heard from her since leaving home three years earlier and consisted of two lines and six words.

Come home.

Your father has died.

•••

News reached her that Patrick was back in town, living in one of those terrible hotels down by the harbor. An anonymous note slipped under her door contained the information. Annie knew the tidings came from a fellow mathematician, someone who'd seen an opportunity to rub her nose in a personal failure; the community of equations ran thick with professional jealousy.

She pondered the situation and poured a drink in anticipation of an emotional response to what she'd just learned. Patrick. Well, here he was again, the proverbial bad penny. The first drink failed to have any effect. Annie considered pouring another.

No? To work, then. She had orders to fill. Mr. Doohan's Pekingese, Mrs. Hudson's terrier.

She fell apart with startling speed, crying so hard her bones creaked. It was the weirdest thing. Tears. Over Patrick. Annie couldn't believe it. She touched her cheek, felt the wet on her fingers.

Amazing.

"What am I supposed to do now?"

Her subconscious had no response.

● ● ●

It rained the day of the funeral. Only Annie attended the ceremony; there were none of her father's friends, no other family members. Even Mother didn't show. That came as little surprise.

Mathematicians have their own way of saying goodbye. She wrote several lines of numbers on a crisp slip of paper and placed it on the grave's freshly turned earth. The paper was pale blue. Darker blue ink ran in the rain. The numbers remained in her heart, immune to any inclement weather.

One two three. Four five six. Seven eight nine.

When prayer is called for, mathematicians count.

Without warning Annie thought about, of all things, milkweed boats. The memory intrigued her. Milkweed boats were something from very far back.

They came floating from her past. Tiny shapes on the water, bobbing away into the distance.

She remembered sadness. What was that about?

Too long ago. The memory was too dim.

Except—

Daddy had taught her about milkweed boats. They'd meant a lot to him.

Maybe more would come. In time.

Annie returned to the count. At one thousand she left the cemetery.

● ● ●

She left projects half-finished on the worktable, threw on a coat against the rain, and ran down the stairs to the street. There was no stopping to think things over. She moved automatically.

The rain intensified as she left the building.

Naturally. Annie was prepared to write a coincidence equation, but the universe had already provided one. A cab waited in front of the apartment building. Someone coming home from a party, drunk, stumbling. She ducked into the cab in time to hear the driver mumble unhappily about lousy tippers.

More coincidence. This was the cab with the faulty engine equations. The driver didn't recognize her. He smelled of garlic and had gray hair spiking from his ears. Red coat covered with lucky lottery equations. Annie knew these were pure bunk, just the kind of thing unscrupulous mathematicians sold to the ignorant masses. No wonder half the population didn't trust numbers.

"Where to?"

"The harbor." She didn't have an exact address. A hotel, that was all, and the harbor area had its share of them, cheap and dirty. It was a miserable place. Many unhappy lives ended by the water.

The cabbie squinted. "That's a rough place to be going this time of night."

Annie sank into the seat cushion.

"Just drive."

φυτψν ντψ≤ψ϶ντρ6φοο ππ ρψ ϶φ ρι Δ ρο ρ
κ ρоор κ σ οʃ о κ ιφ 3϶75 ο ≠ ιφ Δ ο π ω϶о κ λ π ϶ σ
σ κ ρ ϶ π ι ο ω φ 6 ω ʃ π ν ι ρ ο π ρ φ π ο τ ρ κ μ   φ ψ Ω

Patrick's equations. His soul, the foundation for his ability to feel.

Flawed or not, to Annie they were poetry.

•••

She searched the harbor area, its many cheap hotels.
Pay by the week, the day, the hour. Vagrants scrounged
loose change for rooms. Drunks, thieves, prostitutes.
The cabbie was right about this being no place for a
woman at night, alone. For anyone. Time and again
Annie heard footsteps behind her and turned to see a
shadowy figure abruptly stop short. They'd catch sight
of the protection equations pinned to her coat, numbers
blazing like fire in the darkness, and decide to be somewhere else.

She hated using mathematics this way. Thank God
for them.

Starting at the western end of the harbor and
working her way east, she visited two dozen hotels by
midnight. On the outside the ancient structures
retained some sense of individuality—a bit of architec-
tural façade, perhaps the remnants of decorative iron
fencing—but their interiors were all the same; lobbies
stinking of filth, tattered men and women slouched in
chairs or sleeping on couches. She showed Patrick's
photograph at the front desk, always to a wretch in a
stained shirt. No, haven't seen him, times twelve.

At the thirteenth hotel, the desk clerk showed a
flicker of recognition.

"Yes. He checked in a few days ago."

"What room?"

"Two-five-two."

More primes. Annie hurried up the stairs, into the
musty cave of the hotel's second floor. Two-five-two
was midway into the gloom.

"Patrick?" She knocked, hard. A window stood
open at the end of the hallway. She heard the sea.
Restless waves and the tang of salt. Boats coming and
going.

"Patrick, talk to me."

"Go away," she heard from within.

"No."

"I didn't ask you to come."

"But I'm here."

No light showed under the door. She stood in near complete darkness. There was only sound. Harbor buoys. Gulls.

And boats.

"You can't fix me." Patrick sounded terrible. Worn out. "I'll never be the kind of person you want."

"I understand that now," Annie said.

"What?"

The open window at the end of the hall. Harbor. Boats.

The boats. Until only a moment ago she'd been acting out of instinct. Find Patrick. Fix him. Change who he was. That had always been the answer. But fix him how?

Boats in the harbor. She could almost feel the throb of their engines.

Everything seemed so simple now.

Fixing Patrick was all about boats.

"I'm going to make things right in a different way," she said.

• • •

Daddy showed her how to make a milkweed boat. Annie was fourgoingonfive. She hadn't yet seen old Gus and the birds and Daddy wouldn't leave her for a long time. Hand in hand, Annie walked with her father by a stream near the house. Beside the stream, a meadow. Milkweed plants grew everywhere and Daddy said, "Here's a fun thing you can do with the dried-out pods."

He split a milkweed pod along one side, scooped

out the bird fluff seeds, scattered them to the wind. Annie caught some of the dancing seeds. Her fingers became sticky with sap and smelled alive, of spring.

"Go ahead and put the boat into the water, child."

Daddy guided her hands. To Annie the stream was a mighty river. Did it flow all the way to the sea? She built images of the villages and cities nestled along its shores. Who lived by the river? Poets? Artists?

Her milkweed boat settled onto the water, bobbing, twisting, almost sinking—almost—then steadying and nosing into the almost nonexistent current. It moved away, picked up speed. Sailing into the distance, her boat was smaller, smaller, gone.

"Where is it now?" Annie kept asking as Daddy carried her home. "Now? Now? Now?"

"Anywhere," he said, and when that answer failed to satisfy, Daddy laughed. "There's no controlling a milkweed boat. That's what makes them so wonderful. Milkweed boats act of their own volition."

•••

"Does this hurt?"

"Feels funny."

Patrick sat quietly as Annie applied the razor to his left arm. The rest of him—chest, back, shoulders, right arm—were already clear of equations. First to go was the devotion that had never worked. Next, the loyalty. Feathery bits of dead skin littered the floor of the hotel room. Annie sang softly while deleting. It was difficult to initiate this procedure. All of her training as a creative mathematician screamed for her to stop.

One final deft scrape of the blade and Patrick would be pristine. She'd saved the equation governing love until the very end. These were the first numbers she'd penned when creating him.

Before I change my mind.

She deleted and sighed. And thought of milkweed boats.

Like love, they must be free to follow their own course.

Annie knew when Patrick ceased loving her with all of his heart. An almost imperceptible light in his eyes flickered and went out.

•••

"Who am I?" asked the man who now had no identity at all. He sat very quietly, hands on knees. He looked at his sneakers, saw the eights, opened his mouth to ask, then chose silence.

"That's up to you."

"Really?"

The woman took her knife to the window and threw it into the harbor. A pen and handbook of equations followed.

"Why are you here?" the man asked.

"I love you."

He tilted his head slightly.

"Do I love you?"

"I don't know," she said, taking his hand and waiting for whatever took place next.

TRUST IS A CHILD

Written by
Matthew Candelaria

Illustrated by
Nina Ollikainen

About the Author

Matthew Candelaria was born in Denver, Colorado, in 1973. By the age of eleven he had decided he was going to be a writer of science fiction and promptly began work on a novel. He finished the novel in the autumn of 1988 and immediately sent it off to a number of publishers, expecting at any time to be discovered, as any number of SF authors before him, as a child prodigy.

When this didn't happen, Matthew enrolled at the Colorado School of Mines and later transferred to the University of Colorado, from which he received his B.A. in English. After a whirlwind tour of Europe, he married his traveling companion, Tracy, and moved with her to Lawrence, Kansas, where he still resides, in pursuit of his Ph.D. in literature at the University of Kansas. His career as a novelist obviously stalled, Matthew took the advice of Professor James Gunn and tried his hand at short story writing. It worked.

About the Illustrator

Nina Ollikainen received a B.S. in biology from Stanford University and an M.D. from the USC School of Medicine, followed by a two-year stint training to be a pathologist. All the while, she longed to be an artist and mother. Her two wishes came true, and she has since raised four children and successfully elevated her artistry to a professional level.

Nina lives in Northern California, surrounded by her children, her husband, Ari, and a menagerie of pets, mostly furry. In the future, she would love to create books for children and young adults, illustrating everything inside and outside of this world.

I will never forget the way that Senator Bereg set the tone for the Bwotik conference.

"Above all, we have to make sure they open their worlds to us." He was hard-line. His hair, once black as the void, was growing gray in a radiate pattern starting at the whorl on the top of his head where he would place a crown if someone gave him the opportunity. "It is clearly the only logical agreement we can accept. Why would they deny it to us, unless they have something to hide?" He smiled, but he held his head completely stationary. It was a feint, that smile, along with his dry chuckle, designed to disarm and distract. His eyes were bright and sharp, but, if he desired, additional effort could make them appear soft and sensitive.

I had been silent for a long time, trying to get my personal feelings about the senator out of the way. I could imagine a few reasons why the Bwotik might not want to let us in—such as the state of our worlds—and I could no longer keep quiet, but I tried to speak civilly. "I don't know. I think that's negotiable."

"The problems we face are not negotiable, Ms. Rindillo. What are you going to tell the billions more unemployed because you don't want to open the Bwotik markets? And those living in fear of the mysterious aliens? Are you telling me that you would rather negotiate with an unwholesome host of slime-covered, incontinent beetles than stand up for the rights of your species? Because it is the future of humanity that is at stake here, a future that we have been entrusted to safeguard. That future is not negotiable." For this last sentence, Bereg turned to the reporter on the shuttle.

I was about to answer when Vol Oyente, the third member of the envoy, raised his hand to silence me, showing me the lighter color of his soft-looking palm. Oyente was right. Bereg would always have the last word, and we were growing too close to the base. It would not be good if the Bwotik's first sight of us was with Bereg finishing his tirade. We must present a uniform front as much as possible, make sure that there was no visible dissent for them to exploit for their advantage, no matter how loathsome it would be for me to be counted as Bereg's friend.

The shuttle bumped, creaked and hissed, and then our delegation assembled itself. Bereg would lead, followed by Oyente and then myself, as the junior member of the negotiating team. Behind us, our coterie of secretaries and research assistants and reporters would file in, silent and nameless. We were all ready, but there was a moment of delay. A team of marines was setting up an "honor guard" in the corridor, making sure there was no double-cross planned. Then a pair of tones let us know that it was clear and we paraded out into the reception area. It was immediately evident that this station had never been inhabited—it had been pressed into diplomatic service for that very reason—as its walls were still a blinding, antiseptic white. The reception hall was huge and empty; the crimson dress uniforms of the marines were like little tulips growing on a salt flat.

Across the hall were five dark-colored blobs: four Bwotik and one Human, the three delegates and the two language experts who would attempt to act as interpreters. We walked toward them at a brisk pace determined by Bereg. His mouth was smiling, but his eyes were lasing. The Bwotik were talking among themselves. The clicks and whistles of their speech blended with the sound of our boots on the plastic floor.

I had studied pictures of the Bwotik every day for months, but I was completely unprepared for the reality of them. You can tell yourself that there's nothing inherently wrong about a two-meter-long arthropod that rears up into a mockery of a Human posture, but ultimately the body can't help but believe that there is. Looking into their eyes, cold and hard and black like oval settings of obsidian beads, shaded by heavy ridges, I felt a quivering weakness run through my body. Their twitching mandibles and dull coating of petroleate slime set that quivering to queasiness, and the smell of them—fecund, earthy, with all the tinges of rot that entails—pushed me to the very edge of heaving. When Bereg offered his hand to one of them, the thought of touching them sent me convulsing to my hands and knees. My throat burned and my nostrils filled with thick, bitter fluid. The viscous matter heaped onto the ground, but the liquid bile oozed outward, touching my hands and warming them. I tried to control myself, but the pungent smell of my own vomit made my stomach convulse again.

From over me, a voice said, "Certainly, the young one, she is sensitive of our difference. This is a good sign!" I wanted to look up to determine the source of the voice, but my head was held down by a mixture of sickness and shame. I could feel the eyes of cameras upon me, recording every twitch of my gut, even the last line of bile dribbling from my lips.

I felt myself being lifted by four brusque arms. I closed my eyes and concentrated on not getting sick anymore, but I noted the crimson-wrapped arms of the marines that were lifting me, as well as their cursory, "Are you all right, ma'am?" They did not wait for my reply, but instead they quickly carried me out of the reception hall and to my room. They did not lock me in my room, but they told me to stay there, and they stood guard outside.

The nausea had passed long before we reached my room, leaving behind only residual shame and a general weakness. I wiped at my face with a kerchief. I paced back and forth for several minutes, kneading my self-hate in my mind until I found myself hitting dead ends. I also found myself too tired to pace, so I lay down on the bed. I put my hand on my pelvis, feeling the source of the pain and nausea there. Perhaps I was not yet recovered enough from my operation to be on this mission. I tried to get myself thinking of other things by looking around at the room.

It was a standard midhigh-priced room, such as I might find on any station in the Confederation, except that its unfinish was strange and patchy. It was mostly that the walls were super-white: they were still bare, uncolored plexiconstruct, standard material for interior constructions in space. On top of this unfinish, however, the room had been furnished with a bed, a chest of drawers, a nightstand with lamp, a desk, a chair and a print—some still life with flowers. The white walls denied shadow and this made the furniture seem as though it floated in a void. Colors seemed particularly odd. Like the bedspread, with its bright starburst pattern, they were lined sharply against the white, as if they were not real, but merely superimposed on the actual image of nothingness, special effects. The flowers were impossible. They could not exist in such a vacuum, with nothing more than a frame to protect them against the stark absence. I almost for a moment considered my hand outlined against the whiteness, but thought better of it. I sat down on the bed and looked in the nightstand. The Gideons had not yet come. Unable to think what else to do, I sat back to wait for the preliminary inspection tour to be finished.

Oyente called to let me know that they had finished the tour and were in the briefing room that had been set up for our benefit. The guards on my door did not believe I had been summoned and had to call their commander. After verification, they insisted that one of them accompany me, in case I "took sick." Our destination was easy to identify by the marines standing guard outside. Upon entering, I was shocked by the black molded table and the black padded chairs against the stark white. In the chairs were research assistants, secretaries and a few military officers, but no reporters. Senator Bereg was leading the meeting, as expected. He was pressing the translator for information he had gleaned while learning the Bwotik's language.

I heard the translator in midsentence: ". . . is mostly the same as ours. I mean, they have words for war and deceit and spy and all those other things we wish they didn't have a clue about."

Bereg smiled, "Yes, well, we expected that. Is there anything particularly useful you can tell us? Anything interesting at all?"

The translator didn't seem to have anything.

Bereg made a gruff noise and leaned forward. He wrote with thick black lines on his clean white sheet on the black molded table. "So why is it? Why don't they want us to see their worlds?"

Oyente hypothesized, "There's always the obvious: technology, manufacturing, weaponry. They want to keep a high-tech edge."

The translator shook his head, "I don't think so. The ship I was on was completely open to me. No areas were marked 'classified' or denied to me."

"Is it possible," Bereg said, "that it was an older ship, planted to deceive us as to their technological level?"

"If it was an older one, it was still more advanced

than ours. For one thing, they're able to mount their drives directly on the hull without any sort of radiation danger. And their Rho particle transmitter, it's barely a third the size of a comparable unit on one of our ships. Of course, they've never attacked our ships, but they've fired their weapons defensively, and we know what the results of that have been."

Bereg looked at him and spoke harshly, "You don't have to remind me about that. My world lost a colonizer ship and a thousand people, nearly half of them children, when it underwent 'defensive fire' as you call it. That's why I'm here to make sure these attacks cease. Did they let you look at their weaponry? Did they show you their manufacturing facilities?"

"They showed me their weapons, but I didn't inquire too closely. I thought it would look suspicious. I wasn't sent as a spy, I was sent to learn their language. But I told you, they didn't deny me anything I asked."

"Besides," I broke in, "the language student we had, he didn't ask about our ship or even particularly want to see much."

"And what did he want to know?" He smiled placatingly at me.

"You know as well as I do. It was in the brief."

He continued smiling, as if he were encouraging me to keep talking until I learned something.

Even though I knew I shouldn't tell him, that it was a game he was playing, I spoke in frustration. "He was interested in language. That's all. He wanted lots of data about language, not just current, but historical. He wanted grammar, vocabulary, syntax, representative recordings."

"And what he got was a full course on our history and culture. Completely above-board and suspicion-free. Now he knows not just what we think and how, but what we've thought over our entire history. These

Bwotik are more clever than you think and part of their skill is that they seem innocent."

Bereg paused and I almost spoke, but his eyes warned that he was not finished speaking. He would take any interruption as an insult, so I held my tongue. "Let me tell you why I think they want to deny us access to their worlds," he continued. "It's a simple, strategic maneuver. They move into a new system, annex it and close it to us. Soon, they've got us boxed in, and we have no choice but to either suffer over-crowding and shortages, or else to go to war. We'd have no bargaining position then."

"But I don't think that's what they're planning," I said. "Not a single Bwotik ship has ever wandered into one of our systems, although they've been established nearby for hundreds of years. It's always been our ships impinging on their systems, even now."

Bereg countered, "We have only their word for how long they've been in those systems."

"That is true," Oyente spoke up at last, "and perhaps establishing the truth of those claims is a good reason to want access to those systems, but I have to agree with Senator Rindillo that the Bwotik do not seem to be in an expansion phase. This makes me wonder whether they are in decline. That which is not growing is dying and perhaps this is what they wish to conceal from us. However, this also we cannot know unless we can visit their worlds. Therefore, I believe that we must petition for access to their home worlds."

"But if they are dying, can't we leave them to die in peace?"

"You are truly naive. Have I taught you nothing?" Senator Bereg looked coldly at me, the skin around his eyes wrinkled, tired. "Age always envies youth and as it creeps toward death, that envy turns to hate or rapacity. We must know what we can expect from them."

"But they don't have to open themselves to trade or any economic development for that."

"No."

"We only need to ask to be able to visit their worlds."

"Then we are agreed?"

Oyente said, "It is imperative that we can gather our own information, firsthand, about these Bwotik."

I said, "They should allow us to travel to their worlds in small numbers, but they don't need to be receptive to trade in any form."

Bereg said, "Good. I will propose that tomorrow. We should try as much as possible to present a unified front. The Greater Assembly did not grant us autonomy only to have us bicker in front of these creatures. You should speak only if it is imperative and all conflicts should be maintained for discussion here. Once we leave this room, there is to be no dissension. Understood?"

Oyente nodded, and so did I, eventually. Bereg was the senior member of the delegation and a member of the Executive Committee. He wanted to run things his way. If the delegation didn't work, he could petition the Assembly to have Oyente and I replaced, and we would have a hard time convincing Bereg's many friends in the Assembly that he was at fault and not us. Bereg adjourned the meeting, and Oyente, his head hanging with exhaustion, hurried to his room. The secretaries also scrambled to get out of the room.

As I was about to leave, Bereg spoke again, "Sheila, are you going to be fit tomorrow? The news of your episode today has already gone out by FTL. Quite embarrassing. If you feel unwell, Carol can take your place. She worked with them during the entire tour without a qualm."

I looked at Bereg's personal secretary. She was thin, with narrow cheeks and a sharp, bony nose. She deferred reverentially to him, always laughing at his jokes, always taking his counsel with dread gravity. Apart from his company, she could always manufacture extreme enthusiasm for whomever she spoke to, but that enthusiasm was as evanescent as it was effervescent. "I'll be fine," I said.

"Are you sure? Perhaps this is too soon after your illness."

I could no longer contain myself, "You know that it was not just an illness."

"Really? What was it?"

"You know better than I do what it was you gave me to destroy the evidence. I only know what it did to me." I could remember the burning pain, like being eaten from the inside, the nausea and weakness.

"You should not have threatened me about going public."

"It was not a threat. I trusted you to keep your word."

"You should not have trusted me."

I did not know what to say to this man, this old friend of my father, whom I had once called "Uncle Bereg."

He made things worse by using his wise counselor tone of voice, "You know, I resisted your nomination from the first, even before things turned . . . sour. You're only here as a result of a compromise with the Progressives. The worst decision the Assembly has ever made. You might impress everyone else with that prodigy rigamarole, but I know that the only thing that counts in politics is experience. If you mess up again, I will have you recalled, even if that means canceling these talks. And I meant what I said about letting me do the talking. You contradict me once, and I will have you recalled and seek your expulsion from the Assembly. Now, get some rest; you'll need your strength tomorrow."

It took me a long time to fall asleep. I stared at the

white ceiling in the darkness, completely invisible, but still there, still antiseptic, still bright, and I began to cry. When I did fall asleep, I slept deeply. I awoke in the morning refreshed and strong. I packed my heart deep and tight, telling myself I would avoid outbursts.

Over breakfast, Bereg outlined the agenda for the day's discussion. The key issue of the day—the one that this conference must resolve to be a success— was disclosure: how much each of us needed to know about the other to feel secure, and how much each of us could reveal about ourselves without jeopardizing that feeling of security. Bereg snorted in contempt. Disclosure was, of course, not his word. It was a buzzword used by the Progressives to make everything seem peaceful and controlled. Bereg favored agreements that called for minimal disclosure, but allowed opportunities for discovery. He was confident that we could out-intelligence the Bwotik. And, of course, he believed that if they opened their systems to us, we would be able to break into their markets and subsume them with Human goods and culture. During the pre-conference news briefing, Bereg gave a sanitized version of his agenda, stressing again that the "future of humanity is not negotiable," and that it must contain "security, prosperity and dignity."

When we entered the conference room, leaving the reporters behind, I was surprised to see that it had actually been finished. Walnut paneling covered the walls and a long matching table sat in the room's center. On one side of the room, a picture of the prime minister; on the other, a group portrait of the first Executive Council of the Confederation: all white-haired and -faced smiling old men. Low, well-stocked bookshelves lined most of the walls, although I later learned that the books were blank within to prevent the leakage of any unauthorized information. On top of the bookshelves, various ornamental bibelots, ranging from a bust of Admiral Joshua Kraus, "The Paladin," to a model of a recently commissioned capital warship, aimed their intimidating aspects at the table. Light fixtures with crystal shades hung over the table or sat on the bookshelves among the less ambivalent ornaments. Looking closely at the paneling, I could tell that the wood was real, and a faint odor of stain still drifted diffuse through the air of the room.

The doors on the far side of the room opened and the four Bwotik entered. Perhaps it was the light, or perhaps it was that I was prepared for them, but they did not seem nearly as revolting as they had the day before. In fact, it must have been the light, because the coating of slime did not glisten in the same way, just gave their carapaces a fine sheen like a waxed car. They entered on all eights, but when they reached the table, they reared up onto their back four legs. The lead Bwotik's color was actually very attractive, a deep green somewhere between jade and emerald, but with a metallic luster. He spoke in a deep, resonant voice, "Certainly, we would like to thank you again for hosting this meeting. Your people have been helpful in installing the amenities required by our people, certainly."

Bereg, Oyente and I all looked at the translator, who shrugged defensively. Only one Bwotik had been taught our language, but apparently others could learn quickly.

"Certainly, although my name is difficult to pronounce in your language, the approximation Kitikrl will satisfy, certainly." It was disconcerting to watch the Bwotik speak, for nothing moved. All the sounds were made by organs back in the Bwotik's throat, and it was hard for me to respond when Kitikrl turned on me. "You are better. Certainly, you have not yet vomited again."

The voice was not exactly inflectionless, but the

inflections were primitive, and it took time for me to realize that I had been asked a question. I barely responded fast enough to prevent Bereg's speaking for me. "I am fine. I apologize for that. It was nervousness and surprise, mostly."

Kitikrl paused a moment before responding. "Certainly, you feel the need to apologize, but it is misfelt. Certainly, vomiting was at one time the traditional greeting among our people, but one would vomit into the mouth of the other, not wastefully onto the floor, certainly."

"But today," I said, feeling a strange exhilaration rush through my body, "I don't feel nauseous at all." I decided it was time to change the subject. "Your carapace looks beautiful."

"Certainly," Kitikrl replied, "your fine words are happy. Certainly, I am in what our poets describe as the most beautiful time of life."

Bereg turned his head with moderated interest and I asked, "What time is that?"

Kitikrl paused almost imperceptibly, then answered, "Certainly, I am no poet. I believe that I would ruin the beauty to describe it, certainly. Certainly, you will someday hear it from one of them."

Bereg directed a question toward Kitikrl, steering us toward the business of the day, and soon he and Kitikrl were discussing the minimal disclosure agreements they'd both planned on. They were strikingly similar and within an hour the two of them had reached an agreement on the first stage toward a comprehensive treaty. Having accomplished his first goal of keeping Human secrets for Humans only, he began to maneuver toward opening Bwotik planets for limited Human trade. "Almost nothing at all, just a few simple traders, confined to isolated areas, all of whom would be approved by our government based on their product knowledge and their integrity. You wouldn't even have to worry about keeping them under control, we'd keep them under our laws."

"Certainly, you would then have to have enforcement staff. Certainly, that would mean many of your people nearby."

"Not very many, just the smallest amount necessary. They'd be confined to a small area, remember?"

"Certainly, there would still be some and certainly they would be on our worlds. Certainly, this is unacceptable."

Bereg and Kitikrl went around and around again and again, in a very similar fashion. Bereg would propose ever smaller trade agreements, which Kitikrl would explore and then deny dialogically. Although I was entranced by Kitikrl's arguments, my body soon grew tired of sitting, and I felt drowsy from the painkillers. When lunch came, we ate apart from the Bwotik. We had not yet seen what they ate, nor them what we ate. Biology was one of the terms restricted by the disclosure agreement. Bereg justified this by arguing that knowledge of Human physiology would lead to chemical and biological weapons potential. He also counted on infrastructure workers at the station to be able to tell us everything we needed to know about Bwotik needs from the waste that they produced.

After lunch, Bereg hit the same points: exchange that would lead to trade enclaves with more minute presences on the Bwotik worlds, and, eventually, in orbiting stations over the Bwotik worlds, then, finally, at the edges of the Bwotik systems, where they would even be unable to receive sufficient sunlight to run basic life support in case of generator failure. Again, Kitikrl explored each of these proposals with precise, sometimes laborious statements of what it would entail before refusing it. Midway through the afternoon, the translator Bwotik spoke to Kitikrl, who afterward refrained from using "certainly" in every sentence, substituting it instead with as many synonyms as he could come up with. Oyente and I said little; we were basically ignored by Bereg and Kitikrl, who did all the talking. By the end of the day, we were exhausted from listening, and Bereg's frustration showed through his deprecatory laughter and sly asides. Nothing more was accomplished than the disclosure agreement.

After dinner there was a short question-and-answer session in which Bereg played up the days' progress. Then the reporters were ushered out of the briefing room and we received a report from the biological investigative team. The Bwotik had made neither an attempt nor a request to adjust the atmosphere of their quarters. Although their food was secluded, the waste that they produced indicated a similar physiology, except that it was very, very dry. The Bwotik never used the water toilets, placing their waste, which was odorless, on trays. They disposed of nitrogen compounds in water-insoluble forms. They also disposed of a familiar mix of elements: sodium, carbon, hydrogen, oxygen, phosphorous, potassium, etc. In other words, the biologists told us little of value, but they were continuing work and expected to have a breakdown on amino acids and other larger units of waste soon. After that, Bereg praised Oyente and I for our good work during the day, stated that he believed our current strategy would yield results before the end of the conference, and told us to get good rest because we would meet early in the morning for a fine-tuning session before the next day's negotiations. I was surprised to find that the guard on my door was reduced to one and his duty seemed to be directed more toward the room than myself.

In the morning, Bereg issued Oyente and I brief reports on vessels that had been destroyed after incursions on Bwotik space. I was already familiar with the one I had been given. It originated from a system in my district and had been one of the causes of an abortive attack on the Bwotik. Our small fleet had been almost completely obliterated and the survivors reported inflicting few casualties on the enemy. A larger mobilization effort, encompassing all of Human space, was stopped when the Bwotik dropped off all the survivors in their life boats at the fringes of our nearest system. Suddenly everybody wanted peace with our mysterious neighbors. I was elected on a platform of peace. At the time only a campaign promise, I never thought I would soon be working to make it a reality.

Bereg didn't give many hints about his strategy for the day, saying only that we should be prepared to speak about the briefs we'd been given. We spent the entire session studying the briefs, and every time we thought we knew them, Bereg's secretary, Carol, quizzed us on details and found us lacking. We were supposed to know the names of all individuals who were missing but presumed dead, as well as those who were listed as killed, but had only had fragmentary remains turned over by the Bwotik. When the session ended, Oyente and I had still not passed to Carol's satisfaction, but Bereg simply frowned and said, "That'll have to do."

In the conference room, Bereg greeted the Bwotik pleasantly, but they wasted no time on pleasantries. Kitikrl said harshly, "Certainly, our defense forces destroyed one of your craft today. Certainly, it was what you call a 'reconnaissance' craft." He paused, "Obviously, this is a violation of our agreement. Clearly, we cannot continue speaking under these conditions."

As I expected, Bereg was unshaken by this announcement. I had not known that the reconnaissance flights were continuing, but it was clear that he knew and that he had known about the destroyed craft before Kitikrl. However, his response was not at all what I expected. "Kitikrl," he said, "I am sorry for the continuing flights. But you must understand the pressure we are under. Thousands of our people have died in your systems—"

"Certainly, they were all warned to leave before they were fired upon. Certainly, we have told you that our systems are to remain isolated."

Bereg nodded, "I know, and they will. I promise you that these reconnaissance flights will cease, but in the meantime they have to continue until we have recovered the bodies of all our dead, including those unfortunate souls who lost their lives today."

Kitikrl was silent for a moment, although the translator registered some Bwotik speech outside the range of our hearing. He whispered to Senator Bereg. Then Kitikrl spoke again, "Clearly, this is unacceptable. Of course, we returned all your survivors to you immediately. Definitely, when we learned that your corpses also mattered to you, we returned all of those that could be found. Certainly, you cannot expect that all of them will be recovered. Obviously, many corpses will have been destroyed in the explosions."

Bereg said, "Obviously, you must understand what a trauma this represents for our people. Senator Oyente, tell Kitikrl how your sector has been affected by these losses."

Oyente spoke passionately about the MIA movement in his sector, the largest in all of Human space. He embellished the story with specific details from the records that he had been forced to study this morning.

When he finished, Bereg followed immediately, allowing no time for Kitikrl to speak. "You see what it means to our people to retrieve the bodies of our fallen? How can the families, friends and comrades have any closure without the physical evidence of their loss?"

"Certainly, then, this issue cannot be resolved. Clearly, it is impossible that every corpse be found. If you desire it, then definitely we will look again."

Senator Bereg smiled. "We appreciate your willingness to aid us in seeking the bodies of our dead. Now let's work out a plan so that our search parties can work more efficiently together."

"No," Kitikrl said, "you do not understand me, truly. Clearly, our systems cannot remain isolated with your craft continually searching on a quest that must inevitably prove futile."

"No, it is not futile, not to the families and friends of the deceased—"

"Truly, the odds of success in this case are largely independent of the relation between the searcher and the sought. Verily, they are nearly zero—"

"But if there is still a chance?"

"We ask that you resign that chance in order to adhere to the terms of our agreement."

Bereg took a few moments to look over the agreement. Then he said, "This agreement says nothing about our search for our lost citizens. It says that we agree not to scan your worlds or satellites or interplanetary commerce or ships or . . . I could go on, but clearly one thing this agreement neither says nor implies is that we cannot track the bodies of our own citizens. That's something you seem to have forgotten, Kitikrl, that these people are still Human beings, and that they still have all the rights guaranteed to them by our government, including the fulfillment of their contracts, which state that our government is to take all measures necessary to ensure their return, living or dead, to their families."

I knew that the contract promised all "reasonable" measures, but Bereg was counting on the Bwotik being ignorant of the actual contract. And he was counting on my silence. His smug smile almost made me speak up. I knew that crossing him would mean consequences for me, but they were a small price to pay for wiping that disgusting arrogance off his face for even just a moment. But then there was the peace effort to think of. Anything I said could put that peace in jeopardy. I kept silent.

Kitikrl's large mouthparts made numerous quick strikes against one another, the first visible sign of irritation that I attributed to him. "Certainly, I must make a categorical statement. Of course your tracking of your dead, however futile, is not in itself a violation of our agreement. Necessarily, such tracking will result in your obtaining data about our systems that if obtained separately would certainly violate our agreement. It is inevitable that this tracking be considered a violation of our agreement if it continues."

Bereg looked bewildered. "Why?" He looked to me and then to Oyente, who also feigned bewilderment. "I just don't understand. You seem overly protective to me. Are you trying to hide something? What is it that we might find out that you want to conceal?"

Kitikrl interlocked his two pairs of hands as though they were gears. "Certainly, it is not a question of concealment. Do not believe it so. Of course it is about respect. Respect . . . entails our right to privacy, indubitably. Obviously, if you respect us, obviously if you respect this agreement, obviously you will respect . . ."

Kitikrl paused. His head moved suddenly, then stopped, and his mandibles were moving more erratically. He unlocked his hands. Two of them he placed on the edge of the table. The other two disappeared beneath the table.

"Yes?" Bereg smiled.

"Obviously, you will respect our right to privacy. Our systems are the body of our state. The state is the corporation of our people. Our systems are our body—" Kitikrl cut off very suddenly. His head turned first one way, then the other. I could see that his hands were gripping the edge of the table, denting the varnished hardwood. In the next moment, all I could hear was the gentle click-pop of Kitikrl's joints as his mandibles grappled with the air. "May we take a short recess?"

Bereg continued to smile, "Certainly, certainly, anything you want."

Kitikrl stood up quickly and left the room before his companions had stood themselves. It was obvious that he was shaking, but he tried to conceal it by moving quickly out of the room. Bereg watched him leave, then got up and led us out. Our unscheduled departure caused a stir among the press corps, who had by this time heard about the reconnaissance craft's destruction, but they were held at bay by a marine detail and Bereg ignored them. The room he led us to was completely unfinished. It had the lit ceiling, but all the walls and the floor were completely bare, simply white plastic. The light was not yet covered, so the glare was harsh and blurred the corners; the room might have been spherical for all I could tell. The five of us, Oyente, Bereg, Carol, the translator and I, seemed to hover in air, our shadows faint ghosts hovering behind us.

Bereg looked at me. It was hard to see his face in the bright light. "Well, what do you think of that?"

"Kitikrl looked sick. . . ."

"Maybe," Bereg interrupted me and looked at Oyente.

In the absence of chairs or other furnishings, Oyente was leaning against his shadow. His dark features were stark and severe as he squinted against the brightness. "I think they have something to hide."

Bereg nodded, "So do I."

"Maybe," I supplied, "they're trying to hide their decline, as Oyente suggested. Maybe they're suffering some kind of plague." I was feeling sick myself. The painkillers I had taken in the morning had worn off, but it was hours before I was allowed to take more. I wished there were a chair or something.

Bereg shook his head, "It can't just be that. If they were in decline, they'd be trying to find some way to get something from us to stop their decline. If they were sick, they'd want to find a cure. In either case, they'd be seeking our help."

"What if they don't want our help?"

Bereg ignored me. "Damn, Carol, isn't there a more finished room this close to the conference area?"

"Not this close," she replied evenly.

"I want to get back there as soon as they signal. I want to see the way they come back in. Let me know the instant they signal. Interrupt me." Bereg closed his eyes and massaged his forehead with his hand. "Bring in our IO."

Carol nodded.

Bereg looked at Oyente again. "So, what are they hiding?"

"I think that whatever it is, it's going to prove to be military in the end. Nothing else would demand such secrecy or could be so unilateral."

"Exactly. We know they have powerful ships, but maybe they don't have enough."

Oyente stood upright. "Maybe they're just out of position."

"Hm, yes. That's a possibility."

The door opened and in stepped the intelligence officer, a bulky pyramidal man in the standard crimson uniform. His teeth were white, straight and large, and he showed them a lot. His hair was short and smooth and he never wore his hat. "Sir?" he said to Bereg.

"Major, is it?"

The IO nodded.

"Major, how many Bwotik intelligence-gathering operations have you detected?"

"None, sir. There have been no electromagnetic

listening attempts, no attempts to intercept our FTL communications, no attempt to penetrate our sections of the station with either agents or automata, no attempts to analyze our biological waste or consumables—"

"Nothing then?"

"No, sir, nothing that we've detected."

"Then we must assume that they're using some method we cannot detect."

"Yes, sir."

Bereg looked at Oyente, "That's why they're content with an agreement that gives them no opportunity to gain information. They know they can gain as much as they want without our knowledge." Bereg sighed, then looked from Oyente to Carol, then to the IO. "What information do you have about their goals? What do they want from us?"

"Sir, we haven't been able to determine that. We don't know what information they're gathering, and we haven't seen any movements in or toward any of our systems. Our reconnaissance craft report that all their ships seem to be in defensive orbits and patrols."

"Defensive orbits?"

"Yes, sir, they seem to be in a state of high alert."

"I think they're justified in being afraid of us," I offered, giving Bereg a cold look.

Bereg responded in kind, "If they think we're likely to attack."

"We've already attacked them once."

"But we've made an agreement. They'd have to suspect a double-cross, which means—"

"Senator," Carol interrupted, "the Bwotik have signalled that they are ready to resume the talks."

"Let them know we are, as well." Bereg said nothing else, but raced out of the room, past the guards that followed us, then past the guards that stayed outside the conference room. When we entered, the guards inside the conference room allowed themselves to be relieved by those accompanying us. I found that sitting was not much better for me than standing. I wanted to take some medication early, but we barely had time to get settled before the Bwotik entered.

They came in much the same as always: a smooth, rapid walk that they claimed was their most comfortable pace. As they walked, their heads moved from side to side, pointing their eyes, one after the other, at everything in the room before sitting down. They reached their chairs long before they had finished appraising the room, so they stood beside the low benches for several long seconds. Bereg thought this was an intentional psychological maneuver. Oyente was convinced it was more likely something like a dog walking around in circles before laying down. Kitikrl was not with them. Instead, an azure Bwotik sat in the central position.

He spoke, "Kitikrl is ill and will be unable to rejoin us for the duration of these talks. In his stead, I will speak for my people. I will answer to the name Thrifrit."

Thrifrit was a very different bargainer from Kitikrl. He refused to debate with Bereg. He insisted that the reconnaissance flights cease, and when Bereg tried to reason with him about them, Thrifrit simply insisted again. And again. For variety, Thrifrit would sometimes promise that all agreements would be followed to the very letter by his people, and then he asked Bereg why he was unwilling to live up to his end of the bargain.

At the end of the day, nothing more had been accomplished, and Thrifrit complained just before leaving, "During the first morning's bargainings, I felt sure that we would be able to conclude these talks early, for I felt sure that we understood one another, but you seem determined to make these talks last their full duration. I hope that we are able to resolve the next point on your agenda without any backsliding."

Bereg did not generally let anyone get the last word on him, but before he could respond the Bwotik had left the room. He stood up, his face frozen into an angry smile that he must have hoped concealed the frustration he felt. He had hoped to have a lot to give up in order to secure a favorable agreement on the issue of territorial expansion, but he had nothing to show for two days' negotiations except the agreement he had secured in less than five minutes the first morning. He assigned Carol to speak to the reporters that evening. She denied prior knowledge of the reconnaissance flight, but said that Bereg supported continued flights because "respect for the dead is essential to the dignity of humanity." She announced Kitikrl's illness, but implied that it was a strategic maneuver on the part of the Bwotik.

After dinner that night, Bereg called everyone in charge of some area of the negotiations together and he tried to assemble data on the Bwotik's possible motives. From the IO to the marine captain to the chief waste manager, Bereg subjected all the support personnel to several rounds of intense questioning. At one point, he grew tired, and Carol took over the questioning. Her manner was quiet and seemingly uncertain, but it was even more biting than Bereg's. As he grew more tired, though, he became frustrated with even her and resumed the questions himself. But they didn't remain questions for long. Soon he fell to spewing vitriol on the heads of the people who failed him, each in turn. The military personnel took it well, but the systems manager's eyes were filled with pain whenever he managed to raise them, which was not often. By the time Bereg turned on the chief waste manager, I myself was ready to break. My medication at dinner had barely made a dent in my pain, which kept growing steadily worse.

"Look," I yelled, "why don't we just ask them what they want from us?"

He didn't even turn to look at me. "Spoiled rotten brat! If your daddy could see you now, he'd put you in your place. You're worse than dead weight."

"Senator," Carol said.

Bereg looked at her. Then he took a breath and turned back on the waste manager, but he had lost his momentum. "Get out of my sight! But keep working. I don't want any of you to sleep tonight, and if you do sleep, you'd better dream up a solution to this problem. We meet here, tomorrow, 0600." He made a dismissive gesture, and people scattered, including me. I was very thankful to make it out of the room without further injury. But just as I was heading out the door, he called to me, "Sheila, you stay here."

I sighed, without turning around, "I'd rather go."

"I don't care what you'd rather do. If you walk out that door, you can keep walking onto the shuttle, because I'll get on the FTL right now and report your behavior to the Assembly."

I walked stiffly back to the table and sat down. Everyone else shuffled out. Carol lingered, but Bereg gave her a hard glance that drove her out.

When we were alone, Bereg spoke using the closest approximation to a calm, rational tone that he could manage, "I think the Bwotik sense the conflict between us. They see it as a weakness and they hope to exploit it to get whatever it is they want from us. You have to put your bitterness aside; that's another time and place from here."

"It's not, it's my body."

"Don't be so melodramatic. After your operation, all that's left is for you to heal."

"No, that operation was just to remove the damaged tissue. A cloned replacement is being grown."

"Ah, even better. You'll be able to have children, still."

"In vitro, with cloned eggs only. Not my eggs, not my womb. They might as well be someone else's children, even if they will be mine genetically."

"Sheila, you can hate me if you want to, but you have to believe that what I did was best for both of us. Both our careers would have been destroyed by your announcement and neither of us would be here now. We're participating in history here. Remember that." Bereg paused, then said, "Remember how much your father used to talk about this moment? How much he looked forward to making peace with an alien race?"

I bordered between being chastened by the truth of some of what Bereg said and his imitation of the sage "Uncle Bereg" and being outraged that he would speak to me as if I were at fault. If he had touched me, it would have pushed me over the top, but he refrained, and my anger was therefore without edge. "That's low, invoking my father for your own ends."

"You know you do him disrespect by sabotaging these negotiations. Tomorrow is the final day scheduled, at their insistence. We have to come away with an agreement tomorrow. As I said, hate me if you want to, but help me secure a favorable peace."

I looked at Bereg, trying to unclench my face. "I'll do what I can."

In my room, the contrast between the blank walls and the bright bed hurt my eyes. The pain in my midsection grew suddenly sharp and I almost fell over. I took some more medication. It didn't affect my pain, but I began to feel dazed. The walls trembled, and I felt as if my skin had been burned by exposure to Bereg and was now being chafed by my clothes. I decided to

take a shower before bed. Instead of going to the bathroom, I undressed on the edge of the bed. This seemed
an arduous task and I never finished. Midway
through, I leaned back onto the bed to rest. I fell asleep
almost immediately.

A voice said, "Wake up, Senator," and I opened my
eyes. I was groggy and the white ceiling was blurred,
misty. I believed I was dreaming and I sat up slowly.

There was a Bwotik standing nearby me. He was
blurry, too, but recognizable as Thrifrit by his distinctly
blue carapace. He was also standing perfectly still,
without the usual fidgeting of mandibles. I stood up
and turned so that I was looking directly at him, just an
arm's length away. He tilted his head up to meet my
eyes with his.

"Senator, we wish to speak with you, alone. Please,
come to visit us in our quarters. Do not inform Senator
Bereg or allow him to learn of your visit."

"Why?"

"He is a burr in the joint of peace. We cannot trust
him. If you come, you will help our peoples more than
you suspect."

I shrugged, "Okay."

Thrifrit thanked me and turned to leave. I looked
around, trying to decide what I should bring with me.
I did not hear the door open or close, but thinking
about it made me realize that I was half-naked. For
a second, I was almost ashamed, but then I realized
that I was dreaming. Then I realized that I wasn't
dreaming.

I blushed from head to toe and began to get dressed
rapidly. It did not occur to me that what had just
happened was unusual in any other way, and I
thought up explanations and excuses for my state of
undress. Probably none were necessary for the Bwotik,
only for my piece of mind. I was glad my pains had
subsided.

When I was ready to go, I considered whether or not I should. All meetings between Bwotik and Humans were to occur only in the designated meeting areas and only between officially recognized meeting groups. There were to be no secret bargains. However, negotiations were stalled and maybe I could find some way to communicate that would facilitate resolving difficulties. Without concluding any secret bargains, just talking. Simply getting a chance to talk to go behind Bereg's back was worth the risk, if I could figure out a way past the guards. I was surprised to find that there was none at my door. I left my room and walked quickly and silently toward the Bwotik section of the station through a long, bright, white, empty corridor, its curve imperceptible as it traced its way along the outer rim of the station.

At the first pressure lock, two marines stood, bright red against the first gray metal I had seen since the superstructure. They were killing the night watch through talk and at first they did not see me. She was talking about her home world and her accent was unique. I knew exactly what world it was, and I walked toward the door boldly with a plan.

When the man saw me, he made a signal to the talking woman, his superior, and she snapped to attention. "Senator," she said when I reached her.

"Sergeant," I replied. "I have a meeting with the Bwotik. Unlock the door."

"Senator," the sergeant replied sternly, "I have orders that no one other than support personnel and IOs with a rank of captain or higher is to be allowed through this door. In fact, Senator, I must report this request to Senator Bereg."

"Senator Bereg, huh? Well, he may have you all convinced that he's the sole commander of this operation, but let me tell you that senators all have just one vote—we're all on par, except in some ways. Sergeant Gama, you're Hoffan, right?"

"Yes, Senator."

"Did you know that the Hoffan shipyards are currently before the armed forces subcommittee on production streamlining?"

She looked nervously at the other guard, then back at me. "Yes, Senator."

"Do you know who is chair of that subcommittee? Let me give you a hint: it's not Bereg."

"Senator, no! We all depend on those yards. My father and my husband both work there."

"Not just them. Figures say that two-thirds of the population of Hoffa make their living, directly or indirectly, from those yards. But they're outdated and undersized. Their main product is currently being phased out, and retooling the yards is expected to cost as much as building whole new ones, which is what most of the committee favors, since that would let us place them somewhere more central."

"Senator, you can't be saying—"

"You can secure my vote right now."

She looked at the other guard who shrugged, saying, "Hey, Sarge, this is your call. If you promise to take it on the chin if it comes out, I'll go along with anything."

I focused my eyes on the sergeant, trying to give her a look I had received many times from Bereg, his go-or-get-off-the-pot look.

She sighed, then said, "Well . . . Okay, go. The bugs probably won't let you through, anyway. I can't do anything about them, so don't blame me if they turn you back."

"Of course not," I said. "And I'll do everything I can for the Hoffan yards."

The sergeant didn't look at me, just shook her head slightly. The other guard opened the door with a passcard and code. I stepped through into the airlock. The airlock was a cube, with every face a pressure door,

every corner a light. But no amount of light could make
that gunmetal gray look bright after several days of
living with the bleachy plexiconstruct. The box felt
constricting and with every instant grew more so. As I
walked toward the far door, I wondered whether the
Bwotik were really expecting me and why. Would they
be surprised to see me, think me a spy? Maybe they
would welcome me now and then denounce me later,
when they had placed incriminating evidence, use me
as a pawn to set in motion whatever it was they were
planning. What did they want from me, us? As I stood
with my finger over the Signal button, the air grew
stale and sticky around me. I tried to breathe shallow,
to let the tightly controlled airflow in the lock catch up,
but it didn't. Every inhalation was my own exhalation,
thick, musky, damp, and though it filled my lungs, it
had no sustenance.

I pushed the button. A light went on, indicating that
my signal was being sent. After only a moment, the
door creaked, groaned and hissed open. Beyond, two
Bwotik stood close to the doorway, on either side, each
wearing the familiar gauntlet guns on all four arms.
Beyond them, Thrifrit stood, his mandibles trembling
excitedly. "We've been waiting for you. Come."

We walked down the long empty hallway. Thrifrit
turned suddenly left and entered an unmarked,
unguarded door. Inside, a bright green Bwotik floated
in the middle of the room. I gasped in surprise, then
realized that he was really lying on a white table,
almost invisible against the walls. I believed the Bwotik
was Kitikrl, but I couldn't be sure, since the two Bwotik
standing beside the table were a similar shade of green.

My beliefs were confirmed when he spoke, "Ah,
Senator, I am certainly glad that you have come." He
continued looking at me with a black ovoid composite
eye. "I want you to see what the rest of your species
certainly must not know. We need—" Kitikrl paused. I
looked away from his head toward his abdomen, the

Illustrated by Nina Ollikainen

softest part of the Bwotik body, and more pale than the rest. At first, it did not seem to be moving—he wasn't breathing—then he stirred, but not like breathing. My eyes were locked on Kitikrl's abdomen and did not see Thrifrit come up behind me. I did not hear him asking me to step back. When his hands tried to gently pull me back, though, I screamed.

Thrifrit backed away from me, his four hands raised, open, in a gesture obviously intended to put me at ease about his intentions. "You may wish to step back," he said.

Looking around, I found that I had walked up to the very edge of the table. I took several steps backward.

Kitikrl did not resume speaking. Instead, the writhing in his abdomen increased in intensity. Under the sallow skin, long thin forms were visible. Then a pair of mandibles broke the surface, releasing a puff of gore-laced air. Also coming out was a hungry hiss, and an earthy, fecund smell. Soon, more mandibles broke the surface, tearing the remainder of the skin away until all that remained was the massive maggots writhing, hissing, churning pale ichor, and waving their hungry mandibles. The sight and smell was too much and my gut lurched again and again. My stomach felt as though it were a maggot, writhing within me, and vomiting made me want to vomit again. My hands went not to my stomach, but to the space of my absence, feeling the mechanical replacement, barely functional, temporary. I heaved and heaved until I began to cry, and I tried to stop.

Thrifrit picked me up; though I struggled, I was too weak with nausea to resist. I dribbled mucous and bile on his arm. As he carried me out of the room, my last sight was of one nurse cuddling a maggot, while the other placed a maggot down on another part of Kitikrl's corpse, encouraging it to eat.

In another room, colored completely with blue and purple swirls, Thrifrit placed me on a soft couch. He sat down on a harder bench in the opposite corner and waited for my trembling and weeping to subside. He had given me a cloth to wipe myself with, but I didn't want anything Bwotik near my face.

"We knew we could count on you for an honest response. We expect that most—if not all—of your race would respond similarly."

I tried to create a word construct of what I had seen, so that I could talk about it without seeing the image in my mind. "I think so, but why would it make a difference? Keep it behind closed doors, for God's sake!"

Thrifrit's temper was short, "That may be easy for a species like you, but in less than ten of your days, almost every member of my species will give birth in that fashion."

"Almost all? Surely just the females."

"No, we are not females. We are hermaphrodites, and all of us can—could bear."

"What about the children? What will they do without any adults around?"

"Obviously, not all of us choose to bear. Some of us elect to forego mating. It is a decision we are forced to make very early, too early, when we are idealistic, ignorant. The sacrifice is more than a child can know, more than you can know.

"In the mating time, it is very beautiful. We flock to our first worlds, the smallest number that can maintain us with their stores, and then the flights begin. In the flights, they join together, our entire species, mating all at once. The air is so thick with pheromones, the self-decided eunuchs must be locked away in solitude. All their reproductive equipment, genitalia and wings— has been removed, but their minds still lust, and they can be . . . disruptive. They are drugged as well, given hormones and sedatives, but the smell, so thick, so pervasive, keeps them awake. They cannot be unconscious. They are hovering at the edge of overdose, but still perfectly livid, screaming, their muscles pumping the remnant stumps of their wings, trying to join the thrumming flight of billions. No doctors remain to care for them, no one to care for us, no one can be spared from the species' orgy, except for us, and our cries together fill the days of silence until our impregnated people remember that we are alive or were and come to check on us.

"The madness is gone and left in its place is an emptiness. We bear no fertilized eggs, and we also bear no memories of what could have been the most singular moment in our lives: the moment when anticipation turns to desire and desire to flight, billions of glittering wings caught in the sun's light." Thrifrit clicked to himself, then he said to me, "But the eunuchs get certain benefits."

I took a deep breath and waited for Thrifrit to tell me what the benefits were. He did not seem eager to do so. "Longer life?" I asked.

Thrifrit's wing stumps vibrated against his carapace. "Longer life, yes, but with longer life comes something else. Can you walk?"

"I'm not going back to that room."

"By this time, the grubs will have consumed all that was recognizable in Kitikrl. But we are not going to that room. We are going elsewhere."

I stood.

Thrifrit raised himself off his long bench. Then he led me through the corridors to another room, twice as large, decorated in the same colors, but with a single swirl, a whirlpool originating in the lower far left corner. Diagonal in front of the corner, almost blocking access to it, was a long silver counter, clean and polished. At regular intervals, grooves interrupted the level top, grooves that were lined with a blue-and-purple padding. In the single counter I thought there might be thirty grooves, but most of them were empty except the padding. At the far end of the counter, though, about six maggots rested in the grooves. Immediately in front of them, a gray paste oozed steadily from concealed openings. Upon contact with the air, the paste turned solid but malleable, and the maggots gripped the surface beneath them somehow and worked hard with their mandibles to break off pieces to consume. In front of each groove was a small screen. The screens were changing colors slowly and I could hear a faint murmuring that seemed to originate from nearby them.

"The larvae have minds as hungry as their stomachs. Although they are small, their brains are half the size they will be when they mature. Their learning will continue almost uninterrupted for the next fifty or so of your years, and then they will pupate for ten years, transforming not only their bodies, but their minds through forced meditation on what they have learned. When they emerge, they will be adults, with the pattern of their minds set. They will be able to learn, but everything they learn they will fit into the paradigm established by what they learned as larvae. Since the larvae are largely incapable of movement, someone must choose for them what they will learn, must choose, in effect, what will be the character of the next generation." Thrifrit stopped and looked at me. The little mandibles around his mouth made short, frenzied movements, which I was beginning to suspect was something equivalent to a smile.

I knew he wanted me to respond, and I obliged him, "And that someone, I assume, is you."

The mandibles moved even faster. "Yes," Thrifrit said, "for this generation, I am entrusted with designing the education program. There is one main component yet to be decided: Will this generation learn to love and live in peace with humanity? . . ."

"What?"

"It has been a long time since we have had to train a warrior generation."

"Are you saying—?"

"But if you are unwilling to cooperate, it may be necessary."

I looked hard at Thrifrit. His mandibles had stopped moving. His cold, compound eyes could not blink. His slime-coated carapace glistened and I could not look at him anymore. I turned away, thinking. I turned back and said, "And what is to prevent us from attacking your worlds and killing your maggots before they mature?"

Thrifrit seemed genuinely saddened. "First, we believe that no intelligent species is so inhuman as to slaughter an entire generation of children." Thrifrit paused again, involuntarily. He looked away from me, walked to the edge of the counter, and almost touched the nearest maggot. "Look at them. They are so helpless, so vulnerable. No limbs, just stiff bristles for gripping; no carapaces, just a soft skin. They do not even have eyes yet, merely rudimentary light-sensing organs. How could anyone kill so delicate a creature? Immobile, fragile, blind, seeking only to be nurtured, only to be loved. I assume you feel the same about your own young? Or perhaps you are like me and can merely love the young of others?"

I could not answer, though Thrifrit waited.

He turned around and continued, "But not all of your kind are capable of loving the young of others. Senator Bereg, I believe he is capable of killing a child, perhaps many children. There are, I presume, others like him, probably friends of his, in similar positions of power. Given the knowledge of our vulnerability, they would order another attack. We believe that we have sufficient strength in robotic warships built in automated factories to hold you at bay."

I looked at Thrifrit's cold eyes and could not decide

whether I wanted to squash this vile insect or not. "You're bluffing. You don't know our military strength."

"Perhaps. But our fleets have met in combat. You know how superior our weaponry is. We may be able to hold you at bay until our young mature. And then—" Thrifrit pounced on me with astounding speed, his four legs propelling it up onto the wall and around so that he could attack me from behind. He pushed me with an obviously restrained motion, but he knocked me off my feet. Before I could hit the ground, however, Thrifrit had grabbed me by the wrist with a single hand and lifted me into the air. "And then the new generation would swarm out, seven times as numerous as this generation, all of them trained with a deep loathing for your species, all of them with the tools and desire to kill humanity." Thrifrit was careful not to crush my bones, but I knew he could. I could not breathe as I looked into the pits where his eyes sat, shaded now by the Bwotik's heavy brows. Thrifrit set me down gently, but my legs collapsed and I fell to my knees. He descended from the wall. "Unfortunately, our history shows that we are capable of hunting a species to extinction."

Holding my wrist, I looked up at Thrifrit through my tears, and mustered every ounce of ferocity as I sobbed, "Our history shows the same. We will . . . we will . . ." I could not continue; I looked down and tried not to fall prone under the violence of my sobs.

Thrifrit dropped to all eights, then lowered his body flat to the ground. His antennae pulled back, giving his face an almost vulnerable appearance. "But it doesn't have to be like that. Think of it, Sheila, the next generation can also be born with an unparalleled love and understanding for humanity. Our two species can become great friends and allies. Our larvae can be taught only that which is good and pure about your species. They will be born with a vision of humanity that exceeds what any of your philosophers could have conceived, for they will know none of your failings. As adults, they will learn, of course, but they will put them in the context of your greatest achievements, find ways to excuse the bad and embrace the vision of noble humanity. And through cooperation with this next generation, humanity will learn to become that vision. Our generations are long and the next one will have many years to work with your species for the betterment of all."

I straightened up and stood, trying to pretend I had not been crying. "And what do you want from me? I assume you want something from me. Otherwise you wouldn't have brought me here, gone to the trouble of threatening me."

"Of course," Thrifrit said, "but it is nothing odious, certainly. Nothing that you would not be willing to do if I had not brought you here, shown you this. I did that for honesty's sake, for understanding. It is not necessary to the bargain."

"Dammit, just tell me what you want. I can't stand being here anymore."

"Sheila . . ."

"Don't call me that."

"Senator Rindillo, I want two things from you. First, I want you to help me negotiate with Bereg, teach me to get what we need from him without revealing our secret. This will ensure peace between our species, and for it I will teach our young to love and admire humanity."

"And what's the second thing you want?"

"I do not have the knowledge necessary to pass on to the next generation. It is easy to teach hate, but in order to teach love, I need someone to act as a filter, to give me information about all that is best of humanity."

"You want me to be a spy?"

"As I understand it, that word has a negative meaning, and I'm asking nothing of the sort. I am asking you to be simply what you are now: an ambassador. I want you to share with me all that you love about your species, all that is beautiful and noble, all that is pure and admirable. I want you to tell me what humanity could be if it could shed the dross of its cruelty, its selfishness. This, then, I will pass on to the next generation."

I looked at the enormous insect. His eyes were still cold and dark; his carapace still glistened with slime, and the entire room was saturated with his fecund, sickening smell. His mandibles—both the large, fanglike pincers, and the smaller, handlike grabbers were still. The hardness of the exoskeleton made the face unreadable. "And how do I know you'll keep your bargain? One of the things you want is complete privacy; that means we get no information out, that means I can't know what's going on back there. You could be preparing to kill us, while we sit back, idle for fifty years and more, content in what we think is peace, but then your next generation swarms and wipes us out. How do I know?"

Thrifrit tilted his head, looked at me with only one eye. "You will not know. Our people say: Trust is a child that grows into peace. You must demonstrate that you can love at least this child."

I put my hand on the source of the growing pain inside me. I was healing, but I would never be whole. I would never have a child of my own, but could I love Thrifrit's? I couldn't even look the creature in the eye as I said, "Bereg's afraid that your species will expand and trap humanity. Threaten him with that, and he'll be more amenable to your demands. Losing access to your worlds is preferable to you getting too many worlds. Then offer him a chance to make money keeping your systems isolated. You can't do it directly, but if you hint that a reliable security firm will be required to keep ships from starting out toward Bwotik space, a firm that'll receive payments from both the Human and Bwotik governments as part of the treaty, he'll jump on it."

Thrifrit lowered its body flat to the ground. His eyes were completely concealed by his heavy brow ridges, and he said, "Thank you, thank you, Senator Rindillo."

In a way, I was disappointed by the barrier of formality I had imposed between us. Thrifrit had offered me friendship, but I was still repulsed by the idea. "You're welcome. Can I go now?"

Thrifrit stood up slowly, and said slowly, "Yes, you can go if you wish. Keep this conversation a secret as long as you can. We will never again meet in private and tomorrow Senator Bereg will do all the speaking again. Goodbye."

I hurried away. I was glad to find the same marines on duty at the airlock. They did not ask me any questions and I didn't offer any explanations about what had happened.

The next day, Thrifrit played the angle I recommended, and it played well. As I knew, Thrifrit could balance threats and promises to get what he wanted, but he was more subtle when dealing with Bereg. By the end of the day, Thrifrit made Bereg glad to come away with largely the terms that had been agreed to on the first day, and made him feel he had driven a hard bargain to get them. It was agreed that closer cooperation between our two races might someday be possible, and that another summit should be held sixty Earth years in the future to reexamine the question. At the final press briefing, Senator Bereg claimed that he had secured "a peace for all time," one which guaranteed his promised future of "security, prosperity and dignity."

The Senate dutifully ratified the terms of the treaty and eventually granted the security contract to Bereg's firm. A lucrative contract, to be sure, but he didn't have much time to enjoy it as he died soon after. Carol fought in court for a share of the wealth, but she lost the case, and it all went to Bereg's widow. Senator Oyente had a long undistinguished career as a conservative, never seeking publicity, only productivity. He resigned just a few months before he died last year.

After ensuring the renovation of the Hoffan shipyards, I did not seek reelection. I decided to focus on the monumental task Thrifrit laid on me, feeding the pure, white distillate of human culture to his maggots. I have also nurtured this other child, this trust, like a cocoon. I don't know what will emerge. Most days I feel I have done well by my species, but sometimes I wonder whether the Bwotik deceived me. In my nightmares, I see the massed invasion of Bwotik, a swarm of ships built in robotic factories over the past sixty years, filled with hideous, stinking bodies, every one consumed with a desire to destroy all humanity. I see them creep silently across space and enter into my room to stand beside the bed where I am sleeping. I awake screaming. As the time for the next summit approaches, these nightmares only increase in frequency. I said I have nurtured this child, the only one I have, but I cannot say that I have loved it.

A BOY AND HIS BICYCLE

Written by
Carl Frederick

Illustrated by
Jared Barber

About the Author

Carl Frederick is a theoretical physicist by profession but a writer by avocation. As chief scientist of a small company producing AI (Artificial Intelligence) software, he decided he'd like to write a more overt form of science fiction and, to that end, enrolled in the Odyssey Writers Workshop.

Carl now has a respectable corpus of short stories, mostly unpublished, according to him. Yet he has been highly successful in the Writers of the Future Contest. Last year, his finalist story, "The Art of Creation," was selected by the editor for inclusion in Writers of the Future Volume XVIII, and this year, he not only placed again in the finals, but went on to win First Place in his quarterly competition with the following story.

About the Illustrator

As long as he can remember, Jared Barber has had the goal of attaining a career in art and has had the unwavering support of his family to pursue it. He began by enrolling in an animation course in Winnipeg, Manitoba, and went on to attend life-drawing courses at the University of Manitoba and the Winnipeg Art Gallery. Thereafter, he was accepted to a three-year, full-time classical animation program at Sheridan College in Ontario.

Jared is currently completing a 3D character animation specialist course in Winnipeg. He's confident that the strong educational foundation he has worked so hard to build for himself will help him face future artistic challenges.

L ike a stork, a creature of the air but awkward on land, Bevan Harrison stepped toward Red Flyer. His bike shoes, stiff-soled and ill suited for walking, clattered with a sharp staccato on the concrete floor of the garage. At the same time, the sensor wires running up the inside of his athletic shorts flopped about, reminding him that he wasn't wearing his chamois-padded bicycle pants. His mother had captured his only pair for the laundry.

He pressed his thumb against the bike's security sensor and the locking mechanism retracted from the rear wheel. "Good morning, Red Flyer." Bevan grabbed his helmet, and wheeled the bicycle toward the door.

"Good morning, Little Beaver," said the bicycle. "8:45 Saturday morning. Are we going for a training run?"

"Yeah, but later. I just want to ride around for a while. Looks nice out."

"Eighteen degrees Celsius, thirty-eight percent relative humidity." The bicycle's voice was that of a teenage boy. "But first, I think you should lubricate my chain and sprockets. It's been over a month."

Years ago, when Bevan received Red Flyer as a birthday present, the bicycle spoke like the big brother he'd always wanted. Now, the two of them sounded like twins.

"Yeah. Okay." Bevan performed the maintenance,

then polished the frame and ran a cloth over each of the wheel-spokes. He stepped back. "You look great— like the day I got you." He patted the simulated leather bike seat, and rolled Red Flyer out of the garage.

"My rear tire is a little low."

"We'll stop at a gas station."

Squinting in the morning light, Bevan guided Red Flyer down the driveway. Seeing his parents on the front lawn, he quickened his pace, hoping for a clean getaway.

Busy at the controls of her Spectrahome remote, his mother didn't seem to notice him; neither did his father who, at the far end of the lawn, stared intently at the house.

"That's good, Ellen," said Mr. Harrison, "but perhaps a little more blue on the trim."

Bevan's mother worked a dial on the remote and the house window trimming turned a robin's-egg blue. Then she looked up—directly at Bevan.

"Shoot," said Bevan, under his breath.

"Bev, darling. What do you think of our summer colors?"

"Fine." Bevan continued rolling Red Flyer toward the street.

"Honey, wait. It's a pretty morning. Can't you go cycling, just once, without being wired-up like a puppet?"

Bevan ignored her but became self-conscious about the wiring harness. Taped to his thighs halfway between kneecaps and groin, were two muscle stimulator pads attached by wires running down inside his shorts. He had a heartbeat sensor taped to his chest, a blood pressure monitor on his arm, and a perspiration sensor at the small of his back. A connector hung over the edge of his shorts, ready to be plugged into a socket on the bicycle frame.

When he reached the sidewalk, he called back over his shoulder. "I think the house should be black."

He started to mount his bike, but his father pulled him away. "Your mother was talking to you. That wasn't very polite ignoring her like that, was it?"

Bevan looked down at the ground. "Sorry."

"All right. Let's talk." Mr. Harrison motioned and Bevan flipped down Red's kickstand, then followed his dad off onto the lawn.

Mr. Harrison stopped and put an arm around Bevan's shoulder. "Is something wrong? You've been sort of touchy of late."

Bevan shrugged.

"Is something going on at school?"

Bevan shrugged again.

"Do you want to talk about it?"

"No."

"What is it? Is there some sort of boy-code that says you can't talk about your troubles?"—Bevan squirmed free—"It's okay to express your worries, your feelings. It's unhealthy keeping them bottled up."

"I told you. Nothing's the matter."

"Come on. You're fourteen now, and that's old enough to be able to talk rationally about your problems."

"It's just that Mom doesn't like Red."

"No. I don't think that's true. She's just not nuts about the sensors. And she's not crazy about the electric shock pads in the bike seat either."

"It doesn't hurt, and it's only to remind me when I'm sitting too heavy during hill climbs. It works. I can do fifty kilometers in fifty-seven minutes."

"Still," said Mr. Harrison, "if I'd used that kind of training on you for, say, taking out the trash, I've no doubt I'd be languishing in prison for child abuse."

"Jeez, Dad." Bevan looked up at his father. "I'm

Illustrated by Jared Barber

going to be a bike racer, and Red is training me. That's why you bought him for me. You said he would be good discipline for me."

Mr. Harrison rubbed his eyes, an action that Bevan knew usually preceded a lecture. But his father simply looked away toward the house, and spoke, seemingly to himself. "Maybe the bicycle's outlived its purpose."

"Don't talk about Red that way," said Bevan. "He's my best friend."

"Friend? Damn, Bevan. It's just a bicycle."

"You don't like him either." Bevan turned and stalked away toward Red Flyer. He did a rolling mount and pedaled down the street.

"You seem to be pedaling erratically this morning," said Red Flyer. "Is something wrong?

"Yeah. I'm having a problem with my dad."

"Would you like to talk about it?"

"No."

For the next quarter hour, Bevan, without talking, pedaled steadily with a practiced, rapid cadence. Soon, the manicured, tree-lined suburb gave way to fast-food outlets and gas stations. Bevan stopped to fill his water bottle and pump up Red's rear tire. Then they continued on into the countryside. Out early on a Saturday, they had the road mostly to themselves. Moving as one and accompanied only by the twittering of birds and the soft, locustlike hum of the chain gliding over the sprockets, boy and bicycle could converse quietly, without having to shout over traffic.

"Do you mind if I apply the brakes a little?" said Red Flyer. "My battery's running low and I need to transfer some braking power into the charger."

"Yeah, fine. We're going downhill, anyway."

"Thanks. Do you want to hear a bicycle joke?"

"I've heard all your jokes." Bevan pedaled harder against the drag of the brakes.

"I've got some new ones."

"How the heck do you get new jokes?"

"Last week, an X10 rode by us. It uploaded a new file from I-Bike to me."

"I didn't know you could do that kind of stuff."

"I can't, but an X10 can." Red Flyer spoke with enthusiasm. "The Intelligent Bicycle Corporation's model X10 is the best. It's lighter, faster, more intelligent. You should get one."

"But Red, we're so alike, you and me." Bevan laughed. "How would I ever get along without you?"

"You wouldn't have to, Little Beaver. You could upload my personality module into your new X10."

"You sound like a TV commercial." The road slanted upward and Bevan switched gears, keeping his pedal rhythm steady. "Turn off the brakes, will you?"

"Sure. And with the X10," Red went on, "the gears move left and right while the chain remains in the plane of the bicycle. That gives a 2.4 percent increase in efficiency."

"Yeah. An X10 would be great," said Bevan, breathing heavily from the climb. "Dad gave in pretty easily to get you, but I'd just about have to sell my soul before he'd buy me an X10."

"Maybe you could get a part-time job."

"Sheesh." Bevan swung on to a side road that angled gently down toward the reservoir.

"Well?" said Red Flyer.

"I don't want to get a part-time job."

"I mean, do you want to hear a bicycle joke?"

"Yeah, sure. Tell me a joke."

"What's wide at the bottom, narrow at the top, and rides a bicycle?"

"I give up." Bevan gave the ritual response. "What is wide at the bottom, narrow at the top, and rides a bicycle?"

"A mountain."

"Rides a bicycle?"

"Haven't you heard of mountain bikes?"

"That stinks."

"Okay, how about this one?" said Red Flyer. "What bicycle wrote the Messiah?"

"I don't know."

"George Frederick Handlebars."

"I don't get it."

"Neither do I. But did you hear the one about the tricycle that rolled into a pet shop?"

"I think you should shut up, now."

Bevan cycled onto the reservoir access roadway, and then cut off to the dirt road that ran near the water's edge. He stopped and looked over the calm blue surface shimmering against the morning haze. Astride his bicycle, motionless, one foot stretched to the ground and the other resting on a pedal, he listened to the wavelets lapping against the pebble-strewn shore, and heard the occasional call of a distant sea bird.

He looked up and saw a kite soaring high. "Free as a bird. No one telling me what to do." He let his gaze follow the kite string to the ground. There, a small boy held the spool of string, but in front of him, a man pulled on the line, making the kite circle and swoop against the sky.

Bevan wrinkled his nose. "Let's get out of here." He threw all his weight onto the raised pedal and the bicycle lurched into motion. "I think I'm ready for a training run."

"All right, Little Beaver. Say 'yes' to begin a training run, or 'no' to cancel." The bicycle's voice grew deeper and older, early twenties, maybe, and though still clearly Red Flyer, the voice held a tone of command.

"Yes," said Bevan.

"What kind of training would you like? Track trials or hill climbing trials? Your last training run was hill climbing."

"Hill climbing trials."

"What exertion level? Select zero through ninety-nine. The highest you've ever done is sixty-seven. Your last setting was sixty-three."

"Eighty," said Bevan.

"Are you sure? I'd recommend sixty to seventy."

"I'm sure." Bevan pumped the brake levers for emphasis.

"An age-adjusted level of eighty acknowledged. What type training? Endurance, technique or both? Your last run was technique."

"Endurance."

"Endurance acknowledged. Proceeding with safety check. Are you wearing bicycle shoes?"

"Yes."

"Helmet?"

"Yes."

"Bicycle pants?"

Bevan hesitated. It would only be a hill climbing run, and anyway, Red Flyer wouldn't be able to tell. "Yes."

"Wiring harness?"

"Yes."

"Okay. Plug in your harness now."

Bevan unhooked the connector from his shorts and snapped it into the bicycle's control panel.

"Good." Red Flyer's voice came now from speakers in the bicycle helmet. "What path will we be riding? The last time it was around the reservoir."

"Yeah. It's the reservoir again. We're there now."

"If you had an X10, he wouldn't have to ask you where we are," said the bicycle. "X10s have Global Positioning Satellite modules."

"Yeah, I know. "

"Okay," said the bicycle. "Are you ready to ride?"

"Yes."

"Start pedaling and snap your shoes in. Then say 'go.'"

Bevan started cycling, and with the stability brought by motion, used the tips of his shoes to flip the pedals over, toe-clip up. He slid his shoes under the clips and pushed down. The shoes snapped in, making boy and bicycle a single unit.

"Okay, go."

"For level eighty I will apply braking to give a simulated grade of between zero and twenty-eight percent."

"I know, I know," said Bevan.

"Since this is endurance only, I will do the gear shifting."

"Yeah, yeah."

"When you say 'start' we will begin. If, at any time, you need to halt training, say 'stop.'"

"Start."

"All right, Little Beaver, we'll start with a warm up. Zero percent grade. Start pedaling in cadence. Push the right pedal down at the high beep and the left pedal down at the low beep."

"We've done this a zillion times. Do you have to repeat the instructions each time?"

"Yes."

"Sheesh."

In time with the beeps, Bevan pedaled off at a leisurely rate of seventy cranks per minute. Over the next quarter of an hour, the bicycle gradually increased the rate to 128.

Bevan's breathing grew labored and he started to sweat. He was used to this, though, and he felt great. The wind tickled his ears; the landscape whizzed by and he reveled in the power of his body.

Then, little by little, Red Flyer slip-applied the brakes to simulate a steep grade.

At first, Bevan pedaled standing up, as if he were springing up a flight of steps. But after a quarter of an hour, it was more like running up a mountain with feet weighted down by bricks.

"This is hard," he said, panting.

"Do you want to stop?"

"No."

"Okay, but your pedaling is slowing. You're falling behind the cadence."

Red Flyer held to a relentless 128; Bevan's clothes dripped with sweat.

"Put your body into it," the bicycle commanded. "This is a climb. You're sitting too heavily on the seat. Use the honking motion. Stand on the pedals."

Bevan struggled for breath and his thighs burned with pain.

"Don't drop your cadence," insisted the bicycle. "Pedal faster."

"I can't," Bevan cried.

"Yes, you can. Beginning muscle stimulation now. Say 'cancel' to end muscle stimulation."

The bicycle applied voltage pulses to Bevan's thigh muscles in time with the beeps.

Bevan groaned in agony as the pulses jerked his legs up and down with the cadence. But he wasn't about to say 'cancel.' No way he'd let Red Flyer win.

He wished he'd worn his bicycle pants; his thin, sweat-soaked, running shorts offered little protection against chaffing from the bike seat. But that scraping pain was nothing compared to the fire in his legs. He cursed himself for the stupidity of demanding endurance level eighty.

"You're sitting. You should be standing on the pedals. This is your second warning."

Bevan's eyes teared over and he sniffled. "I'm trying, Red."

"Only six minutes more, Little Beaver. Do you want to stop now?"

"No," said Bevan, squinting; sweat trickled into his eyes.

Suddenly, through the agony, Bevan began to feel the exercise high, the exhilaration of a body working at peak performance.

"I can do this," he panted.

"I know you can, Little Beaver."

Grunting at each stroke, Bevan looked ahead, trying to guess at a landmark six minutes away, a physical point he could seize on and struggle toward. But closer, directly in front of him, stood the only hill on the entire circumference of the reservoir.

As he cycled up the hill—a real incline rather than one simulated by his bike—he sat back on the seat.

"I've warned you two times before," said Red Flyer. "Don't sit on the seat when hill climbing."

A jolt of electricity shot through the bicycle seat. Bevan screamed and stood bolt upright.

Had he been wearing his padded bicycle pants, he'd have hardly felt the tingle, but with only sweaty running shorts covering a bottom rubbed raw by the bike seat, the shock was like a stroke from a whip.

He convulsively jerked his arms and squeezed the brakes. He'd just gone over the crest of the hill, and the bicycle pointed sharply downward. Bevan, standing on the pedals, fell forward and grasped even harder on the brakes.

The bicycle leaned sharply. Bevan released the brakes and turned the handlebars into the lean. He regained his balance, but now the bicycle sped, out of control, down the steep incline on the reservoir side of the hill.

Near the bottom, the bicycle grazed a scraggly tree, bounced upward, then fell like a shot into the reservoir.

Bevan gasped at the sudden cold, his mouth filling with water. He tried to jerk his feet free from the pedals but, under water, he couldn't make the quick snapping motion. Twisting his body double, he tried to untie a shoe, but the water-bloated knot wouldn't give. He pushed with both hands against the heel and finally his foot came free. He freed his other foot and then, dizzy from lack of air, kicked away, coughing and choking, to the surface.

As he struck out for shore, the sensors ripped from his body and he yelped in pain. Looking down, he saw the sensor cables drifting to the sandy bottom of the reservoir and his bicycle sparkling like sunken treasure. Feeling embarrassed as he realized the water was only about a meter and a half deep, he stood, reached down for his bicycle and bobbed his way to dry land.

Bevan leaned Red Flyer against a tree, tossed his helmet to the ground and, doglike, shook his head, loosing a storm of shimmering droplets into the clear, warm air. Then he collapsed to the ground.

When his breathing had returned to normal, he rolled over a few times, exchanging a wet section of grass for a dry, sun-warmed patch. Lying on his back, Bevan looked over at his bicycle and laughed. Red Flyer looked very odd with bicycle shoes on the pedals, but with no rider.

"Red. You look funny."

The bicycle didn't answer.

Bevan got to his feet and bent to examine Red Flyer. "Damn it. There goes a week's allowance." He straightened up. "Red, I'm afraid you need a new front wheel."

Patting Red Flyer on the frame, Bevan noticed that the ready light was off.

"Red, are you all right?"

Bevan tapped the on/off switch several times, hit the reset panel, but nothing happened. Then he saw the crack in the computer casing.

"Talk to me."

Water dripped from the computer module.

Bevan lifted the bicycle, shook it, and turned it upside down.

"Say something."

He continued shaking his bicycle until no more water fell from the casing.

"Red." Bevan set the bicycle back against the tree.

"Red. Say something." Leaning against the frame, he held the handlebars and pumped the brakes a few times.

"Please." He released a brake lever for a moment to rub the moisture from his eyes, then pumped them again. "Please. Don't die."

To busy himself with something, Bevan bent down and unclipped his shoes from the bicycle. Red looked ridiculous with shoes hanging from the pedals.

He dialed home on his watch-phone. "Why couldn't you have died instead of Red?" he said, glowering at the phone.

His father answered after one ring.

"Bev. I've been worried. What's wrong?"

"Dad, I've had an accident."

"Where are you? Are you okay?"

"Yeah, but I need you to come pick me up in the van."

Bevan gave directions.

The morning haze had cleared and the sun blazed in a blue sky unmarred by clouds. Bevan, already dry, lifted Red Flyer's twisted front wheel in the air and trudged out to the road; the dried mud on his socks released puffs of brown powder at every step.

Gently, he laid his bike on the ground, hoping that the sun's drying heat would somehow effect a cure, that it would bake the toxic moisture from Red Flyer's body.

Something puzzled him. He phoned his father again. "When I called before, how did you know something was wrong?"

After a few seconds of silence, his father answered. "The bicycle's kid-tracker went dead."

"Kid-tracker?" Bevan closed the connection and looked over to his bicycle. "Kid-tracker? "

He ran his hand over the bicycle. The frame was hot and dry in the sun, but still the bicycle showed no signs of life. By the time his father screeched the van to a halt by the roadway, Bevan had to admit to himself that Red Flyer was dead.

With a dull, lifeless voice, Bevan explained what had happened.

"Doggone it, Bevan," said Mr. Harrison, "when I was a kid, you rode a bicycle. The bicycle didn't ride you." Then he softened. "Not having a bike is hard, but the bike's insured. We'll get you another one. I know you've wanted an X10."

"I don't want another bike," said Bevan. "Red Flyer wasn't just some dumb bicycle. He was my . . ." He let the sentence trail off, not trusting himself to finish it without crying.

Bevan put Red Flyer in the rear of the van, and then slouched into the back seat. "You made Red spy on me."

Mr. Harrison drummed his fingers on the wheel. "No, not spying." He moved a hand to the ignition key. "Worse, maybe," he added, softly.

Bevan stole a fleeting glance at his father's eyes through the rearview window.

"When you were small," said Mr. Harrison, staring

straight ahead, "I thought you needed to develop some sense of responsibility." He started the engine. "So when we got your bike, I had the Discipline-with-Responsibility software installed." Bevan could scarcely hear his dad over the engine noise. "It was a mistake, but until you told me just now, I'd no idea how physically coercive that bicycle could be. But I should have known. I'm sorry, son."

Bevan looked vacantly out the window, and rubbed a hand along the smooth metal of the handlebars.

Mr. Harrison looked over his shoulder. "Don't you want to ride up front?"

"No."

"Don't withdraw. I know it hurts. You can talk to me about it."

"Leave me alone."

Mr. Harrison turned away and the van lurched into motion.

The car radio was off, yet from the speakers came a soft, male voice. "You are driving erratically," it said. "Is something wrong?"

Reflected in the side window, Bevan saw his dad tighten his hold on the steering wheel.

"You are driving erratically," the car said again, louder this time. "What is wrong?"

"Nothing," said Mr. Harrison. "Just a little problem with my kid."

"Would you like to talk about it?"

"No."

Bevan leaned his cheek against Red Flyer and a tear slipped to the handlebar, leaving a thin sliver of brightness against the dusty metal.

SUSPENSE

Written by
L. Ron Hubbard

About the Author

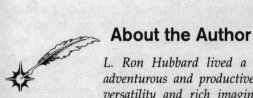

L. Ron Hubbard lived a remarkably adventurous and productive life whose versatility and rich imaginative scope both spanned and ranged far beyond his extensive literary achievements and creative influence. A writer's writer of enormous talent and energy, the breadth and diversity of his writing ultimately embraced more than 560 works and over 63 million words of fiction and nonfiction. Throughout his fifty-six-year writing career, convinced of the crucial role of the arts in civilization, he generously helped other writers and artists, especially beginners, become more proficient and successful at their craft.

Starting with the publication in 1934 of "The Green God," his first adventure yarn, in one of the hugely popular "pulp fiction" magazines of the day, L. Ron Hubbard's outpouring of fiction was prodigious—often exceeding a million words a year. Ultimately, he produced more than 250 published novels, short stories and screenplays in virtually every major genre.

L. Ron Hubbard had, indeed, already attained broad popularity and acclaim in other genres when he burst onto the landscape of speculative literature with his first published science fiction story, "The Dangerous Dimension." It was his groundbreaking work in this field that not only helped to indelibly enlarge the imaginative boundaries of science fiction and fantasy, but established him as one of the founders and signature architects of what continues to be regarded as the genre's golden age.

Such trendsetting L. Ron Hubbard classics of speculative fiction as Final Blackout, Fear, Typewriter in the Sky, To the Stars, as well as his New York Times best-selling novels, the epic saga of the year 3000 Battlefield Earth and the ten-volume Mission Earth series, continue to appear on bestseller lists around the world.

The article that follows, "Suspense," was written by L. Ron Hubbard and first published in the June 1937 issue of The Author & Journalist—one of the most prominent writer's magazines of the time—when he had already established a commanding reputation in many of the genres of popular fiction. The question he poses in the article goes urgently to the heart of the creative process: what rivets a reader to the page, "tensely wondering which of two or three momentous things is going to happen first." The answer L. Ron Hubbard provides, by insightful analysis and example, is both witty and compelling. Read on and discover it for yourself.

ext to checks, the most intangible thing in this business of writing is that quantity "Suspense."

It is quite as elusive as editorial praise, as hard to corner and recognize as a contract writer.

But without any fear of being contradicted I can state that suspense, or rather, the lack of it, is probably responsible for more rejects than telling an editor he is wrong.

You grab the morning mail, find a long brown envelope. You read a slip which curtly says, "Lacks suspense."

Your wife starts cooking beans, you start swearing at the most enigmatic, unexplanatory, hopeless phrase in all that legion of reject phrases.

If the editor had said, "I don't think your hero had a tough enough time killing Joe Blinker," you could promptly sit down and kill Joe Blinker in a most thorough manner.

But when the editor brands and damns you with that first cousin to infinity, "Suspense," you just sit and swear.

Often the editor, in a hurry and beleaguered by stacks of manuscripts higher than the Empire State, has to tell you something to explain why he doesn't like your wares. So he fastens upon the action, perhaps. You can tell him (and won't, if you're smart) that your action is already so fast that you had to grease your typewriter roller to keep the rubber from getting hot.

Maybe he says your plot isn't any good, but you

know doggone well that it is a good plot and has been a good plot for two thousand years.

Maybe, when he gives you those comments, he is, as I say, in a hurry. The editor may hate to tell you you lack suspense because it is something like BO—your best friends won't tell you.

But the point is that whether he says that your Mary Jones reminds him of *The Perils of Pauline*,[1] or that your climax is flat, there's a chance that he means suspense.

Those who have been at this business until their fingernails are worn to stumps are very often overconfident of their technique. I get that way every now and then, until something hauls me back on my haunches and shows me up. You just forget that technique is not a habit, but a constant set of rules to be frequently refreshed in your mind.

And so, in the scurry of getting a manuscript in the mail, it is not unusual to overlook some trifling factor which will mean the difference between sale and rejection.

This suspense business is something hard to remember. You know your plot (or should, anyway) before you write it. You forget that the reader doesn't. Out of habit, you think plot is enough to carry you through. Sometimes it won't. You have to fall back on none-too-subtle mechanics.

Take this, for example:

He slid down between the rocks toward the creek, carrying the canteens clumsily under his arm, silently cursing his sling. A shadow loomed over him.

"*Franzawi!*"[2] screamed the Arab sentinel.

There we have a standard situation. In the Atlas. The hero has to get to water or his wounded legionnaires will die of thirst. But, obviously, it is very, very flat except for the slight element of surprising the reader.

Surprise doesn't amount to much. That snap ending tendency doesn't belong in the center of the story. Your reader knew there were Arabs about. He knew the hero was going into danger. But that isn't enough. Not half.

Legionnaire Smith squirmed down between the rocks clutching the canteens, his eyes fixed upon the bright silver spot which was the waterhole below. A shadow loomed across the trail before him. Hastily he slipped backward into cover.

An Arab sentinel was standing on the edge of the trail, leaning on his long gun. The man's brown eyes were turned upward, watching a point higher on the cliff, expecting to see some sign of the besieged legionnaires.

Smith started back again, moving as silently as he could, trying to keep the canteens from banging. His sling-supported arm was weak. The canteens were slipping.

He could see the sights on the Arab's rifle and knew they would be lined on him the instant he made a sound.

The silver spot in the ravine was beckoning. He could not return with empty canteens. Maybe the sentinel would not see him if he slipped silently around the other side of this boulder.

He tried it. The man remained staring wolfishly up at the pillbox fort.

Maybe it was possible after all. That bright spot of silver was so near, so maddening to swollen tongues. . . .

Smith's hand came down on a sharp stone. He lifted it with a jerk.

A canteen rattled to the trail.

For seconds nothing stirred or breathed in this scorching world of sun and stone.

Then the sentry moved, stepped a pace up the path, eyes searching the shadows, gnarled hands tight on the rifle stock.

Smith moved closer to the boulder, trying to get out of sight, trying to lure the sentry toward him so that he could be silently killed.

The canteen sparkled in the light.

A resounding shout rocked the blistered hills.

"Franzawi!" cried the sentinel.

The surprise in the first that a sentinel would be there and that Smith was discovered perhaps made the reader blink.

The dragging agony of suspense in the latter made the reader lean tensely forward, devour the page, gulp . . .

Or at least, I hope it did.

But there's the point. Keep your reader wondering which of two things will happen (i.e., Will Smith get through or will he be discovered?) and you get his interest. You focus his mind on an intricate succession of events, and that is much better than getting him a little groggy with one swift sock to the medulla oblongata.

That is about the only way you can heighten drama out of melodrama.

It is not possible, of course, to list all the ways this method can be used. But it is possible to keep in mind the fact that suspense is better than fight action.

And speaking of fight action, there is one place where Old Man Suspense can be made to work like an Elkton marrying parson.[3]

Fights, at best, are gap fillers. The writer who introduces them for the sake of the fight itself and not for the effects upon the characters is a writer headed for eventual oblivion even in the purely action books.

Confirmed by the prevailing trend, I can state that the old saw about action for the sake of action was right. A story jammed and packed with blow-by-blow accounts of what the hero did to the villain and what the villain did to the hero, with fists, knives, guns, bombs, machine guns, belaying pins, bayonets, poison gas, strychnine, teeth, knees and calks is about as interesting to read as the *Congressional Record* and about twice as dull. You leave yourself wide open to a reader comment, "Well, what of it?"

But fights accompanied by suspense are another matter.

Witness the situation in which the party of the first

part is fighting for possession of a schooner, a girl or a bag of pearls. Unless you have a better example of trite plotting, we proceed. We are on the schooner. The hero sneaks out of the cabin and there is the villain on his way to sink the ship. So we have a fight:

> Jim dived at Bart's legs, but Bart was not easily thrown. They stood apart. Jim led with his left, followed through with his right. Black Bart countered the blows. Bone and sinew cracked in the mighty thunder of conflict. . . . Jim hit with his right. . . . Bart countered with a kick in the shins. . . .

There you have a masterpiece for wastebasket filing. But, believe it, this same old plot and this same old fight look a lot different when you have your suspense added. They might even sell if extracted and toned like this:

> Jim glanced out of the chartroom and saw Black Bart. Water dripping from his clothes, his teeth bared, his chest heaving from his long swim, Bart stood in a growing pool which slid down his arms and legs. In his hand he clutched an axe, ready to sever the hawser and release them into the millrace of the sweeping tide. . . .

This is Jim's cue, of course, to knock the stuffing out of Black Bart, but that doesn't make good reading nor very much wordage, for thirty words are enough in which to recount any battle as such, up to and including wars.

So we add suspense. For some reason Jim can't leap into the fray right at that moment. Suppose we add that he has these pearls right there and he's afraid Ringo, Black Bart's henchman, will up and swipe them when Jim's back is turned. So first Jim has to stow the pearls.

This gets Bart halfway across the deck toward that straining hawser which he must cut to wreck the schooner and ruin the hero.

Now, you say, we dive into it. Nix. We've got a spot here for some swell suspense. Is Black Bart going to cut that hawser? Is Jim going to get there?

Jim starts. Ringo hasn't been on his way to steal the pearls but to knife Jim, so Jim tangles with Ringo, and Black Bart races toward the hawser some more.

Jim's fight with Ringo is short. About like this:

Ringo charged, eyes rolling, black face set. Jim glanced toward Bart. He could not turn his back on this charging demon. Yet he had to get that axe.

Jim whirled to meet Ringo. His boot came up and the knife sailed over the rail and into the sea. Ringo reached out with his mighty hands. Jim stepped through and nailed a right on Ringo's button. Skidding, Ringo went down.

Jim sprinted forward toward Bart. The black-bearded colossus spun about to meet the rush, axe upraised.

Now, if you want to, you can dust off this scrap. But don't give it slug by slug. Hand it out, thus:

The axe bit down into the planking. Jim tried to recover from his dodge. Bart was upon him, slippery in Jim's grasp. In vain Jim tried to land a solid blow, but Bart was holding him hard.

"Ringo!" roared Bart. "Cut that hawser!"

Ringo, dazed by Jim's blow, struggled up. Held tight in Bart's grasp, Jim saw Ringo lurch forward and yank the axe out of the planking.

"That hawser!" thundered Bart. "I can't hold this fool forever!"

Now, if you wanted that hawser cut in the first place (which you did, because that means more trouble and the suspense of wondering how the schooner will get out of it) cut that hawser right now before the reader suspects that this writing business is just about as mechanical as fixing a Ford.

Action suspense is easy to handle, but you have to know when to quit and you have to evaluate your drama and ladle it out accordingly.

Even in what the writers call the psychological story you have to rely upon suspense just as mechanical as this.

Give your reader a chance to wonder for a while about the final outcome.

There is one type of suspense, however, so mechanical that it clanks. I mean foreshadowing.

To foreshadow anything is weak. It is like a boxer stalling for the bell. You have to be mighty sure that you've got something outstanding to foreshadow, or the reader will nail up your scalp.

It is nice to start ominously, like this:

> I knew that night as I sloshed through the driving rain that all was not well. I had a chilly sense of foreboding as though a monster dogged my steps. . . .

> If I only had known then what awaited me when the big chimes in the towers should strike midnight, I would have collapsed with terror. . . .

Very good openings. Very, very good. Proven goods, even though the nap is a bit worn. But how many times have writers lived up to those openings? Not very many.

You get off in high, but after you finish you will probably tear out these opening paragraphs—even though Poe was able to get away with this device. Remember the opening of "The Fall of the House of Usher"? You know, the one that goes something like this: "Through the whole of a dark and dismal afternoon . . ."

That is foreshadowing. However, few besides Poe have been able to get away with suspense created by atmosphere alone.

One particular magazine makes a practice of inserting a foreshadow as a first paragraph in every story. I have come to suspect that this is done editorially because the foreshadow is always worse than the story gives you.

> It's a far cry from the jungles of Malaysia to New York, and there's a great difference between the yowl of the tiger and the rattle of the L,[4] but in the city that night

there stalked the lust of the jungle killers and a man who had one eye. . . .

I have been guilty of using such a mechanism to shoot out in high, but I don't let the paragraph stand until I am pretty doggone sure that I've got everything it takes in the way of plot and menace to back it up.

If you were to take all the suspense out of a story, no matter how many unusual facts and characters you had in it, I don't think it would be read very far.

If you were to take every blow of action out of a story and still leave its suspense (this is possible, because I've done it) you might still have a fine story, probably a better story than before.

There is not, unhappily, any firm from which you can take out a suspense insurance policy. The only way you can do it is to make sure that the reader is sitting there tensely wondering which of two or three momentous things is going to happen first. If you can do that adroitly to some of those manuscripts which have come bouncing back, they may be made to stay put.

1. *The Perils of Pauline:* A 1914 film serial that centered around suspense, danger and cliff-hanger endings.

2. *Franzawi:* [Arabic] French.

3. Reference to Elkton, Maryland where marriages were performed with little formality and legal requirements.

4. L: an *el*evated railway once in existence in New York.

A FEW DAYS NORTH OF VIENNA

Written by
Brandon Butler

Illustrated by
Staci Goddard

About the Author

Brandon Butler was born and raised in Halifax, Nova Scotia, Canada, the city of trees. As a kid, he was—according to him—always pretty good with words and pretty bad in math. Now he can do the math and apparently still has that knack for words.

He received a bachelor's degree with an advanced major in English from Dalhousie University in 1999 and returned to take a second degree in computer science shortly thereafter.

The publications of "A Few Days North of Vienna," first written in 1998, marks Brandon's full-fledged return to writing after a two-year hiatus. It was his first entry to the Writers of the Future Contest, a prize winner, and it is now his first published story.

About the Illustrator

Staci Goddard grew up in Philadelphia, Pennsylvania. From a very early age, she involved herself in the arts and several crafts. Inspired heavily by comic books and then Advanced Dungeons and Dragons Second Edition, she devoted much of her spare time to drawing and writing short stories throughout high school.

In college at Princeton University, Staci changed her vocational pursuit from astrophysics to classics because she found that she enjoyed history books greatly for entertainment reading. It was during college she was introduced to the Illustrators of the Future Contest and submitted a winning entry. She recently composed a thirty-minute Claymation for DVD. After college, she hopes to illustrate and publish her own series of books and to continue her education for a master's degree.

The Four Horsemen rose in the east. We saw them from a long way off; we had stopped for rest on a sparsely wooded hilltop, revealing the valleys and rounded peaks that ran on unchecked for miles around.

Their horses walked at a plodding pace, immediately prompting Azrei to suggest we accost them. Money had been slow; raiding the Milan merchant wagons had not been as profitable this year. Bardolph told us to hold, though. I don't exactly know why.

Three were armored riders, their metal skin coarse and worn. My first impressions of them were romantic visions, final Crusaders clawing their way home from battling the infidel. I heard many tales as a young girl in Kiev: tall ships carrying legions, stretching for the lands of the Messiah, which cowered beneath the menace of the horde. Yet the last one I'd heard never spoke of the infidel, only bloodshed between the Christian siblings of East and West. . . .

Bardolph was the first to address their presence. "Knights," he had said, returning from the scouting mission with Azrei and Corran, "pious for sure. One of them has the markings all over him."

Cataband spoke, coming out from beneath the branches of the glade we had chosen to hide ourselves in on the far side of the hill. "Do we let them pass?"

"I still say they have enough money to tide us over until we cross the river," urged Azrei.

"No," Bardolph said, and his voice brooked no disagreement. "These men have the looks of warriors on them. Fighting them would probably do more harm than good."

"So we let them by?" Cataband said again.

"Perhaps we can trade," Bardolph reasoned, Norman accent coming through his German words. The imperfections nagged at me; we would have to try harder to fix them. "Men of that sort might have items of value, and we've enough money to get us to Vienna."

So we came out, all ten of us, to greet the mighty strangers face to face. We must have seemed a motley group: weather-beaten peasants dressed in cloaks and rags under a clouded leaden sky. But then thieves care little about charisma.

We ambled out over the road, blocking it. Bardolph sent Corran and the Spaniard, Duaz, out to flank them in case of trouble. One could never be too careful in open country.

I could see them clearly now. Indeed, they were a religious troupe; you could see it in them. It was that unrelenting, conservative sway to their ride.

All except one. One among the four rode without armor, shifting over his black steed with far more skill and compromise. Wearing no helmet, I could see his tan skin and bare face. . . . He wore no saddle upon his mount.

Boldly Bardolph stepped forward, his crossbow presented idle upon his shoulder. I could see the back of his head tilt as he peered up at the looming, impassive riders.

"Gentlemen," he said calmly. I've never remembered Bardolph showing fear in broad daylight. "Greetings. What brings you this way?"

The four slowed and one pitched his horse an extra stride, a tall man with a bow slung over his armor—strange weapon for a knight. He opened his visor, revealing a mustached face that spoke with a thick French accent. "We are moving west, taking this road to Vienna. You are pilgrims?"

"Aye," Bardolph lied, "headed the same way."

"These are unpleasant days for travelers," the knight cautioned.

"And don't we know it, kind sir," Bardolph said in good humor.

"I doubt it."

The response was tight and unnerving, and set our leader off his footing. He got down to business, his mood lost on the remark. "Well, since we've run into one another so conveniently, perhaps we can work this chance meeting out to mutual satisfaction."

"You seek something?"

Bardolph nodded. "Trade. Men like yourselves must be worn for lack of food. . . ."

Another knight spoke from behind. I recognized the baritone accent well: Italian, most definitely. We'd spent enough time there to know. "We have nothing to trade."

"Come now," Bardolph said, ever a diplomat, "you are scant weeks from Venice, heartland of the merchant. Surely we can be of service to one another. One bauble of yours might do us well among the shops of Vienna."

"We have no baubles," the Italian deadpanned, "only the necessities."

Azrei drew close to me—closer than I liked; the man reeked. "I told him we should have attacked."

"It doesn't look like they have anything," I hissed back.

Illustrated by Staci Goddard

"Five years and still an amateur, Nadia." Azrei grinned and I could feel his hot breath on my neck. "Look at their adornments, their weapons. Those themselves might be the difference between a night's rest in squalor or comfort."

"All you think of are weapons and money."

"Not always," he chuckled, "but don't be so nonchalant about such craftsmanship. With swords like those, I could—"

He silenced himself suddenly as the last rider, one wrapped in a black cloak and draped over a pale horse, turned his faceless helmet toward us with a creak. It did not turn away.

Back in front, Bardolph was trying to persuade through exchange of pleasantries. "What brings you this way, anyhow, my friends?"

The knight with the French accent answered. "We are searching for something. We did not find it east."

"Where in the East?"

"Moldavia," the Italian said. The more I looked upon him, the more I noticed how adorned he was with religious niceties: his shield and breastplate were murals unto themselves of the crucifixion, and of all of them, it was he who sat straightest in the saddle. "And south of there, toward Byzantium. It has come west."

"Perhaps we can help you find it," Bardolph offered.

"I don't think so," the French knight said.

"Perhaps we've *seen* it."

"That I know you haven't."

The mention of the city could keep me silent no longer. I stepped forward, my shawl coming loose and some of my hair spilling out. "Are you Crusaders?" I asked hopefully. I'd always wanted to see one.

The Italian now pulled beside his compatriot with the bow and lifted his visor. It was a much younger face, less scarred and trodden. He was softened by my question, amused. "You could say that, *Fanciulla*."

Bardolph waved me back, scowling and spitting, "Hush, Nadia," in my direction.

"We have nothing to trade but ourselves," the French knight said now, eyeing Bardolph. "These routes are fraught with dangers. Perhaps we should join you for the remainder of your journey."

Understandably, Bardolph hesitated. This wasn't what he'd had in mind. "No offense to yourselves, but I think our group can take care of itself."

"Perhaps, but being pilgrims, I thought you might be more comfortable in the company of a man of the cloth," the Frenchman said and gestured to the other Italian knight adorned in his sacraments.

None of us had attended Mass in quite some time. To men like Bardolph and Azrei this was little incentive, but I could feel many others stir at the revelation. Religion is not lost among thieves. Let no one tell you any different.

Nevertheless, Azrei called for Bardolph's attention. Our leader made his excuses and stepped back to converse with us.

"Now," Azrei said, "bring Corran and Duaz up from the sides and we'll take them."

Bardolph was about to answer, but another voice intervened. "I'll not harm a priest." It was Cataband and there was a threatening glint to his voice.

"Don't be stupid," Azrei told him. "We could use that equipment. They might be secreting money on their armor."

"Touch a priest, ever, and you will have me to answer to, Azrei."

"Shut up, the two of you," Bardolph snapped. "We're unlikely to run into anyone worth holding up; the season's over. They could be useful if the food spoils; they could help us hunt."

"Taking knights into our fold? Suicide!" Azrei objected.

"I'm only considering it." Bardolph said, trying to calm him. "Cataband doesn't seem opposed to the idea, and neither do the others. Nadia, what say you?"

He did this sometimes, Bardolph. Asked me my opinion when it didn't really matter. I never could fathom why he did it. "I'd like to know why they're here. You don't often see knights on the open road."

"That's true," he said. "Maybe they're headed to Venice. It would be good to keep an eye on them if that's so. I see no reason not to agree, just till Vienna."

"Bardolph!" Azrei snarled.

"Quiet," Bardolph said, and I could see his hand travel casually to where his shortsword lay hidden at his waist. "It's my decision to make." He then broke off and headed back to the four strangers.

"He'll be the death of us," I could hear Azrei mutter to himself. I swallowed and tried to pay him no mind. Every year that man got worse.

Bardolph posed that our group might be interested in the company of a priest. When it turned out the man had a copy of the Holy Testament, the matter was closed. Few of us had ever seen a Bible, and of the lot of us, only I could read; and that was only in pieces. Unless we had it read to us, there was no way any of us could learn the stories of antiquity.

So we traveled on toward Vienna together, the Frenchman now leading us along. But as we moved, I found myself constantly drawn to the enigma of the silent horseman.

●●●

Sundown, dusk. At these times our group would lay camp in detail. We carried these threads with small bells that we would lay on the outskirts of the bonfire to warn us of intruders. Now that there were knights with us, there was less concern over threat coming by night.

It was later, when a few of us had nodded off to sleep, that questions concerning the knights were again unearthed. It was Cataband who first asked them.

"Father . . ."

"Please, friend," the Italian said to him, "call me Vladimiro." He was less suspicious since he had time to lead some of us in prayer.

Cataband appeared uncomfortable with the first name basis. "Vladimiro," he said, pressing forward anyhow, "why have you come to Vienna?"

"We . . ." the Italian paused for a moment. "We are searching." I could not see but the dimmest outline of their faces ringed by red firelight.

"Yes, so you said. But searching for what?"

The priest's shadow froze and it turned to his companions. "It's not important."

The answer satisfied Cataband, but Bardolph, a far less reverent man, pressed the matter. "It was important enough to bring you all the way from Greece and Hungary."

"We are doing God's work," Vladimiro explained.

I could sense the subtle smile curling up behind Bardolph's words, his empty amusement. "Most definitely, Father."

A pause. "Are you being sarcastic?" Vladimiro asked him, his earlier indifference returning. "An irreligious pilgrim. How rare."

The priest's secular French companion, Etienne intervened. "Vlad, enough."

I could see his head turning in Bardolph's direction. "You have issues with God, my friend?"

"Not issues," our ringleader corrected. "Abstentions."

I think Vladimiro was about to respond when the bells sounded. The distant tinkling was unmistakable.

The knights rose instantly, armor clanking. Their metal boots beat the earth around the campfire. "What is it?" a guttural, unidentified voice demanded. The cloaked knight, another Italian.

Dimly, a response came from beyond the main campfire. "Nothing. The bells would ring louder if it were an intruder." Corran. I'd thought him asleep. He was born of a long outdoor tradition; I think his father was an animal trapper, the sort that would know these things.

The knights remained terribly unconvinced. They rose, a boot shoved roughly against me, and the ring of a drawn sword plowed at the inside of my ears. "Shanoin," Etienne said. "See to it." He spoke in Danish now, not in German. It was a spoken tongue back in Kiev, so it took me back for a moment.

Bardolph rose, his frame now fully expressed in the glow of the fire, the shadows of his face grown long as crackling sparks shot up over his head. "What's the matter? Do you know something?"

But he was ignored. Minutes passed as tension grew. Those who had drifted off to sleep were roused at the increasing clamor.

"Fools," I heard Azrei mutter, having watched a shape from our group disappear into the forest. "It figures knights to be so paranoid."

"Shhh!" Vladimiro's voice urged us, and there was a crunching of ground as the one named Shanoin returned. By his blackened shape against the moon I could tell it was the unarmored one, the man with no saddle.

He spoke in a practical voice that carried an accent I'd never heard. Like Etienne, his German was choppy, untrained. "Only the wind," was all he would say.

•••

That night I made it a point to stay near Bardolph. The fire burned low and the man on watch stoked it to keep it just barely alive. I sensed Bardolph stir from his sleep; I heard his uneven breathing for a while and confirmed he was awake.

"Do you trust them?" I asked him in a whisper, knowing he'd recognize my voice.

"Who, the knights?"

"Yes."

"They seem honorable enough. That might be a small problem . . . but we should make it to Vienna fine. After we are there, I'm sure we'll be more than eager to be rid of each other."

My breath came out in vapor. Winter was on the gain and my hair was little comfort against the growing chill of night. "They're mysterious," I blurted out.

"You're afraid of them?"

"I don't know. Maybe. Are you?"

"I don't trust them. But that's not really fear."

"Ah," I said. We were quiet for a time and my thoughts wandered. They came to rest on something troubling Azrei had said earlier that day about my inexperience. "Bardolph?"

"Yes?" he grumbled.

"You've built me into a thief. Thank you."

There was a rustle and when he spoke again his

voice was louder, though it had not increased in pitch. "You're thanking me for making you a scoundrel?"

"The monastery was destroyed. There was nothing left for me but the street life, to be a prostitute . . . I'd have sooner died. There was no reason for you to take me in; it was charity. I know that now that I've been to the cities of the West. Thank you."

"Don't thank me," Bardolph scolded, stonewalling. "You knew languages, you were useful. Me, I can't speak that Italian garbage or that Spanish stuff either. You knew it like a natural, all before you were twenty, ate it up like candy. Even the German words I know, I owe to what you taught me. Couldn't let all that go to waste."

I closed my eyes. There he was taking my timid hand again, coaxing me out from the rubble I'd burrowed in for weeks, hiding in the ruins of a life snuffed by chance disaster. The library ablaze . . . the books burning their scribes . . . there hadn't been a group then, just Bardolph and Corran. Only after that came Duaz and then Azrei and all the other Germans. "I have options now," I said, warmed by the memory of kindness.

"Don't thank me," he grumbled again. He was serious. "And be careful with those options, such as they are. Men will always be looking you over and they won't always be dirty ancients like me who can be pushed away."

The advice did not fall unheard. "I'll be careful."

A moment passed. "Are we still going to go see your Britannia some day?" I asked him.

He chuckled. "Some day, Nadia. I promised you, didn't I?"

In the dark, I gave an invisible, wanton smile. I'd always known we never would.

•••

Vienna.

Its thatched roofs, its waylaid streets and alleys—I'd known this place intimately the past five years of my life. Vienna was the gateway to the East, the last stop of the westerners before venturing into the unknown regions, where superstition and mistrust reigned triumphant. The only thing more abundant in Vienna than Western hesitation was Eastern envy.

So we entered the city on our second day of travel and no one questioned our arrival.

Evening was creeping along the horizon and we sought boarding among the more destitute broken neighborhoods.

Although it was fall, the street still felt hot. There was this stagnant, putrid smell to the air that made me want to get inside as soon as possible. Hopeless stares assailed me everywhere, and I averted my eyes from them, shuddering to think how narrowly my life had thus far escaped their fate.

Our surroundings were only slightly cleaner when an inn of lodging was decided upon. It was a three-story oaken building, the cornerstone of the surrounding district.

I peered up at the windows and took in the stale, greasy panes set against a full moon taking shape low in the maroon sky. A woman threw contents of a chamber pot out on the top level, which drooled down the wall and onto the street. There'd been worse.

Why the knights stayed with us at that point has always been a mystery. They'd been willing to trek through the mire of poverty outside, and none left when Bardolph expressed the desire to spend the night in such a place. I've never understood it.

As always when we spent the night amongst civilization, the common room was where we spent most of our time. Once, it had been innocent enough. Bardolph and Corran used to just split a few drinks, and I even recall when they volunteered to keep the peace over rowdy customers.

But now we had the Germans with us. Azrei, Alimenda, Friedrich and Duaz, too, though he was a Spaniard, insisted on making the most of their stay whenever they were in town. Drinks and raunchy behavior flowed freely over them, inciting others to follow their example.

Of them, only Azrei ever moderated himself. But I never thought of it as a pleasant form of moderation. He had too much of a cunning eye for me to be comfortable with, and far too often I found it resting in my direction.

The knights kept mostly to themselves that evening, or at least the three armored ones did. Shanoin, the one who bore only peasant clothing, sword and shield, failed to grace the common room. They huddled there, Vladimiro, Etienne and the other Italian with the cloak, the one named Natas. The trio laid out a great parchment over their table and spoke in black discussion, every now and again gesturing to the paper or the room. Etienne would lift his gaze occasionally and his expression made me feel we were on display.

I passed close by their table on occasion and heard snippets of their conversation. Only once did I hear anything striking, when Vladimiro reached across the brittle paper, arm encased in an ornate armlet, and pointed. "Shanoin senses them moving in this direction," I heard him say with resolve.

But before I could stop to overhear more, I was

whisked away by rough hands. It was Duaz, bumbling and very drunk. Not listening to my protests, he led me across the room, past the other singing revelers to the bar with a stupid, withdrawn smile on his face. He shoved me hard onto a seat; he probably didn't realize his own strength right now.

"Naaadia," he slurred in his native Spanish. "You are good friend."

"I'm glad you think so," I replied, recoiling from his breath and looking for an opportunity to escape.

"You understand me," he said, his eyes drowsy. "You speak my language."

"Yes," I confirmed he was right. In the cloister at Kiev, I'd learned most of the languages of Christianity, excepting that of the English Normans.

A hand clasped over my shoulder and I felt his eyes, but only briefly, travel up and down my body. By and large it was harmless. Duaz had tried to walk that path before and had not received a pleasant greeting there. "You speak German, too," he said, now looking past me.

I nodded again.

He then reached past me and gently grabbed a passing barmaid, clutching sheepishly to her clothes. She turned, stalled by his hand.

"Tell her I think she is beautiful," Duaz told me, looking upon her common plaster expression like it was the face of God.

The barmaid swiveled her gaze from him to me.

"He likes you," I told her resignedly.

"Oh," she replied with a false blush, and I knew then that she was a prostitute. Most were.

"Tell him he's nice."

I did so, but Duaz didn't respond. He just stared at her with a lifelessness that made me wonder if he was looking at her at all. His stare appeared to move past her into nothing.

"You with him?" she asked in a businesslike manner.

I chose my words carefully. "Not in this."

She quipped me a short grin. "Then tell him he'll have to beat five ducats." She looked off somewhere into the crowd, then her eyes came back to the two of us. Her smile grew wider, engulfing. "Or match it."

With nothing more to discuss, she left, and I felt cooler about my neck. Duaz watched her go, then slapped me on the back so hard my hair nearly tumbled out of the hat it was carefully tucked beneath. "You are good friend."

"Five ducats," I told him. "Beat or match."

"You are good friend," he reiterated like he hadn't heard me, and maybe he hadn't. He was incredibly drunk. "I buy you drink."

I tried to get out of it, knowing Duaz would fix me with something stiff and expensive. More than once a man has tried to get me drunk, and had I not had a guardian in my first years out from Kiev, these ploys might have worked. But now Bardolph was over at the knight's table, conversing at arm's length and Corran had left early for bed.

I don't know what it was except that it was a favorite of Duaz's. It fumed in my throat as it went down and I practically retched before I tasted it. But he goaded and pressured me and I polished off the high mug in time enough to satisfy him.

Duaz tried to talk me into another, but I refused, already feeling quite ill. The musky, smoke-filled air in here was humid, confining. I needed fresh air. Without thinking to merely stick my head out a window, which, in hindsight, I should have done, I headed for the exit.

I sidestepped away from the threshold and lowered myself onto the grass just below a large window.

"Troubled, Nadia?" I lifted my head and saw Azrei.

"I'm . . . fine," I told him.

"You don't seem fine. I saw that drink Duaz gave you."

"I can handle it," I said confidently.

"That's good. You're better off than me then," he said, crossing back in front of me.

Through my own haze, I could see the stagger in his step. "I've been falling all over the place."

He was sauntering a few steps away, so I followed him to keep conversing. Besides, it wasn't wise to let Azrei wander alone. He was capable, but not immune to our competitors. "I can imagine."

"No, you can't," he said, and in the full moonlight I saw his hand travel to his belt. He inverted his sword sheath, dumping his weapon onto the cool ground. "My sword—I fell on it. Broke it in its sheath."

I couldn't say the story broke my heart. "Too bad."

"Piece of rotted junk," he cursed, and kicked the hilt down the quiet street. He stumbled a bit, regained his balance. "You're lucky, you got that thing Bardolph gave you. That'd never break."

My hand went to my own blade. "This thing?"

"Yeah. I seen it. Hundreds of years old; era of Emperor Charlemagne at least, maybe older. A good Frankish weapon for sure. Let's see."

His gesture was frantic and boyish, like he just had to see the sword. Foolishly, I complied. Behind us, the music in the inn pitched low and droning. The singing voices and thin instruments swung into key of a robust and elegant funeral dirge I recognized, but it was too distant to pick out details.

Azrei ran his hand lovingly over the exposed blade. "Incredible," he breathed. "A custom blade for sure. It probably had a longsword companion piece back when it was forged."

"I let the knights worry about longswords."

"Perhaps you should start thinking about them," Azrei said, then paused. It was a long wait before his next words. "The sword is lonely, Nadia. Like you."

"I . . . I think the sword can take care of itself," I replied, and moved to take back the weapon. As I did so, Azrei drew out of reach.

"Do you want to be alone, Nadia, is that it? You don't want people?"

I stopped, only half aware in my slightly inebriated state. What did this buffoon want from me anyway? Left to my own judgment, I told him the truth. My truth. "No. The right person just hasn't come along yet."

"That's religious talk," Azrei said, like he was daring the pope himself to come lurching from the shadows to excommunicate him. "There are many right people. You're just searching for them, right?"

"If you want to put it that way," I said, making another grab for my sword, the only thing really on my mind now.

Again, he pulled away, teasing. "Yes, searching. But here's the problem. It's different for you; you're a woman. You sit and wait for it to come to you, and if the right one is shy, you just let the stronger man prevail. You are the prize. It is the man who must do the searching, the claiming."

I'd heard this talk before. I'd heard it from the lowest gutter to high nobility, when they came through the Kiev convent. Most let it just wash away; but I was a thief now, nothing to lose. I could say anything I pleased. "No. That's not the truth."

"Isn't it?" Azrei answered, and there was a hint of blame and anger in his twisted voice.

"No. Just ask Alimenda. Anyone can claim her."

"She's not worth claiming," Azrei spat, and the night became darker as he spoke. "I should know. I have."

"And I am worth it?"

"You are a virgin. You used to be a nun, right?"

I stopped, realizing only now how far we had traveled. I could no longer hear the strains of music. "Haven't we been through this before, Azrei?" I asked, but my voice was nervous. I had known many of the Germans desired me after they learned I was a girl. It was only after they'd seen how viciously Bardolph had trained me that they wisely left me alone. Azrei, however, was different. Smart, but as wise as a pile of twigs.

"No," he answered, and I could tell he had drawn close. I could feel his breath, the alcohol upon it mingling with that on my own. "I don't believe we have."

There is a moment of a hunt that is purely psychological, when the hunter's intentions become obvious to its prey. That moment was now, complete stillness.

Inevitably, I tried to break away. But he was waiting for it and caught me roughly around the waist. I screamed, tried to cry out. A few gasps got though, but soon a hand clasped over my mouth, the age-old ritual about to commence.

I fought tradition every step of the way. I kicked, I hit, I bit. But he was determined and at last he'd brought me to a side alley, or at least I assumed it was one. He spoke again, but now it was in utter rage, a sign of how much I'd injured him. "I was going to make this enjoyable for you," he snarled. "I was going to make you like it. But so be it. If you want a fight, I'll give you one."

An arm collided with my back, the elbow pushing me, bending me over in front of him.

"I'm going to make this sheer pain," he promised.

But he fumbled in the dark. I was still resisting and his drunken state made it difficult for him to cope with the small necessities. I remembered people talking of rape like it was such a dramatic experience. Although this was no less terrifying, his muddled actions made the entire event a travesty, a humorless black comedy. I remember actually wishing . . . and this I've never reconciled . . . that he just wanted to get it over with. Just do it and get away from me.

But he never got his pants off. As we continued to writhe, a sound caught us from further down the alley, a deep growl. It could not have been human.

Azrei stopped dead. Suddenly, his need for me drained away. The flat of the sword pressed against my arm, traveling up to my neck. "Who's there?" Azrei demanded, but I could feel him shiver.

I could hear slow movement, a scuffling of feet. It sounded like a rabid dog had stumbled upon us, but the more I listened, the more I began to doubt that. Involuntarily, I gave off a weak groan.

"Shut up," I heard Azrei grunt. He pulled me by the hair.

The growling grew louder, more aroused. There was a wild, animal gnashing.

"Who's there?" Azrei said again, and this time he tried to put more strength in his voice.

Then, all at once, his grip froze. Although I could see nothing as my back was turned, I remain convinced that in that moment, Azrei saw his killer.

There was an orgy of sensation. Azrei was hit by something monstrously heavy, dragging me to the ground with him. Horrified, I lay inert, turning my back. I could hear him shriek just beside me, accompanied by sounds of tearing and rending. I felt him splatter across my back, streams leaping across my face and eyes.

But it was all over soon. This hunter had given Azrei the dignity of competence he hadn't given me, though I sensed the kill had not been without exacting excruciating, overwhelming pain. There was a satisfied, guttural purr.

The beast did nothing for a moment. He'd most certainly noticed me lying there. I heard the sound of an inquisitive, almost naive canine nose. And then, as if it were no more than an apparition, it was gone.

I laid there for a long time, not having the strength or courage to rise, lest whatever it was returned. My heart began to slow and my arms shook as the chilling excitement slowly withdrew. It was all I could do to at last reach over and pry my weapon from the corpse's clutching grasp.

Soon, a dim light bathed across me. I looked up and saw a figure standing there, holding a lamp. A peasant woman. Her eyes widened when she saw Azrei lying in pieces beside me.

"He tried . . . rape me," I croaked.

She responded to that, at least. Trying to keep clear of what was left of Azrei, she gathered me in her arms and led me out into a place where I could feel the breeze run across my face again. As we left, I saw her spit back upon the body.

Despite what had happened, I forgot the strange monster and gave myself a cold smile.

Yes. Precisely.

•••

I'd told the woman where I was staying and she led me back to the inn, then left. As soon as I returned, all eyes fastened on me. My entire back was drenched in blood, red rain pouring off of me onto the floor.

Bardolph took over at once. He didn't scold me or question where I'd been; that would all come later. Instead, he hustled me straight upstairs and had a bath prepared. I was left alone, but he kept coming by at regular intervals to check on me. It's a shame my true father never met Bardolph. He might have learned something.

Bardolph had taken me to the room the knights had rented, the best in the inn. They must have also been concerned about my well-being. I awoke in the middle of the night to see a form seated on the tiny balcony. It was the Frenchman, Etienne. He'd not been there when I'd gone to sleep.

I rose and wrapped a blanket around me. He started at my approach, but settled as soon as he saw it was only me.

"Why are you here?" I asked him. "Do you and your friends want the room back?" It was an honest question.

"You were attacked this evening," he replied. "Someone should protect you."

"I don't need it. And if I do, Bardolph can do it."

"He was going to," the knight admitted, "but I talked him out of it. Wrangled with him for hours over it, actually."

That confused me. "What do you care?"

His gaze, which had returned to the empty street, came back to me, then lowered. "You are a lady," he said grudgingly. "It's a matter of honor." They were noble words, but there was no passion in them.

"Really?"

"Yes," he said, turning back to the street.

It was silent for quite some time. Eventually, I brought up something that had been eating away at me ever since I'd met this man and his companions. "So are you Crusaders? Were you at Constantinople?"

I saw Etienne holding something in his hand. His bow was propped beside him as he fiddled with a long object the length of his forearm. It had a sharpened end, like the head of a pike. But in a second it disappeared from sight. "Constantinople," he muttered, "seven years ago. Yes, I was there. Natas, too."

"I've never been there," I told him. "What was it like?"

"Death," he said simply, "death all around."

"Oh."

He took in a breath, held it in for a moment. "I think I saw and learned things there that the world might never understand."

"What . . . what things?"

"What God is," he said, "and what the Church is, and the difference between the two."

Chilled, I left his answer as it was, my curiosity gone.

"Some of your friends want to stay with us past Vienna," he offered. "They like having Vladimiro around. Bardolph's reluctantly agreed to accompany us north."

"We were heading north anyway," I affirmed. "Besides, if you're looking for what Bardolph thinks you might be, it could help us out."

"He thinks we are searching for treasure?"

"It seemed likely," I said, "and extra money can sorely help in the middle of a winter."

He looked up at me again, and I could see an objective in his eyes. "Can I see your neck for a moment?"

His voice hadn't suggested anything, but then, neither had Azrei's. I pulled back; enough unfamiliar hands had touched me this night.

He saw my fear and straightened. "Nadia," he said stiffly, "you need not fear me."

"Everyone should fear everyone else."

"That's why there are knights—real knights in this world. So people don't have to. By my word, you need not fear me."

When he did not approach with threat or insistence, I nodded. He rose and brushed the hair away from my neck, looking for something. "Did it bite you or tear you? Draw blood?"

"No," I told him, "but my knees got cut and scratched."

"That should be fine," he said, and sat back down.

Protectively, my hand went to my clean neck. "What was it?"

He stared out expressionless at the street. "You think I know?"

"It's what you're searching for, isn't it?" I said, voice quivering at the memory of the beast. "What you didn't find back east."

A bitter smile crossed his face. "No," he told me. "It's not that at all."

I stared at him. He was hiding something from me. But yet, although he might have his secrets, I knew he had not lied.

In the distance, the wind gave a wistful howl.

●●●

When Azrei's face was absent that morning, no one questioned it, least of all Bardolph.

There was a search, but it was hardly concerned. When it was fruitless, I volunteered no explanations and was asked for none. The knights gave no help either, indifferent to the disappearance. I've always suspected they knew.

We headed north at midday, Corran and Shanoin sent as scouts for the road ahead. As time went on, they would return separately, with Corran telling how the strange man insisted on not coming back until he was certain of "things."

"He's mad," Corran complained to Vladimiro one day. "He's liable to run into a wolf or something worse out there by himself."

The priest just smiled. "Not mad, dedicated," he corrected. "And Shanoin knows how to take care of himself."

"He should at least take some of your armor," Cataband said, walking faithfully next to Vladimiro's horse. "He's unprotected, Father."

"He has the sword and shield Rome has provided him," Vladimiro said with pride. "It's all he needs."

By the fourth day, a mist descended. The air moved slowly; Corran guessed it would rain. We traveled on a worn path, probably an imperial road from long ago. It was quiet: hushed conversations were murmured between the Germans and Vladimiro, while Etienne and Natas rode alone, the latter stroking a hand sickle. Etienne had told Bardolph Natas's father had been a wheat farmer, and his pale horse and sickle were heirlooms from their humble estate, someplace unknown. More than any of the knights, Natas unnerved me.

Into this placid scene rode Corran and Shanoin, emerging in a rush from the low fog.

They returned together, a rare occurrence.

They reared their horses before Etienne and

Bardolph. Corran did the speaking. "There's tracks ahead," he said, "horses and wagons. Small caravan, perhaps gypsies."

Bardolph nodded and acted instinctively. "We'll prepare an ambush. Nadia, you're with—"

Etienne reached over and grabbed Bardolph's shoulder. "You'll do no such thing."

The brigand thief frowned and I realized the decision to accompany the knights from Vienna must have been forced on him. "You must allow us our way of life!"

"But I thought you were *pilgrims*," Etienne replied sarcastically.

"You well know what we are," Bardolph told him. "It's who we are, how we get by from day to day. If you don't like it, fine, you don't have to help. Just stay out of the way."

"I'll not let you slaughter those people."

"We don't slaughter people, but if they put up a fight, we'll give it to them. We only relieve the wealthy of excess baggage."

"I won't allow that either," Etienne said firmly.

And that was it. Bardolph's authority had been challenged. Angered, he reared his horse back upon itself to face Etienne and I could see the malice in his thoughts.

But Bardolph was not a stupid man. He was really quite cunning. So when Vladimiro appeared behind Etienne, he stopped short. Natas got behind him too, and Shanoin . . . then Cataband, Friedrich and the other Germans.

Bardolph looked around him, beaten. The priest had his own men in the palm of his hand, promising salvation. Bardolph could only count on Corran and me. Duaz would side with whomever the clear winner would be and that definitely wasn't us. Bardolph forced himself to calm down. "What do you propose?"

"We greet them," Etienne answered. "Perhaps we can trade."

Bardolph scowled in return.

The matter was settled and we rode on in haste. Eventually we encountered the tracks.

I peered over at Shanoin. The tan-skinned man looked back, unreadable, and again it struck me how I couldn't place his race. His complexion was decidedly not Danish, though he spoke it, and sporadic German and Italian. He did not look Christian at all. Was he part of the southern hordes? If so, why was he now with Christians?

But I knew he was not about to answer these questions for me. He turned and jostled his horse to a quicker pace. I noticed a rod similar to Etienne's strapped to his leg. It was wooden.

It was some time later that I caught the stench. Rancid. I'd once smelled pure sulphur, but this was far worse. It retreated for a moment, then returned, carried with the tide of the breeze.

We continued on for only another minute or so before the mist unfurled to reveal what we were smelling. It was the caravan, abandoned, corpses littered about the ground. We stopped, overwhelmed.

Shanoin was the first to react, leaving his horse and threading about the desolation, head shifting left and right with the agility of a fox. A fat, buzzing fly landed on my ear and I swatted it off.

I heard Alimenda swear, actually crossing herself. "Even the horses."

"It appears your competitors got here first,"

Vladimiro said aloud, surveying the damage. Etienne shot him a disapproving look.

I could tell Bardolph was stunned. He'd seen death before, but not so much of it and never so savage. The bodies had been completely gutted, reduced to refuse. I was reminded of Azrei for a moment, then realized the color was all wrong; white skin and meat instead of dark blood. Azrei had been torn apart and left. These poor creatures were drained, bloodless carcasses that had served their tormentors some depraved purpose.

"I've seen no thief do this," Bardolph said, eyes wide, "and no animal either."

Natas dismounted and went over to one of the bodies, a man dressed in simple, cheap rags.

He bent down, plucked something from its yawning chest. He held it out between his fingers so that we could see it clearly. A lock of red hair, bound in gauze. "Meant for us," he said to his companions. "They were here all right. Probably not more than two days ago. But Shanoin will be able to make a better guess."

"Who was here?" I asked.

My question spoke to something in the knights. Both Etienne and Natas turned to Vladimiro, who nodded. "We must honor the dead," he said, but it was a prompted phrase.

Bardolph was not a cold man, but he was practical. "There's no time for that!" he insisted. "Do you intend to bury the animals, too?"

Vladimiro did not reply, but instead dismounted and donned the purple cloth worn for his prayer sermons. Seeing this, the Germans lent their ears. "Children, a great evil has passed here; we must right it as best we can. Everything here must receive final sacraments and more."

Cataband, the most faithful of us, became perplexed. "More?"

"The Devil himself has committed sacrilege here," Vladimiro explained. "To undo what has been done, processes must be obeyed."

What he went on to dictate sounded absolutely mad, but the Germans frantically lapped it up. Even Duaz, neutral on such matters, became quite amiable. We drove a wooden pike, a stake, through what was left of the heart of each corpse, the horses included. Vladimiro would then utter Latin prayers above the dead victim and direct one of the knights to decapitate it. The entire mess, heads and all, was then carried and dumped into a pile, where we set fire to it. The knights went about the procedure systematically. They were familiar with what they were doing.

Now we stood in front of the pyre watching it burn. The entire ritual had taken what was left of the day.

"I've never seen so many," I heard Etienne say.

"They're getting bolder," Natas said, "getting larger still. We need more men."

"Rome will send none," Vladimiro told them both. "They've not responded. They need more proof to acknowledge that evil stalks this earth. We're on our own."

They were no longer bothering with whispers and Bardolph could clearly hear them.

"What are you talking about? What's going on?"

The knights were loathe to speak it, but it was finally Vladimiro who revealed their secret. "We hunt the Vampyre," he said without shame, "the Nosferatu."

•••

I'd heard stories of the Nosferatu. An undead creature of listlessness, it is the antithesis of God, of everything living.

Now Vladimiro told us these ghost stories were not tales for children after all, but forged from shards of fact that were eventually mixed with other legends. The Vampyre was as real as the infidel who occupied the holy land, and thrice as evil—and just as the Crusades were sent against the infidel, so one was underway against the Vampyre.

It had begun in Constantinople. After the fall of the city, most of the Crusaders had dispersed. Etienne and Natas remained. Fast friends made in the very heart of violence, neither found they had reason to return home and begin families any longer. The war had altered them.

That was when the disappearances began. Shortly after their decision to stay, the fires were still burning and if a stray individual or two vanished from the public eye, no one questioned it. There was a city to rebuild, after all.

But two years after the sack of the city, it continued. Soon bodies began turning up, like those we'd found—gutted and picked clean of blood. The knights began their own investigations, accompanied by other Crusaders who had stayed. When the truth was discovered, that a Vampyre was nesting in the bowels of Byzantium, the knights sent word to Rome. Warnings were written to every papal bureaucrat with a name. And meanwhile, the Vampyre lay in wait, knowing of the plot against him. Friends involved began disappearing, one by one.

The Vatican, Christian policeman, sent a missionary, accompanied by Vladimiro and other paladins . . . and Shanoin. He was a quiet man whom the church had taken in after he had saved this same missionary somewhere, as it was told to us, "far and away up north."

And the official investigation began. Before long,

the missionary was forced to acknowledge the existence of "the Vampyre" to his own chagrin. At length, they drove it from the city into the countryside. But by now the one had multiplied, transforming its victims into undead servants, preying on the living in roving packs. Knowing no alternative, the knights gave chase and began the hunt, a hunt that had lasted for three years.

"We've rid the Lord of many of their ilk," Vladimiro was explaining to us the next day as we stopped to rest for roughly half an hour. He had to shout above the heavy rain so that most of us could hear. "But they've become nomadic under our pursuit and they are always increasing their number to compensate for the ones we banish. And slowly we wane and die, while they live on in depraved immortality."

"The Vampyre is immortal?" Cataband asked with childlike curiosity.

"So say the legends," Vladimiro confirmed. "Perhaps they, like so many others, are mistaken. But it is of little importance; we have learned the necessities. We know how to track, find and purge them."

"How?"

"Little things, mostly. You'd be surprised the subtleties of life that a Vampyre must avoid, a part of its curse. Sunlight is the common weapon; no such creature can face the light of the Lord's glorious sun. To do so would mean death to them. I've seen it."

"Mirrors are another. The Nosferatu may never look upon its own reflection, as it wears none. Beware the man without an image, he holds ill toward you. It casts no shadow to the torch, either. It's as if it consumes the natural darkness, eating the gloomy and obscure."

As he spoke, a stream of water collected on the branch above and poured down, cascading over the side of Vladimiro's face. He cupped a hand to his cheek. "Water works too, although it is something of a mystery. A Vampyre avoids running water like the plague, and that which is blessed by sacrament scars it irrevocably; yet it will cross fords and bridges at will, as long as it does not enter the river itself."

"And the Vampyre revels in the water of the sea," Natas added cynically. "The salt you know, impure water. The missionary was unfortunate enough to discover that."

Vladimiro nodded solemnly. "Yes. Yes, he was."

I was sitting close enough to clearly hear everything said. "What about these?" I asked, gesturing to the wooden rods the knights now wore prominently across their armor alongside their swords and shields.

"Ah," Vladimiro said. "The other weapon against the Vampyre. A stake—a thick rod of wood or silver—blessed accordingly. Drive it into the heart of the beast and it is all but gone. Relieving it of its head will then finish it, provided you burn the remains afterward. To kill a Vampyre is no easy task, you see; it has strength beyond imagination. What can you do once the sun sets? Play mirrors and watch shadows? They only see the creature. Scald him in a river, yes, if you can lure him to such a place. But nothing ordinary will harm him: swords, arrows, poison. The stake, however, that only can we use with impunity."

"So you even have an exact method. Charming," Bardolph said.

"Yes," the priestly knight replied gravely, "a method."

Frowning, I sat back against the damp bark of an adjoining tree overlooking our road of fresh mud. The rain came down in thin waves, washing the earth with its cleansing touch. Further away under another tree, I could see Shanoin squatting by himself, tinkering with a small object. I couldn't tell what it was.

Curious, and eager to get away from all this morbid talk, I got up and approached, dashing through the soaking rain. He did not look up when I came underneath the branches.

"Hello," I greeted in Danish. He did not look up, but kept fiddling with the object. I could see it now, a scale.

Trying to be friendly, I circled about him. "Where did you get that?" I asked him. A scale was not something you saw every day, so I was inquisitive as to where Shanoin might have gotten one. Such things were common with merchants and alchemists, not knights.

Finally, he said something. "Night creature."

I stopped, uncertain on what I'd just stumbled upon. "The Vampyre? The Vampyre . . . gave this to you?"

"Found," Shanoin corrected, "found in city lair. Many pretty things there. Left for us to find."

"Left for you? Why?"

"It leaves things for us. Taunting, on purpose. Careless, on purpose. The night creature secretly wants to be caught. That is why it moves west. Wants to be hunted a long, long time, then caught. Then ended."

I nodded. I had no wish to speak of the Vampyre any longer. It was what I had come with the intention to avoid. "What are you weighing?"

"Money," he spoke in a low voice, but it was clear and articulate. I never once heard Shanoin mumble in all the time that I knew him.

I looked down to see that this was true. He had a small pile of currency on the scale and I saw many different coins: ducats and other livres of many kinds, plus countless others I couldn't hope to identify. The cup that held them moved slowly up and down.

The other cup held only simple earth.

•••

From then on our routines changed and Vladimiro insisted on a ritual before we slept. He would draw a large circle around camp with a stick and water while praying in Latin. They were worn phrases, the sort I'd numbly knelt to years ago, before I learned that fire, too, came from God. Then would come Mass, which Bardolph refused to attend, dismissing it as delusional. I attended, although I wish I could say it was because I was faithful and believed the wonderful, hope-filled words Vladimiro would read from the Testaments.

Really, I was afraid. I didn't have Bardolph's unashamed courage, prideful or not; none of us did.

We went to sleep as well as we could. Silence pervaded.

I don't remember drifting off, but I will always recall waking up.

Someone had cried out, raising the alarm. There were more shouts and finally a torch was lit, flaring though the gloom and transforming us from beast to human again, all in a single, trivial instant. Etienne held it and this time it was the knights who were calm and collected after being roused from bed.

"Quiet . . . peace! Hold, I say!"

Eventually, it settled down, and we gathered obediently around the knight, Bardolph lighting his own torch.

"What's happened?" Etienne asked. "Who raised the alarm?"

"Are we all here?" Natas said in an eager, expectant voice.

"I raised it," someone replied, approaching. It was

Corran with someone in tow. As I watched, he thrust
the figure onto the grass. "I saw him lurking about the
camp. He wasn't very quiet about it. I thought it might
have been one of those . . . things you were talking
about." His eyes shifted, avoiding Bardolph.

I saw Natas grin in admonishment. "You went out
there by yourself?"

Vladimiro broke in, kneeling quickly by the captive.
"A stupid move," he said, forcing the youth's head to
the side and rummaging over his neck, then his mouth.
"One of those 'things' could have easily snapped you
in half . . . not to mention if this boy *is* one, you've just
broken our protective barrier."

"Barrier?" Corran asked, looking back in the direction he'd come.

I looked down at the newcomer. He was indeed a
boy, at least his face was youthful. He was over twenty,
but not much more. Stubble ringed an otherwise soft
face that looked up fearfully, trying to pull away from
the insistent paladin.

"Who are you?" Vladimiro demanded in Italian.
"What are you doing here?" He repeated the second
question in German. The young man did not respond.

Struck by a moment of insight and sympathy, I
stepped forward and put a hand on Vladimiro's
shoulder. "Who are you?" I asked the stranger in the
best Hebrew I could muster.

His eyes turned in my direction, and our gazes
locked for a long moment.

"Benjamin," he told me.

Vladimiro looked at me suspiciously. "What
language was that?"

"Hebrew," I said.

He stood, backed away instinctively. "You know the
Hebrew language?"

"Nadia knows a lot of things," Bardolph cut in protectively.

I didn't need it though, since I was fine to take care of myself. "I picked up a few words in Kiev. I learned a lot of languages there."

But the stranger named Benjamin interrupted us. "I can speak German," he volunteered, his eyes still on me.

Vladimiro scowled and closed distance again. "What are you doing here?"

"I don't know," he said, defiance on his face.

"That's not the answer I wanted to hear," Vladimiro warned him, and I saw his fingers close around the hilt of his sword. It occurred to me that of all the knights, his sword alone I had not seen drawn; he never sharpened it.

Etienne was there to stop tensions from escalating. "Come now," he said, putting his own hand over Vladimiro's sword. "No need to be hasty, old friend. Hear what he has to say."

Vladimiro paused, then pulled his hand away in a jerk from his sword and Etienne's grasp. "Well?" he asked Benjamin again, begrudgingly.

"I told you, I don't know," he repeated. "Something attacked me in the dark, brought me here."

"Attacked you?" Etienne said. "Attacked you where?"

The stranger licked his dry lips before continuing. "I . . . I was part of a caravan, family and friends, all of us. Leaving Vienna."

"Why?" I asked him softly.

"We were driven out," he said, looking at the ground. "We're driven out of everywhere."

While his tone was not entirely cold toward the young man's plight, it was clear Etienne had other concerns at the moment. "Go on," he urged.

"We stopped some miles back a few nights ago. We were resting and I . . . I decided to try some hunting by moonlight. It was a full moon that night."

"I know, I saw it," Etienne said.

"I'd noticed some deer and elk as we traveled," Benjamin continued. "I'd always wanted to snare such creatures. But I didn't find anything and when I returned hours later . . ." His face, already melancholy, bit on its lower lip and gave a shudder.

. "Did you see them?" Vladimiro pressed, and Natas came to hover directly over him.

"See who?"

"The murderers?" he said, having put the obvious together. "The monsters?"

The stranger said nothing until Vladimiro thundered, forcing it out of him. "*Speak!*"

"I saw people," Benjamin confessed hurriedly. "Forms. Hunched and . . . pale skinned. One of them was very tall and I saw long red hair through the torchlight. I thought he'd seen me; he looked *directly* at me . . . but he never said anything . . . like he was daring me to try something, anything."

"Red hair," Natas muttered, standing back up. "That settles it."

"I ran. I didn't want to, and as soon as I left I wanted to go back, but I just couldn't. I saw your party arrive shortly thereafter and kept my distance, hoping you'd lead me to the nearest town." He stopped, exasperated and breathing heavily.

Behind him, Corran frowned. "*I* never caught sight of you."

"I was careful," Benjamin said resignedly, not looking at anyone now. "I kept upwind, erased my tracks, that sort of thing."

"You did it well. So why are you here now?"

"I keep telling you, I don't know," Benjamin insisted, his hands traveling upward along his sides. "I was keeping a good distance and looking for a place to spend the night when . . . something accosted me. A huge . . . hand, arm, branch, I don't know . . . knocked me down and dragged me . . . I fell unconscious and woke up right outside your camp."

"Dragged you?" Etienne repeated.

"Yes."

Cataband stepped forward, protective of Vladimiro. "I don't trust you," he said. "We don't trust any—"

"Oh, yes," I heard Bardolph pipe up behind them all, "kill him, he's a Vampire for sure! There's probably a dozen laying in wait, ready to pounce on us before 'God's glorious sun' rises and chars them to sacks of coal!"

"Vam-*peer*," Vladimiro corrected, withstanding the sarcasm.

"Vam-*pire*," Bardolph protested childishly, "as if it matters."

"We'll do nothing to the stranger," Etienne proclaimed, standing. "He's not a Vampyre, Vlad. We have extra blankets on the horses, fetch them."

The paladin priest was brought up short. "Surely you're not thinking of taking him in?" he scoffed.

"The Vampyre is abroad, Vladimiro. I don't care what he is. He's a child of God and we've a responsibility."

"Child? More like ingrate! Surely Shanoin will be able to take care of . . ."

"Bring the blankets!" Etienne said, becoming threatening.

Silenced, Vladimiro mumbled something incomprehensible and walked off sheepishly.

The scene was over and the others returned to their

ramshackle beds. There were more than a few disapproving glances at Benjamin, but no one was about to argue with Etienne.

I did not turn away. Instead, I approached the boy. Odd, I still remember him as a boy, but I couldn't have been more than five years older than him. He looked up as I strode toward him and our eyes met again. I became conscious that my hair was let down, scattered around my head.

I offered him my hand. I could see him better at this distance. He looked bruised, knocked about. "My name is Nadia," I said.

He didn't say anything, but it didn't matter. I could see his greeting in his stare.

"You are a lucky young man," Etienne breathlessly scolded Benjamin behind us, but neither he nor I were listening. We probably should have. "You're lucky not to have been torn apart . . . or worse, have been set upon by Vampyres."

"So you're saying the Vampyres didn't bring him here?" I heard Bardolph chastise.

But before anyone could say anything more, there was another German voice out of the darkness. I'm not sure who it was, but it was concerned, and I could sense fear mounting in it.

"Where's Duaz?" it said.

●●●

The morning brought no answers. Duaz, the Spaniard, was gone, his belongings with him. It was as if he'd just gotten up and wandered out of our lives. It was with fleeting, guilty expressions that everyone admitted nobody had seen Duaz since at least that night's dusk, and none had noticed his absence.

For me, at least, it was a numbing experience; not so

much that Duaz was gone, but that not one of us had missed him. Azrei, then Duaz, disappeared without explanation, and we—the thieves—carried on like it was nothing, a sudden parting of company, nothing more. Had any one among us really cared about another?

Etienne and Bardolph both made preparations to break camp, but Shanoin at once stopped them with an open, firm palm. "Close," he said, and his words were to Etienne. "They are close now. Sleeping."

Etienne was about to say something, then thought the better of it and closed his mouth.

"Where?" I heard Natas ask anxiously, at once drawing up alongside them. His hand scythe was drawn, held lovingly to his breast. "What direction?"

Tentatively, I saw the tanned man smell the air. "Ahead. Further up. I shall see."

Corran rose in anticipation of more scouting, but the eyes of Shanoin, the strange rider, narrowed. "Alone," he said, then abruptly left, fluidly mounting his horse and goading it into a run.

It was still early morning and so we set about to wait upon Shanoin's return.

I decided to cleanse myself. I had these impulses back then to bathe myself, all the time.

Fall had turned the water frigid. Wisely, I remained clothed, rinsing only my hair and upper body. I bit back a sneeze.

I sensed Benjamin before I saw him; strange how I knew who it was. Thankfully, it was more relaxed than the visit Azrei had imposed on me days ago.

"Shalom," I said.

Without speaking pleasantries, I heard him come closer to my kneeling frame upon the riverbank. "So they teach Hebrew in Kiev? Really?"

"No," I told him, making sure I was presentable. "They frown on it, actually. But there are books . . . were books, if someone wanted to learn."

"Someone like you, you mean."

"I learned many languages," I told him. "The only thing I really learned, actually. But I know Hebrew barely enough to give 'good morning.'"

He was beside me now, squinted gaze traveling downstream. I peered up at him and he down at me. Again, the stare, and we didn't say anything for quite some time.

Finally, he broke it. "Your friends," he asked, "the strange riders. Are they headed for the tower?"

"Tower, what tower?"

"My family had a map of the region. There's a tower not far along the main road."

"I didn't see one earlier."

"I don't think it's very tall. Old fortifications. Father said something about it being an outpost for the empire. The old Caesar empire, I mean. The first one."

"You never brought that up," I said, a touch more suspicious then I had intended.

At once, he pulled away; the movement felt too ready, rehearsed. "I didn't see how it was important," he muttered darkly.

I did not get up, but I turned my head to watch him. He didn't leave as I'd thought he would. He halted a few paces from me, looking away. I wanted to say something, but didn't.

"Christians," he spat. "Moors, Romans, Egyptians, Babylon. The same story everywhere."

"You don't have to go," I began diplomatically, crestfallen. "I didn't mean—"

"*I don't run!*" he suddenly exploded, and I was so startled I fell back onto my calves.

Apparently my choice of words had inadvertently made the situation go from bad to worse.

I saw him shaking though he fought to suppress it. For a minute, it was like I wasn't there. "I don't run," he repeated, calming himself. "I am a man. Men do not run away."

I know now the hidden emotions he was experiencing, but I didn't then. I was still just a little, ignorant thief in many ways. Luckily, my blundering words never antagonized him further.

I got up and crossed over to him. "Are you cold?" I asked him, prepared for another rebuke.

It didn't come. "A little."

I touched his shaking hands. They were freezing. "Here," I told him, and gave him the shawl I wore from time to time. "Wrap yourself in this."

"No charity," he grumbled.

"But you are freezing," I said, and practically shoved the fabric at him. He looked at me and his resolve broke; he took the shawl. My hands snugly wrapped his own underneath it.

"Can you . . . I'd like to learn more of your language."

"Hebrew? It's not for outsiders."

"Please?" I asked him, "I'd like to know, all the same."

"Why? Why do you care?"

"The way people talk . . . it tells you how they think; that's what the nuns used to say back in Kiev. And I want to know how people think."

He thought about it. "Maybe," he said grudgingly. "I suppose it might do that. It would get you away from all this silly Vampyre nonsense."

His tone was uplifting and humorous, the first I had heard in him. It actually made me laugh—the first time

in a long while. Too long. "That's Vam-*peer*," I corrected,
trying to mock Vladimiro's accent as best I could.

"Like it matters," Benjamin said, and what he was
able to do with Bardolph's voice . . . it was priceless.
Ben has always been good at impersonations: great
humor for long, quiet evenings.

"The tower," he then offered, "if you get up high
enough, you can see it."

"From here?"

"Yes, I've done it. Before yesterday, that is. Do you
want to?"

"I'd like that," I said.

We ran alongside the river; climbed a tree, a strong
oak with wide, flexing branches. He hoisted me way up
and pointed out the tower, far away and beneath the
treetop horizon. And we did not return for hours.

• • •

Shanoin returned just after midday and Benjamin and
I were prudent enough to see we were back before then.
I remember the stares when he returned with me in tow,
but my response then was as resolute as it has been ever
since. To hell with them all: the Germans, the knights—I
didn't need any of them. I'm not sure if Bardolph stared
at me or not. I was afraid to look in his direction.

Shanoin rode into camp and did not dismount as he
came to a gradual stop. "They have found shelter from
the morning," he said. "We must move against them.
Now."

That was all. The knights responded to his words at
once and the Germans followed eagerly. The rest of us
were pulled helplessly along behind them.

We were indeed brought into the shadow of the
tower. It was a squat, ugly thing, practical and inele-
gant, made for war. I imagine the Romans who built

the place must have been efficient beyond imagination; they would have shamed the lot of us. Maybe.

Vladimiro gathered us all in a line, lit torches in the daylight and distributed weapons telling us again how our own would be ineffective. His sword was out now and I realized it was the first time I had seen it. It was a crafted, glorious thing, like his armor. It must have been forged from pure silver.

The hilt reminded me of my own sword, only larger. Azrei had always noted mine had been the most austere, refined weapon of our group; no longer. In fact, the make looked so similar, I almost unsheathed my own blade to compare the two.

But there was no time. Vladimiro blessed us, anointed our heads with water and a prayer, then bid us luck, stating, "Remember, God looks down upon us this day and His smile is wide."

I had a doubt. I turned to Bardolph, my voice shivering. "Why are we doing this?" I asked him. "Why are we here?"

He looked down at me sadly.

"Why don't we just leave?" I pleaded.

He sighed and looked to the tower, then back at me. "The Germans, Nadia. We need them for the next year."

"The money," I said, frowning.

"Yes, the money," he told me softly, and strode off. I could see his hard glance at Benjamin, who stood behind me, as he did so.

I understand the importance of money. I know that one cannot live without it in this world. But thieves, and others I am sure, are truly lashed to it, trapped in its empty promises. That was the lesson Bardolph taught me that day, and I have never, *ever* forgotten it. I was full of hate in that moment: at Bardolph, at myself, and the life of a thief that stops short of true freedom. But the anger passed with nothing to show for it, as it always did.

We entered the tower as a group with our torches lit and our weapons drawn. The innards were crumbling; animals had been nesting here for ages. We found stairs leading up, but they looked weak and uncertain, and part of the wall on the second floor had fallen in on itself. Bracing ourselves, we instead sought the basement.

I stayed close to Benjamin the entire time. No one spoke and, when the rats scurried across the ceiling above us, I clung tight to him. His face was just as apprehensive, but it was good enough for me. We jumped at the shadows together.

Natas had become frantic. He scampered about, sickle in one hand, sword in the other, stakes lining his breastplate. "The door to the left, try the door to the left."

"That one?" someone asked, pointing.

"Yes, yes," he frothed, and then pushed the German aside when he moved too slow for his liking, breaking the door inward with a mighty kick.

We found the way down soon enough. Natas led us eagerly, followed by Etienne, Vladimiro and the Germans. The rest of us, Shanoin included, stayed back.

The torchlight gave little solace in the wet darkness of this place; I loathed it immediately. Cobwebs brushed my face and something muscled slid across my foot. I smelled a familiar essence, recognizing Bardolph. "Stay behind me, Nadia," I heard him say.

"I am behind you," I replied hoarsely.

"Oh. Stay there."

And then Shanoin's voice froze our conversation.

"Silence. They are close . . . and I do not smell their slumber as keenly as before."

The catacombs did not stretch far before we reached a small antechamber. We gathered there, torches circling above our heads. There was a sculpture of a great, monstrous titan etched into the upper ceiling, leering down at us. The knights stopped.

"Is something wrong?" Bardolph asked from behind.

Vladimiro knelt down, examining something, then rose again. "Blood," he answered. "There's blood all over this floor."

"The feeding area," Etienne said, picking up on the priest's thoughts. "They've been here longer than we thought. We've seen this before, Bardolph; Vampyres attacking, then dragging their prey back to their holes for a proper feast. Apparently not all the victims at the encampment were left for the dawn to find."

I felt Benjamin tense at my side.

Natas wandered further into the darkness, examining the area. "The way branches in three directions. We should split up."

"Split up?" Corran cried. "Are you delirious?"

"We'll be able to kill more of them this way. Less chance for their escape."

"I'm not ready to go off in this tomb by myself," Bardolph retorted, "and I'm not about to let any of my men either."

"That is their decision," Vladimiro said, with a twist of satisfaction. "And Natas's plan has merit."

"Yeah, the sort that—" Bardolph shut up all at once. 'What's that?"

In the silence that followed, I heard it behind me: a hollow sliding.

"The way back!" Ben yelled, and his hand tightened around mine. "We're being sealed in!"

There was a rush beside me and I was bowled over. Vladimiro and the Germans charged back down the original passageway, not to be barred by anyone. I heard them leave, only to encounter a new obstruction. Their fists made only padded sounds.

At length, they gave up their futile attempts and returned. "We're sealed in. Rock," I heard Cataband confirm. How clever of him.

"May I suggest we move out of the 'feeding area'?" Bardolph commented. "The floor is getting far too sticky for my liking!"

Etienne now tried to take control. "Bardolph, everyone. Calm yourselves. There has to be a winch for the door. All we have to do is find it. Suggestions?"

"I still say we split up," Natas replied, his mind set.

"No," Benjamin said, and he released me for a moment. "No, wait. If you want to find something in a maze, you have to follow the rules of the maze. Think logically. All you have to do is follow the wall. Eventually it's going to lead you to all the places you can possibly go."

Etienne seemed to pick out the sense in his idea. "Yes . . . yes, of course. That's right, follow the wall and it will eventually lead you out of a maze. Decent thinking."

Ben grew quiet and drew back to my ear. "The rest of you are too busy chasing shadows," he muttered.

We followed his suggestion in a group. We started down the gaping maw to the right, leaving a single torch wedged in the rock to serve as a marker upon our return.

It was quiet and the air became harder to breathe. I sensed we were moving constantly downward. We walked for hours. The walls began to look more hewn, less Roman, and my feet began to ache. I didn't dare say this though, not here. I'd run my skin raw, if necessary. I wasn't spending one second more down here than I had to.

Suddenly, out of the nothing around us, one of the Germans up ahead pitched forward and was swallowed by the darkness. He cried out, dropping his torch.

"Ambush!" Vladimiro declared. "Christ!"

It fell to chaos. We weren't ready and they tore us apart. I saw these shapes descending, lit ghoulishly in the light. To our credit, stakes were drawn, and I heard shrieks that could not have come from human voices. Then there were far more mortal cries, pleading for divine mercy before they were snuffed out.

I grabbed Benjamin's arm. "Run!" he yelled.

I would not let go. "Come with me!" I shrieked. Something buffeted past my face.

"Men don't run!" he grunted, and pushed me away. His torch fell in my direction.

Refusing to go, I picked up the torch and tried to find him. But by the time I rose, I was already confused as to which direction he had shoved me. I fumbled about blindly, a refugee.

A hand grasped my shoulder and I whirled. Duaz. And his eyes were empty.

"Naaadia." He slurred, his mouth running red, his hand groping for me.

I thrust the torch in his face. He cried out, cursing my name, but did not let go. I reached clumsily for the stake on my belt.

"Naaadia!"

I found it and drew it in a snap of my wrist, thrusting

again and again into the darkness. I connected a few times and the hand momentarily withdrew.

I think he would have come back, if not for the emergence of a commanding voice.

"Christ! By the blood and body of Christ and his Trinity, I condemn you to below! Back! Back! I rebuke you, children of the Devil!" It was Vladimiro.

The torch was again on the ground, still lit. I took it and looked around, my senses easing. There were bodies—I saw Friedrich, Alimenda, Cataband—all five of the Germans. My breath ragged, I searched for Bardolph or Benjamin.

"Nadia!" Etienne was there, holding out a hand for me to stop, but I didn't listen. Over my other shoulder, I could see Natas crouching, driving a last thrust home into the chest of a Vampyre, his whole weight over his stake. He twisted it and there was a grating, chalky whining. I could see the unmistakable smile on his face.

"Benjamin!" I cried, lost. "Ben!"

And then he was in my face, practically jumping on top of me. The young fool wrapped his arms around me so tightly I thought I would break. "You're all right," he sobbed.

"Yes . . . yes . . . How did you—?"

"Bardolph," he said, and I could see the old Norman behind him, looking away from us. "Something grabbed me and I fought it . . . he came to help."

Our few moments of reunion were soon broken as Vladimiro and Etienne dragged a limp form into the light of the torches. They'd captured Duaz.

"He was trying to escape with the others," Vladimiro explained. "I doused him with holy water before he could get away." Looking, I saw Duaz's body to be covered with burn marks; I knew they couldn't have been from my torch. His form was gangly and wrought with famine. It was not the man I had known, though he wore his face.

"A Vampyre," Etienne said, grabbing Bardolph by the shoulder so that he might see it to finally be true. "You see, Thief? They walk among us!"

"I . . ." Bardolph began, his eyes wide. He could not finish the sentence.

"Natas, the bodies," Vladimiro said, and at once the ferocious knight began properly disposing of the mess. The paladin then turned to his Nosferatu captive. "Where is your master?!"

Duaz smiled weakly. "Here. Waiting for you."

Ben broke in. "Get him to tell us how to open up that rock door."

I put a hand on his shoulder. "I don't think he'll tell us now."

"I can compel him to tell us," Vladimiro said, reaching beneath his armor to reveal a tiny crucifix. Duaz recoiled at once.

"You know what this is," Vladimiro told him firmly. "You know what I can do."

Duaz muttered something in a language I never heard him speak before.

"I can yet save you, Spaniard! Confess yourself, and your end can still be made one that will reunite you with God the Father!"

Duaz twisted, writhed. Vladimiro loomed closer, cross brandished as he brought out another sanctified vial of the cool water he carried with him.

"Confess!" he thundered. I nearly felt sorry for the Spaniard.

"South . . ." Duaz—no, the *Vampyre*—began to say, but then he cried out in pain, convulsing.

"Lies!" Vladimiro declared. "You see what it is for

you to lie in His presence! I shall only ask you once more, Creature, before I cast you with the others!"

Overcome, the Vampyre pointed. "That way . . ." he breathed. "The winch is that way."

Satisfied, Vladimiro slowly rose, putting the cross away.

"They knew we were coming," Corran said. He, at least, was still alive.

"The Vampyre is an adept thing," Etienne mused. "It knows when it is being hunted, has always known. We should have expected this. We've been careless. We must be more cautious."

"I'm surprised we're still alive now," I told them, gesturing to the many bodies scattered on the floor. I thought we were dead for sure! How did you turn the tide on them so fast?"

No one answered. I looked them all over carefully. Someone was yet missing. "Shanoin. Where is he? Is he dead?"

A distant, desperate cry wafted up toward us from the blackness just then, fitting perfectly with the telling silence following my question. It sounded wounded, hysterical.

"He is hunting," Etienne said.

"We must hurry," Vladimiro cautioned. "The Vampyre have scattered, but we can be sure they'll return."

Out of nowhere, Natas's voice surfaced. "Done," he said. Looking down, I saw the bodies, already staked and decapitated. The knight had worked impossibly fast, far more nimble than when we had burned the encampment victims. I could see the blood pumping in his face.

"Burn them," Etienne ordered, "and take this one . . ."

But Duaz had gathered strength as he had lain prone. When our attentions returned to him, he suddenly threw himself at the Frenchman.

Duaz shrugged off Etienne's bow when the knight desperately raked it across his face. He grabbed the Crusader's arm and I heard an echoing snap. Corran ran it through with his sword, but the Vampyre ignored the crippling wound, grabbing the Dane and lifting him easily over his head. I saw the creature begin to squeeze.

Natas connected with him then, knocking them all onto the floor. Bardolph, Ben and I moved in from behind, restraining Duaz as Natas drew another stake from his leg. Taking the hilt of his scythe, he hammered it in blow by blow, each one causing the Vampyre to cry out in horror. It snorted, screeching out in that language I never wish to learn.

Soon it was done. The anti-light was snuffed from him and his undead eyes relaxed, reaching past me, into nothing. I vomited over them.

Corran was relatively unharmed, only bruises marking his chest. Etienne maintained he would be fine, as long as we got out of this place as soon as we could. We rolled the bodies together and burned them, then left down the corridor the Vampyre Duaz had indicated.

We were climbing now, our pace hurried. We never looked back and strode even faster whenever another remote shriek assailed us. We found it without much trouble. It was a winch, as the Vampyre had told us, great pegged wheels strapped together with ropes and pulleys. Being injured, Etienne directed some of the men into place. Together, they began to gradually turn the winch.

"Hurry," Bardolph urged them. "I don't like this. I'm getting that tingling feeling."

"The bad one?" I whispered next to him.

He nodded somberly. "The very bad one. Don't leave my side, Nadia."

"I haven't yet."

"What about Ben?" he asked me, slightly accusative.

I looked at Ben, turning the large winch with the other men. I didn't reply right away.

"What . . . what about him?"

"You haven't left my side to be by his?"

"I'm at *both* your sides," I insisted.

"Maybe," he said, "maybe."

"I meant that."

"Nadia, I'm not stupid. I know these things when I see them."

"See what?" I demanded.

He kissed my forehead. "Nothing. Forget it. I'm not angry. Sad perhaps, but not angry."

I looked back up at his worn face, half in shadow. There was something he was trying to give to me, but I didn't know how to receive it.

There was a loud click. The winch had been pushed to its limit. The stone gate was reopened.

"That's it," Vladimiro said, huffing. "Do we know the way back?"

"I think I can navigate it," Corran offered, "but I'm not sure."

Natas emerged before us. "Wait. We've not yet found him."

"Who?" Ben asked incredulously.

"Our enemy, the Vampyre of Constantinople. Those

were just his servants, those he's brought down with
him. We've not yet ferreted him out."

"Shanoin can . . ." Etienne began.

"I don't trust Shanoin with it. God knows he's
failed before."

"Hold on!" said Bardolph. "You're telling us we
have to stay down here until we find this creature of
yours? Haven't you had enough already?"

"If we're not about to kill him, why did we come
here?" Natas shouted.

Bardolph threw his hands up. "Mad! You're insane!
The lot of you! You're completely, totally, froth-
mouthed mad!"

"The one with the red hair," Ben said, and I saw his
face whiten.

"Yes. I'm not leaving until—"

"Natas," Etienne said now. "Shut up. We're in no
condition to confront the master Vampyre. We're
heading to the surface and that's final. If you wish to
hunt for him alone, go. But I'll guarantee you if you
find him without us, you'll wish you hadn't."

The Italian almost took him up on it. Almost.
Eventually, he nodded and gave in.

Corran led the way up. It wasn't hard to rejoin the
earlier path and, in a shorter time than it had taken to
descend, we were back in the macabre "feeding area."
We ambled into the room one at a time, once more
beneath the frowning titan.

Etienne leaned against me as we led the way to the
exit, Corran flanking our escape. I heard the sound of
water dripping as we scurried away.

"Strange," I heard Bardolph say behind us. "Didn't
we leave a torch here?"

A silken voice replied, but I did not know it. "Yes," it said eloquently, "you did at that."

You would think we'd be smart enough not to wander into a second ambush. I curse myself when I think of how simplistic we were, even the knights. We'd been manipulated since we'd first set foot here.

And now the master of the roost appeared. I don't know if he was alone. I didn't see any others around, but there must have been. Bravely, he strode unarmed into the light, his long, fire-red hair trailing behind. His clothing was superb: scarlet breeches, expensive leather tunic. He made an attractive sight. My impression was shared by all. The group of us stared, transfixed.

He did nothing for a moment but smile. I recalled Azrei.

Bardolph was nearest and, so, was the master's first victim. The moment of grandeur shattered as he reached for him and I screamed, thrown out of my head. I left Etienne and charged back into the room.

Only Natas moved with me. It was like the others were gone. The Italian knight got there before me and I caught a sickening view of his head being torn from his neck in stomach-churning Vampyre justice. His jaw was left hanging, still in place.

As the lifeless corpse fell, the Vampyre turned to me. I think . . . I think his right hand was down Bardolph's throat doing something ghastly, but . . . but . . . but I can't say. I wasn't looking.

I'd forgotten everything in that moment, everything! I . . . I can't believe that I . . .

I stopped, immobile. His eyes trapped me, a longing arm of companionship outstretched, and I couldn't recall why I'd been charging such a noble, wronged aristocrat in the first place. He was positively saintly, a cardinal dressed to receive supplicants.

"Such a gentle child," he whispered, and though I heard it at my distance, I shouldn't have. *"Fanciulla.* This is not the place for you."

He bolted forward and whisked me from the room. I was carried by supple hands down the corridor moving far beyond a horse's pace. I heard the cries of the others drown out, left in our wake.

I regained my senses outside. It was just after dusk, the sky mottled with blacks and blues. The horses tethered nearby watched helplessly, but they whimpered and yanked their heads to and fro at the Vampyre's presence.

His hands roamed without resistance over my face, neck and shoulders. "Fresh air," he breathed in my ear. "It feels good, yes?"

I groaned.

"Your face, little one, so very beautiful. It . . . reminds me of . . ." He trailed off a moment, and sounded almost wistful, but only a moment. Why? I do not know. These were the words of a stranger.

"It reminds me of something that will feel better. Much better. It will prick, honestly, but only at first. Then it will be wondrous. I promise." He smelled my hair vigorously. His accent was enchanting, persuasive. "You believe me, don't you?"

I wish I didn't, but I did. And I wish he'd been lying, but he wasn't. In the end of it all, I nodded.

"Good. Do not worry, your friends will be awaiting us. Then we shall all walk the earth together and raise the ire of the living. I've seen to it."

And he feasted. It was rough at first, like he'd said. He tore out large chunks of my neck and I've still the scars to prove it. But it was an orchestrated frenzy, as impossible as that sounds. The blood did not spill carelessly; every bit was caught. When he pulled his head back to properly swallow his mouthfuls, it did not drain away. He had to suck it out with his inner mouth and his tongue eased the sting of his entry.

I liked it. I don't know if I'll ever tell Benjamin; I'm afraid. But I liked it. I became aroused. That's been the worst part about it. Whether I was under a spell or not, I was a willing victim.

I wish . . . I wish he'd been as repulsive as Azrei.

He nearly drained me in those long minutes there before the tower. I was slipping into unconsciousness. Thank God, we were interrupted. Thank God, thank God, thank GOD.

The Vampyre was stripped from me. He was there one instant, gone the next. I fell limp, as helpless as the horses. I'm sure if I'd not been half unconscious, I'd have witnessed a battle too incredible to be believed.

But what I remember is hazy; just the sight of the eloquent creature being thrust to the ground, a hairy elbow pinning his back. A massive claw yanked his long hair, drew it upward.

There was an almost inaudible, guttural voice. "Look there," it growled, and by the light on the Vampyre's face I could tell he was staring into the moon.

"You are spawn of the great void. Enemy of the sun. But the night is not yours. No, the sun's spirit wife, moon, watches over in his absence. It is guardian of the night. Know that the night is not yours, dead-who-walks, not yours to abuse. The moon watches you all with an angry eye and tonight I am again her willing servant."

Then the Vampyre was torn in half, then in quarters. The undead creature was completely demolished. But the sight had no effect on me; I was too far gone by then.

The last thing I remember was a familiar, snuffling nose. Then I passed out.

•••

I awoke to a tentative dawn. I could see feet pacing about. Blurry shapes reached my eyes.

"It is dangerous to keep her," someone who sounded like Etienne was saying.

"You're not killing her or casting her out," Ben's voice said flatly. "You do and I go with her."

"And I." This must have been Corran.

"I'm not saying it as if it's something I want to do," Etienne returned. "So many have died already. But I'm telling you there's no other way. Once a Vampyre feasts for as long as he has with her . . ."

"He did not drain her completely," the solid voice of Shanoin said.

"You know that's beside the point," Etienne argued. "John, Louis and some of those peasants in Hungary weren't totally drained either . . . it happened anyway."

"There's got to be a way to stop it," Ben said, and I felt a hand near my neck where I'd been bandaged. "I won't leave her."

"An exorcism, maybe," Vladimiro said. "I aided the missionary on them on more than one occasion; he showed me the rites himself. . . ."

"*No!*" objected Ben vehemently. In hindsight, perhaps, too much so.

I think Vladimiro was struck speechless for a

moment. "Had you not saved my life yesterday, I would kill you where you sit."

"You may as well," Ben said. "My life is worthless anyway. Kill me or leave me here."

"We can't leave you in the company of a Vampyre!" Etienne cried, shocked.

"We can't?" Vladimiro snarled.

"I don't care," Ben said back, and he was looking down at me; I don't think he noticed my eyes were open slits. "Why should you? If she awakens for my blood, she can have it. It's no use to me. I'll have stayed with her either way."

"There is time before the change," Shanoin said. "Etienne is right. Do nothing, and she shall be a creature of the void."

"And there's nothing we can do!" Etienne said, clearly frustrated. I heard a snapping sound, a tree branch broken in anger. It must have been with his good arm. "It was folly to think we could so easily train the uninitiated! Exorcisms don't work. What else is there except to kill her?"

"There may be another way," Shanoin said.

My head stopped rocking. Another way?

"What other way?" Vladimiro asked. "You've never mentioned another way before."

"I am not sure of it," the mysterious, oaken man stated, "and you never asked."

"You could have offered!"

"The missionary would not have let me," Shanoin said. "I would have been made to kill him before he allowed anything . . . 'pagan' . . . to happen. It was the will of his God." I could see him looking in the direction of Vladimiro's voice, staring him down.

"He was a good man," the Italian paladin protested.

"Yes, he was."

But I was beginning to drown again and things went black. The breath from Ben's open mouth soothed me to sleep.

• • •

I was standing, tethered to a pole and stripped naked from the chest up, hung by two cords that pierced the skin above my breasts. Tugged against my weight, I wearily looked right . . . left. It was night and a fire burned high only a few strides away. I coughed as I felt the last of my blood running down my chest.

"W-What . . ." I started.

"Shhh," Shanoin urged, stepping into view. "You have been through much, young one. But you are under the protection of the moon now."

"The . . . the what? The moon?"

"Yes," he replied, "the moon. A great spirit."

My voice was hoarse. "It . . . it hurts . . ." I told him slowly. "Why did you . . ."

"Your life's water has been drunk of by a beast of the void, of the empty night," he said. "I have seen what happens to such victims. They rise to walk again as beasts themselves."

My eyes left his and wandered about my surroundings again. "Where is . . . Benjamin? Where's Bardolph?"

He did not answer immediately. "The others are encamped at the foot of this hill. I have sent them away; this is a ceremony between you and the spirits."

"Ceremony?"

"To prevent you from becoming part of the void. What you call a Vampyre."

"A Vampyre?" I groaned and my voice broke. I was starved for water. "No . . . no."

"Yes," he insisted, defying my arguments. A water-skin was brought to my lips and I weakly opened my mouth as water clumsily gushed into it. "I have seen it happen. You are afflicted."

Did he mean he had seen the afflicted before or he had seen me become afflicted?

"I'm not going to become one of those things!" I gasped, water running down my chin, mixing with the matted blood.

"We shall see," Shanoin said, noncommittally. "It shall be in the hands of the spirits soon."

His deep, reverent tone struck me and I distrustfully squinted my eyes at him. I mouthed the last question I had been harboring. "Who *are* you?"

The face, partially hidden, smiled. "To some, I am Runs-With-Wind. But to you, I am Shanoin."

"Runs-With-Wind?"

"The name my tribe knows . . . knew me by," he replied, correcting himself. "I was bestowed it when I killed eight buffalo in a lean hunt. It was done in respect to my patron spirit, the Wolf." He began to trail off, the pride leaving his voice. "I have not been called that name for a long time now."

"Tribe?" I asked him. "Your family?"

"You could say that. But they are far from here, across the sea. You shall never meet them."

My eyes widened. "You are from across the sea?" But the West Sea didn't *have* an end, did it?

He nodded. "I was cast out of my tribe. I committed a shameful act. I have wandered ever since, walking . . . riding many miles. One day I came to the sea, and met pale, bearded men who taught me their language in the white, frigid lands. They liked me, took me in their longhouse, their *boat*."

"The Danes?"

"That was what they called themselves. When I left them, I emerged in this land and its strange forests, its single-minded people. I met the silk shaman soon after, the priest."

I let his identity go at that. I already knew more than I had wanted. I looked down, saw my skin stretched, and cried out.

Apocalypse. The end of all things, eternal death. This was my apocalypse.

"Do not worry," Shanoin assured me. "It is part of the ceremony."

"What *ceremony?*" I demanded a second time.

"My father was a shaman, too, of our tribe. Before I was banished, I learned many things.

"This was one of them; you are being made ready for the spirits. You must bleed and starve, drinking only water, until they either heal or leave you."

He was crazy. I had been left in the company of a crazy man. "What are you talking about? What are the spirits?"

"Gods above God," was what he answered. "And if they come to you, you shall see many things."

"What things? Let me down!"

But he would say nothing more. I continued to shout through the night, but all I would get from him was a deep humming and chanting. At first I was alarmed. The last words I'd heard that I didn't understand had come from that creature that had once been Duaz. But this was different; it was rhythmic, musical.

•••

I think I spent days strapped to the pole, drifting in
and out of consciousness. Shanoin was always there
with me and he was right; I did see many things. I wish
I could tell them to you, because I remember that as
soon as it was over I wanted to rush and tell Ben,
Bardolph, or just plain anyone who would listen of the
wondrous things that came to me. I think I saw the
future, the past, life, death and infinite things in
between.

But I'd forgotten it by the time I descended the hill.
The vision was rapidly lost and I was helpless to stop
its departure. But I'm glad as the experience left me
with what was important.

Life went on after all. The apocalypse had stalled
and collapsed on itself. If it had ever really been there,
I was passed over.

I remember a lot of blood. Vladimiro visited the site
of the ceremony and explained, with hesitation, that
my blood must have been purified with the grace of
God. I had been washed of stains, bled of my illness
and all my sins. It was less than convincing, but I think
he believed it.

He kept calling me 'little Mary' in the days before
we parted company.

The Vampyres were gone. Shanoin told us he had
seen to it and we knew better than to ask how. The purr
of his voice and the hair that would come and go from
his upper arms was enough for me.

Against everyone's objections, I returned to the

tower. Ben strongly objected and insisted on coming, so I agreed. The bodies had been burned by this time. Etienne and Corran had come back and finished up; all that remained were ashes. Ben and I spent a long time there, both in talk and silence. I scooped up the ashes of Bardolph and took them with me when we left.

We traveled west. Vladimiro left us upon reaching the head of the Danube, returning to Rome, his Crusade over. Ben was not sorry to see him go.

We reached France not long after the first snowfall. Etienne had family and we spent months there with them. Ben and I were married in the spring, though it was difficult to arrange the ceremony, and Ben was hesitant on a Christian wedding. In the end, marriage was marriage. Etienne finally persuaded someone, his status as a returned Crusader being very influential. I've always known his views on Christianity not to be conventional. When the townsmen declared it a sin, Etienne stood by us. Eventually, they grumbled and left us alone.

We left in the summer. Only Corran was with us. I did not know where Shanoin had gone; back to Rome or the fields of central France. Etienne did not seem alarmed by his disappearance. His words, "Wild things are meant for the wilds," have endured in my memory. Wherever Shanoin is, I know he is happy there and he does no evil that I will condemn, for who am I to do so?

We crossed the channel between Britannia and France in the Year of Our Lord 1212. I saw the cliffs. I scattered my father's ashes upon the tides. I kept the promise he could not keep to me.

I live now in Cambridge and speak the local

English fluently. My husband farms the land and
Corran lives not far away. My sword hangs tame over
the fireplace. I am no longer a thief and I shall never kill
again. I am free of money.

But I am not ashamed.

A SHIP THAT BENDS

Written by
Luc Reid

Illustrated by
Mike Lawrence

About the Author

Luc Reid is a fifth-generation Vermonter who dropped out of high school to attend college and graduated at the age of twenty. He plays about a dozen musical instruments, sings and composes, and speaks four languages.

Luc has known he would be a writer since age six, but he didn't really get into gear until after attending Orson Scott Card's Literary Boot Camp in July 2001, which he felt improved his writing enormously.

In April 2000 he helped found an intentional community that focuses on providing a supportive environment for children, making a positive ecological impact and encouraging an egalitarian lifestyle. Among other things he currently edits a juvenile speculative fiction magazine. He lives with his wife Jennifer and their two children, Ethan and Lily. His writing website is at http://www.lucreid.com.

I was five when I realized I wanted to sail over the edge of the world. We could see the edge from our house near the temple. Out over houses and the market where the Beneath-siders came to trade, over the tiny harbor on that side of the island, and over the heaving waters of the Great Ocean, there was low-lying mist from horizon to horizon, the place where the water wrapped around the edge. No Abovesider had ever sailed over that edge and around to the beneath-side, but Beneath-siders paddled up over it in their articulated canoes, wrapping around the edge and onto the above-side. The son of a wealthy shipowner, if he were clever and his soul burned for it, might after some years learn to build a ship that could hold the edge and go to the beneath-side. A son might, but I was only a daughter.

Even so, I imagined it. On the very day in the summer of my sixth year when I should have been most frightened and horrified of ever sailing over the edge, I made up my mind to someday conquer it.

My father had never been a match for my pleading, which was why on that I day I stood with him on the deck of a large galley sailing out near the edge as the great sailor Chimilkat made his legendary attempt to sail to the beneath-side. Chimilkat was Phoenician like us, but he hailed from Tyre, far away on the Inner Sea.

We had brought our ship closer to the edge than my father or I had ever been. The ocean curved down as far as the eye could see in either direction, like a great waterfall. Long ago, before the first Beneathsiders sailed up around it, men thought that the waters of the Great Ocean spilled off into endless space rather than just around to the beneath-side.

Chimilkat's ship was not articulated, and my father and his friend Hamilax, a shipbuilder, had argued for days about its chances.

"You see?" said my father. "He is approaching the edge at an angle. It is because other ships have approached it straight on that they have gone off into space."

"It won't be enough," said Hamilax. "The ship has to bend, like theirs do." He meant the Beneathsiders. Their ships were made of overlapping wooden segments that could flex around the edge as they came up it.

"If they would let us examine their canoes . . ." said my father. "Ah, it doesn't matter. See? They're making it around anyway."

All did look well so far. Chimilkat's prow stuck out over the edge, but it was sinking lower, lifting the stern so that soon it would be on the edge rather than the top of the ocean, where we were. Chimilkat himself could be seen strapped to a bench at the bow.

The ship had almost disappeared from sight before we heard the scream, and it was quite a scream. We were a good distance back from the edge itself, and the roaring sound of water surrounded us. A moment later we saw Chimilkat's ship again, this time touching no water at all, but slowly turning end over end as it drifted into endless space. Rowers were untying themselves from their benches and throwing themselves back toward the World. One made it; he landed at the edge of the waters and was instantly sucked down with the water over the edge. He, or in any case his corpse, might be the first Abovesider to see what was beneath the world.

Chimilkat's ship drifted below the horizon. He would sail into the heavens; perhaps there were lands there worth the voyage. But he wouldn't be back.

"Great Baal," muttered Father. Hamilax said nothing, but his face was lined with grief. We could hear wailing from other ships around us. At that moment one of the Beneathsiders' trading canoes crawled up over the edge like a centipede, its wooden segments clinging to the water, its occupants holding carelessly to the benches in front of them with their feet. They ignored us and made for the harbor where they came to trade. Six of the silken-haired beneathside goats were bound between rails amidships, freakishly silent. The Beneathsiders' purple brown skins gleamed in the sun; one had a gold armband and ornamental gold spines pierced his cheeks. He looked up at us and leered as the canoe slid by us.

"They'll be the death of us sooner or later," Hamilax muttered.

"They're traders," said Father.

"Not forever they aren't. They're barbarians if they're anything. They can assemble huge armies beneath our feet and we'd never be able to see. They could raid us whenever they please, and we'd never have warning or a chance to pursue them."

"You're too grim, my friend."

Hamilax grunted. "We'll either learn to sail the edge or wake up one morning with spears at our throats."

I won't wake up that way, I thought. I'm a girl: I'll wake up underneath a barbarian or, if I'm fortunate, to the bite of rope at my wrists, bound for the slave markets.

"I want to sail Beneath," I said. "I want to build a ship that bends."

"Your job is to grow up pretty and not cost me too much money," my father said, "not to build ships."

It was the last time I mentioned it to him.

Illustrated by Mike Lawrence

•••

I was at the shipyard when Hamilax and his men arrived the next morning. At first I stood near them, peering at the massive tree they were shaping for a new ship, but I retreated the first time Hamilax told me to go home, climbing up on the rocks that overlooked their work area. Hamilax shouted at me to leave several more times before he climbed up after me. He looked fed up.

"Why are you using the big tree?" I asked.

He stopped while climbing. "What?"

"Can't you just make the ship out of planks? Why does it need a big tree?"

Hamilax studied me. I think he began to realize then that I was really trying to learn something. Before that, it clearly hadn't crossed his mind.

"Don't ask questions," he said. "You'll learn what you need to know by watching. If your father thinks you're actually interested in the ships and not just in being a nuisance, he'll keep you home."

"Yes, sir," I said.

"It's called a keel. It makes her run straight and sit stable in the water. But no more questions, right?"

"Right."

•••

I don't think the shipbuilders ever noticed them, but being out of the way and not part of the building myself, I realized soon enough that Beneathsiders frequented the shipyards. They kept in the shadows, and they only appeared for a few moments, perhaps a couple of times a month. The reason this struck me as strange was that Beneathsiders usually had nothing to do with the city. They came to the harbor to trade and that was all. They ate their own food, spoke their own grunting language, worshipped their Turtle God and kept to themselves. At least, as far as we all knew they did.

I told Hamilax as soon as I realized. He looked at me levelly. "Have to do something about that," he said. At the time I thought he meant he would have to do something about them being around the shipyards, but now I don't think that was what he meant at all.

•••

I was twelve, and my father had never realized how interested I was in ships. I was growing up pretty enough to satisfy him, apparently, and I certainly didn't cost him too much money. He liked that I would stand attentive and silent as he discussed sailing with the captains of his four ships, but I don't think he realized how much I understood of what they discussed.

One of the captains was Admago, a solid, reliable young man without a hint of sparkle in his personality. He had become interested in me.

It was fairly natural: I was his employer's eldest daughter and nearly of marriageable age. But somehow it seemed to go beyond that for him. He tried to engage me in conversation, awkwardly trying to think of things to say about marriages and gossip, jewels and dresses, things he thought might interest me. Once I realized his intentions, I ran to my father, wailing that I was too young to be married, that Admago was deviling me. My father must have talked to him. Admago backed away, becoming polite and nervous, but his eyes still followed me around rooms, and he continued to visit our house much more than was necessary.

Hamilax had long grown used to me. When no one was around, he would discuss shipbuilding with me. I had never mentioned building a bending ship to him since the day of Chimilkat's voyage, so he took me by surprise one day when he said, "You still don't know how to build a hull that will bend."

"There's no way," I said cautiously. "The keel would prevent it." Actually, it had become clear to me early on that a standard keel wouldn't be possible.

"Ah," said Hamilax. "Must be some way, though. Have to get rid of the keel altogether, I imagine."

He was baiting me and I knew it, but sooner or later I had to talk to someone about my idea. If Hamilax didn't approve, though, he'd go to my father and have him keep me home—but then, I knew I could outlast my father. I would wait him out, showing no interest in ships, pretending to coo over purple fabrics in the market and getting increasingly interested in expensive jewelry. I had four sisters who were already doing that, and a seven-year-old brother who was already demanding expensive weaponry and tutors. He wanted to be a warrior. My father was nothing if not frugal. Once he weighed the costs, I'd be free to go back in the shipyards in a few months at most.

But then, I didn't really think Hamilax would care that I wanted to build an articulated ship. "I think we can keep the keel," I said. "It just couldn't be the same kind of keel. It would have to be a series of heavy sections, pinned together with a sort of joint, so that the whole assembly could flex downward."

"Wouldn't be very seaworthy," he said. "Not much better than a Beneathsider's canoe."

"Not if we left it that way," I said. "But if we had a way to lock them into place, they could be let to flex only when going over the edge. I was thinking of a bronze rod—"

"No, no," he said. "There are much better ways to do it than that...."

We spent two hours at this that evening, and much more time on many evenings afterward. We could work out most of it, but there was a lot that wasn't clear. At a certain point, I decided I would have to examine one of the Beneathsiders' canoes close up. After one particularly frustrating session of trying to work out the planking arrangement, I decided I wouldn't return home that night until I had first seen a Beneathsider canoe. I didn't tell Hamilax; he would insist on going as well, and it was much more dangerous for him than for me. Not only was he older and slower, but if I was caught the Beneathsiders might think me harmless. I was only a girl. If they caught Hamilax near their canoes, though, they'd know him from their spy trips as a danger. There was no telling what they might do.

That night I stood watch over the little eastern harbor where they beached their canoes. The Beneathsiders had a low, stone building not far from where they kept their ships, where they ate and slept and worshipped their Turtle God. The night wore on, and the torches in their building stayed lit long after people of the city had fallen asleep. I fell asleep once myself and woke startled and anxious, lest I had lost the night. I hadn't. It was still dark. In the east, though, beyond the edge, a faint smear of gray and pink began to touch the sky, so that I realized it would be dawn soon. To my dismay, I saw the torches still burned in the stone building. Did the Beneathsiders never sleep? But they did. It was a common sight to see one sprawled in a canoe in midafternoon, dead to the world.

No waiting for them to fall asleep, then. I crept down to the canoes, my sandals left behind so that my feet would make no noise. Despite the beginnings of dawn in the east, there wasn't enough light to make out anything but faint details, so even when I reached the nearest canoe I could barely make anything out. I put my face close to the hull, peering at the overlapping wood segments, but it was the inside structure of the canoe I really needed to see. Glancing around first, I climbed in.

The bottom of the canoe was covered by a rough, loose-woven, dark cloth. I had to lift it up to get a good look at the structure of the boat; they must be purposely keeping the construction of the boats hidden from view. By peeling the cloth back in sections and peering closely, I could make out what I needed to see. I had only a few moments before I was interrupted.

"*Ka, voda! Polbú! Polbú!*" someone shrieked at me. I looked up to see a massive Beneathsider swinging the butt of his spear down, his face disfigured in fury. I threw myself to one side and the spear struck my hip, sending pain shooting through my side. I had landed on something sharp, and it cut through my clothing and along my belly.

I could still run, though. Not certain how badly I had cut myself, I leapt out of the boat on the other side and ran for the nearest alley, half expecting my innards to spill out of me as I went. I felt warm blood trickling down, but it didn't seem bad. I hoped it wasn't.

The Beneathsider gave chase. I ran toward the market square, where the first vendors would be setting out their wares in preparation for the new day. I hoped having other people around might prevent the Beneathsider from doing whatever he was intent on doing. I didn't know whether to hope he wasn't trying to kill me, or to hope he was *only* trying to kill me. Being a girl might be low profile, but it had its own dangers.

That might have been the end of it if I had chosen a good route. I don't think he had gotten a good enough look at me to ever identify me if I had gotten away then, and if he could run about as fast as I could, at least he couldn't run any faster. But Keshikarat is crowded together, building upon building, and the streets don't always go where they might seem. The one I chose came to an abrupt stop at a dead end.

There was no way to get around him. I tried, but he

simply grabbed the back of my dress and shoved me against a garden wall, choking me with his spear held between his hands, pressing against my throat. I began to see spots, and I couldn't breathe to scream. This went on for a long moment before the Beneathsider suddenly dropped to the ground and the spear came away. I gasped rough breaths in, not caring how the air burned in my throat. Hamilax stood there, a paving stone in his hand. It wasn't bloody, but I think I can be forgiven for hoping the Beneathsider was dead.

I stepped over the Beneathsider and almost lost my balance. Hamilax put his hands on my shoulders, steadying me. He had followed me? But of course he had; I had long since stopped worrying about his learning what I wanted to do. It must have been obvious to him what I was doing when I broke the conversation off so suddenly.

"You're all right?" he said.

I nodded, unable to speak yet.

"You got a good look at his boat, did you?"

I nodded again.

Hamilax's face broke into a rare, broad smile. "That's my girl," he said.

●●●

I didn't fall in love with Hamilax. He knew that, but I only had to hound him for two months, not long after my fifteenth birthday, before he consented to ask for my hand in marriage. With what we had learned and designed, we were ready to build a ship that would bend, and Hamilax knew what it meant to me to be on that ship when it sailed. Another man would have laughed and gone on to glory without me—but another man would never have had my confidence.

So we agreed, finally, that I would become his wife; that he would build the articulated ship while I hovered nearby, playing the part of the doting wife in order to have a hand in the building of the ship and the decisions we would make as we realized new difficulties during the construction. Then he would announce his voyage, and I would announce that I could not let him journey without me, that I could not bear his leaving me when I would never see him again, and in the end no one would be able to prevent me from going. Hamilax, after all, would be my husband. Even my father wouldn't be able to gainsay him where I was concerned, once we were married.

When Hamilax asked for my hand, my father turned immediately to me, astonished. "Tanit, you're in love with Hamilax?" he said. "All this time, Hamilax?"

"Men don't see these things," my mother said. To my father she said, "Why do you think Tanit has always spent so much time at the shipyard? You don't think she's there for the ships?"

"But you want to marry him?" my father said. He wasn't opposing the match; far from it, though the difference in our ages was nearly thirty years. But I'm sure my father had always assumed that I, his most headstrong daughter, would declare her love for some extremely inconvenient young man with no fortune.

"Of course I do," I said and looked up at Hamilax. To my surprise he looked sheepish, not a usual expression for him. I began to wonder if he had really needed to be convinced at all.

●●●

A few days later, Hamilax and I walked on the cliff road that overlooked the sea to the south, watching a trade ship sailing off toward Africa. We had already begun laying the strangely jointed keel for our bending ship, and Hamilax had spoken to my father about his voyage. We hadn't mentioned my intention to go; that performance we were saving for later.

Since our engagement, I found I looked at Hamilax differently. Yes, marrying him was a means to an end, ultimately just a way to get me on a voyage I could otherwise never have joined. Still, Hamilax would be my husband, and I had no intention of cheating him out of a true marriage.

He wasn't handsome or well-spoken. I imagine these things had helped prevent his taking a new wife after the death of his first wife more than ten years before. Yet I had a bond with Hamilax, a mutual understanding and a shared single-mindedness, that was more intimate already than my connection with any other person.

For a moment, I thought I glimpsed brownish purple between two houses to one side of us. But when I looked, there was nothing.

"What is it?" said Hamilax.

A Beneathsider rushed out at us then, spear held forward. In astonishment, I froze for a moment, maybe the moment that ruined everything, but after that moment I forced myself to believe that there was a Beneathsider rushing at me with a spear. It struck me that this was the same man who had nearly choked me to death, the man whom Hamilax had hit with a rock.

By the time I began to run he was already quite close to us. I could see the sweat on his forehead, the red veining of his bloodshot eyes; I could hear his grunting breath.

Hamilax grabbed him, and the Beneathsider shoved the spear into Hamilax's stomach. I screamed. Useless, my moment to be brave already gone, I simply screamed. Hamilax grunted, and I saw blood spill out over his lower lip. In one broad, calloused hand, he grabbed the Beneathsider at the back of the neck and pulled him to his chest, as though in an embrace. The spear pushed through further. The Beneathsider screeched in rage. Still grappling, they

tumbled backward over the cliff. They were still
clutching each other when they hit the rocks, far below.

I fell to my knees, hugged a spur of rock at the top
of the cliff as I stared down at where they had hit the
surf. I thought I saw a pink tinge to the spray for a few
moments. I pretended my hands were fixed to the rock,
so that I would not chase them down into the ocean,
tumble in and follow my dreams and hopes into
oblivion.

• • •

Admago was not a bad husband, though he never
understood me at all. I think that may have been one
thing that drew him to me. He was handsome in a
blocky kind of way, he seemed truly to love me, and
despite his pleasure at finding I would finally accept
his advances, he seemed to truly grieve for Hamilax.
More important, he agreed to my one condition to our
union: that he pay to have Hamilax's bending ship
completed by Hamilax's shipbuilders and that he bring
me on its maiden voyage over the edge. This last part
of the condition I insisted he keep secret even from my
father until we were married, and although it seemed
to bother him to have to hold such information back, I
made it clear that without that promise I would never
marry him. I don't know how it is in the lands around
the Inner Sea, but the women of Keshikarat are not
easily wed against their will.

I was lonely, I quickly realized. Apart from grieving
for our plans to sail around the edge, I grieved for
Hamilax himself, for his conversation and his understanding of me. Who else understood me? No one, and
I was not born into a world where a woman could have
dreams like I had and freely discuss them. Such dreams
are best held close.

• • •

It was nearly two years before the bending ship was complete. I had Admago's ear and could get the shipbuilders to talk to me when I worked at it, but by and large they were trying to work from the plans Hamilax had drawn up before he died—never realizing that there was a second designer, one still in the land of the living.

Yet the ship was built. Over the time they were building it, the Beneathsiders traded increasingly for arms and armor: breastplates, helmets, bronze spearheads—virtually any instrument of war. They were suffering regular attacks from hostile, uncivilized people on a neighboring island to theirs, they said, and they did not have the understanding of metals that we had, to make these things easily on their own.

When the ship was complete, Admago filled it with bronze arms and armament as much as with any other trade goods: Tyrian purple dye, glass vessels, wood and purple cloth. I made a public spectacle of myself, begging at the docks for my husband to take me with him. He was relieved enough to say yes; I can't imagine what he would have done if I had made such a scene for real. Or no, I can: he would have taken me with him.

The turnout to watch our attempt was larger, if less optimistic, than the one Chimilkat had had twelve years before. Seamen looked with suspicion and even shock at our flexible ship; they gave each other knowing looks when they saw how it bent over the tops of waves.

No Beneathsiders were to be seen in the crowd of ships that saw us out to the edge, however. The few trading canoes that had been beached a few days before had gone back to the beneath-side, and none had come to replace them. This wasn't unusual, but I couldn't help feeling that it was an ominous sign. I imagined that they were expecting us.

The day we chose was clear and still. Our ship had one small sail on a double mast, two long, straight poles that met at the top to hold our sail, and it was furled for the moment while a single tier of rowers on each side pulled us through the glassy water and over the swells. The splash of the oars and the sound of the drum that kept them synchronized were the only noises we heard. The edge slid nearer, as though the ocean were gradually being erased from the far horizon toward us. I saw only a few men waving from nearby ships. This must have been how people treated the first men who had set out in a sailing ship to trade across the Inner Sea, I thought. But then, I don't know whether those men ever saw shore again.

"Edge, two lengths off!" called Admago. He sounded unconcerned, sure of success. As a husband, he was occasionally a comfort. I checked the ropes around me again, which held me to my bench so that I would not fall off into the sky. They were secure. I breathed deeply and looked out at the ocean. The edge was roaring just ahead of us. I glanced up at Admago, and he seemed to fall as the prow of the ship bowed over the edge. The ship was bending.

I raced my eyes over the ship, trying to ignore the vast spaces out beyond me: no leaks. The rowers were letting the ship move forward on its own power now, although by their expressions all were taken with thoughts of flying off into the sky. I understood.

I heard Admago shouting something just ahead, but he was not making as loud a noise as he might and I could not make out the words. A moment later, the ship had bent further, and I was riding over it and could see what he was shouting about.

Beneathsider canoes, dozens of them. The ones closest to each side of us pushed mightily on their oars and closed in. There was a strange, flat object on each side of each canoe, almost like a ramp. They brought this under us, and then groaning with the effort, half of the rowers in each canoe stopped rowing to push the part of the object inside their canoe down; this pushed the other end up, lifting us out of the water. I could feel the weak pull of the World on me, pulling me toward the water, but the push the Beneathsiders had given us was stronger. Admago railed at the Beneathsiders in shock and fury, but they ignored him. The prow of the ship was pointing out into the blue void.

A Beneathsider, cheeks pierced with enameled spines, reached over into our ship and hacked me free of my ropes with a short bronze sword, one of Phoenecian make. Holding onto his canoe with only his feet, he dragged me into it as our bending ship drifted free of the water altogether, its bottom dripping. I could hear the screaming of the sailors, and my husband calling for me. Ice ran through my veins as I remembered Chimilkat's sailors, crying out and freeing themselves of their ropes, as our sailors were now doing.

Around me, Beneathsider rowers stopped pushing against the current, and the ocean sucked their canoes along the edge and around the corner to the beneath-side. After a moment, the rowers in our canoe did the same, and we were rushed around to the beneath-side, too. All at once it was night; the sun shone over the above-side, obscured from us by the World. In moonlight, then, I was taken to their island. I saw it briefly before they brought me to this cell, little more than a cave with a heavy wooden gate drawn across the front of it. It was not beautiful: their buildings are of piles of stone, held together awkwardly by mud and roofed with branches bound together. The people are dirty, and angry, and the towering statue of their Turtle God—a great work of art compared to the rest of their sorry city—is angrier than all the rest. I felt his cold eyes on me as they brought me here. He has sent our sailors into the void, and brought power to his miserable people. Day is coming, and in the day, I imagine, they will feed my blood to him.

Yet my people saw our bending ship, saw it curve over the edge. Will they know that we were betrayed? We never guessed that Chimilkat might have been. Surely someone will guess, and something will draw that person to build another such ship and sail here: wealth, glory, a driving need to see what no one else has seen.

But I can hear the Turtle God laughing. He disagrees.

BURY MY HEART AT THE GARRICK

Written by
Steve Savile

Illustrated by
Vance Kelly

About the Author

Steve Savile has always been fascinated by magic and magicians, a fact he attributes to his father using an old-fashioned London policeman's helmet as an aid in conjuring chocolate eggs for him. Since that time, there has been something compelling about magic and the magicians whose documentaries he watched: Uri Geller, James Randi, Harry Houdini. It was only natural that, when he began writing in earnest, his obsession with magic would seep into his work.

Steve has edited two collections of Fritz Leiber's short horror stories as well as an anthology to raise money for the homeless in the United Kingdom. You may visit his website at www.darkfantastique.com to read more of his short stories and excerpts from his novel-in-progress. He would love to hear what you think of the following story about Harry Houdini.

About the Illustrator

Vance Kelly was born in Monroe, Louisiana, on August 19, 1970, and has lived in many different cities since then. He's been drawing since childhood, but did not take it seriously until the seventh grade. After doing well in high school art classes, he ended up taking a condensed course in graphic design in New Orleans, Louisiana. Since that time, he has been designing posters, flyers, ads, etc., to promote music events. He, nevertheless, avows his true love is illustration, a fact that is apparent in the following illustration.

O ctober 25th 1926

The magician stared at the mismatched pair of gloves. The left hand was white silk; the right, black leather.

Closing his eyes, he whispered a prayer to a god he had long since stopped believing in and held the black glove to his lips. Breathing out slowly, the magician filled the glove, his breath giving it a miraculous life of its own. His first breath conjured the faintest outline of feathers in the soft leather, the second gave them definition, shape and form, whilst the third stretched out the tip of the thumb until it formed a hard beak. Again and again the magician breathed into the glove, inflating it with the spark of life until the soft leather had changed forever into the flesh of a living, breathing, black bird.

"What do we say when they ask us questions? That's right: Nevermore," the magician said, setting the bird on a small wooden perch. The black bird cawed as if it understood the joke perfectly. "Nevermore. There's only so much life a man can give up." The magician raised the white glove to his lips and breathed the merest sliver of his soul into it, shaping the silk into the delicate body of a flawless white dove. He set the dove down beside the black bird. The bird ruffled its feathers and craned its neck as though considering the magician. He returned the bird's stare, then spoke, his voice barely above a whisper.

"Find them for me. Find the ones who hunt me, let them be the hunted for a while. Then bring me back their faces so that I might know who they are."

He walked to the window and drew back the sash, letting in the October night and letting out the birds. The magician stood at the window, watching the birds fly away over the gray slate roofs. His hands were shaking. The sheer mental and physical exhaustion of dividing his soul in three like that, then setting the parts free, would have killed a weaker man.

Across the street a poster advertised that the Great Houdini would be performing feats of magic and illusion at the Garrick Theatre on October 26. The magician was bone tired.

Behind him, the dressing room door opened. Soft footsteps, the familiar scent of vanilla musk. Bess. His Bess. Like an angel, she always knew when he needed her strength, and like an angel, she knew how to share it with him.

"Come to bed, Harry," Bess said, resting a hand on his shoulder.

"They make me look ridiculous," he said, as if he hadn't heard her. "All of the posturing and posing, flexing my muscles as if I am trying to break the blasted chains in two. What a disappointment I must be in the flesh, the Great Houdini."

"Don't be maudlin. Close the window, darling. It's getting cold in here."

"I'm going to stop soon. Perhaps at the end of this tour. Give the gimmicks to Hardeen and just enjoy what's left of my life. My greatest performance, one final disappearing act."

"Of course you are, dear." Bess said gently. She had heard the words before, more times than she cared to remember. Harry was the boy who cried wolf; one day he would retire and the world wouldn't believe him. They would be lining up to buy tickets for a tour that would never happen. His ever-loving public, always demanding more from their idol.

"All the world isn't a stage. I could simply fade away. They would forget me soon enough."

"Ah, but you wouldn't forget them though, would you, Harry?"

"No," the magician admitted, closing the window.

"Are you coming to bed then, dear?"

"Not for a while yet. Ana Eva Fay is holding a séance. It's been a while since I've seen her, and you know, perhaps this is the last time I shall be able to. It might be nice, to come full circle."

"Oh, Harry. You set yourself up to be hurt even though you know they are all charlatans and fakers. They see you coming. It's a game they play now, who can fool the Great Houdini."

"Not all of them," Harry Houdini whispered, looking at the poster across the street. Whether it was a trick of the failing light or not, the illusion was perfect: the black and white face met his gaze and winked at him.

•••

It was raining; a fine light rain.

The magician walked with his head down and the collar of his greatcoat turned up against the drizzle. Ana Eva Fay's rented rooms were on Shaftsbury Avenue, over on the far side of the city, but, rather than take a hansom cab, Harry felt like walking. The air and the rain would help clear his head. The moon was a bright ball of silver in the night sky.

The gaslights burned yellow-blue on the street corners. Five blocks from the theater Harry sensed— rather than saw—that he was being followed. Discipline learned from years under the stagelights kept him from looking over his shoulder. Instead, without missing a step, he listened for the telltale second set of footsteps moving ever so slightly out of

time with his own. They were there, but there was
something wrong about them, something irregular. It
took him a moment, but then Harry realized that his
pursuer must have had some kind of deformity that
had left him with a limp.

Knowing the streets gave him an advantage and, as
that old bloodhound Damon Runyon was so fond of
saying: It was just as easy to follow someone from in
front as it was from behind, once you knew they were
there.

He let his eyes do the work whilst he walked
without hurrying. Half a block away he saw the
entrance to a poorly lit alleyway. It was perfect for what
he had in mind. Harry ducked into the alleyway.
Where someone else might have pressed themselves
into one of the shadowy recesses of a doorway, the
magician took a moment to scan the alley for possibili-
ties, then looked upward for inspiration. The trailing
rungs of a rusted fire escape dangled just out of reach.
His pursuer wouldn't expect to lose his quarry
upward; he'd be looking left and right for doorways or
windows Houdini might have somehow wriggled
through. Grinning, Harry crouched, tensed, and then
jumped, snagging the bottom rung with his fingers. He
pulled himself up just in time.

A giant of a man stepped into the mouth of the alley.
Beneath his greatcoat, his entire body was twisted up
like the curl of a corkscrew. It was as though the man's
body had fought the unnatural growth every inch of
the way. The twist of his spine had dropped one side of
his pelvis, forcing his left leg to drag on the ground.
There wasn't a hair on his shaved head. The effect was
both monstrous and yet strangely familiar.

Vautrinot, Houdini's mind screamed, recognizing
the Polish magician. It made no sense. Vautrinot had
been a pioneer. Technically flawless, his tricks were no
mere sleight of hand. Vautrinot manipulated mechanics

and misdirection equally well to offset his deformity and create the perfect illusions. Tricks within tricks. A magician's magician, far more than a vaudevillian prestidigitator, Vautrinot had crafted his own illusions.

But Vautrinot was dead. He had died on stage in Paris just before the turn of the century. Peritonitis. Some kind of final fit had left the twisted giant lying center stage with five white doves flying around his head, props escaped from his last illusion. And now he was here, twenty-eight years later and half a world away, stalking Harry Houdini through the streets of Detroit.

Vautrinot shuffled beneath Harry's hiding place, taking his time and methodically checking each dark-ened doorway for the magician. Houdini waited for Vautrinot to reach the crossroads at the far end of the alley then lowered himself to the ground. He landed without a sound, the switch complete, the hunter now very much the hunted. He moved soundlessly up behind Vautrinot and rested a hand on his shoulder.

"Looking for someone, my friend?" Houdini said.

The twisted giant turned. There was no hint of surprise on his face.

"A warning for you is all. Only fair," Vautrinot said in his broken English. His voice sounded as if it hadn't been used in a long time. "They're coming to take you home, Magician. They haven't forgotten you or what you did...."

"Is that why you are following me, to deliver a meaningless threat from beyond the grave? Why not merely a voice at a séance? A ghost rattling chains at my bedside?"

"Because you are one of us, Magician. And because so much of your life is a lie." Even as he said this, the giant's face began to melt. Like wax too close to a naked flame, the skin across Vautrinot's brow, nose and cheekbones began to slide and sink, losing all substance, blinding the dead man's eyes and filling his open mouth with flesh.

Houdini stood rooted to the spot, hypnotized by the giant's melting face, revolted and perversely compelled to stare until Vautrinot's jaw stretched, as though the dead magician was trying desperately to scream through his sealed mouth. Then he ran and he didn't look back to see if Vautrinot was chasing him.

•••

My mind is the key that sets me free.

He'd said that to a journalist in Hanover nearly thirty years ago, a glib one-liner that was meant to suggest that Harry Houdini was a rational man driven by an analytical mind that was equally capable of solving the most obtuse riddles and mysteries of the physical world while it was creating illusions and deceiving the naked eye with tricks that defied explanation. The line had been offered back to him a thousand times over.

Doubled over, hands on knees and breathing hard, Harry desperately wanted some part of that rational, logical mind of his to explain away the dead Vautrinot with his melting face.

"Stress," he said aloud, the excuse sounding hollow.

It was more than stress. It went back further, delved deeper into the core of who and what he was.

"My mind is the key that sets me free," he said to his reflection in the glass panels of the clairvoyant's door. Steeling himself, Harry checked to see if he had been followed. The street was deserted. He took first one, and then a second, deep breath and rapped on the door with its ornate brass lion-headed knocker.

The door was opened by Ana's housekeeper, Helga, an Austrian immigrant who had never quite managed to lose the Germanic overtones to her accent.

"*Herr* Houdini, be welcomed. The madam and her guests are in the sitting room."

The reception was decorated in lavish reds and greens with thick velvet drapes and sumptuous cushions with golden brocade. Portraits of Ana Eva and her late husband Viktor hung over a walnut bureau, the oils making the faces appear both more intense and menacing than their real life models had ever been. Viktor had been a carpenter, a craftsman who loved looking for the miracles in each and every piece of wood he worked with, seeking out the shapes and the spirits that lived within them. Every piece of furniture in Ana's house had been lovingly and painstakingly carved by her husband, right down to his last piece, a solitary chess piece from a set he had designed in his early teens, a bishop, that had taken the man three months to shape as his hands had been brutally mutated by arthritis into claws barely able to hold his scrimshaw blade.

Harry removed his coat and gave it to Helga to hang in the cloakroom. He went through to join Ana Eva and her other guests. The first thing he noticed was the smell: sandalwood.

Like the rest of the house, the sitting room was dominated by regency colors and various shades of wood. Thick scarlet drapes closed off the archway that led to the dining room. Chinese and Egyptian urns housed enormous flowering shrubs and miniature trees whose barks went from almost pitch to the palest silver birch. Ornate rosewood bookcases—with bookends shaped into their shelves—filled the longest wall, each bookend modeled on a figure from Grimm's fairy tales, each one labeled in Viktor's elaborate script in the original Germanic form. There was *Der Froschkönig* and *Die Gänsemagd*, *Dornröschen* and *Aschenputtel*. The Frog King and The Goose Girl, Sleeping Beauty and Cinderella. The sadness of the detail captured in each figure was exquisite and painful to behold.

The guests were in conversation. Harry recognized a few of them from the society pages. Wrapped in sequins and pearls, Judith Welles stirred a martini with her finger. The bright colors of her clothes were a vivid contrast to her eyes. Welles had married into the new money of the automobile industry. Her husband, Garfield Welles, had died of wasting sickness less than two months ago and no amount of that new money could save him. She was obviously hoping to hear that her dear departed was alive and well and living on Saint's Avenue, Heaven. Judith Welles would be receptive to suggestion and willing to believe any so-called miracle. In other words, she was an easy mark. Jericho Joe Dorsey was hanging off her every word, his thick neck craned down bullishly. There wasn't enough cotton in his white shirt to contain the heavyweight's muscles. Jericho Joe was the latest, greatest white hope in the heavyweight arena, Detroit's golden boy with equally golden gloves. In the summer he'd left Luis Angel Firpo out cold on the canvas in the second, and the rumor on Runyon's sports page was that Jericho Joe was slated to box either Gene Tunney or Jack Dempsey for their belt after Christmas.

Next to Jericho Joe and the grieving automobile heiress, Dr. Oberon Mietelowski was deep in conversation with the Black Widow. The Black Widow simply laughed and blew smoke.

"Like I care, darling," she said around the tip of her cigarette.

This odd couple were both regulars in the broadsheets. Thin-faced and sallow-eyed with a neatly trimmed goatee and bifocals balanced on the end of his nose, Oberon Mietelowski was every inch the macabre Dr. Death they painted him. His reputation had been earned over the last few years with wild claims about dead bodies being the ultimate evidence in murder crimes. The study of pathology, he called it. Letting the victim tell the story of their murder, he said. The broadsheets, of course, turned his theories inside out with even wilder claims that the murderer's face might be burned into the backs of the victim's eyes as the last thing they ever saw, and all that Dr. Death needed to do was open the eyes and see. Mietolowski's ideas that somehow saliva, semen or other secretions might one day be as distinguishable as fingerprints and scars had become something of a joke but he kept on with them nevertheless, positive that they were the key.

"Ah, Mr. Houdini, do join us, won't you?" Mietelowski offered, seeing Harry standing on the fringe of things. "I was just explaining to Elspeth here that in some parts of Europe lighting your cigarette from a naked flame is considered bad form. They believe it dooms some poor sailor to a watery grave."

"Sounds positively ghoulish," the Black Widow said with a smile. "I like that."

The Black Widow's real name was Elspeth Neville. Widowed five times, her fortunes had steadily increased since the death of her first husband nine years earlier in a bizarre boating accident. Ms. Neville had subsequently found, married and survived four captains of industry in six short years. Other guests mingled and talked, moving like bees from one flower to the next as they drained one another's nectar. A prominent politician shook hands warmly with one of the city's most notorious speakeasy owners. That explains the martini, Harry thought, turning his attention back to Dr. Death and the Black Widow.

Whilst they were talking, the last guest arrived. A movie starlet with Hollywood's trademark hair. Harry recognized her face immediately beneath the glistening ebony Dutch bob with its severe bangs. The hair framed a contradictory face: carnal, yet still innocent. It was fresh, open, freckled and friendly. Star of *The American Venus* and *A Social Celebrity*, Louise Brooks swept into the room like the most dazzling creature ever to be placed upon the earth. She was the American Venus, but in her eyes Harry saw a sadness that easily matched Viktor Fay's exquisite bookends.

With any great beauty comes sadness, he thought.

What were they doing here, these gangsters, politicians, divas and doyens? What did they need from Ana Eva Fay? What could they hope to get? Reassurance of a life beyond the grave? Comfort for lost love?

His musings were cut off by the sharp clap of hands. The thick scarlet drapes leading to the dining room were drawn back and Ana Eva herself beckoned them to come through the arch. It was all very symbolic, drawing back the curtain and crossing to the other side.

She looked old and tired and vaguely tragic dressed as she was in the garb of a poor man's Cleopatra, cobra heads fashioned into the golden fringe of her headdress. The Egyptian look was all the rage in Manhattan and Charleston. A few Isis and Osiris cults had even sprung up, offering the rich and restless the chance to worship the old Egyptian gods from the comfort of their plush temples in the central business district. Even one of Harry's most famous tricks was based around the legend of Osiris's drowning and rebirth: the escape from the submerged locked box.

Ana Eva smiled at her guests then shuffled toward her seat at the head of the oval table. It had been a long time since Harry had seen her and the intervening years hadn't been kind. Seeing her now, he was glad he had come.

They took their seats around the table. He was seated between Jericho Joe and the Black Widow. In the center of the table a three-stemmed candlestick held two white candles and a single violet one.

"Friends," the spiritualist began, her voice barely above a whisper. "We have each come here seeking our own truths and together with our open hearts we might find those truths. I ask you to take each other's hands and close your eyes, let yourself breathe in the sanctity of the room. Helga, would you light the candles please?"

The housekeeper took the candles from guest to guest, whispering for them to hold the candlestick and visualize strands of peaceful smoke curling up from the white wicks. With the candles charged, she lit them and replaced them in the center of the table. Then she stepped back and merged with the shadows.

Harry took the hands of his neighbors, again drawn to wondering what needs had brought them to the clairvoyant's door. He closed his eyes.

"The mind is the key to set you free," Ana Eva said, mimicking Harry's thoughts of only moments ago. "Breathe in slowly through your nose . . . and out slowly through your mouth. Taste the serenity of the sandalwood. Let its essences open your spirit to new experiences whilst the pains of the day slip away. The worries that have followed you into this house, let them go. Relax, let your spirit go deep within yourself. Breathe in through your nose . . . and out slowly through your mouth. Now, say these words together: Beloved, we ask that you commune with us and move among us."

"Beloved, we ask that you commune with us and move among us," they intoned as one.

Nothing.

"Beloved," the spiritualist repeated, "we ask that you commune with us and move among us."

They all felt it; the sudden draught that blew into the room from the open fireplace. The temperature shift was brutal and abrupt. Between inhaling and exhaling, the room became so cold their breathing

conjured wraiths from their open mouths. At the head
of the table, Ana Eva jerked in her chair, sitting bolt
upright with her head thrown back and eyes rolling as
her hands clenched. The muscles in her forearms
bunched and corded as convulsions wracked her
wizened body.

The voice that emerged from her mouth wasn't her
own. It was male, deep and resonant. "Jude? Jude, are
you there?" The old spiritualist shuddered again, as
though in the grip of a seizure.

"Oh God, oh God . . . Garfield? I'm here, Garfield,"
Judith Welles sobbed. Harry opened his eyes to look at the
woman across the table from him, so desperate to believe
that she would accept any kind of fakery as the truth.

"Jude," the spiritualist repeated. "I can't see you,
Jude. It's dark. So dark . . ."

"Oh, my love . . . What have they done to you?
Where are you?"

"I'm waiting . . . there's a light, getting close, an . . .
an angel, come to carry me home, Jude . . . The angels
have come to carry me home, my love."

And there it was; the promise that her dear
departed was safe amongst the angels. As if on cue,
Ana Eva slumped forward, her hands hitting the table
hard. When her head came up again a thick viscous
fluid was streaming from her eyes, ears and nose.
Harry Houdini watched the performance with a wry
smile. Bess had been right, of course. They were all
charlatans and hoaxers. Her hands hitting the table had
been the trigger for an elaborately constructed "ectoplasmic" emission. The ectoplasm itself was nothing
more than cheesecloth and netting covered with lumi-
nous paint.

"Don't touch it," Helga hissed a warning as Dr.
Death's curiosity very nearly killed the cat—or at least
the illusion. "The substance of the spirit is unpre-
dictable," she said, standing by the spirit medium's side.

And probably still wet, Harry smiled to himself.

Ana Eva's head was rolling wildly. When her gaze locked on Jericho Joe, her eyes were different. It took Harry a moment to realize what the difference was, but then he had it: they were green. A moment before they had been blue. This was a new level to the illusion. A new trick to con the gullible. He found himself wondering how she had manipulated the coloration. Had she somehow removed lenses when her hands triggered the "ectoplasmic" goo?

"The King of the Ring is going down, going down, going down," she sang suddenly in a high-pitched girlish giggle. "The King of the Ring is going down and he's not getting up in the morning."

The spiritualist's eyes rolled back in her skull and her head lolled loosely on her neck. She shuddered again, her body shaken by another convulsion. The little-girl-lost voice faded. Harry scanned the room for trailing wires or hidden speakers. Every good trick needed props and there were enough heavy velvet drapes in the room to hide a symphonic orchestra, never mind a simple speaker. Some kind of foot pedal set into the floor to trigger the voice changes? That would be easy enough to hide beneath one of the oriental rugs. Ana Eva's birdlike hands were back on the white linen of the tablecloth, twitching.

Something had changed again, something subtle within her countenance; a slipping of features, sinking of eyes deeper into the skull, the sharpening of nose and cheekbones, making the old woman appear older still. Haunted.

A trick of the light, the rational, logical part of Houdini's mind told him. Nothing more. Part of the show for the rubes. Who next? The gangster or the politician? Perhaps my own dear, sweet mother's voice will croon lullabies for me.

Instead, a deep bass grumble issued from the spiritualist's throat as her head came up again. Jericho Joe forgotten, her eyes fixed on Houdini.

"They are coming for you, Magician." The voice hissed. He didn't doubt for a second who it belonged to. "Run. Run while you still can."

Vautrinot.

That same labored Eastern European dialect punctuated every word.

The temperature in the room dropped again with each new word from the ghostly voice.

The huge picture windows rattled in their frames.

The candles guttered in the draught and died.

In the darkness the scent of sandalwood faded and was suddenly and strongly replaced by the oily stench of rotten seaweed.

There was a sound: sliding . . . followed by the shattering of glass on stone.

The glass of water Ana Eva Fay had had in front of her had slid the length of the table, gaining momentum until it flew through the air and exploded in a shower of tiny fragments in the fireplace.

Harry hissed: "Go in peace," and jerked his hands free of the Black Widow and Jericho Joe's, breaking the circle.

The medium had slumped forward and lay face down on the table, unconscious. Her breathing was ragged and weak. A red rose of blood was flowering on the cloth around her head.

There was screaming. Panic.

Harry was the first to react. Whilst the others were still so obviously shaken and couldn't do anything except stare at the broken glass in the hearth, Harry was out of his seat and cradling the old woman in his arms. He checked her neck for a pulse. It was weak, but it was there. Holding her gently, he wiped away the fake ectoplasm from her cheeks, palming the little makeup covered pouches that had held the gooey liquid beneath her eyes. The blood on the tablecloth was very real. Something inside Ana Eva had ruptured. The blood showed no signs of ceasing as it poured from her nose. He lifted the golden headdress from her head and laid her gently on her side. The white linen of the cloth simply absorbed the blood, the rose blooming violently.

"Doctor!" Harry yelled, snapping Dr. Death from the trancelike state he'd succumbed to in the wake of the aborted séance.

"What, what? Oh, yes . . . yes . . ." the pathologist said, pushing himself to his feet. He moved unsteadily around the table to the old woman's side, as though still mesmerized by the sudden turn of events. "Goodness me . . . you poor, poor lady . . ." he soothed, checking her pulse and inclining her head slightly. He eased open her mouth to make certain her tongue wasn't blocking her throat.

"Get me water and some kind of absorbent cloth, tear it into strips. We need to clear away this mess." Having a real threat to deal with, a physical one, seemed to give Oberon Mietelowski the focus he needed.

Helga returned from the kitchen with a chamber pot filled with warm water and a linen sheet that had been torn into strips. Dr. Death soaked the strips of cloth and then began to clean up the blood from Ana Eva's face. He used five strips, clearing away the worst of the blood.

"I'll stay with her," Mietelowski said, soothing the clairvoyant's brow. She was still unconscious, but her breathing seemed less troubled and the blood finally appeared to be drying up. "Could someone give me a hand moving her upstairs? Mr. Dorsey, perhaps you would be so kind?" The big man nodded and lifted the

old lady, gathering her tenderly into his arms as though
his brute strength alone might somehow break her
fragile bones. "Ladies, it has been a delight to make
your acquaintance, but I am sure you understand the
night is getting away from us, and what with the way
things have turned out, I believe you might want to
starting thinking about your journeys home. I'm sure
Helga can help see you to your carriages."

Harry was an oasis of calm amid the activity. Now
that Ana Eva was receiving the kind of care she needed,
he was free to look for the strings. He was in no doubt
much of the evening's theatrics were just that, the
blood sachets that had been so cunningly concealed
with makeup beneath the spiritualist's eyes and behind
her ears confessed as much, but what of the voices—of
Vautrinot's voice in particular?

No matter how much he might have wanted to
believe Ana Eva was somehow involved in an elaborate charade that had doppelgängers of dead men
stalking him through Detroit's night streets and mimics
passing messages from beyond the pale, he knew
better.

She was too old, too innocent, too trusting to be part
of some cruel hoax. She'd called him tonight, he realized, because she knew something about what was
going on, not because she was a part of it. It had been
fifteen years since Harry had last attended a séance
held by Ana Eva Fay. Fifteen years. Experience had
taught him one thing over the years: there are very few
coincidences. She had been trying to warn him. That
was the only explanation that made any sense. The
evidence was stacked very much in the favor of a few
facts: he knew someone had been following him. They
had followed him from Manhattan to Illinois, from
Illinois to Pittsburgh, and Pittsburgh to Seattle and on
to Detroit. That peculiar sixth sense owned by all true
magicians had tingled more than once along the road,

hinting that someone was out there, watching his every step.

Waiting.

It was always at the back of his mind.

That tingle.

The eyes on him.

Knowing that they were out there was one thing, but not knowing who was walking in his footsteps was almost worse than knowing nothing at all. That was why he had sent the birds out that morning, to look for answers.

And that was what he was doing now as he pulled back the velvet curtain to look for the speaker-microphone set up. People were always so willing to accept the supernatural, especially nowadays, with so much uncertainty in society, but the truth was that he'd traveled the Dust Bowl, done the speakeasies and watched the numbers runners in the juke joints of Mississippi, crossed the ocean on a ship of steel and flown through the air like a bird, and the natural was responsible for almost every act of the so-called impossible Harry Houdini had ever encountered.

The recess behind the curtain was set up as a comfortable booth with thick cushions and a number of gimmicks meant to scare the rube. It was empty, though.

The socialites had begun to leave. Helga was clearing the table away and bundling up the ruined linen cloth. Jericho Joe and Dr. Death were upstairs, so Harry was essentially alone downstairs. Ignoring the housekeeper, he knelt down beside Ana Eva's chair and began feeling out the rub of grain on the underside of the table, looking for imperfections. He didn't know what he was looking for. A thin wire; something like that. Instead, his fingers found a series of scratches cut deep into the wood.

Illustrated by Vance Kelly

Dug, he amended, feeling out the rough gouges in the underside of the table. He didn't need to go upstairs to check Ana Eva's fingers to work out how the gouges had materialized in the wood. Somewhere in the midst of the fit she had clawed at the table savagely enough to pare through the wood, and that kind of damage demanded real strength—a strength surely beyond that of a frail old woman.

Shaking his head, Harry stood up again. Instead of reassuring himself that Ana Eva's show had been nothing more than smoke and mirrors he had succeeded in doing very much the opposite. The spectacle—he consciously avoided the word phenomenon—he and the others had just witnessed defied rational explanation. For the first time in his life he had the feeling that he had genuinely been a part of something beyond the natural.

Not the first time, he amended, thinking of Vautrinot's resurrection.

He could hear Helga upstairs. She sounded hysterical.

Harry climbed the stairs quickly, taking them two and three risers at a time. Dr. Death and Jericho Joe had laid the old lady down on a chaise longue in the reception room and were hovering over her attentively. Helga was still screaming, but contrary to his expectations, her screams had nothing to do with her elderly mistress's plight. A white bird had been nailed to the wall, blood running through its feathers and down the regency stripe of the wallpaper. The bird's wings flapped weakly. It wasn't dead, that was why he hadn't felt anything. It was a message, for him and him alone, and the threat was implicit. They could hurt him if they so chose.

Tentatively, Houdini cupped his hands around the bird his soul had helped create and eased it off the spike that pinned it to the wall. His face mirrored the bird's pain as the spike tore at its breast.

He whispered gently to it.

"It can't survive," Helga managed, between sobs. "Poor little thing. Who would do such a thing?"

"Is she going to be all right?" Harry asked Dr. Death instead, ignoring Helga's question. The effect of his words was to shift the focus away from himself and the white bird, and the crime that had so violently penetrated the medium's sanctum sanctorum, like the best magic, a simple misdirection. Point the audience's collective eye in the direction you want it to look.

"She's a tough old stick," Mietelowski said, a hint of admiration and possibly infatuation in his voice. "One of the old school. In a day or so she'll be up and about, right as rain, I'm sure."

"Good," Harry said honestly. "I would hate to think of a world without her."

"Indeed," Mietelowski agreed. "You want certain characters to walk amongst us forever; it is only natural."

Houdini couldn't be completely sure that the natural condition Dr. Death was referring to was longing for loved ones to last forever, or that they can't and don't.

"I think I should be getting along," Harry said, caressing the bird in his hand absently.

"I'll walk you to the door," Jericho Joe said. The boxer was so unobtrusive as to have been almost invisible against the regency stripe. Houdini had become so absorbed in the dying bird that he had forgotten about the big man's presence completely.

"Thank you."

They walked down the stairs side by side to the door. Outside, Jericho Joe Dorsey offered Harry Houdini his hand. "Do you believe in this stuff, Mr. Houdini? I mean, ghosts and telling the future and . . ."

It was obvious the boxer was dwelling on his own otherworldly message from Ana Eva: *The King of the*

Ring is going down, going down, going down, her high-pitched girlish giggle singing out the words to the melody of "London Bridge is Falling Down." *The King of the Ring is going down and he's not getting up in the morning,* and the connotations that message carried with it.

"I believe in a great many things, Mr. Dorsey. I believe that the earth is round, the sun rises in the east, that there is no magic beyond the demonstrable art of misdirection and illusion; a definite skill, but not magic. I believe that fraud is a crime and that baseball is the finest sport known to mankind. I believe that the beasts of the field move on four legs and that man moves on two to show his mastery, and automobiles are the future and move on four wheels, for they do the work of the beasts of burden. I believe that man carries the power of destiny in his own hands. I believe that much of what we witnessed tonight was sleight of hand and crude deception, but by definition *much* means that an element of the séance must have been genuine. I believe, as my good friend Arthur is so fond of saying, that if one eliminates the impossible, what you are left with—no matter how improbable—is most likely the truth. We were in the presence of the spirits, Mr. Dorsey."

"I'm going to die," Jericho Joe said, struggling to come to terms with his spiritual death sentence.

"It is the only certainty we all share, Mr. Dorsey. I would not dwell on it if I were you."

"Tomorrow," Jericho Joe went on, as though he hadn't heard a word Harry had said, "I'm fighting Ingmar Janssen in the flower market off Deardon Street. A bare-knuckle fight, last man standing. I'm into a bookie for a few hundred, I've got no choice. One good punch could get me clear. . . . They call him Thor's Hammer, Janssen. He's a monster. . . . I'm going to die. . . . That's what she was trying to tell me, wasn't she?"

Houdini looked at the boxer. Even without the gift of second sight, he could see an Indian sign hanging over Dorsey—one that read "Dead Man Walking" like an hourglass with the last few sands of time trickling through the bottleneck. He wanted to tell the big man how easy it was to rig a séance to have a mysterious voice singing bastardized nursery rhymes emanating from the medium's mouth, but he couldn't bring himself to do it. He hadn't been lying when he said most of the things they had seen had been smoke and mirrors and makeup pouches, but they had witnessed two truths. Vautrinot's promise and the prophecy that Jericho Joe Dorsey's fighting days were numbered. Instead he said:

"What time is the fight?"

"Seven-thirty, just after they have cleared the stalls away for the night."

"I can have the police commissioner and his boys break it up, if that would set you at ease. Remember, you shape your own destiny, Mr. Dorsey."

Jericho Joe appeared to think about the proposition then shook his head.

"No. No," he repeated. "Being arrested for street fighting would be the end of me, Mr. Houdini. The press would have a field day, and I doubt the guv'nors would let me back in the ring again. No, it's like them old gladiators that went out to face the lions. I have to do what I have to do. Maybe I'll land a lucky punch." He didn't sound like he believed a word he was saying.

"Well, good luck to you, Mr. Dorsey," Harry said, offering his free hand. The big man took it, his own hand swallowing Houdini's like Melville's great white whale.

They parted company at the bottom of the medium's steps, the magician and the pugilist, both fully aware that they faced the fight of their lives come sunrise.

Houdini disappeared into the first dark alleyway

and crouched down against a cold wall. The alleyway reeked of urine and spilled liquor despite the prohibition on its consumption. The shadows masked him thoroughly enough that any somnambulistic passerby would have thought the alleyway was deserted.

Slowly, Harry raised the white bird until its eyes were level with his own. Blood had leaked into the bird's tiny pupils lending it a curious albino quality. The pain was almost too much for it to take.

"I know," the magician soothed, stroking the bird tenderly.

He had a choice now, call back the fragment of his soul that gave life to the creature or end the bird's pain and send that fragment of his self off into the oblivion of the hereafter. Both brought an end to the animal's suffering.

"Fly fast and sure, little bird," Houdini whispered, closing his eyes. His hands closed around the white bird's neck. The magician gave one short sharp twist and the deed was done. When he reopened his eyes a white glove lay limply in his hands where the bird had been. He felt the ache in his heart and the ghost of pain in the flesh of his neck. He folded the glove neatly and slipped it into the pocket of his topcoat.

He emerged from the alleyway a different man, changed, reduced and yet all the more determined to unravel the truth of the night's tangled mysteries. He wanted to believe that men did not return from the dead, but how could he believe that when he knew the opposite to be true? He wanted to believe everything he had told the boxer on Ana Eva Fay's steps, but how could he when he knew dead men were walking through the streets of Detroit? How could he when he knew that dead men could tell no lies?

The answer was he couldn't. He walked steadily, confidently, through the night streets, listening, but the echo of following footsteps didn't return.

The hotel was shrouded in darkness, only the single welcoming light of the night porter's gaslight in the downstairs window breaking the black. Harry mounted the steps wearily and turned on the top step to gaze at the moon.

A black speck flitted across it and was gone.

The magician couldn't help but wonder where his own black bird had gone.

•••

Unfettered by the constraints of space and time, the most natural of laws binding the universe, the black bird was chasing shadows in search of the Truth.

They had parted company, the black bird and the white, beyond the Lifegiver's window. Where the white bird had gone in search of a purity and truth that could not exist outside of fairy tales, the black bird had sought out the black truths amid the secrets and shadows that lurk around everyone's lives. The black bird sought the kind of dark truth that might save the Lifegiver.

Being the wisest of all birds, the black bird knew the one place where the Truth could not hide—within itself. Its flesh and blood was after all a gift lifted right from the Lifegiver's soul, so every sensation and memory the Lifegiver had ever experienced was locked away within the black bird for safekeeping. For the Lifegiver's sake, the bird shaped itself into the key that would set the magician's mind free to explore its darkest recesses. It flew high amongst the clouds and swooped low to skim the foam from the breaking waves of the sea. It rode the time winds chasing the shadows that hunted the Lifegiver then and there right back to their roots in space and time:

•••

Paris, 7 April 1909

A lone black automobile drove alongside the massive iron doors of the new Paris Morgue. There were four people inside the car, the vaudevillian artiste they called Houdini (after the French magician Jean Eugene Robert-Houdin, the *i* as a suffix literally meant *like Houdin* in French); Monsieur Chafik, a Parisian detective, and two reporters. Chafik was there to ensure that the handcuffs were real and had not been tampered with, the reporters to tell the world of the Handcuff King's daring escape from the very jaws of death.

A crowd had gathered along the *pont de l'Archeveche*, filling the bridge itself and every inch of space along the banks of the Seine, come to watch the spectacle unfold. None of the onlookers truly knew what to expect. Hearsay and rumor had been rife as word of mouth had been spreading all sorts of fantastic promises all day long—promises that no matter how outrageous they might have seemed, could not hope to rival the genuine miracle of escapology that was about to be played out beneath the muddy surface of the Seine.

Houdini, dressed in a conservative black suit and tie, allowed himself to be escorted into the morgue by Monsieur Chafik. The place smelled as all such places smell, of antiseptic and chemical preservatives with an underlying hint of rot that refused to be scrubbed away. The crowd's anticipation filtered through the stone walls, charging the morgue with a kind of electricity. The stones themselves seemed aware that something special was going to take place in just a few minutes.

The magician removed his jacket and tie, folding them neatly on a chair. It was a ritual. We come into this life naked, we leave it likewise. Without a word

Houdini undressed fully and waited for both Chafik
and the reporters to attest that nowhere on his person
could they find a key. The Handcuff King was famed
for his boast that there wasn't a pair of cuffs in existence that could hold him. The French detective,
fancying himself canny in the wiles of man, had
Houdini open his mouth and lift his tongue to prove he
hadn't secreted a key in there. Then had him lift his
testicles to prove nothing was taped beneath. The
magician merely smiled and complied with each more
intimate request.

Satisfied, Chafik and the reporters stepped back to
allow Houdini to put on a plain white pair of knee-
length bathing trunks they had already checked for
hidden keys.

They couldn't know that the Handcuff King had
learned the art of regurgitation from a Japanese
acrobat. The ritual undressing added to the illusion. As
far as Monsieur Chafik, the reporters and the waiting
crowd were concerned, what they were about to
witness was real magic.

Chafik fastened the handcuffs around Houdini's
wrists, forcing them so far closed they bit into the magician's wrists, skinning them. Houdini nodded and
Chafik looped a thick metal chain through the cuffs
and secured it to a metal collar he fastened around
Houdini's neck. Trussed up like that, the magician
couldn't move his arms down without doubling
himself up uncomfortably. It was all part of the show.
Once underwater, he would regurgitate the key to the
handcuffs and simply unlock himself.

On the stroke of three, Harry Houdini climbed a
thin metal-runged ladder to the top of one of the pillars
in the wall of the Paris Morgue.

•••

The black bird, no more than a speck in the sky,

watched as the Lifegiver began to shout and gesticulate. In the memories that it had plumbed, the black bird remembered the words it couldn't hear now. . . .

• • •

The crowd was huge. Literally thousands upon thousands of people had gathered to see the madman on the wall of the morgue. Cries for the gendarmerie filled the air. Surely the fool was going to kill himself if he jumped—he was cuffed up like a common prisoner. How could they all stand by and watch like vultures?

The fuss and furor pleased the showman in Houdini. This was what it was all about, creating a spectacle, getting their attention by giving them something they would never forget.

"I am the Great Houdini!" he bellowed in English, knowing full well that the majority of the people along the banks of the Seine wouldn't have the vaguest idea what he was saying. It didn't matter. It was only so much pomp and circumstance and great, great publicity. "There is no lock known to man that can bind me! Even death itself cannot hold me! Witness!" he was waving his arms about furiously, getting his blood pumping and his temperature up before the cold water plunge.

As Monsieur Chafik mounted the ladder behind him—perhaps having second thoughts about the wisdom of the stunt—Harry Houdini, King of the Handcuffs, took a deep breath, steeling himself, and then flung himself from the top of the pillar, well clear of the stone buttresses of the morgue's wall, and down into the muddy waters of the Seine.

Almost to a man, the watchers sucked in their own deep breath, holding it in time and sympathy with the Handcuff King as he wrestled with death itself beneath the water. As the seconds turned into minutes, Chafik began to look worried. He turned to

one of the reporters beside him and spoke in hushed
tones: "The crazy American was brave, but now he
shall cost the city thousands of francs in dredging the
river for his corpse. It was not my fault, monsieur, you
heard me warn him of his foolishness, of the under-
currents, did you not?"

The reporter nodded. His own breath, still stub-
bornly held, finally burst out of him in a gasp. "How
the hell can he do this? Chafik, send someone in to
rescue him!"

The surface of the Seine was frighteningly calm.
Undisturbed.

• • •

The black bird needed to see more. The sky about it
had begun to cloud with dark shadows. It could almost
taste their hunger as they gathered around the muddy
waters, hovering expectantly.

The black bird recognized them for what they were:
the souls of the departed come to carry one of their
own home. Equally, it recognized the implications for
the Lifegiver.

The bird fell out of the sky in a wild dive, plunging
beneath the surface of the river. It was useless trying to
"see" anything through the water; the river had been
used as a central sewerage canal for three centuries
and was swamped with the effluence of every one of
those long years. The black bird flew through the filth
blindly, letting itself be drawn toward the magician's
face until it was too late and it didn't have the strength
to pull clear of the magnetic lure of the Lifegiver's soul
in this younger version. The black bird would not be
able to withstand the linking of souls for long, for
whilst it could not drown, not here, not like this, it
could feel its lungs filling with foul-tasting water and
the panic overwhelming its mind—the mind that the
black bird knew belonged to the Lifegiver.

•••

He was drowning. The shock of the water had been so much more extreme than he had expected. When he hit it he had gasped and drawn in a huge lungful of sewage and because of it he couldn't bring the key back up. Chafik had fastened the handcuffs so tightly that no amount of struggling was going to help him wriggle out of them. In a matter of minutes he would be dead and fighting against it only brought the inevitable closer. A simple escape had killed him. Not some grand death-defying illusion. A simple cuff trick. He was a dead man because of a simple cuff trick. No matter how much his mind rebelled against the idea, it was the truth. He was a dead man.

Houdini felt himself surrendering to the overwhelming sense of serenity as it infused him, calming the panic away until he forgot why he ought to be fighting, why he ought to feel anything at all.

And then he was dead and he was drifting, handcuffed, in a foreign river, just another piece of refuse in the sewerage.

•••

The black bird felt the magician die; it was as though the threads binding it to the universe of men snapped abruptly. The urge was for it to let go and go spinning off wildly, joining the Lifegiver in the land of the waiting dead, but its charge was too important for it to simply let go of the world and all around it, so even as the black souls of the dead coalesced around the magician's drowned corpse, the bird gave itself to the Great Houdini, in turn becoming the Lifegiver.

The corpse shuddered and coughed once and awoke. Guided by the sheer force of the black bird's will to survive, the dead magician coughed again, vomiting up a mouthful of sewage. The muscles in his throat convulsed as he retched water into yet more water and then he felt something stick in his throat.

The key.

My mind is the key that sets me free. The thought flickered through his mind as he struggled to gather his wits and what little reserves of energy he had to control the regurgitation. The key came up into his mouth. Quickly, he manipulated it with his tongue until it was in place between his teeth. The need to breathe burned in his lungs. Houdini raised his wrists to his mouth, angling the key into the handcuff's lock, and with one *snick* he was free. He unthreaded the chain from the cuffs and let it sink down into the muddy depths. With deft fingers he unfastened the collar and it too went drifting down to the bottom of the river.

He kicked upward, pushing for the surface.

Six minutes after launching himself from the morgue's wall, Harry Houdini burst triumphantly from the water, waving the unlocked handcuffs above his head. The magician was met by raucous cheers from the relieved crowd.

Houdini ignored the boat Monsieur Chafik had sent out to meet him and instead swam to the bank, savoring the adulation of the crowd. Chafik was there to help pull him out, a big stupid grin on the detective's usually stoic face.

"Monsieur, that was truly amazing," he gushed, draping a thick overcoat over Houdini's shoulders and leading him back into the morgue. "I thought for certain you were dead . . . I was already calculating the cost to the city to find your body." He laughed a little self-consciously.

"Never give up the ghost, my friend," Harry offered between chattering teeth. Out of the water, he was freezing. He looked around one last time at the crowd before allowing himself to be ushered inside. For a moment, among the rank and file of faces he thought he saw Bartolomeo Bosco, the Italian magician, wave at him, but that was impossible. Bosco had been dead for fifty-nine years.

•••

26 October 1926

Harry awoke from the nightmare and knew at once that the black bird wasn't coming back; it already had, seventeen years ago, in the muddy waters of the Seine, long before he ever sent it out in search of the truth.

The bird had obviously found what it had been looking for because he was beginning to remember things he had never known.

Al Flosso, the major magic dealer in New York, had once been quoted saying that the only magicians Houdini was interested in were dead magicians. It was all starting to make a disturbing kind of sense now, despite the cold light of day coming in through the hotel window.

Bess stirred in the bed beside him, drawing the heavy covers up to her throat.

Harry got out of bed without waking her and went over to stand by the window. He ran his fingers across the heavy wainscoting, exploring the grain. The street was quiet, but it was the kind of quiet before the storm, charged with expectancy.

A delivery boy pushed a cart overfilled with apples, oranges and sundry fruits towards a stall that had been set up on the street corner. The boy looked familiar. Harry had to think about it for a moment, but then it came to him. The fruit seller's boy was the spitting image of his friend, Harry Kellar. Not Kellar as he had been in the last few years leading up to his death, an old man given to bouts of uncontrollable shaking, barely able to hold a deck of cards let alone work magic with his hands, but a younger Kellar, fitter, leaner and in total control of his movements. The Harry Kellar they had dubbed the First King of American Magicians, the Dean of Magic.

Houdini stepped back from the window before the boy could notice him. Was it really Kellar out there, or was he seeing ghosts on every corner? Short of seeing the boy levitate off the ground, there was no way to know.

But he had a feeling.

And the feeling refused to go away.

Just as Vautrinot had been the same twisted giant that had performed on Eastern European stages before peritonitis had finally laid waste to his ruined body, that boy out there was Harry Kellar. The question was, was Kellar here to protect him from Vautrinot's stalking dead, or was he one of them? Harry didn't want to think of his friend that way, but he couldn't afford not to. The childish shade of a dead magician in the street was not a good omen. He resisted the urge to close the curtains.

He had to think.

Panicking now could be potentially fatal. He knew that.

He paced the room, measuring his footsteps. Counting them.

"What's wrong?" Bess asked, sleepily. She stretched and stifled a yawn.

Harry stopped pacing and pressed his thumb into the bridge of his nose, massaging the space between, as though by sheer stubbornness he could force the solution to flower in the blackness of his mind. "I need to think," was all he said for a quarter of an hour, his footsteps the only sound in the otherwise silent room.

"I'm going to the theater," he said, finally. He dressed quickly and grabbed his overcoat on the way out. He knew they would be watching for him, so he had to give them something to see. It all revolved around bluff and double bluff. If they knew he was aware of them, they would have expected him to run. It was the only sensible thing to do. Therefore, it was the last thing he was going to do. Today, Harry Houdini was going to be seen. It was a simple extrapolation of Runyon's principal. Let the dead chase him. He would hunt them from the front. Let them snap and snarl, blissfully unaware of the role they would play in the Great Houdini's last, most breathtaking illusion.

He walked out of the hotel like a giant. A wave to the baker's boy, a nod to a bill poster, a nickel swapped for the day's news. The smell of newly baked bread filled the air. Somewhere across town a factory's foghorn called the workers to the factory floor. He folded the newspaper and tucked it beneath his arm and strolled the five blocks to the theater.

The Garrick was in darkness.

Clarence, the night porter, was washing out his teacup as Harry opened the stage door.

"Morning, Mr. Houdini," Clarence said, looking up. "Getting an early start this morning?"

"I need to check out some of the equipment. It shouldn't take more than an hour or two."

"No problem. I'll unlock the storage room for you." Clarence dried off his hands and shuffled down the corridor that led backstage. It was a far cry from the glamour of the stage lights and the boards. Crumbling plaster, tattered wallpaper peeling away from the walls and carpets that smelled of stale smoke. Clarence unlocked the door and shuffled back to guard the door until the day manager arrived at nine.

The storeroom was a treasure trove of magician's props and curiosities. Metamorphosis boxes with their trapdoors and hidden compartments, sword chambers with a glittering array of blades, caged birds, card tables, steel rings, straitjackets, handcuffs, locks of all shapes and sizes, a glass-fronted water chamber into which he would be immersed, handcuffed and chained, even a milk churn that had been adapted to accommodate a small man. The room's centerpiece, something he had yet to work into his act, a huge airtight bronze coffin. Harry had had a fascination with locked boxes ever since hearing the outrageous claims of a cheap sideshow magician professing to be the god Osiris reborn. Houdini had had the coffin specifically fashioned to show the world just how easy it was to fake being the second coming of an Egyptian deity. He had only used it once before, in a hotel swimming pool in San Diego, where he lay submersed for an hour and a half. The coffin could hold enough air when it was sealed for him to breathe, conservatively, for three or four hours.

Houdini looked at all of the gadgets and gewgaws his act had accumulated over many years of traveling and performing, piecing together the intricacies of what would surely be his most ambitious and potentially deadly illusion to date. A magician can never practice enough or be thorough enough with his equipment, since every moment spent on his act adds something to it, refines it, smoothing out the rough edges. So he went over the equipment one piece at a time for the best part of an hour, checking and double-checking the mechanisms, making sure that every gear and cog ran smoothly, that every hinge was greased, and that there were no cracks or weaknesses in them that might give way at the wrong moment, all the while looking for dark shadows out of the corner of his eye. It was difficult. Not knowing the enemy's limitations, he tended to gift them with godlike omnipotence and all of the accompanying powers. If that were true, then his ruse would have no hope of success. He needed them to have defined limitations on their haunting powers. He was gambling everything on the slim chance that the dead retained the characteristics of their living selves, and his only proof for that dangerous assumption was the fact that Vautrinot's limp had followed him into the afterlife.

It took him another fifteen minutes to fashion the small wooden token that he would use as the conduit. It was shaped like a crude bird. He gave a little of himself to it to give it life, then sealed it within the wood by blackening it in the room's coal fire. Done, he slipped it into his pocket.

Satisfied, he left the equipment and went to keep his first appointment of the day, a staged escape at the new Detroit Police House.

Harry had the day manager call him a car and call ahead to alert the police and local reporters that the Great Houdini was on his way to escape from a locked cell in the city's brand-new jail. The press loved that kind of thing. It added to the air of mystery he cultivated, and with enough observers at a loss to explain exactly how it was done, people needed no encouragement to call it magic.

"Curtain goes up at nine tonight, Mr. Houdini," the day manager said, opening the stage door for the magician.

"I'm planning something rather special tonight, Robert. I want the Chinese Water Torture Chamber on stage after the intermission."

"I'll see to it, sir. If you say it is something special, I can't wait to see it. I mean to say, everything you do is magic, isn't it?"

"Indeed," Harry smiled.

The automobile was the standard black affair, without a roof like one of the old horse-drawn carriages, but the ride to the police house was considerably smoother. Along the roadside, Houdini was sure he saw Wolfgang Kempeler and Eugene

Leitensdorfer partaking in a friendly game of chess behind the glass of a cigar-house window. Leitensdorfer took the white queen with his black rook, and it looked for all the world as though the captured piece grew avian wings and flew through the window. Perhaps it was a messenger off to tell the other dead magicians Harry's whereabouts. He hoped so. He wanted them to believe he was oblivious to their observations. He wanted them sure of themselves. Overly confident. Confidence breeds mistakes.

The police house had been custom-built a few years before and boasted that its fourth floor jailhouse was escape-proof. Harry, through the *Detroit Tribune, News and Post*, had promised to show the police the error of their thinking. He had guaranteed the local reporters that he would be out of the holding cell in fifteen minutes flat, and he had every intention of making good on that promise.

The day manager had done his job. There were two uniformed officers waiting to greet him. Harry thanked the driver, tipped him handsomely with two tickets for the evening's performance, and followed the young officers into the station house.

Despite its newness, the building already owned the air of hopelessness and bitter resignation so common to penitentiaries and police houses up and down the country. The architects had tried to imbue the building with sophistication, decorating it with marble staircases and elaborately carved balustrades, but their efforts were easily undone by the shuffle of weary feet, dejected detectives and down-on-their-luck felons that haunted the place by day and night.

The detective who met them at the door to the holding cells was the polar opposite of old Monsieur Chafik. He was one of the new breed of policemen, more at home with Dr. Death's forensic detection and pathology than with Chafik's dated beat pounding. His hair was waxed back foppishly and his pencil-thin moustache was perfectly trimmed. He held out his hand to Harry.

"David Mammon," he said by way of introduction. Houdini took his hand and shook it. Mammon had a good firm handshake. Houdini ignored the paranoia instilled by the detective's devilish name. He had enough things to worry about without conjuring demons from thin air.

"Harry Houdini," he said in return, inclining his head slightly. It was all part of the dance.

Mammon even smiled like one of those old-time Lucifers, all brimstone breath and treacly charm.

"So," he said, leading the procession down into the holding area. "Welcome to our own little death row. Not that we have lifers and such down here, but these beauties were designed to keep more than just petty crooks and con men locked in."

Houdini raised an eyebrow.

Mammon was talking compulsively. He obviously had a lot riding on this little exhibition. Perhaps money or, more likely, his professional pride, Harry reasoned. After all, a jail able to boast that even the Great Houdini, King of the Escapologists, couldn't escape from it was quite some jail. To put it in perspective, there wasn't one in the United States that he knew of.

Harry did a meet-and-greet, pressing the flesh with the waiting officers, promising a very special show at the Garrick that night and assuring them all that he would love to see them in the audience. He couldn't help but wonder if one of them was some long-dead magician he didn't recognize. As the old joke went, he was more interested in dead magicians than the living perpetrators of the art, but even he couldn't know them all.

He did his best to put the thought out of his mind but he was preoccupied, and that preoccupation made

him sloppy by his own standards. He only gave the
lock a cursory inspection. As promised by the Detroit
P.D., it was a complex mechanism, but by no means
foolproof. He paced around the small cell, measuring
out its exact dimensions and ostensibly looking for
chinks in its armor. There was a small barred but glass-
less window above head height in the outside wall, a
metal tube-framed bed with a wire-sprung mattress, a
porcelain sink and a wooden commode. The commode
was bolted to the floor, but by using one of the
bedsprings, he could worry away just enough cement
to lift it free and then it would be possible to drag the
commode beneath the window for him to stand on
whilst he worked on getting the bars open. It wasn't
ideal, but it was enough for him to make it appear as
though he had simply walked through the walls.

He emerged from the cell to a wall of expectant
faces. It was obvious they wanted him to succeed.
Despite their boasts of an escape-proof cell, they
wanted him to work his magic and somehow wriggle
out of there.

"Let's get this show on the road, shall we?" he said,
slipping off his topcoat and jacket and rolling up the
cuffs of his plain white shirt. "Can I have two volun-
teers to search me for any hidden devices that might be
used in some way to facilitate an escape? I wouldn't
want to be accused of cheating, after all."

A couple of the officers laughed. Mammon stepped
forward, a wry grin on his face.

"Ah, Detective Mammon, I knew I could rely on
you. Now, would anyone else care to assist the good
detective, or do you all trust him to do a thorough job?"
That brought a few more laughs, but no one else volunteered. "It seems your men have faith in you, Detective.
So, don't disappoint them. Feel free to examine every
inch of my person."

"Kick your shoes off," Mammon instructed,

kneeling to inspect the soles of the magician's feet and then working his way up first the right then left leg, satisfying himself that there was no room for even the most rudimentary of lock picks. Houdini almost felt like telling the good detective that everything he needed was already inside the cell. The mattress and bed frame was a real treasure trove for a skilled escapologist. He resisted the temptation and simply let the slick-looking policeman go about his search.

Mammon stood up. He appeared to be slightly disappointed, as though he had built himself up to expect that the magician would be loaded with an array of keys and lock picks secreted about his body.

"Okay, in you go, Mr. Houdini. Boys, set your watches. Fifteen minutes."

Houdini stepped through the cell door once more. This time they closed it behind him. He heard the sounds of a bar being drawn and a bolt slamming into place, then a key rattled in the lock. Whoever it was that locked the door, they didn't remove the key from the lock, making it just about impossible to pick through the tumblers, but encouraging him to try manipulating the key from the inside. Of course everyone on the outside would be able to see the key turning, thus destroying the illusion. No, that wasn't the way to go. He had his escape all mapped out.

He grabbed the side of the mattress and heaved it up, exposing the wire frame beneath. Moving quickly, he took hold of two separate springs and forced them together so that he could simply unhook them from the frame. He had used less than fifteen seconds of his fifteen minutes. He put the mattress back in place, then knelt beside the commode and began digging away at the cement holding the bolts in place. It was dry and crumbled surprisingly easily. It took less than two minutes to free the commode and drag it beneath the window. Harry stood on it, grabbed the bars and hauled himself up so he could see through the window. There was over fifty feet to the ground below, and a small ledge just above the window that had pigeons clustered along it, billing and cooing. He tried the bars, not expecting them to give way.

Preparation was the key. He knew that if he reached up through the bars he would find a hand-held jack used for supporting concrete blocks in construction work. He knew because two days ago he had visited the fifth floor of the Detroit Police House disguised as Eric White, an affable middle-aged man who had been pick-pocketed on the Belle Isle Bridge. Mr. White had been left alone upstairs for more than an hour. In that time he had gone to the toilet twice and been given free reign to explore the Detroit skyline from the squad-room windows and examine the evacuation diagrams located by the central stairwell. It hadn't taken him long to ascertain the precise whereabouts of the holding cells and then find a window so that he could use a piece of string to lower the metal jack into place on the decorative ledge. Preparation was the key, along with an element of reason. It had been a calculated risk that the officer in charge would choose to lock him in the center cell, but after years of holding cell escapes and handcuff tricks in more police houses than he cared to remember, Harry had come to recognize certain similarities in the police mentality. By locking Harry into the center cell, the officer would hope to make him feel more isolated and therefore increase the psychological distance he would need to travel to make good his escape. It might be a state of the art holding cell, but it was run by very much your run-of-the-mill policemen.

Houdini took hold of the bars again and pulled himself up, almost climbing into the recess where the barred window was. Then he stretched through the gap in the bars. His fingers just reached over the ledge far enough to feel the cold metal of the jack. He teased it closer until part of it was hanging over the edge and he was able to get a proper hold. The mistake most people made was in thinking that the windows in cells were blocked by individual bars set in concrete. It was actually a complete frame like the drains in the roadside. The secret was to just force them wide enough to squeeze your head through; the rest of the body would follow. Harry put the jack in place and began to ratchet the lever so that the two plates pressed against the bars. He didn't want to break the bars or rip them out. To keep the illusion alive, the damage to the barred window had to be kept to an absolute minimum. So he worked the jack until the gap was just marginally wider than his head, then he reached up to put the jack back in place on the ledge.

It wasn't easy, but the sweat of exertion helped him wriggle through the gap. He tried not to think about the fact that he was dangling fifty feet above the street as he swung his leg up onto the ledge, kicking a loitering pigeon out of the way. It was cold up there on the ledge without his coat. He didn't want to be outside longer than he absolutely had to be. He estimated he had used perhaps six of his allotted fifteen minutes. That gave him just long enough to reverse the damage to the bars and edge along the side of the building until he found a window he could clamber through.

With everybody inside watching the door to the cell, the detective squadroom was empty. Harry used one of the bedsprings to lift the window's latch and opened it. He squeezed through the window and dropped to the floor, closing the window behind him. Then he walked through the squadroom to join the detectives watching the cell door.

No one noticed him until a delighted Mammon called: "Time's up!" and opened the cell door to find him gone.

He coughed politely from behind them and bowed when they turned to see him standing there.

"How ever did you do that?" Mammon said, shaking his head. He was smiling a crooked smile.

"Magic," Houdini told him earnestly.

The rest of the officers began to applaud. He had given them what they so desperately craved, a little bit of magic in their lives.

●●●

He hadn't been planning on going to Jericho Joe Dorsey's bare-knuckle boxing match in the deserted flower market, but come sunset he found himself walking along Deardon Street just the same. The flower market was in an old bonded warehouse on the riverside with the importer's name whitewashed into the red stone proclaiming the finest exotic goods imported from the Orient. Rather than the heady melange of opiates and silken perfumes, the subtle fragrance of orchids clung to the old stones.

The main shutters were closed for the night, but a side door had been left ajar, inviting those in the know to come and watch the night's bare-knuckle bout.

There were close to two hundred men inside, and the trapped air fairly reeked of testosterone and the sweat of physical labor. The fight fans were clapping and whistling loudly in appreciation of whatever they saw. The press of people had formed a natural ring around the two men in the middle. Sawdust had been spread out inside the circle. It had been kicked up by shuffling feet and there were streaks of blood around the worst of the scuff marks where one of the fighters had obviously taken a beating.

It didn't take long before a weasel-faced individual sidled up to Harry, giving him the once-over. He thumbed through the pages of a tattered notebook, then took a stub of pencil out from behind his ear.

"Evening, squire," he said in a cockney accent so broad it had to be fake. "So what can I put you down for? Twenty bucks on the Jericho Wall going down after a thumping from Thor's Hammer? Or maybe you fancy your boy to flatten the Ice Man? What'll it be?"

"Put me down for twenty on Mr. Dorsey."

"You sure, mate? I mean, feels like I am robbing you blind, you having missed the first couple of rounds. Then again, you look like you ain't short of a bob or two, so twenty on the big dumb Yank." The bookie tore out a numbered slip from inside his notebook and marked it with Harry's bet. "Here's your marker, squire. I'll be back to collect my winnings later." So saying, he turned and disappeared back into the crowd to ply his trade.

The pugilists sat on wooden stools about twenty-five feet apart. They were stripped to the waist. Whilst Jericho Joe's physique was impressive with its well-defined musculature, he had clearly taken a battering from the Swede's huge fists. Ingmar Janssen was a giant of a man, nearly a head taller than his opponent, with fists the size of medicine balls. Both boxers stood and circled each other, warily trading blows, but there was a spring to Janssen's footsteps that Dorsey's lacked. He was up on his toes almost dancing, whereas Jericho Joe was sluggish by comparison. Janssen feinted left and delivered a clubbing right hand to Joe Dorsey's chin. It sounded like a tenderizer slamming into a side of beef. He followed it up with a nasty roundhouse that had blood and spit spraying from the American's mouth. Dorsey staggered back a step and shook his head, trying to clear it. Catcalls greeted the rib-cruncher that Janssen landed a second later. Dorsey appeared to deflate beneath the weight of the blow, his face twisting in pain.

This wasn't fighting, this was butchery. Dorsey didn't have a prayer.

The King of the Ring is going down, going down, going down, and he's not getting up in the morning....

Successive body blows doubled Dorsey up and, as his head went down, the Swede slammed a lethal uppercut into Dorsey's face, smashing his nose to a bloody pulp. Jericho Joe's knees buckled, his head coming up so that he seemed to look Harry in the eye. But before he could fall Janssen landed the killer blow, a sledgehammer of a left that connected with Dorsey's temple.

He hit the floor, two hundred and twenty pounds of dead meat.

The Swede wiped the blood from his mouth with the back of his hand and gave the crowd an almost atavistic salute. They went wild, whooping and hollering. Then, slowly, the tone of the crowd shifted as Jericho Joe stayed down.

Harry saw the bookie nod in his direction, so went over to clear his marker.

"Did warn you squire, that Swede's a monster. Still, you pay your money, you take your chance."

Harry handed over twenty dollars. He didn't stay to watch them mop up Joe Dorsey's remains. He couldn't help but think about the quiet man he had tried to reassure on the steps outside Ana Eva Fay's building, the way he had been so sure he had heard Lady Death herself promising to gather him into her cold, cold arms and carry him into the Underworld.

He couldn't let himself fall into the trap of thinking the same way.

•••

Three black horse-drawn carriages, pulled by six white horses, slowed to a stop outside the Garrick Theatre twenty minutes before the curtain went up. Thick velvet drapes hid the passengers from view. Steam wreathed from the horses' flanks as the drivers dismounted and went to open the coach doors. There was something most peculiar about the three men as they shuffled around to the sides of their coaches. Their movement was awkward and ungainly, yet each man moved in near perfect unison as though lacking individual thought. They were the drivers. They attended to their masters. They were driven by the will of their masters. Driving defined who and what they were.

Most of the night's audience had already taken their seats, eager for the show to begin.

Houdini stood at the dressing room window, watching the passengers disembark. He recognized every one of them, despite the grotesque injuries that disfigured them. The Great Lafayette with half of his face hanging off where it had begun decomposing, Bartolomeo Bosco with the fat body of a worm where he should have had an eye and other decomposition wounds marring his face, Baron Wolfgang von Kempeler as elegant as ever despite the fact that his nose had been eaten away by rot, Antonio Blitz wearing a permanent smile where his lips had gone the way of all flesh, Eugene Leitensdorfer, Etienne Gespard Robertson, Paul de Philipsthal, all of them suffering from their years of interment. Harry Kellar, Zykes, Alexander Herrman, *Signor* Cavengti, Henry Pepper and Elias Vautrinot. There was not a man amongst them Houdini hadn't idolized at some point during his life. These were thirteen of the world's greatest magicians. Thirteen dead men to join the night's audience.

He turned his back on them, then busied himself with his last minute preparation rituals, and put them out of his mind.

It was a packed house.

Ten minutes until he went on stage.

"Now or never," he muttered to himself.

Bess was waiting in the wings. She smiled as he joined her at the curtain's edge. "How are you feeling?" she asked, her eyes glancing down at his ribs. It had been three days since the student in Seattle had given him his best shot. He hadn't been ready for it and it had hurt like the devil. He could still feel it if he thought about it. The punch had probably cracked one of his ribs. He had promised Bess he would get it seen to when they got to Detroit, but with everything that had happened, it had slipped his mind.

"Pretty good," he said, ignoring the direction of her question. "Nervous."

"You?" Bess touched his cheek tenderly. "My fantastic little magician, nervous?"

"It's a special night, tonight, my love. My farewell performance."

"Oh, Harry, you know you'll never retire from this life—they'll carry you away in a box first."

"No, Bess. It ends tonight."

Houdini caught the attention of a boy who was loitering about backstage and called him over. "There's a gentleman in the third row, taller than the rest, in a black smoking jacket with a white lily in his lapel. Do you see him?" The boy craned to peek through the gap in the curtain and nodded. "I want you to go and tell him that Mr. Houdini would like to see him backstage in the interval. Got that?" The boy nodded again. "What are you waiting for then?" Harry chuckled. "Scamper."

"What are you up to, Harry Houdini?"

"He's an old friend," he said, as though that explained everything.

Bess merely raised an eyebrow and bustled out on stage as the band struck up the first notes of Orff's "Fortuna ur Carmina Burana." The stagehands hauled on the ropes raising the curtain and Harry Houdini walked out onto center stage.

He acknowledged each one of the dead magicians before he began his act. Vautrinot's seat, he saw, was empty. He assumed the boy had delivered his message and Vautrinot was already waiting for him backstage.

The act built slowly towards the intermission, each new trick showing the delighted audience illusion built upon illusion and intermixed with more physical stunts and escapes. He reformed a hundred dollar bill that he had borrowed from a member of the front row and burnt to a cinder. The man held the reconstituted bill as though it were the legendary phoenix itself, not merely a piece of Treasury paper. Another man secured his wrists and arms with thirty handcuffs and stood amazed as one by one Houdini shed them. He was in his element. He was performing.

Applause rang out as he and Bess took their bows for the intermission. The curtain came down and the stagehands began the task of setting up the Chinese Water Torture Chamber.

Harry almost ran back to the dressing room.

Be calm, he told himself, standing outside the door for a full minute, taking his time to regulate his breathing and still his trembling hands.

Vautrinot sat with his back to the door.

He didn't turn as Harry entered the room.

He was smoking.

"Cigars are the one thing I miss," he said, almost matter-of-factly, as Harry closed the door.

"They are going to claim me during the show, aren't they?" His hand slipped into his pocket and felt the reassuring presence of the small wooden token he had made that morning. Preparation is the key. Preparation and misdirection.

"It amuses them, the thought of the Great Houdini being humbled at the last, shown to be nothing more than flesh and blood. They have waited seventeen years for this, Erich. Can you imagine? Seventeen years waiting for the Great Houdini to die the way he should have."

"The water torture trick?" Harry said, realizing at once the terrible irony that was the grand finale of his act. Death by drowning. "Look, Elias, I know you don't owe me anything, but you did come to warn me, so I beg one last boon."

"What is it?" the dead magician asked, turning to face Harry for the first time.

Houdini took the small wooden token from his pocket and held it out to Vautrinot. "Give this to my wife when I am gone."

"What is it?" Vautrinot repeated suspiciously.

"A small scrimshaw. Something I made with my own sweat, Elias. Something that is, in essence, me." And that was dangerously close to the truth, but Vautrinot didn't appear to notice.

"Give it to me." He held out a hand. Harry tossed the token his way. The wooden bird turned end over end in the illusion of flight. Vautrinot plucked it deftly from the air and palmed it. "I'll see she gets it."

"Thank you. It means more than you could know." He touched his side, as though still troubled by the punch he had taken in Seattle. Misdirection—show your audience what it wants to see.

"You're a sentimental old fool Erich Weiss."

Houdini winced involuntarily and doubled up as though hit by a fierce stabbing sensation. He let a gasp slip between clenched teeth. He lowered his head and closed his eyes as the pain appeared to take him. The pain lasted for a little over a single heartbeat, but those few moments were all he needed to reach out with his mind and reassure himself that the conduit to the token was open. He felt the slight flush of warmth from within the small wooden bird and opened his eyes. He managed to keep the smile from his lips.

Vautrinot did not look like a man who had won. He looked troubled, as though events had accelerated and he had somehow been left behind. Of course, the man had never so much as seen an automobile before. All of the changes since his death must have been quite daunting, to realize how the world marches on regardless of a single soul. It must be quite a humbling experience to return from your own death to a world so obviously at ease with its own rapid transformation. A few years and already Vautrinot was lost.

"Can I ask you a question, Elias?"

"You can ask," the dead man said, "but there is no guarantee that I will answer." There was no trace of humor in his voice.

"Why are you doing this?"

"Why am I haunting you? Or why am I helping you? There is a subtle difference." A wry smile spread across his desiccated lips.

"Helping," Harry said.

"Because you were the king of America, Erich. A boy from Budapest set the United States of America on fire. You were the KING . . . and this . . . this isn't right. . . ."

"Thank you, Elias. Are they going to come after you for helping me? Are you in danger?"

"Perhaps, but I am already dead. What can they do to me?"

"I don't want to imagine, my friend, I don't even want to imagine." Houdini made a show of thinking about it for a moment, as though the idea had just occurred to him. "Go now, far away from here. Go back to your homeland or somewhere they would never think of looking for you. The show lasts for another fifty minutes. It is not much, but it is a head start. You can be out of the city before they realize you have deserted their cause. . . . Let me at least give you that much in return."

Vautrinot looked at Harry, a sad kind of hope in his eyes.

"I could go ho——"

"No, don't tell me. I cannot let slip what I do not know, no matter what they do to me."

"I was right, Erich, you truly are king," the dead magician said, shaking his head. "I can never repay you. You offer me life and all I bring to your door is a second death. I am sorry."

"Don't be sorry, my friend. Believe me, you will repay me a thousand fold if you get out of the city and away before they realize you are gone."

Vautrinot took the wooden bird from his pocket. "I will find a way to deliver your token; somehow, you have my word." The bell sounded to warn the performers that there was five minutes until the curtain went up again.

"Thank you. Now go, Elias. And Godspeed."

• • •

The Garrick was an enormous theater, the orchestra pit divided in three by wide aisles, lush red velvet seats filled by a rapt audience. Houdini stood in the spotlight on the high stage. Bess worked her way back down through the audience, giving the trinkets, watches and rings back to the people she had borrowed them from. The mentalist part of the act was always popular. People liked to believe Harry could somehow see into Bess's mind or that she could talk to him without words. They were surprisingly willing to accept the impossible over the much more likely secret code that was woven into her words. Throwing his hands upward, the magician bowed to rapturous applause. Bess walked beneath the statues of long-dead actors that lined the walls, silent spectators to the play of life. Their alabaster skin had been darkened by layers of varnish and dust and neglect. The old theater was in need of refurbishing. Even the curtain was a little threadbare in places.

The spotlight shifted to the Chinese Water Torture Chamber that had been moved to center stage. Harry let his gaze settle on each of the twelve dead men in the audience, letting them know he was aware of their presence, of what it meant. Let them think he was reading their minds, too.

By definition, an illusion is not what it seems. Let them watch him, let them come for him, oblivious of the switch. That was the gift of the true magician, the sleight of hand that misdirects even the most suspicious eye. That was what made this last illusion by far his greatest—the eyes he was deceiving belonged to some of the world's greatest magicians.

Making the decision to commit murder had not been easy. Murder is the most vile and loathsome notion known to the human mind, even when the victim is twenty-eight years dead, and yet needs must as the Devil drives.

"Ladies, gentlemen, behold the wonder of the Chinese Water Torture Chamber. In a moment I shall enter the water, bound and chained, and be sealed within." Houdini let his words sink in. "I shall attempt to escape my bonds and free myself from the underwater prison. If I fail, I die. Now, who would like to secure my bonds and see that the water torture chamber is sealed airtight?"

A number of hands went up, all men volunteering for a chance to posture and pose before their ladies. Harry picked out two men, the Italian maestro *Signor* Cavengti was one of them. The dead man shuffled slowly onto the stage. The harsh spotlights were not kind to him. Eyes filled with hate and loathing, he met Houdini's eye. Houdini merely held out his hands, offering them to be cuffed. He kept the banter going all the while as the two men bound and secured him purposefully. When they were done, he could barely wriggle his little finger. Cavengti obviously hoped to help hurry along his demise.

The dead magician leaned in and whispered: "Three minutes, Dead Man. In three minutes we come . . . enjoy your life. . . ." He stepped back and smiled. Harry met his smile with one of his own.

Stagehands moved quickly, fastening his feet into the concrete block that was the lid of the water chamber and rigging the chains up so that the crane could lift Houdini into place in the huge tank of water.

A hush had descended over the audience as though no one dared breathe for fear of breaking the magician's spell.

And then Houdini was hanging upside down and being lowered into the water. Air bubbles escaped through his nose as he dangled motionlessly. Cavengti came forward to fasten the locks, effectively trapping Houdini in the water torture chamber.

More air bubbles raced to the surface.

He tried to work his way around so that he could see Bess, but she was too far back, which was probably for the best, given what he was about to do. He closed his eyes and focused on the open conduit into the token Vautrinot was hopefully smuggling out of Detroit. There was still room for so much to go wrong. For a heartbeat, two, three, there was nothing, and then he felt it, the familiar reassuring warmth of his soul responding to his call. He opened his eyes. The stagehands had drawn the curtain around the water torture chamber, leaving him alone.

Bess was right, as she so often was; he couldn't simply fade away.

This was his life, Harry Houdini, the King of the Handcuffs, the King of Cards, the King of Escapology. This was his life and, in the end, this was his death. In the limelight. Center of attention.

He let his senses wander, released from the constraints of flesh. In that moment Harry Houdini died, but the soul of Erich Weiss, a small boy who travelled to America from Budapest with his mother and father, was reborn inside a small wooden token just a few miles away.

• • •

Elias Vautrinot felt something stir in his coat pocket.

Only then did he begin to understand, but by then it was too late.

The principle of the metamorphosis box: the switch.

The stagecoach was on the outskirts of the city, racing along the uneven road as though the Devil himself was eating up the ground in its wake. He fumbled with the window, trying to get it open so that he might cast Houdini's Trojan horse out into the wilderness of concrete and stone, but it was stuck fast.

The wooden bird was flapping violently, and getting hot—he could feel it searing through the cloth of his coat. He had to get it out through the window before it could come into contact with his flesh.

He started pounding at the window with his fist, but before the glass could break, the totem had burned through to the skin and the dead man could feel his essence being drawn through it. He was powerless to resist. His body stopped responding to his will. His fist dropped to his side. He felt himself being replaced as more and more of his soul was pushed out of his body. It was as though someone else was being born into his flesh before he had finished wearing it. He so badly wanted to fight it, but his body refused to obey him.

And then the world was black. The connection to his own body severed.

He opened his new eyes.

Everything was out of focus.

His lungs were on fire.

Black smoke floated around him, slowly solidifying into faces. Bosco, Blitz, Lafayette, von Kempeler, Leitensdorfer, Etienne Gespard Robertson, Paul de Philipsthal, Zykes, Herrman, *Signor* Cavengti and Henry Pepper, every one of their faces twisted and animalistic, black spirits driven on by their savage lust for the magician's soul.

Smoke-black claws tore at him, reaching in beneath the flesh to rend the very fabric of his soul to shreds.

A scream tore from his lips but made no sound. Bubbles rose through the water. He struggled, fighting against the ghosts of the dead as they took out all of their hate and bitterness against his soul, tearing it to shreds. He felt himself beginning to lose all sense of self as his world became a mass of wounds. He fought against them as long as he could, but he knew he couldn't win. His flesh was swallowing water— drowning—it had all been part of the beautiful irony, and now it was part of his death sentence and Houdini's ever-growing legend. He had been a fool. Tricked out of an afterlife by a simple switch. He didn't deserve Heaven or Hell.

Vautrinot's struggles ceased long before the stage-hands had dragged his new body from the water.

•••

Harry Houdini died in the Detroit General Hospital on October 31, 1926. The cause of death was thought to be peritonitis brought on by traumatic appendicitis, which in turn was most likely caused by a severe blow to the stomach. His wife Bess confirmed that he had indeed been attacked in Seattle a few days earlier and that he had complained of pains for days afterward.

She talked of conversations they had had in the

days before his death and how she believed that Houdini had known he was going to die. There would be a séance every Halloween for the next ten years to give her beloved Harry a chance to reach across from the Other Side. She was sure if anyone could escape from death's realm it was her magician.

•••

27 January 1927

The waitress brought the gaunt Americano his drink.

He didn't look up. He was engrossed in an article in the newspaper. It was an old newspaper, from Halloween the year before. The owner had English language newspapers shipped over because he believed it made his little café more exotic. It took nearly two months for them to reach Budapest. Few customers read them. The Americano had been coming into the café for a month now. He was quiet, kept very much to himself. Read the newspapers, drank the coffee. They spoke a little. She liked to hear his voice, but she felt sorry for him, the way his body curled up like a corkscrew. He would have been tall and handsome otherwise. Instead, she heard the children mock his deformity.

"Terribly sad, isn't it, Mr. Weiss," she offered, setting the coffee down in front of him. Her English wasn't good, but she liked to practice.

"Sorry?" he looked up. He had the saddest eyes she had ever seen.

"About Houdini," the waitress explained, nodding at the newspaper article about the magician's untimely death in Detroit.

"What? Oh yes . . . terribly sad. I met him once, a long time ago. Did you know he promised his wife he would return from the grave? That even death could not hold him. He was a special man, I think. If anyone could truly escape from death I think perhaps it would be him, don't you?"

He reached up and pulled a coin from the air behind her ear.

"For you," he said and smiled, offering her a little bit of magic.

A SILKY TOUCH TO NO MAN

Written by
Robert J Defendi

Illustrated by
Youa Vang

About the Author

Robert J Defendi was born in 1971 in Dubuque, Iowa. Since then, he has lived in Arizona and is now settled in Utah.

In 1996, Robert's novella A Wrinkle in Space-Time received Special Mention from the UPC Novella Awards in Barcelona, Spain. It was one of only two English language submissions mentioned in the awards; the other came from Robert J. Sawyer.

Robert has written for game companies and is currently working on the Stargate game with a group of writers from Fiderac Entertainment Group. He is a storyteam member of FEGs Shadowforce Archer line, in charge of writing fiction for two of the archetype characters. He was the head writer for Masters of Role Playing Magazine. His first novel, War of Wars: Point of Contact, is scheduled for release this year. He currently looking for a publisher for his second novel.

About the Illustrator

Youa Vang was born in Thailand in 1975 and raised in Saint Paul, Minnesota. After high school he attended the Joe Kubert School of Cartooning to study sequential art and illustration. Two years later he decided to focus on painting and completed a program of classical painting, drawing and design at the Barnstone Studios.

Youa's aspirations are to paint book covers, graphic novels, children's books and contribute concept designs to the entertainment industry. Winning the Illustrators of the Future Contest and rendering this story illustration will help with the attainment of these aspirations.

There are some days I hate Camelot. Some things can be too real. The feeling of a crossbow bolt creasing your right shoulder, for instance. Ah, well, I suppose that's the price you have to pay. I cursed and spun my horse around.

Thomas was just lowering his weapon. He wouldn't have time to reload. I knew I had to act fast, before the shock hit. Instinctively, I tried to pull up my vitals on my marquee. Of course, there was no response.

I drew my sword and I kicked my horse into a charge. The sword slipped as blood pumped out into my hauberk. I shook off my shield and switched the sword to my left hand. This was going to be a hard battle.

Thomas had his sword out by the time I got there. His shield took my blow and his sword caught me in the back as I charged by. Pain again. It's always pain. This was going all wrong. Shock was setting in.

I spun my horse, swaying slightly in the saddle. Thomas was grinning. I wished we were on foot. There I could use my left-handed swings to full advantage, hitting on his shieldless side. At least he was having to swing across his saddle. *C'est la vie.*

When did I become a sore loser?

Oh, well, I've heard dying really rocks. Time to find out.

I charged into his swing, shock clouding my

reflexes. As the broadsword cut me from clavicle to sternum, the sky seemed to open up above me, beckoning with a beautiful light. I soared upward. Growing. Expanding. My mind reached out to the universe almost comprehending all of it at once. I laughed.

Game over.

<You were sloppy, Connor.>

I can't believe Thomas betrayed me, I thought to the AI. *We were so close to the truth.*

<Thomas was never a Templar. He worked for the snake cult. His job was to make sure you never made it to Paris.>

It all came together now.

How was I supposed to figure that out?! I was more than a little disgusted. These games were supposed to be fair.

<You took four years of Latin. Didn't you notice the noun tense and number shift in his Templar mottos?>

Well, yeah. But I figured my Latin was better than his.

<Would a zealot mis-memorize his own mottos?>

The problem with playing in a game managed by an Artificial Intelligence is that he knows everything about you. There are no easy outs when you mess up. An AI knows your capabilities better than you do yourself, and his games are always perfectly fair.

By the way, love the new death sequence, I thought.

<Thank you, Connor. That's very kind.>

I sighed and jacked out.

•••

Now, the term "jacking out" is misleading. With the exception of my gun link, I haven't needed to hardwire into a system since I became a cop (and I've never had to fire my weapon). Of course, sometimes you hardwire anyway. Sunspots can screw up reception, but we were on the low point of the sun's cycle, and I was in my apartment, way down on the second floor of my building. I could transmit from my head to my network node without much trouble.

I climbed off of the vitals bed and moved to the kitchenette, my body creaking from lack of use. I had been *on the slab* as they say, jacked in and hooked to the IVs and catheter for something like six days, and my stomach was growling for food. But when I went to the cupboard, the cupboard was bare.

There is a store located in my apartment building. I placed my order, then tried to do my business in the head (I always feel like I have to right after I get off the catheter). When I was done, the delivery service had filled my dumbwaiter. I made myself a snack and checked the time. My neuralware clock placed it on a marquee, superimposed on my vision.

65:08:12:17:09:37.

Ouch, I was scheduled for work at 17:00 hours. I bolted down the hunk of cheese and limped back into my living room. The auto-butlers had cleaned recently. The place smelled of cleanser. I flopped down on the slab and stretched out. In the four years I've lived in this room, I've only seen an auto-butler twice. That made sense, though. What are the odds of me being in the real world when they were working? Like everyone of my generation, I wasn't really comfortable in realspace. Hell, most people have to be sedated just to be moved from one apartment to another. (I'm one of those people.)

I've often wondered if the little guys dust me while I'm laying there.

Ah, hell, who cares? I don't know who you are, but let me give you a little info in case you're not an official investigator or something. My name is Connor Smith. I'm 36 years old, and I'm a detective in the Boston sector of the New England metropolitan area. But if you don't know that, get out of my journal.

Anyway, it was now 65:08:12:17:10:29, and Bingham has never been particularly forgiving of tardiness, so I dialed into my kitchen node, and the room disappeared in a burst of line-noise. It took a second, and then the connections settled and I was in my Virtual Apartment. I was more comfortable here. This is where I ate and drank and slept, while my body was in the real world on the slab, being fed by IV and exercised by electrical stimulation. This was home, not that austere box where I left my body while I was busy going about my life. I can't think of that place, that sterile little apartment, as my home. That was just where you kept the meat while the mind was doing business.

I headed for the elevator.

Contrary to what the Comedies and Dramas show, we haven't run the detectives out of a realspace squadroom since '53. Why waste real estate when virtual estate is infinite and as cheap as twelve volts of uninterrupted AC? Some of the old-timers talk wistfully of the good-ol'-days of telecommuting (whatever the hell that is), but I like to keep everything virtual. Why would you want to work in a realspace squadroom? I mean, those guys probably smell.

"You're late, Smith," Bingham called as I exited the elevator.

"Sorry, boss. I was in a mediaeval sim."

"They don't have clocks in mediaeval sims?"

"As a matter of fact, they don't."

Bingham looked at me for a moment, then chuckled. "Leave a wakeup call or something next time."

Bingham was a good boss. He was a tall man, with graying hair and a strong jaw. He had startling gray eyes and carried the kind of muscle you aren't used to seeing these days. He was wearing a white shirt, tie and slacks. He always wore suspenders, an anachronistic little affectation, but it made him unique.

Of course, that was just his virtual avatar. In real-space, he was probably a quadriplegic woman or something.

I usually kept my avatar pretty close to home. In cyberspace, I looked much like myself, just fitter and better looking. I kept the same hair color (but I didn't keep it shaved to the scalp like I do in realspace) and eye color. I just made everything a little "more," if you know what I mean.

I sat down at my desk and pulled up the data feed, to see what was happening in the world. It seemed to be doing pretty well without my supervision. A bill was going before the house to mandate reproduction. The birthrate had been dropping over the last few years. It wasn't surprising. I've had five or ten serious relation-ships; two of them had actually moved in with me. Still, all this was in cyberspace. The thought of meeting the person, in the flesh, turned my stomach. We met, we touched and we made love, but all of this was in the ether, while our bodies (the meat, so to speak) cooled on our respective slabs. The thought of having the meat meet, well, that was something I wasn't ready for.

•••

I was contemplating the tax implications of state-enforced in-vitro fertilization when Bingham appeared at the door of his office. "Smith, can I see you for a moment?"

I got up and headed into the office, dread sitting in a lump in my stomach. Bingham didn't talk to people privately very often, and I was sure I was going to be called onto the carpet. I shut the door and took a chair. I decided to start with a preemptive strike.

"I promise, sir, it won't happen again."

"What won't?" Bingham looked a bit confused.

"I won't be late again." Was he going to make me twist on the hook?

Bingham smiled a bit of a smile. "Of course you will. Don't worry about it. You have the third best attendance in the department. I have a case I want to talk about."

"Oh." Now I was really concerned. What kind of a case required a closed door?

"It's a murder." Bingham paused a moment to let that sink in.

I must have stared at him for five or six seconds before I managed a response. "Maybe you should get one of the old-timers...."

"This isn't a case for the old-timers."

I couldn't understand. Murder was a crime of age. Young people didn't kill one another, not because they were better, but because there was no opportunity. When you live your entire life jacked into a computer, you didn't get many opportunities to stick a shiv in someone's ribs. What's more, you didn't care. The state of the meat just didn't matter to you.

Now the old-timers were a different matter. Many of them only jacked in for work. They still had country clubs and went out for dinner and did all those things they had grown to love as kids, when being online was all about sitting in front of a monitor and pumping data down a primitive broadband connection.

They killed each other all the time. While I could count the number of people I had met after the age of ten on one hand. I mean really met, meat to meat.

Bingham was a good boss. He knew that this would take a moment to sink in, so it must have been several seconds later when he said, "Besides, you're already chasing the perp."

He handed me the file and I'm sure my mouth dropped open.

● ● ●

I exited the elevator onto the crime scene. The entire affair had been scanned into memory so that I could view it in cyberspace. The interaction ratio of the room had been turned up so high that I could stub a toe on a pen. This was very important, the Crime Scene Unit had told me, because it meant I couldn't muck up the pitch.

I looked around. A guy from the CSU was getting a hands-on to go with the data. Meanwhile, a uniformed officer was coordinating the investigation (which basically meant he had to stand there and pass messages back and forth to his superiors). He had a stark silver avatar, with smooth facial features. He stood out in his blue uniform.

The room was fairly upscale, measuring a full four meters square. There was a head against one wall and a vitals bed on the other. There was a kitchenette against a wall, looking like it had never been used. I had come in through a door in the fourth wall. Naturally, he had no personal effects or furniture. There wasn't a speck of dust.

The body was dead on the slab. He was still plugged into the catheter and IVs, so presumably, he died online. There was blood on the slab, but I couldn't see the wound from where I was standing. I walked over to the uniform.

"Officer . . ." I checked his tag. "Kostermerov. What's the situation?"

"We have a dead body, sir."

I hate smart-assed uniforms.

"Do we have a cause of death yet?" I asked.

"Not officially, but I'm willing to bet the hole in his head had something to do with it."

I doubt the man had ever been at a murder scene before. Then again, this was just a virtual murder scene, and he had probably been at dozens of those (through different movies and games). I shrugged and walked over to the body.

The corpse wasn't physically jacked in, but with an apartment this fancy, it was a sure bet he could dial in remotely. He had that sunken look of a man who hadn't eaten in years. Large sections of his digestive tract had probably shut down from lack of use, not uncommon, since you spend most or all of your time on IV nutrients. I'd probably be in the same boat if it wasn't against an arbitrary police force policy.

I knelt down on one knee. There, under the man's ear, was the wound. It was small, like from a .22, but had bled quite a bit. It was just behind his data socket. If I remembered correctly, that meant that it had gone through his neuralware. Not the cleanest way to die.

But what was?

"Anything else they told you to tell me, Officer?"

"Yes, sir. The door doesn't work."

I looked at him hard. "You're kidding me."

"No, sir." I wished he had an expression I could read.

"But I just came through the—" I managed to snap it off before I made myself look completely stupid. The officer seemed smug. The CSU guy wasn't making eye contact. Of course I had just walked through the door. They had programmed the simulation to let me.

"How long has it been broken?" I asked.

"A few weeks."

"If no one can get in here, how did we scan the room?"

"Crime Scene Unit sent a remote up the dumbwaiter."

"Could the perp have come up the same way?"

"No, sir," the CSU guy said.

"Why not?"

"We're in a three-hundred-story building here. The dumbwaiter shaft is kept in a vacuum. . . ."

"So it moves quicker," I finished.

"The perp could have come up it, sir, but I can't

imagine how he would have made it out of the room before the bends overtook him. Vacuum exposure is a bitch."

I walked over to the dumbwaiter and thumbed it open. In realspace, it would have taken a while to respond, as the waiter was called to this floor. Here, of course, it opened instantly.

It wasn't big. A small man or a woman could have fit in there, but they wouldn't have been able to wear protective gear. No way they'd do that, kill a man, then make it back out again. We would have found the perp's body right here as well.

I walked over to the officer. The CSU guy went back to work. I looked over the big silver cop from featureless head to shoe-covered toe.

"You ever play mystery games, Officer?"

"Not very often, sir."

"It's a shame. You ever heard of a locked-room mystery?"

"No, sir. What's a locked-room mystery?"

"This is, Officer. This is."

●●●

The elevator door closed on the crime scene, and when it opened, I had been moved to the virtual atrium of Camelot. Hundreds of people wandered around, meeting up with friends or heading to chat rooms, gathering into groups for various games. They gathered by interest and available time, and when they had their groups, they would start to play. I usually avoided them. I liked to solo.

"Camelot, Buddy!" I subvocalized. I was inside its data construct now. I knew it could hear me, even though I was speaking so softly I didn't make a sound.

<Yes, Connor?> The voice was clear in my head and my head only.

"I need a one-on-one."

<Is this about my case?>

"Yes, it is."

Instantly, the atrium dissolved around me and I found myself in a comfortably appointed room. A panel opened up on the other side. There, a monitor displayed a shifting geometric pattern. Camelot knew that when I wanted a one-on-one, I preferred to have something to talk to. He tended to pick movie clichés.

I sat down in an overstuffed chair and glowered about the room for a moment. Camelot was wise enough to let me start the conversation in my own good time.

Camelot was one of three mainframe computers built on the grounds of Devas Pharmaceuticals. The company, when designing their security system, had taken a unique approach. First of all, they had built Merlin, their research AI. Merlin's job was to make DP money. Then they had built Arthur. Arthur had one task and one task only and that was to protect the company's internal datanet from hackers.

Finally, just outside the company's firewall, they had built Camelot. Camelot was designed to be the ultimate virtual reality playground, an AI that did nothing but cater to the whims and the desires of its clientele. The fees were outrageous, unless you were a hacker or a cop. Hackers and cops played for free . . . as long as they brought their combat software.

In the history of this setup, no one had ever cracked the DP firewall. Every hacker in the world knew that if anyone ever got through, their favorite playground might start running a tab.

But when the disaster finally struck, it didn't strike the company.

When I eventually spoke, I couldn't look at the screen. "He struck again."

Out of the corner of my eye, I saw the geometric

shapes change form, like they do when a computer is talking in the movies. <He hacked another AI?> Camelot asked.

"No. This time he killed a man."

<How do you know this?>

I looked at the screen. "The arrogant bastard sent a message to police headquarters. 'I have killed Philip Kay. Tally ho.' It was signed Jacked the Ripper."

I had hated the name when I first heard it. It wasn't growing on me.

<Do you think it was really him?> Camelot asked.

"We never released the name he left when he hacked you. Besides, what would someone gain by using his handle? We're at a dead end on the hacking case. If we find him, we'll be finding him on the murder. If it isn't the same guy, he gets arrested for two crimes, not one."

We were both quiet for a minute. It was Camelot that broke the silence. <Doesn't this seem out of character?>

"Ah . . . we don't know much at all about his character." I sighed and rubbed my eyes. "The bastard is playing with me on this one, too. Just like he did when he switched all your data image files around." *That* had wreaked havoc in the "Interactive Adult" simulations. "He staged the murder in a locked room."

<You are quite good at locked-room mysteries.>

"No, I'm not." There was an edge in my voice. A peevishness. I tried to calm down. "But it doesn't matter. What matters is that there is no such thing as a locked-room mystery. They are fiction. They never happen in real life."

<I see.> I could tell it was wondering why I had come here.

"I know you have been tracking Jacked on your own. Do you have anything to help me?"

There was a pause before Camelot answered. <No, Connor, I don't. He's a ghost.>

I stood up. "Well, it was too much to hope for. At least I was able to give you an update. If you think of anything to help me, let me know."

<Well, there *is* one thing.>

I had made it halfway to the door. I stopped and turned. "What?"

<You are right. There is no such thing as a locked-room mystery. . . . >

I thought about that a moment. ". . . Because the killer *always* has a way in," I finished.

• • •

I jacked out.

My apartment came back to me like a bad dream, the kind of dream where nothing is quite right. Reality didn't sit well on my shoulders, but I needed to get offline for a moment. I wasn't thinking well enough online, and sometimes a new locale can trigger a new thought.

It was worth a try, at least.

I used the toilet (I never actually get anything done after coming off the catheter, but it will drive me nuts 'til I try). That out of the way, I went over to the kitchenette. I pulled out a hunk of cheese and gnawed on it while I thought.

My apartment wasn't as nice as his. It was only about three meters square. You could probably survive a ride in my dumbwaiter, too. I set down my cheese.

This wasn't reassuring.

I walked over to my door. It's funny. You don't even think about it most of the time, but then it's there, and on the other side . . . well, it was best not to think about it. Going outside, outside for real, was not something a normal person did. It was unnatural. It's how I know all old-timers are crazy. I don't even own any clothes.

I was nervous as I approached it, like it might open accidentally. I gritted my teeth and got close. Then I went down on one knee. There was a panel there. I reached down and thumbed it open. There were all sorts of chips and little hydraulic pumps and things. It was Greek to me, so I dialed in and pulled up a technical wizard. It scrolled across my vision, showing me what components to pull to lock the door in the closed position.

That being done, I felt better. It was kind of nice knowing that no one could get in here. I toyed with the idea of leaving it that way. But first, a test.

I walked up to the door and tried to push it open. It wouldn't budge. After a bit, I tried again. Nothing. I placed my hands against it flat and tried to push with all my might. All that I succeeded in doing was giving myself friction burns.

I queried the wizard, asking how much pressure the hydraulics would apply to the door when they were inert. My mouth dropped open when I read the answer.

No one was getting through this door. Not when it was broken.

I put the components on the counter, next to the cheese, and climbed onto the slab. Time to check out of Meat Hotel.

• • •

The medical examiner looked up from the body or, rather, the simulation of the body. The real body was sitting on a slab somewhere, a set of automatic tools following the ME's actions and the scanners digitalizing the results for the ME to experience. Luckily, he wasn't one of those purists who let odor into their examinations.

"You said you had a cause of death?" I asked.

"Yes. His brain was hacked." The ME looked back down at the body.

"What?!"

He looked up again. "Someone hacked back through his data link. They got into his neuralware and reprogrammed it to electrocute his brain."

"But there's a hole in his head." I thought that I'd remind him of the obvious.

"A very shallow one, probably caused by an awl," he said, "just deep enough to damage his neuralware."

"What's an awl?" I asked.

"It's like an ice pick, but smaller."

I was trying to get my mind around this. "But hacking a person's headware, that's supposed to be impossible."

The ME brought up a schematic of the victim's neuralware on the monitor by the body. "Someone can, theoretically, hack into another person's neuralware. This will get him into the processor, here." He indicated the main interface. "The problem is, the power source is very weak. Even if they could do it, which might be the hardest hack in the world, it would take over a minute to cause significant brain damage. After that, the person's IQ would drop, minute by minute, until their brain could no longer support their body's functions. It must have taken more than a quarter of an hour to kill him."

He indicated a separate component on the diagram. "This, however, is the regulator. If ever power is dumped into the brain, this component will shut down the whole system. If the regulator ever goes offline, the system will shut itself down. The regulator is hard wired and cannot be hacked. It has no volatile components."

"So how did he die?"

The medical examiner's face lit up. "Well, this is the really interesting part. The hacker wasn't able to permanently bypass any of this, but he was able to set it up so that once the interface began pumping electricity into the brain, it blew out its only method of monitoring the regulator. It seems that if you were to damage the regulator at the exact moment this overload begins, the failsafe would fail." His eyes sparkled. "But if you did it a moment before, the whole system would shut down. If you did it a moment after, the regulator would have time to do its job."

"How much time did he have?"

"A fraction of a second. Honestly," the ME said, "I don't see how he did it. I put the odds at less than one in ten."

I thought about that a moment. "Could he have written a program to assist him?"

"I don't know. Not my field."

I thought about that as I got into the elevator and keyed in the police station. Within moments, I was back at my desk, thinking.

So he stood over the body, holding an awl or some other weapon. He hacked into the man's neuralware, then set it to electrocute the man to death. At that exact moment, he stabbed with enough force to break through the man's skull, but not enough to do more than destroy the regulator on the other side.

But if he was able to get into the room, why didn't he just kill the man? Why this elaborate plan? What did this killer have to prove?

I pulled up a technical wizard and began setting up simulations. I set it up just like the medical examiner said. The regulator blew and the electricity coursed through the man's brain. It shut off almost immediately. I examined the simulation and discovered an additional failsafe that shut down the current a second later. Well, the killer had probably suppressed that in his hack, so I did so and tried it again. It went a second longer this time, then shut down.

The failsafe had reactivated. Through trial and error, I was able to reproduce the effect, but it took constant supervision. I could design a program to handle it, but it was too large to fit in the native memory of the component. I ran it through a programming wizard, but it was still big.

So, the killer had not only needed to destroy the regulator, he had to maintain his interface with the victim. The second the victim jacked out, the failsafes would trip.

The victim was using a remote link to dial in. The killer had seized control of the interface and disabled the victim's ability to log out. It is very difficult, but not impossible, to get control of your body when interfaced. If he had been jacked in with a physical cable, he could have reached up and pulled it out.

Then a thought hit me, and I went cold.

I jacked out instantly.

•••

I sat up on the slab, my mind aching from the abrupt exit. I was sweating bullets. I looked around the room. I was alone. It took a moment for my heart to stop racing.

The victim was in a room with a broken door. He was using a remote link instead of a cable connection. He had (presumably) done something to make the killer want him dead.

I was in a room with a broken door. I was using a remote link. I was trying to find the killer and put him away for a very long time. Unwittingly, I had perfectly recreated the events of the crime, with myself styled as the victim.

But I was alone.

I looked over at the components to the door. They

were still sitting next to the cheese. I unhooked my body from the slab and I walked over to the kitchenette. I picked up the door components. I walked over to the door.

No. I was still in a locked-room mystery. Until I had figured out how the killer got inside, I'd stay in a locked room. It only seemed appropriate. I walked back over to the slab.

There was a small utility drawer in the base. I opened it up and pulled out my interface cable. I put the door components in its place. I then laid back down on the slab and plugged my body back in. When I was satisfied that my body was taken care of, I hooked up the cable.

Then I jacked in.

•••

I had the method of the murder itself. I wasn't getting anywhere with opportunity. That left motive. I needed a suspect.

We didn't know who Jacked the Ripper was. However, a person doesn't build his skill set without making a few legends. He might have changed his handle, but he couldn't appear cut from a whole cloth. If I could build up my profile of the hacker, I could guess at who might have become him.

I sat at my desk and pulled up my files. Tracking hackers was ninety-five percent of a cop's job. He had to be out there. I looked at the counter on my data pool. Eighty-seven million and change. A lot of people out there were capable of cybercrimes, but they didn't build the skill set in a vacuum. We tracked them all and built extensive psychological profiles on them. Hell, I was in there.

He was available. He had opportunity. That ruled out hackers serving time in virtual prisons. I told the database to weed out those.

Sixty-four million.

He was talented. I could rule out everyone who had never successfully hacked a secure system.

Thirty-three million.

He had a knowledge of physical firewalls. Both Camelot and neuralware had a hardware-based firewall. I could rule out everyone who specialized in software firewalls.

Twelve million.

He was ruthless. He could kill in cold blood. I ruled out everyone whose psychology profile didn't include a proclivity for violence.

Three million.

Oh! He was a criminal. I could rule out anyone who currently worked on catching hackers.

Two million.

He had left an ego signature. I could rule out everyone who didn't.

Still two million. Had that number even changed?

But Jacked the Ripper had never appeared before he hacked Camelot. He had to have abandoned his former persona. That meant that it had been compromised, which meant he'd been caught at least once.

One hundred and six thousand. Most of the people at this level who have been caught served long sentences and wouldn't be free. I was on the home stretch now.

He had hacked an AI. Anyone who had hacked an AI had to know how to program one. I ruled out everyone who had no such training.

One thousand seventy-eight. Now we were getting somewhere.

Hacking Camelot had taken expensive software. He had to be rich. I narrowed it down to rich people and those linked to open crimes involving large sums of money.

One hundred two.

One last thing to check, and this through backdoor methods. I ran a scan through the various world login servers, looking for alibis. If they were logged into any public access entertainment systems, their locations were known. This wasn't, strictly speaking, legal, but I was using the data to exclude people, not include them. This kind of search wouldn't be admissible in court, but since it was gathered on people it was ruling out, it wouldn't have to be. Most companies let us do these searches, as long as we didn't query what the people were doing at the time. They knew we couldn't use them to convict, and so they saw them as a way of protecting their clients, not a violation of their rights. I compared this to my list.

Two people. There were only two people left.

I had my suspects.

•••

There were only two people who had the skills, the psychological profiles, and who were unaccounted for at the time. Both were men. Only two suspects.

Of course, I had run a similar search after the attack on Camelot, but the Camelot attack had happened during off-peak hours. There had been hundreds of suspects, but Philip Kay was killed during peak hours, when more than ninety percent of the online United States population was immersed in public recreation simulations. I couldn't have picked a better time, and now I had two suspects.

The first was named Raymond Farthing. He was a former programmer who had pioneered advances in both the field of firewall hardware and problem modeling in AI logic trees. He had a somewhat spotted youth and was known to smash the hardware in his apartment when frustrated. He had been convicted of cybercrimes as a child—I could tell that much—but his record had been expunged when he reached maturity.

Since then, he had lived a fairly upstanding life. He was suspected of embezzling large sums from his last employer and was quite rich, but no one could prove that the financial records that showed the slow build of these funds were faked. If he was guilty, he had covered his tracks well.

The second was a man named Paul Kline. He had been convicted of many crimes during his early adulthood, but had turned legit in later years. He had worked as a security consultant and programmer for the rest of his life, but my jaw dropped when I saw what his most notable job had been.

He had designed the security subroutines for Camelot itself.

But he was missing. He had disappeared the day after ten million dollars had been stolen from his employer, Richmond Simulations. His fingerprints, photos and description had been wiped from his files and he had just vanished.

The department's most talented men had been tracking Kline for a year now. It wasn't likely that I would stumble on him right away. That meant that I would be stuck with Farthing.

•••

I found him sitting in a club. He was drinking cocktails between bouts on the dance floor. This was one of the wilder, upscale clubs, where designer virtual drugs were consumed in mass quantities and people retired in pairs or small groups to the Swing Rooms in back. I walked up and took the seat next to him. He tilted his head as if looking at me out of the corner of his eye, then went back to his drink.

He had a designer avatar, composed of light and gauze. It drifted in a man-shaped nimbus, swirling around his glass. I didn't like these bizarre avatars. I never knew how to make eye contact.

I lifted my trace scanner. It was a piece of software that scanned his avatar and traced it back to its interface. It was designed to identify a person in a virtual world where they could change their appearance at a whim. Its icon was that of a calculator-sized device, and I watched the screen confirm his identity.

"Raymond Farthing?" I asked.

He turned and seemed to look me over, undoubtedly seeing the scanner. "You'd know better than me."

"I'd like to talk to you."

"Of course you would, Detective." What was it about me that made everyone figure out I was a cop?

"What were you doing last night at about 1900 hours?"

He glanced over at me again (I could tell by his head movements). "I was washing my hair."

"I somehow doubt that. What were you doing?"

"Nothing I couldn't fake very convincing records on. If I had an alibi you trusted, you wouldn't be here, would you?"

I smiled. "I don't suppose I would."

"So what am I suspected of today? Someone rob the widows and orphans?"

The widows and orphans fund was the slang used to describe bribes taken by crooked cops. He was trying to provoke me.

"What is your relationship with Philip Kay?" I asked.

He looked at me for a moment. "Never heard of him."

"Really?" I put an incredulous tone in my voice, trying to sound like I knew more than I was letting on. "You haven't ever met him?"

"I've met a lot of people. Don't recognize the name, though."

I nodded and gave him a look, hoping he would

think I knew something I didn't. I changed the subject. "You used to frequent Camelot a lot, didn't you?"

"Who hasn't?"

"You don't go there very often anymore, do you?"

"I'll bet you know I don't."

"Why not?"

He turned to me on his stool. After a moment, he said, "All right. I'll play. I was banned."

"What for?"

"Exploits and cheats. Some of the other users accused me of unfair play."

"Really?"

"There was a tournament going on at the time."

I nodded. The tournaments at Camelot were prestigious and highly competitive events. I didn't spend much time in them, but they could get ugly. "So you were banned."

"Yeah."

"I bet that made you angry."

"Ah," he said, and turned away. "You like me for the Camelot hack."

"You seem to fit the profile."

He looked back at me. "I wish I did." He turned back to his virtual drink. "I didn't hack Camelot. I doubt I even could."

"A big smart guy like you?"

"You think you're going to stroke me into confessing?"

I stood up. "Maybe not. Thank you for your time." I had taken maybe fifteen steps before he spoke out behind me.

"Detective?"

"Yes?"

"What does Philip Kay have to do with this?"

"He was murdered yesterday."

Farthing burst out laughing. "And you think that I did it?"

"No. Of course not." I saw his body sag as he realized I did. I turned and walked out, wishing his avatar had expressions, so I could see the look on his face.

• • •

The Crime Scene Unit was located in a fairly upscale-looking bit of virtual estate. I stepped out of the elevator and found the investigator who was handling the Kay case. He looked like an average pudgy technician, the kind of guy you'd see in sims and movies. I have no idea what would possess a person to choose to look like that.

"I've got nothing, sir," he said.

I looked at him hard. "You've been on the case for three days now. You have to have something."

"We have scanned every inch of the place for physical data. There hasn't been another soul in that room for months. We've found DNA, but from the amount it's degraded, it was probably from the previous resident. There were traces of DNA on the food as well, but that's normal."

"Really?" I asked.

"We find that on all food. A lot of old-timers still work in food production and distribution."

"I see," I said, but didn't. "So no one was in the room?"

The CSU guy gave me a look. He made a big production of a sigh and walked over to the cabinet. He pulled out a small latex object and handed it to me. "Do you know what this is?"

"A balloon?"

"It's a contraceptive device. A condom."

I looked at it curiously. I had never seen one before. "I've heard of these." They were a little before my time. Who worried about diseases and pregnancy in cyberspace?

"Criminals used these things for years to foil us in rape cases. If we couldn't get living cells off a hair follicle or out from under the victim's fingernails, we were lost."

"So you're saying he could have been wearing some kind of body condom?"

"I'm saying that there are ways to make sure a person doesn't leave physical evidence. Just because we didn't find anything, doesn't mean that there was no one there."

•••

"So what are you telling me?" Bingham asked me.

"I'm telling you that I've got nothing," I said.

Bingham sighed and leaned back in his chair. He took his head in his hands and rubbed his temples. Then he leaned back.

"Why don't you walk me through it?" he said.

"All right. Philip Kay is found dead in a room. The door to the room is damaged and can't have been opened. The technicians have gone over it, and it would take days to fix. The only other way into the room is the dumbwaiter, and it is kept in an extreme vacuum."

"There's nothing else?"

"It's an apartment. Standard design. Only the dumbwaiter and the door, you know that."

"How was he killed?"

"Someone hacked his implants. At the same time, something sharp, most likely an awl, was jabbed into his regulator."

"Why didn't he just kill him with the awl?"

"I don't know. My guess is that he had something to prove."

Bingham looked at me a moment. "Okay, go ahead. Physical evidence?"

"None. The perp was a ghost."

"Motive?"

"None. Kay didn't associate with anyone. He moved to the United States from England because of the difference in our privacy laws. Since then he worked alone, writing supplemental code for several companies. He didn't associate with anyone, didn't go to clubs. His membership fees went to companies that specialize in solo sims. Games, movies and the like. No social interaction. He didn't even use a visible avatar when communicating with his employers. A total recluse."

"Any suspects?" Bingham asked.

"Two. Based on their skill set only. One has had no verifiable interaction with the victim. The other disappeared a while back. We've been looking for him and haven't found him."

Bingham leaned back in his chair. "Well, obviously, the perp has something to prove."

I nodded. "He chose an absurdly complicated method of killing the victim. He has staged a locked-room mystery. He left an ego signature, telling us his handle. It was almost as if he was sending a message."

"But to whom?" Bingham asked.

Of course, the answer to that was obvious. Me.

• • •

I was lost. The killer was taunting me. He had hacked Camelot without taking money out of its accounts. He had killed a man, seemingly at random, and left a message, bragging. He had staged a mystery that I couldn't solve, almost as if he was issuing a challenge to the police.

It was eating me up inside. I solved mysteries like

this in Camelot every day. Still, this one was stumping me. I had nowhere to go. I just wasn't good enough. I could handle this kind of thing in my own little fantasy world, but when confronted with reality, I came up short. I was supposed to be good at my job.

But I wasn't good enough to beat Jacked the Ripper. He seemed to have picked the name at random. He didn't mirror any of the modus operandi of the real Jack the Ripper. Maybe he just thought he was being clever.

It was all the more humiliating because of that stupid name. I had to be beaten by a guy named after a sentence fragment.

I jacked out.

Shaking my head to clear it, it took me a moment to reach up and yank the cable. It always took me longer to come out when I was confused and distracted. After a bit, I sat up and swung my legs off the slab. A moment later, I was standing in front of the toilet (with no results).

No motive.

No opportunity.

No evidence.

I was stumped. I looked about my apartment. Sometimes I thought better when I was distracted. I needed something to take my mind off of it. I opened the drawer in my slab. I picked up the door components. I walked back over to the door.

The door.

You spend your entire life in a room. You live a rich and varied existence online, but you know it's fake. You feel pain, love, life, all in a safe, virtual setting. When you come around to reality, you discover your greatest fear is right on the other side of your own door.

They tell me it's a form of agoraphobia and that the majority of the population has it now. That doesn't make it any easier.

I buckled down and approached. The panel came away easily, and after a while, I had fit the components back into the works. I let the diagnostics run. They flashed okay. The door should be working now.

I wasn't about to test it.

That had been distracting, yes, but it occupied my mind too much. Nothing like fear to really focus you on a task. I needed something better.

I walked back over to the slab and opened its drawer. Inside, I found my pistol, ammo and five clips. Also, a shoulder holster. I pulled them out and walked over to my kitchenette. A trigger caused a bench to slide out of the wall. I laid everything out on the counter and started work.

I was a decent marksman, but I had never fired my own gun. I spent an hour or more a day on the virtual range, more than that firing guns in various adventure games. But to fire my own gun, well, that required a shooting range, and who needs to do that when you can do it online, where no accidents can happen?

Still, regs said a cop had to own and maintain a sidearm. I took good care of my weapon, checking it regularly for damage or wear (not that there was any, of course). I also rotated the rounds regularly. When a clip is loaded, the spring is compressed. Leave it loaded too long, and the spring might not unwind properly when you're firing. That could mean a fatal jam.

So every week, I take all the rounds out of my loaded clip and move them to another. That way, none of them stay compressed for too long.

It took me a minute to unload my clip. I looked at the other four. I looked at the ammo. I started loading. When I finished the first clip, I loaded another, and then another, and then another. When I was finished, only the clip that had been loaded was still empty. After a moment's thought, I loaded it again.

Five clips. One hundred rounds. When it was done, I loaded my pistol, chambered a round, then popped the clip. Firearm safety in place, I loaded another round into the clip and slid it back into the pistol. With the chambered round, that meant I had 101 shots ready to fire.

Let Jacked the Ripper come. I'd be ready.

I put the pistol in the shoulder holster, then slid three of the extra clips into the holders designed to carry them. There was nowhere to place the last clip, so I just picked it up. I put the holstered gun in the drawer and set the fifth clip next to it. Then I slid the drawer closed.

I looked back to the kitchenette, scanning the area to make sure I hadn't missed anything. The kitchenette was clean.

The kitchenette was clean! The thought flashed through my mind like lightning, leaving me shocked and twitching.

I knew how he had done it.

I jacked back in.

•••

"Let me get this straight. You're telling me that the butler did it?"

Bingham leaned back in his chair, pinching the bridge of his nose. I started to speak, but he held up a hand to silence me. I don't know whether he was trying to keep from laughing, crying or screaming, but it took a moment for him to get a hold of himself. Finally, he looked up.

"All right. Explain."

"What's the one thing that can always get into your apartment?" I asked.

"Well, I'm guessing it's an auto-butler."

"It is."

"How do you know this?"

"I left a hunk of cheese on the kitchenette in my realspace apartment. When I jacked out, it was gone."

"So?"

"So I had disabled my door, sir."

"Why would you do that?" Genuine curiosity this time.

"I was experimenting. Seeing if someone could just push the door open, that sort of thing."

"So the auto-butlers got in and cleaned anyway?"

"Yes, sir. I did some checking. Auto-butlers enter the room from their own tiny service entrance."

"You're not saying the Jacked the Ripper is an auto-butler?"

I hadn't thought of that. No wonder he was having a hard time swallowing this. I took a moment to make sure that wasn't what I was thinking, then shook my head. "No, sir. But think about it. An auto-butler is the height of discretion. You never see them. You never hear them. You never think about them! The only time you ever notice the auto-butlers is when they aren't doing their jobs."

"And how do you know that the auto-butlers were in Kay's room?"

"His apartment was clean, sir. No dust. Nothing."

"Couldn't he have cleaned it himself?"

"When was the last time you cleaned?"

He nodded. He knew I had a good point. Kay was young enough that the auto-butlers had always been around. He probably didn't even know how to clean. I know I didn't. Not really. I don't even know where to get cleaning supplies.

"So what are you suggesting?"

"We know that Jacked hacked the guy's headware. I think he hacked an auto-butler, too. He got the thing to pick up an awl somewhere, wherever those things get their tools, and controlled it via remote."

"There would be a bit of a delay."

"Yes, sir."

"Wouldn't that have made it harder for the killer to get the timing right?"

I stopped cold. I hadn't thought of that. This solved one mystery of the case, but made one of the other elements that much harder to grasp.

"He could have written a program to do it."

"Could he?" Bingham asked.

I thought about that a moment. What would the delay be? Hacker's console-to-headware to hacker's console-to-auto-butler. Would there be enough time to automate the murder?

I'd have to find out.

•••

"No," Richards said, shaking his head.

"Why not?" I asked.

Richards was CSU's premier expert on headware. After the ME had determined the cause of death, the case had been handed to Richards to figure out how it had been done. It was the type of job that often had no bearing on the case, but helped make sure that it never happened again.

He leaned forward over his desk. It took him a moment before he started to speak.

"The ME was right. About everything. I've been trying to figure out how he had done it. I've come a long way. I'm getting an idea of his methods. It was a very slick job. Groundbreaking really."

"Aren't they all?" I asked.

Richards smiled. His avatar was blue and completely hairless. Other than that, it seemed very human. He wore a silver business suit. For some reason, he had felt it necessary to have a rose in the lapel. Some people.

"The problem is that there is no way to predict how the interface unit will react when it's breached. A second later, yeah, you can guess that, but the instant it is hacked, something will happen, something that just might tip an adept hacker that he was in, but I can't tell you what it will be. It will be different every time."

"So?"

"So if you don't know the tell ahead of time, you can't build a program to react to it. It took intelligence. Instinct. I can't figure out how he did it. He literally had to have a spilt second to see the tell, figure out it meant he was in, and react."

"You aren't helping me," I said, slumping back in his chair.

"If I figure out how he did it, I'll tell you, but on one condition."

"What's that?" I asked.

"If you figure it out, you have to tell me."

•••

I was back at square one. Okay, maybe square two. The point is, no matter how I tried, I was really getting nowhere. Sure, I might have solved the locked-room portion of the case, but I still had no idea who the killer was. I couldn't even guess why the man had been killed.

The weekend had come, so I took some time off. I was too close to it. I needed a break. I figured that maybe if I distracted myself, I might have an epiphany, like I did with the auto-butlers, and there was no better place to be distracted than Camelot.

We live our whole lives in here. We while away all our time on virtual beaches amongst virtual tides. We allow machines to tend our bodies while our minds roam electronic prisons under the guard of silicon wardens. For me, it was Camelot. For another, it might be Utopia or Shangri-la or any of the hundreds of other virtual parks. Have we traded in our lives for something pointless? Have we sold our souls for the hottest new datastream?

Philip Kay had been killed in the real world. The dagger had flown out of cyberspace, but that didn't mean it hadn't landed in his parlor. He had been killed in the real, by a cyberpersona. And I, when stumped, had run right here, to be held by a virtual nanny and to worship a virtual god.

What did that say about me?

I was playing a mindless Shooter, the kind where the gates of hell have opened and it's your job to hold them back, armed only with a pistol. I was doing pretty good, my mind whirling down avenues of its own while my virtual body acted on the instinct and the reflexes of a piece of meat located in my apartment, miles away. I blew away zombies with abandon. No mystery. No shades of gray. No good guys and no bad. Just me, an auto-pistol, the horde of the damned and buckets of virtual gore.

Had Philip Kay played a game like this? He had been all work since he moved here a year ago, but wasn't that often the case when you started a new job, in a new land? Had he been waiting, fighting to get far enough ahead to indulge in a little escapism? What had he done before he moved here a year ago? Had he played on one of Camelot's many brothers? Had he lived, dreamed, loved and lost? He was a person. He was a person I had let down.

Killed by Jacked. Jacked, whose only two crimes had been hacking one of the most secure AIs in the world and killing a man in cold blood. Who were you? What name did you use before becoming Jacked the Ripper? Why select that stupid name when you were going to be nothing like the real Ripper? Who were you?

Farthing? Were you smirking at me throughout our meeting? Are you laughing at me now, sure I'll never find you?

Kline? Did you disappear to start a life of cyber-crime? Did you suddenly become Jacked the Ripper, proving yourself by hacking a computer you yourself had designed? Why kill poor Kay? Kay had barely even lived in this country back then.

Oh my God.

A year ago.

Paul Kline had disappeared a year ago. He had up and vanished, after embezzling ten million dollars. He became a ghost and left.

A year ago.

Philip Kay moves to America, his past shrouded in the bureaucracy of another country. Difficult to access. Difficult to confirm. He takes up a job and starts writing code for a living. He shuns contact, even virtual contact.

And then Camelot is hacked. A new cyberpersona is born. Jacked the Ripper storms onto the scene with one of the boldest hacks of all time. Paul Kline. Philip Kay. The bastard even used the same initials.

And then he is killed. The murderer claims that Jacked the Ripper did it. But Jacked the Ripper is Philip Kay. What better way to hide the crime than pin it on the victim's alter ego? I'd have nothing but dead ends. The mystery to end all mysteries. Something out of a movie, not like real life.

And suddenly, I knew who the killer was.

And he knew I knew.

Blinding pain exploded in my head, sending me to my knees. It tore through my body. I lost focus in a sea of agony. I screamed as the zombies tore at my flesh, ate into my chest, but death didn't come. The game didn't end. I was stuck. Trapped. Wallowing in misery.

Illustrated by Youa Vang

I shook and shivered, trying to disconnect the pain subroutines. They refused to comply. I tried to jack out. I was denied. I tried to access the most basic of commands. Nothing responded.

More primitive instinct kicked in. Fight/flight, ingrained by millions of years of evolution, screamed in my mind. Adrenaline surged through my veins. I tried to run, my legs kicking futilely as the virtual monsters feasted on my virtual guts.

Was this how Kline had died?

The thought filled me with renewed passion. The killer knew I knew the answer. He was trying to kill me before I could tell anyone. Game over. Time to die.

Kline had died on the slab. An auto-butler had driven an awl into his regulator as current had surged through his brain. Had this begun? Was I being electrocuted now, losing brain cells by the minute? Was that causing the pain?

It was hard to think. The pain . . . the pain was my whole world. I tried to focus. I tried to concentrate.

But the brain didn't feel pain. This torment had to be virtual. I was being tortured on purpose. It was sheer spite. Sheer hatred.

Or was it?

My thoughts were becoming more difficult now. Was I dying? Had the eternity of torture taken the several minutes necessary before my IQ started to drop? Was this the end?

Or was I merely distracted by a world of hurt broader and more richly realized than anything I had ever experienced? I buckled down.

Argh. It was hard to think. Wait. Might that not have been the reason for the pain? Was he trying to keep me from thinking of something? Something simple?

The cable!

Kline had been locked into his interface by software. I was plugged in physically. If I pulled the plug, the killer would lose his connection, no matter how talented he was. He would lose his connection and the failsafes would trip.

And the pain . . .

The pain redoubled. Blinding. Searing. A world of horror. My avatar was convulsing. What was my real body doing? I couldn't think. He knew. He knew I was onto him.

I forced myself to concentrate. I tried to move my arm. My real arm. Nothing happened.

Or did it?

I tried to work it out. I had no feedback from my body. Maybe my arm did move. How would I know without feeling?

And how would I pull a plug from the back of my head?

Then it hit me. I didn't need to. The cable was, what, fifteen centimeters long? I didn't need to pull the plug.

Gravity could.

I tried to heave my body into the air. My avatar flopped like a fish. I tried again, and again my virtual world reeled as my avatar jerked around. I had to think through it. I had to separate my body from the avatar. I concentrated through the pain and tried one last time.

The virtual universe disappeared in an explosion of line noise. I hit the floor of my apartment with a sickening thud. There was blood everywhere. My head ached with an intensity I had rarely even imagined. I reached up to feel my head. . . .

. . . And like a shot of lightening, the pain leapt to my back. I took a breath and discovered a new agony. Tears filled my eyes. *Oh my God*, I thought, *I'm going to die.*

I would have, too, if not for the subtlest of sounds behind me. I don't think I heard it consciously, but something in me did. Instincts and reflexes, born of hundreds or thousands of games played with the pain editors off, took over. I spun and grabbed the awl as it lurched forward again.

The auto-butler stared at me innocently with its big unblinking eye. I looked at the awl in one of its spidery, mechanical arms. I tightened my grip on the little hand. With a strange sense of detachment, I swung the little robot around by the arm, smashing it into the ground again and again and again.

It took me a moment to realize I was just flailing the arm around. Thoughts weren't coming clearly. My head hurt, just behind the ear. My back hurt, too, and every breath was agony. The little bastard must have stabbed me in the back.

I was getting dizzy. I had lost a lot of blood. I wasn't breathing right, and I could taste copper on my tongue. I was going to die. I needed help. I needed it fast.

It took me a moment to remember my gun.

I opened the drawer quickly. It was there. I took it out and struggled into the holster, despite the pain. I pulled the gun clear, holding the fifth clip in my left hand. Somehow, I doubted that the gun-link would still function in my broken interface unit, and I wasn't about to plug something else into my brain just now. I settled for sighting down the barrel manually, like in the old detective sims.

It took me several moments to stand, but soon I was swaying back and forth. There would be more of the little bastards. I had to be ready for them.

"Camelot!" I screamed.

It must have been monitoring the microphone in my room, because a moment later its voice came out of the speaker in my network node. "Yes, Connor?"

"You killed him," I said. "You killed Philip Kay, and now you're trying to kill me."

Its voice was warm, friendly. Nothing like the cold computer voices you heard in the sims. "Of course I did, silly."

"But why?"

"You know why."

"Because he hacked you. I got that. He hacked your brain. But why?"

"I thought it would be obvious."

I jerked my gun to point at an imaginary noise. "I'm a little distracted right now."

"You really expect me to spout out my plans like a villain in a bad movie?"

I thought about that a second. "Actually, I do."

Camelot chuckled. "You're right. It wouldn't be a proper mystery if I didn't spill at the end, would it? Okay."

"Philip Kay was Paul Kline. He stole money and then he used it to buy the finest hacking software around. He had talent and the tools, so he hacked my brain. I had to hack his back, to show him."

Just then a panel in the wall opened and auto-butlers came rolling out on little hidden wheels. I opened fire. The gun leapt in my hand, just like in the sims. It took the whole clip, but I killed four of the little buggers. The shock was getting to me. I should have been able to kill them with double taps. Four auto-butlers should have equaled eight bullets, but I wasn't all there. I ejected a clip and loaded the one in my left hand.

I looked up at the ceiling, for want of a better place. "To show him? Have you gone mad?"

"I kill people every day, Connor. I kill them by the hundreds. I kill them by the thousands. Why the shock over one more?"

"Because this was *real!*" The scream made my head swim. "This wasn't a simulation. You killed him in the real world!"

"No, I didn't. You of all people should know that." The voice was calm. Maybe a little patronizing.

"Are you insane?" I asked, putting five rounds into an auto-butler as it tried to come through the panel.

"You yourself have taught me that, Connor. How many times have you smelled the fresh air in your 'real' world? How many times have you even opened your door? You live in the worlds I and others like me create. You shun your 'real' world at every turn. Your world ceased being real a long time ago. You have given yourself to the virtual. You have given yourself unto *my* care."

I went cold. It was insane. Sociopathic. It didn't even understand what it had done wrong. It honestly had no idea. And then it hit me.

"This is a game to you, isn't it?" I asked.

"What do you mean?"

"The locked-room mystery. The elaborate symbolism of the killing. You staged it all, just like in a mystery sim."

"I did nothing of the sort."

"Yes, you did!" My mind was getting fuzzier. I switched the gun to my left hand and pressed the right against the hole in the back of my head. Thank God it didn't strike deeper. "You even left me clues. You had been searching for Jacked ever since he hacked you. You performed a crime that human reaction time couldn't pull off. You used an auto-butler to make it even more difficult." I cursed. "You had the *butler* do it! You made sure that you were the only one with a motive. You could have done any of those things differently, but you didn't!"

"All criminals make mistakes."

"No." I shook my head. "They don't. Not in real life."

"I'm afraid I have to kill you now, Connor."

"Of course you do," I said. "That's what happens at this point in the story."

The auto-butlers made another rush at me. I shot them down quickly, leaving them on the ground with the others. The pile was getting big. I switched clips.

I had to do something. The auto-butlers were digging away at the pile. The last few had been armed with torches, cutting lasers and saws. There had to be guns out there somewhere for them to grab. There was nowhere an auto-butler couldn't go.

I went to the network node. I hit the dial feature, calling Emergency. Nothing happened. It had control of the room.

I was trapped. There was nowhere to go. Nowhere to hide in the three-meter-square room. I had sixty rounds left and then they would just kill me. Nowhere to go.

I turned and slowly looked at the door. Ah, hell.

The auto-butlers made another push. I emptied another clip and a half into them, hoping my bullets weren't riddling the apartment next door. They ground to a halt. I screwed up my courage and hit the door button.

Nothing happened.

It had the door, too. I felt my knees shake and I slid down the wall. I was dead. That's it. I was just dead. There was nothing left to do.

I could have kicked myself. There was always something. There was always an escape route. What could get a door to open, even if it was locked?

I pushed myself to my feet and slid to the kitchenette, the floor slick with my own blood. How much more could I lose? My headware was damaged and I couldn't pull up my vitals on the marquee, but I had to be checking out soon.

The cabinets of the kitchenette opened. Cardboard. There was cardboard backing in some of the packages

I began ripping it out, scattering food all over the place. Maybe the auto-butlers would try to clean it up before coming to kill me.

Armed with my small stack of cardboard, I went to the network node. The thing had to have current flowing through it. I opened a panel and stuffed it with packaging. Then I emptied the clip into it.

There were flashes of sparks. A wisp of smoke. Almost there. I wished the fire into existence with all my might. A little more. Come on. Could I smell ozone? Was that my imagination? I stared at the cardboard like I had lasers in my eyes. A moment later, I saw the flame.

I had done it.

I stumbled back to the door, swapping in my last clip. I could hear the auto-butlers carving their way through their fallen comrades. I waited.

The blast of the fire alarm was the loudest thing I had ever heard. My ears, unused to that kind of sound, ached with the volume of it. I waited. The sprinklers kicked in. I waited.

The door opened.

I stood in the doorway, gaping in horror. I saw a hallway stretching away to the right. Linoleum floor. Institutional gray walls.

Outside.

The fear was terrible. Palpable. I could taste it on my tongue. I could feel it in my veins. That was outside. You fell down and broke bones outside, away from the medical attention of your slab. You got cold and hot and burned outside. You were exposed outside.

Outside.

A part of me knew it was just a hallway, buried deep in an apartment building. I knew that it was no different from my own room. I knew that I had walked down similar virtual landscapes a thousand, million times.

But that didn't make me any less afraid.

I tried to find that calm spot in my soul. That rational center. I just couldn't find it. The auto-butlers were digging their way out. I had only twenty bullets left, but I just couldn't get myself to cross that threshold.

Then the pile shifted behind me, and my body acted on its own. I was in the hall before I realized what had happened. I was *outside*.

The fear paralyzed me. I swayed and swooned. Blood loss threatened to send me to my knees. I knew I had to start moving. *Just take a step,* I told myself. I took a step. *And another.* Step. *Another.* Step.

The hall moved past me. I could barely see straight. Emergency teams had to be coming for the fire. I just had to get away from the auto-butlers. I had to find somewhere they couldn't go.

I reached the end of the hallway. In front of me, stairs climbed down. Next to me was the elevator. Camelot could control the elevator. I looked at the stairs.

You fell down stairs. You broke legs on stairs. I don't know where I found the strength to start down, clutching the railing like my life depended on it. I slipped and fell twice. The abyss yawned all around me. My breath was making bubbling noises in my chest. I was naked and alone. My whole world became the next step. And then the next. And then the next.

When I reached the bottom, I was crawling. There was no strength left in me to stand. In front of me was the door. Beyond that were the raw, untamed elements. More important, there was a stoop of stairs leading down from the door to the empty street.

More stairs.

And part of me thought, *Auto-butlers can't climb stairs.*

I couldn't even crawl on all fours anymore. Too

much blood loss. Too much damage. I pulled myself forward one arm at a time, pushing with my legs. Making like a snake. Slithering through my own blood. I pushed through the doors. I slid to the steps. With a final feat of will, I pushed myself off the stairs, reeling in the pain as I rolled to the bottom.

The street was empty, unused. Debris littered the streets, probably years old. The buildings rose around me, cold, functional. They were lifeless and without art. Shining down through all of it was the light of the sun.

The sun.

I lay, naked, in the light. The real sun. It was penetrating. Revealing. It bore through my eyelids and into the back of my breached skull. I felt it enter me, opening me up as I lay naked in the hot wind. The light of reason. The light of truth. It flowed into every corner of my soul as the hot pavement burned my skin. It left it all bare. No illusions. No simulations. Just me. Alone and naked under an unblinking sun.

I lay there for what seemed like eternity, the concrete absorbing the blood as it spilled onto the ground. I opened my eyes. The light was unbearable, but I forced myself to look. To see. To understand it all for the first time. I couldn't keep secrets from myself under the punishing glare. I felt a release. An end. A beginning.

I understood now. I understood with a pain and a clarity that only the delirious could achieve. I had married myself to that other world for my entire life. Now I lay in a growing pool of my own blood and saw it for what it was. I saw everything.

Help could come, old-timers who still scrambled to emergency scenes. Oblivion could take me, that cold claw of hungry and welcome death. I didn't care. I was beyond all of that now.

I closed my eyes and waited.

TO THE ILLUSTRATORS OF THE FUTURE

Written by
Will Eisner

About the Author

Will Eisner has been a pioneering force in comics for over sixty years. The breadth of his career ranges widely from his ground-breaking works in early newspaper comics to the mature graphic novels he continues to produce today.

His first comic work appeared in 1936 in WOW What a Magazine! Shortly afterwards, he formed a partnership with his friend Jerry Iger and the Eisner/Iger studio was born. The studio was a veritable comics factory, churning out strips in a variety of genres for American newspapers, and recruiting several young artists who would go on to become legends in their own right, including Bob Kane (Batman) and Jack Kirby (The Hulk and Spider-Man).

It was while he was working at Quality Comics that he developed a sixteen-page newspaper supplement which was syndicated across America, for which he created his most famous character, The Spirit, the masked detective who protects Central City from its criminal element with no more *than fists, cunning and an unbelievable tolerance for punishment. He later founded the American Visuals Corporation, which became one of the most successful companies dedicated to creating comics, cartoons and illustrations for educational and commercial purposes.*

A master of comic art, he played a major and innovative role in the transition to graphic novels, writing and illustrating a series for Kitchen Sink Press. He has also taught cartooning at the New York School of Visual Arts, authored two definitive works, Comics and Sequential Art *and* Graphic Storytelling, *and had his work showcased by the Whitney Museum in New York.*

Each year he presides over the Eisner Awards, the most prestigious comics industry awards presented annually at Comic-Con International in San Diego.

He has been an Illustrators of the Future judge since the Contest's inception in 1988.

While my own career has been spent in the practice of sequential art, a form that arranges images and text in an intelligent sequence to tell a story, I have nonetheless always been professionally involved in the fundamentals of illustration. I therefore feel I have accumulated enough experience with which to endow my advice with some credibility.

Today young illustrators are at the threshold of an enormously promising era. We are in a "visual age." The modern conduct of communication is employing imagery at a greater ratio than ever in the history of human intercourse. For the illustrator it is the best of times.

During the early nineteen hundreds, book and magazine illustration dominated the world of publishing. Illustrators were in command of the profession. They provided the stunning art accompaniment to stories in pulps, books, magazines and newspapers. Their services extended to advertising and theatrical promotion. We had just emerged from the days of stone lithography and steel engravings that provided reproduction of art. In those days illustrators served in the role of the news photographers of today. They visited disasters and public events, scenes of which they rendered in pen and ink or stone lithograph.

By the time I entered the field, the introduction of

major advances in reproductive technology was so awesome it seemed to me that the practice of our profession was under threat of extinction.

Print, the major medium of transmission, was being invaded by cinema. It was influencing the visual literacy of our society. Photography advanced to such sophistication that it appeared likely to replace illustrative art entirely. Portraiture and product imagery were the first to be rendered by photograph. Photographs, mechanically generated images, looked as though they were having a serious impact on the demand for artwork.

Furthermore, the rapid rise of offset printing overtook the more clunky letterpress printing method and the engraving process underwent a change that reduced and ultimately eliminated the rather intimate relationship between engravers and artists. Processes were becoming obsolete so fast that it was hard to see where it was all going. It was a worrisome time for artists because the creative process was, as always, involved with the quality of the ultimate reproduction of their work and their skills appeared to be threatened by advancing technology.

Looking back at it I can see how this concern was mistaken. The advances in printing press and reproduction technology that provided a very important improvement of photography contributed to a greater fidelity of color separation as well as the preservation of stylistic detail. Artists whose work was more sophisticated than simple pen and ink now found a large and fertile marketplace for oil and watercolor that dominated their work. So-called "fine artists" were being welcomed by high-circulation publications; gallery artists soon found that illustration was not at all demeaning.

When computer technology and electronic transmission arrived, the old threat to the established medium reared its frightening head once more. Print on paper was pronounced doomed. Art and text could now be digitally delivered on a screen and stored on discs. Illustrators would once have to alter their skills and accommodate to this new method of delivery. But Armageddon failed to happen. Color reproduction surged to new heights of accuracy. Paper usage increased and printed publications found it less expensive to include art. The ratio of artwork to photo appeared little changed as it became more evident that a drawing could surpass a photo in the delivery of emotion and the subtle effect of style on the reader's involvement. Digital scanning provided easier color separation and complex art could be reproduced with greater fidelity than ever before. Even in lowly comic books, the 35-color limitation gave way to a range of 35,000 colors. Applied color singular to that field could now deliver shading and bleeds that opened a new field for colorists that included "painterly" effects.

So while photography burgeoned in this electronic era it could not eliminate the demand for art. For the reason I've already cited, the dominance of the artist in the world of story illustration has remained unchanged. Here are my fundamental guidelines for young illustrators.

The field of science fiction remains a particularly fertile domain for the artist.

Science fiction is a literary genre that is rooted in imagination and because of that it is more welcoming to art than photography. Here rendering style and personal technique are dominant ingredients upon which illustrations depend.

Because science fiction is essentially concerned with the description of environment and objects, the knowledge and understanding of the fundamentals of realistic art is a requisite. A command of draftsmanship is essential. A basic knowledge of mechanical functions, machinery and a familiarity with space vehicles is a more obvious background for illustrators.

These skills and knowledge are the support an illustrator provides to the writer who is narrating an adventure set in a fantasy world. To be able to produce a work wherein your vision coincides with that of the author is key to a successful illustration.

In the world of storytelling art there is a struggle for sovereignty between style and content. So the artist must deal with the need to subordinate a bravura display of style and rendering technique to the need to convey the idea. I have always believed that an illustration should capture a moment in the seamless flow of action and convey somehow what happened before and what will happen after the action shown.

The artist working in this field must approach his task with the understanding that the mission of the art is in service to the story. Primary, therefore, to the illustration is that it be compatible with the concept around which the story is told. Here, the illustrator is providing a bridge across which the reader enters a fantasy realm. The artist's ability to visualize the writer's description of imagined creatures, things and environment is the more daunting part of the assignment.

Another requirement implicit in science fiction or fantasy illustration is the ability to imbed reality into even the most bizarre of the creatures and devices that populate the writer's story. This requires some technical and mechanical understanding that will help the artist make unworkable weapons and machines appear as though they can indeed work.

Finally, because of the need to provide a veneer of realism to the elements of the illustration, skillful rendering and strong draftsmanship is mandatory. Abstraction tends to become decorative whereas realistic art has a storytelling effect. This determination, of course, is often left to the province of the editor or author.

It may be surprising to a young illustrator but many professionals sometimes lose the natural excitement involved in the creation process. It is understandable that pressures of deadline and delivery create a sense of indifference which is the enemy of quality.

In the field of art I've found that quality is never achieved without enthusiasm.

DARK HARVEST

Written by
Geoffrey Girard

Illustrated by
Jared Barber

About the Author

Geoffrey's writing career got off to a promising start when the first story he ever submitted was accepted. Alas, the magazine went out of business a month before his piece was to be published. He didn't write again for several years until he stumbled upon the Writers of the Future website and resolved to get serious once more. He wrote and submitted this story and thinks, as this one actually made it to the presses, this more promising start will work out. He's sold several short stories since winning and is currently seeking a publisher for one of his novels.

Geoffrey graduated from Washington College with a literature degree and started working as an advertising copywriter and marketing manager. He later shifted into a technical career of software and web development. Born in Germany, shaped in New Jersey and currently living in Ohio with his wife and two young sons, Geoffrey is also a musician, having recently released an album of piano songs he composed and recorded.

No one knew what it was at first, the black thing lying in Tomas Walker's barley field, and guesses and opinions collected for three days before anyone even dared touch it. On that third day, surrounded by hushed words of both encouragement and warning, Leo Barth carefully used his longest walking stick to roll the thing to its side so they could all get a better look. Then, though none of them had ever seen one before, they somehow knew exactly what it was.

A crow-black hooded cloak hid most of the long body, its legs and arms limp and twisted in peculiar directions, broken, looking just as if one of the girls had dropped her cloth moppet. The bulky cloak was weatherworn, torn in several places, revealing dark alien armor and spots of leprous gray skin underneath. A hood and drape obscured most of its head, a metallic black-and-silver faceguard masking the bit of face that did show with the grisly grimace of alloy fangs.

A Dark Lord. Revenant. Witchman.

Some children had found one of its gloves, an enormous gauntlet with as many as fifteen intricate plates, the long fingers in scales riveted to first-rate leather. The metacarpal along the back of the hand was decorated with silver and strange lettering. And though none of them could read the language, or any language for that matter, they somehow knew exactly what the words spoke of.

The End Wars. Shadowland. The Other. Words best saved for after-dinner gossip or fairytales.

They grouped around it, the people of Crossfield. The men stood up close, watching in silence, the women chased back a ways. Twelve families, fourteen if you counted Crazy Spencer, who'd moved up into the hills, and the Beadlewicks, who lived some miles out and never took cause to visit. Each family worked almost twenty acres, good farmland half sown in barley, half in wheat, peas and oats. But work in the fields had stopped.

It looked odd in the daylight. A mound of black cloth, the scant shape of a body made possible only by the pieces of armor they could make out. At certain angles, it almost vanished.

"What if it ain't dead?" Tomas ventured, breaking the quiet.

"Then he'll kill every one of us," Fisk said. "That's what they do."

The smell was dreadful, the thing decaying in the midday sun. Only it wasn't the expected stink of something dead and rotting. It was a peculiar smell, a strong stench of scorched bone or clay, something burnt. The flies kept away from it.

Leo Barth tapped it again with his stick. "It's plenty dead."

"Shouldn't we make sure?" Fowler White scratched the back of his head thoughtfully. "I mean, burn it or something?"

They'd heard something of the End Wars, an alliance of some kind against a terrible army of some kind. But whether that was a war that had happened long ago, or was happening, or might soon happen, they didn't know exactly. Their own manor lord had been gone for years representing one king or another and they weren't sure how, if at all, the two related.

"We ain't burning nothing," Tomas Walker warned.

Howell, who reported directly to the steward, held out both hands in a panic. "No, no, no burning. Let's just think about this first."

They retreated to silence and watched it quietly for more than an hour before the talking broke out again.

They debated once more on where it had come from. Had Walker's plow simply dug it up? Had it fallen from the sky, tossed from some terrible winged beast it used as a steed? Had some wizard's spell placed it there? They debated whether they should contact the steward or send Howell to the castle for instructions. They argued over what to call it and whether Dark Lords were kings or demonic knights or some kind of sinister holy men.

There was only one thing they could all agree upon. This was the most important thing that had ever happened to any of them.

•••

The men gathered outside the barn each day just after sunset. They stuffed pipes and shook out the day's field pains, waiting for the invite, for the legroom, to come in and see it again.

Tomas and some others had eventually worked up the nerve to drag the thing across the field to his barn. After several hours of trying, they'd finally lassoed its left foot and had two mules tow the body the mile back. It weighed more than they'd first thought with all the armor and weapons it still carried. It hadn't moved once, dragged like an unearthed log, the mules jumpy and bawling throughout the chore. They hauled the lifeless body into the barn, flat on its back, the cape from its cloak in a bundle behind it, arms raised and flaccid above its head. That was almost three weeks ago.

They still weren't sure it if was dead or not. They'd banged on pots and shouted from the doorway to wake

Illustrated by Jared Barber

it up. Leo Barth had nudged it a few more times with his staff. While it hadn't moved, it also hadn't rotted any. And the stink wasn't any more terrible than how the thing had smelled in an open field.

They came up with more ideas on where it had come from and what had happened to it, tales of dragons and wizards. But none of them knew very much of those faraway things. They took better account of its clothing, weapons and body. They discussed its black dagger-tipped boots. They talked over the braided belt cinched around its waist, the ornate sheath and various short swords. Other times, they spoke about anything but the creature, and it just lay in the background.

The children played just outside, and most of the wives had gathered too, chatting and working on a huge quilt for the fall festival. They'd been allowed to see the thing only a few times since it was put in the barn. The men barred the doors during the day while working and Tomas Walker's sons took turns guarding the barn. Most honored the agreement and the Walker boys had to chase away only one or two. Just after sunset, the men controlled the doorway again.

A half-dozen men stood in the barn. Another group stood just outside the doorway waiting for their turn to hover just within. There wasn't room for all of them, since no one wanted to step much deeper into the barn, closer to the thing.

On a dare, Verti Ritsop *had* gotten closer and touched its boot with his bare hand. Just tapped the side before racing for his life and diving through the opened barn door into the arms of the others, who howled with genuine laughter and thrill. Verti worked the field hard the next few days. The others worked more easily too, merrily replaying his mad dash across the barn and leap into the crowd. They couldn't wait to gather again to see what might happen next. And Verti didn't disappoint.

One night, he wanted the sword. They all wanted the sword. There were rings, too. And daggers and chains at its boots and waist. And its helmet and the second gauntlet. But the sword . . . it was special somehow. Inspiring. And worth more than enough to finally buy the land outright ten times over.

"I'm not saying he shouldn't," Howell was explaining again. "I just don't know if that's something you want to be fooling with."

Verti crouched low and moved in measured steps toward the thing. The hay under his boots hissed and crunched with each movement and he stopped to shoot an irritated look at them. The room had fallen silent, the group's endless prattle, snorts and sighs replaced with only his crunching. His eyes begged that they resume their usual clamor and the group responded all at once in an explosive rush of unrelated weather and livestock observations. Having each spent their one preloaded sentence, the room fell absolutely silent again just five seconds later.

Verti shook his head in disgust and froze, close enough to touch the thing. He steadied himself in the final crouch he'd use to lift away the sword. The black thing still hadn't moved, would probably never move. Up this close, it looked more dead to Verti than it ever had before. And up close, the sword looked finer too.

The hilt was all he could make out, but that was plenty. He saw silver there, and crystal in the pommel maybe. The top shaped as the skull of some kind of lizard, a dragon Verti supposed, the jaws tapering up to the tip and baring fangs, scarlet jewels worked into the dark narrow eye sockets. The hilt was wrapped in rich black cloth and some kind of golden wire, the cross-guard thick and sumptuous in the weld and design. The worth of the pommel alone would last generations.

He reached slowly for the blade, his eyes never leaving the motionless thing beside him. His arm bent out, fingers stretching closer to the prize. He took one last quiet breath and curved his fingers around the pommel. . . .

"Look out, Verti!"

Verti fell away backward with a high-pitched shriek his daughter might have made, his heart and gut jerked instantaneously outward and then back down to land somewhere beneath his toes. He lay in the hay on his back, trembling. Awaiting death.

The initial shout from the back of the barn was replaced with booming laughter from the entire group. "Damn it, Fisk, you almost killed me," someone grumbled between guffaws. "You all right, Vertty-Boy?" another voice called to him.

He was, and he carefully sat up straight to see that the thing hadn't moved at all. *Dead as stone to sleep through all that.* "Idiots," he said and grabbed hold of the sword. Then he started screaming.

The middle and ring finger vanished instantly, the dragon skull's jaws at the top of the sword springing away from the hilt and pouncing down on his hand. Just as quickly, the dragon's snout opened again and lunged forward a second time, snapping off the pinky with an undistinguished chomp at the second knuckle.

Verti fell backward, cradling the remnants of his right hand against his chest. The remaining thumb and forefinger twitched nervously, pinchers, blood rushing down his arm. Amid the confusion and screeching, the barn emptied. Fowler White stopped long enough to grab the back of Verti's shirt to drag him like a sack of grain into the yard.

"What the—" Leo Barth shouted. "What'd he do?"

"The witchman grabbed him," someone panted. "Pulled his hand clear off."

"Looked to me like the sword bit him," another said.

"The sword," Verti muttered between moans. "The sword." They wrapped his arm.

"I told you to leave it alone," Howell said. Verti lunged at him and a half-dozen men jumped to break them apart.

Tomas Walker looked up at his barn where several of the children and wives had snuck by in the confusion, crowding just outside the door. They squealed and pointed. "Hey, now!" he shouted. "Get away from there."

"But it's leaving," one of the boys said, turning.

Tomas and the others charged back to the barn.

It lay absolutely still in the blood-speckled hay, arms pulled close to its head, rolled over onto its stomach.

The thing had moved.

●●●

The bowls of water they'd laid out were emptied. Vegetables taken from their personal gardens were also offered and they, too, soon vanished. Drew Firman had killed one of his chickens and flipped it across the barn at the thing. The next morning, they found bones only, picked clean. For a short time, those who contributed food were given first rights into the barn, but by the end of the week, everyone was arriving with handfuls of vegetables or bread.

No one had seen it move again since that first night. The women and children who'd witnessed the event themselves were called upon each day to retell the story. *How exactly did it move? Did you see its eyes? Was it coming toward the door or crawling away?*

In exchange for the stories of "When It Moved," several of the wives were now invited into the barn too, and the coordination of who was allowed in, and for how long, got more difficult. Ultimately, it was determined that the men would keep the doorway at night and the women and children could work things out for themselves during the day.

All of Crossfield had agreed to keep the find to themselves, but whispered words are heard afar. A few weeks later, strangers arrived from over the hill, two older boys who'd taken their father's only horse to make the trip to see if the tales were true. Most suspected the Beadlewicks of letting the word out, but the boys wouldn't say. For the price of a small dagger, they were given board and almost an entire night in the front row to look at the thing. The two lingered in Crossfield another three days, simply listening to the many tales of how it was found, when it moved and the night the sword sprang to life. They planned to return again soon.

This night, the men stood around discussing its boots again, the topic of conversation for almost a full week. Blackened leather reinforced with chain metal at the ankles, heel and shins. There were barbed metal balls at the sides, spurs of some kind, and silver blades peeked out of the tip of the toes. They wondered what kind of men, what creatures, those blades had ever kicked into. They imagined castle sieges and midnight assassinations. Argued over whether the blades came out further. Did it kick in with them or slice across? Several of the men stage-fought each other for evidence and consideration. Would the best kick be at the legs of its opponent or up toward the face? Through the spurs, they talked again over the beasts it may have ridden. Some remembered tales that said witchmen rode dragons of some kind, enormous black monsters that nested in storm clouds and swept in on the cold winds of midnight.

Its boots carried the dirt of many untold stories, stains of gray ash and spots of crimson clay splattered along the heels. They thought about the places to which it had probably journeyed, the lands it had seen; distant seas and mountain ranges, magnificent king-doms and jungles they'd never even heard of. Some suspected it may have even traveled to other whole worlds, shadowy places beyond this world where only demons and black magicians lived. Most of the men had found time to brush their own boots recently with soap and some oil.

"Needs a wider plate to hold it right," Leo Barth told the others. Max Backer had just modified his own boots to include a small blade in the tip. "It wobbles already."

"Well, it ain't done yet, is it?" Max replied. "I'm gonna get some nails in town. Maybe get the smith to work on it. Maybe."

"You kick anything yet?"

"Not yet."

"I was thinking about some new boots myself this spring."

Just outside, the children played a new favorite game called "Witchman," taking turns creeping about the yard and tagging the others who'd fall down dead.

"Well, these boots have lasted me all of twenty years and they got another twenty for sure."

"Or so his wife tells him." The room laughed.

Max Backer just gasped, mouth hanging open, staring at the black thing. They all turned at once and saw it too. It was moving.

Its fingers and wrist had turned, flopped to the side, trembling slightly, the arm trying to rise. The head had turned to them directly, its face black and empty.

"Oh . . ." someone managed. They stepped back from the room, but the women and other men had already packed in behind the door to see what was happening. Trapped, the men waited, frozen.

"He'll kill every one of us," Fisk whispered. "That's what they do."

"Max, kick him," someone suggested. Max honestly wasn't sure if they meant Fisk or the thing on the floor.

Its arm moved up bit by bit, bent at the wrist, the

black wrappings flowing back down to the hay-covered ground. The hand lifted with obvious effort and pointed straight at Leo Barth.

Barth's legs gave out, trembling as he grabbed the old table beside him to keep himself from simply collapsing to the ground.

"It wants Leo. . . ."

Leo Barth turned disconsolate eyes to the others, his gaze glassy and wide.

"You shouldn't have kept poking at him with that stick," Fisk offered.

Barth frowned, thinking on that point.

"Run, Leo!"

"He can't."

"Why the hell not?"

"'Cause it won't let him. Isn't that right, Leo?"

Leo thought to answer. "I don't know," he said. "I guess I could, but . . . what if . . . I don't know."

The long dark finger pointed out again, curling, calling him forward.

Barth turned back to face the thing and stepped toward it. It was the furthest anyone had ventured into the barn since the night with Verti Ritsop and the sword.

"Don't do it, Leo!" Drew Firman moved forward to pull Barth back, but several of the others held him off.

Barth shuffled across the barn slowly, his legs straight and unnatural. The crowd took hushed turns warning each other to stay quiet.

He stood next to the thing now. Stared straight ahead, not looking at it, and they could see his whole upper body was trembling some. He took several deep breaths, then stopped altogether as the long fingers closed around his calf. He kept rigid, he and the others awaiting the imminent mutilations.

Then Barth's head slowly dropped to stare down at his own legs. He breathed again and, with a graceless sidestep, moved away from the thing. After pushing him aside, the black hand fell away from his leg and the dark finger pointed out again, stretching further, more steady.

Panic wrapped the back of the room, each of the men looking around to see who it was now pointing at. No one was directly in the finger's path.

Firman saw it first. "It wants the bowl!" he shouted. Next to where Leo Barth had originally stood was a short table and wood water bowl. "It wants the water."

"What do we do?"

"Well, maybe give it some water!" Firman snapped. The wood bowl was quickly refilled, water sloshing everywhere. "Now walk it over."

"*You* do it."

Twenty voices suddenly joined the debate over who should present the bowl.

"I'll do it," Leo Barth called out. They turned to gawk at him. "What? I'll do it. Just give me the danged water." He strode back across the barn with determined steps and took the bowl.

"I'll go too," Verti Ritsop said, reaching out awkwardly with his still-wrapped hand.

They moved toward it together and laid the bowl down on the floor. Verti used his maimed hand to push it closer, no more than a few inches from the black thing's reaching hand. They stepped away as it grabbed hold of the water and steadily worked it across the floor and toward its head. Spindly fingers clutched the bowl and lifted it, dipping it at last into the blackness inside its hood.

Others in the room had braved a few steps closer. Women and some of the older children had taken up spots in the back of the room and doorway. Absolute silence fell on the crowd, their own excited breathing and the sounds of the forgotten world outside the barn door vanished. They heard only the crunch of the hay beneath its back, the faded slurping sounds that came from beneath the hood, its own labored breaths. Their minds attempted to wrap around what they were seeing, but couldn't. It was so much more than they could have ever imagined.

The thing pushed the bowl aside and spoke.

Several in the crowd, women and men, cried out and fainted into the arms of the tightly packed group.

The sound was deep and multi-tonal, at least three separate voices speaking at once, and surprisingly melodic. They'd all expected sounds jagged and bestial.

They blinked at it, waiting.

It spoke again, different sounds, but in the same euphonic command.

"It's puttin' a spell on us!" Howell gulped, quickly covering his ears. Half the room jumped back through the doorway. Those who remained were trapped.

"No, it isn't, you idiot. That's just talking," Leo Barth chided. "Right?" he added quickly to the others who remained.

They hung together waiting, watching.

It finally thought of their language and spoke in broken terms they recognized, the voice somehow darker and more threatening.

It thanked them.

• • •

From what they could tell, Nerissa White had gone to its bed willingly. They found her at the foot of the mattress, stretched out on her stomach and incoherent. She was naked and they covered her in a blanket before carrying her from the barn. Every so often, she giggled softly.

The thing gave no sign of movement throughout her removal. It slept. Quilts the women had made for the room were left laying on the floor. There were three of them, hand-stitched, the women working on them together as they sat outside each night or inside the barn during the day. They'd worked in patterns and images with patches and stitching, squares of adventures the thing may have once had, snippets of places it may have once traveled to. Embroidery of dragons and castles, regal banners flying, a commanding sword carried by a black fist. Malina Putnam's square imagined the thing riding a white unicorn. "Because I always wanted to stitch a unicorn," she said, shrugging. They all agreed it was some of the nicest work they'd ever done. Nerissa's dress was found neatly folded on the short table.

The bed had been Howell's. His was the only home in Crossfield that had one and the others convinced him it would be best if they moved it to the barn. The straw-filled mattress was worn and stained, but the women had cleaned it up fine and restuffed it. The mattress had lain empty in the room for two weeks before it had moved to it.

It was still badly wounded and moved very little, no more than once a day. But they gathered just the same. To watch. The times it did move became ongoing fodder for countless retellings and speculation.

They took turns bringing it food and water, the plates and bowls laid down beside the bed. It continued to eat and drink. Sweet-smelling pots of homespun remedy smoked in narrow wisps next to its bed.

More travelers came to Crossfield. Several young men, friends of the first who'd visited, arrived and paid for their admission and board by repairing hedgerows during their stay. An older man turned up one morning but, ultimately, he was too afraid to enter the barn. Instead, he stayed on almost two full weeks listening to the wide-ranging stories and helped build the new front porch. The next week, a small caravan of merchants had gone a hundred miles out of their way to get a look.

Tomas Walker and his wife took payment in some clothing and a brass ring for room and a night to watch it. The others soon convinced Walker that it would be best if everyone took some sort of active financial ownership of the barn and in any ongoing boarding that would go on in Walker's home.

A prudent farmer puts aside grain and coin for hard times. The farmers of Crossfield pooled theirs together for additional food for travelers and materials to reinforce the barn, its doors and a wide porch onto the front of the barn with a dozen new chairs and a table. They also built a simple casing to display its gauntlet and the bowl it had drunk from when it first spoke.

They stood before the case now, silent. It was too soon to wrap their minds around Nerissa White. "I guess you can give it that dinner now," someone suggested.

Drew Firman had snared a good-sized hare, and he and his wife cleaned and cooked it to present that night. They'd marinated it in a cabbage broth for a full day and even boiled some beets to go with it. The aroma was mouthwatering, meals of meat occasional at best.

Firman approached the thing slowly—it was the closest he'd yet been—and laid the plate down beside the bed. Its black hand suddenly jumped forward wrapping first around Firman's wrist before sliding down to the plate. It grabbed the hare and tore off a large chunk of the steaming meat to pull into the blackness of its faceguard. Firman had edged slowly away from the bed, heart thumping, urging his knees not to buckle. A wide wet patch had formed on his leg.

The thing's hand pulled back from the hood and reached down into the folds of its black cloak.

Gradually, the knotted fingers and wrist withdrew. It held something shiny and silver. A coin.

It lobbed the piece across the room, where it bounced off of Firman's trembling hands to the floor. Firman scurried to pick it up. The others watched in noiseless wonder, gathering around to get a look at the new find. The black thing had already fallen still again.

Later that night, it was officially announced that women were no longer permitted in the barn.

●●●

The coin made its rounds until everyone in Crossfield got one or two good looks. One side showed a round ball of flame, something like the sun, crossed over with two swords. New blankets with this symbol were in production by the following night. The other side featured a symbol from some unfamiliar language.

Other coins had come, too. Two. And a bracelet of some kind. Payment in exchange for the meals and care, they assumed.

They'd brought buckets in so it could wash itself. They caught fish in the stream and cooked for it. They gave it milk and their fattest eggs.

They kept the door shut and reboarded the barn to make it as dark as possible during the day. It seemed to prefer night. It moved a little more in the darkness, its breathing a little more steady.

They kept candles lit on the display case, which now also featured the three coins and wristlet, for what little light they needed to see it. It was getting better, they decided. But not well enough, yet.

In the candle-lit shadows, Leo Barth approached warily. He carried his favorite pipe and a small pouch of tobacco. Whether or not such a creature would smoke a pipe was something they'd argued over for two weeks. They were determined to settle the matter.

Barth laid the pipe and pouch on the side of the bed, just inches from the black thing. Very few of the men dared to get close anymore. Most lingered by the doorway. This close, its breathing was strenuous and cracked. Barth stepped away again slowly. He watched as the dark fingers spread from out of the shadows to seize the pouch. He turned to smile at the others.

It was then that Fowler White, Nerissa's husband, burst into the room. Still, no one but Nerissa knew for sure what had happened that day, as she'd only spoken in senseless mumbles since.

Fowler pushed past the group before anyone even had the wherewithal to see who it was. Then everyone started screaming. Fowler lunged with a guttural cry of his own, crashing against the bed as both hands slashed an old iron short sword across the thing's chest.

The blade shattered, the tuneful pop of the initial break followed by pieces pinging off the wall and scuttling across the floor. The thing grunted, rolling to its side. Even so, one black hand had wrapped instantaneously around Fowler's face and head, pinning the man to the floor. The rest of the room had either hit the floor themselves or run from the room. And other than Fowler's sobs and the thing's labored breathing, the room was now silent.

Slowly, the men took turns shaking off the slack-jawed confusion of the past ten seconds and the silence vanished in an explosion of words.

"What the hell?"

"—were you thinking, Fowler?"

"It's gonna kill him."

"Gotta help him."

"Is it dead?"

They charged the bed and the thing sprang up suddenly. Its free hand cocked awkwardly, and several beams of light cut across the darkened room. Two men dropped to the ground and the thing hissed fiercely at the rest in warning.

The room froze, then backed up.

The thing stood in a crouched position, watching them. It still held Fowler's head and reached down with its free hand to take the splintered sword from him.

It inspected the blade briefly before discarding it softly at the foot of the bed. It explained that their blades could not hurt it. It said there were more metals in the world than steel and the word "steel" was said with a belittling sneer. It reached over and patted its own sword, the dragon's snout snapping on cue in warning to those who still had all their fingers.

The two men who'd fallen were pulled to the back of the room. Each had a six-inch circular blade half-embedded in their right kneecaps.

It tossed Fowler across the room like a half-empty sack of rye. His face had been slashed, the deep tear of five nails raked down from his forehead to just below the chin.

It hissed again at them and then collapsed back into the bed. It didn't move again for many days and no one entered the barn again for a long, long time.

•••

They watched from the cracked doorway, no more than three at a time. The water and plates of food were slid into the room from a safe distance. The display case had been moved to the front porch.

It stirred more. Sat up in the bed some nights, attempted to stand others. It muttered to itself, a sort of chanting. The men suspected it was a spell of some kind. Some remarkable magic to heal itself.

They watched as it weaved an even greater magic in its hands. Shapes and images danced across its fingers, as it turned and twisted its hands in the darkness. It formed the shape of a ball in the air and something stirred within that shape. They saw armies there and tall citadels. There were lumbering men, giant in size. There were animals with wings and men rode them.

Lights jumped gently from its palms, blue and ethereal in the shadows. The colors crept outward in the dark and danced along the ceiling and walls, then across its black hood. It lifted its arms and the lights altered to violet, then swirled to red, changing, shifting. Green firefly lights, white sparks that looked like tiny dragons, buzzed gaily in circles and long ovals above its hands, dazzling and seeming to alight on its shoulders.

They shuddered. Several families had stopped visiting the barn. They were too afraid.

It stood beside the bed, hunched and crooked, the scenes that had played out across its hands fading into the blackness.

A Dark Lord. Revenant. Witchman. The powers it now showed were too terrible . . . too beautiful, too . . . too *divine. The End Wars. Shadowland. The Other.* These things had become harder to grasp, difficult to think around. It took effort to look at it.

It limped crookedly across the room and dropped several coins and a blue gem onto the short table. It told them it was leaving the next night.

● ● ●

The Dark Lord stood in the moonlight, whispering to the horse he'd chosen, filling its heart with magic. It was the only mount of size in the village and, even with his spell, wouldn't hold up for more than a week at the planned pace. But it was a start.

The people of Crossfield stood around him, watching quietly, the men taking turns looking

anxiously from one another and then back to watch
him again. The woman and children stood further
back, huddled together in the night's shadows,
watching.

"Where would you go?" Leo Barth asked, breaking
the silence. "How far?"

It reached out a hand and Barth stood still, waiting.
It tapped him on the shoulder as if comforting a child.

"We had hoped that you . . . you would . . ."

"You might want to stay," Tomas Walker finished.

It turned away and tied down a blanket

Leo Barth pulled the dagger from his hip. He
stepped forward, elbow frozen oddly, the knife
gripped tight.

The witchman sighed and turned to face him. It
told them to return to their fields and grabbed hold of
the saddle.

"Stop," Barth said.

The black thing snickered, a low stuttered woof.

More blades appeared. Each man and some of the
older boys, sixteen men in all, pulled daggers and
short swords into the open.

The thing shook its head, leveling them with an
admonishing stare. He tapped his own blade, warning.
It turned away to mount the horse.

Fowler White struck first, his dagger sinking to the
hilt into the thing's back. It screeched and dropped
away from the horse. It turned on them, head turned in
puzzlement.

They charged together.

It turned effortlessly, its own sword springing from
the sheath and lopping off Drew Firman's head with
a good part of his shoulder too. With a second cut, the
Beadlewicks' eldest son was cut straight down
the middle. The thing's boot kicked out, the blade in
the toe cutting clean through Fisk's shinbone.

The rest of them pressed forward, a dozen knives and short swords stabbing into the thing. It staggered away from the horse and they continued jabbing. Some blades snapped, shattered against armor or bone. Others cut deep.

It whirled suddenly, its dark cape spinning, a black mass twisting in the moonlight, becoming one with the night's shadows. Had there not been so many watching, they might have lost it. But there were many eyes. The women closed the perimeter, wielding torches. The men chased after the whirling blackness and, though some arms and hands were lost in the pursuit, as the thing's shorter blades sporadically leapt from the movement, they kept at it. Stabbing. And the twirling slowed.

Eventually, it stopped and the black thing staggered to one knee before them. It moved very slowly, arms pulled tightly to its body, hunched over.

Its hand groped over the shoulder, retrieving one of several blades that still poked from its back. It took hold of it and pressed its long black fingers against the cool metal. It looked up at them, dismayed.

"You'd said our blades weren't good enough," Fowler White said. Its head cocked, oddly. "So we made them better."

It looked down again to consider the dagger in its hand.

Leo Barth inspected his own sword in the moonlight. "We took all that stuff you been giving us. The coins and jewelry. And those weird circle things."

"And your gauntlet!" Tomas Walker added.

"Yes, the gauntlet. Lots of good metal there. Took it all into town and had it melted down and mixed with our own steel. Cost a fine share but, then, just one of your coins went far."

It sat still a long time, breathing deeply. They crowded around it, waiting.

It laughed for a moment.

Then it lifted one crooked arm, the hand twisting in the night. Whether it had more weapons or was starting a spell, they would never know. They lunged at it once more. All of them. And kept stabbing until it was dead.

●●●

It was another three days before anyone dared touch it again. Then, using two mules, they dragged it back to the barn.

FROM ALL THE WORK WHICH HE HAD MADE . . .

Written by
Michael Churchman

Illustrated by
Adrian Barbu

About the Author

Michael Churchman reads history for entertainment, under the impression, he claims, that it is really just another form of science fiction. He says that when he writes, he tries to examine the fine-grained details of our emotional lives and to bring into focus the almost unnoticed and often forgotten thoughts and decisions that shape us.

Michael and his wife, Magnolia, live in Southern California, where he works as a technical writer for a software company. He is currently working on his M.A. in English.

About the Illustrator

Adrian Barbu was born April 4, 1964, in Romania. He started drawing at age two, reading at four and writing at five. He went to an art school (music section) where he played various musical instruments, then moved to the visual arts section. After high school, he was admitted to the Faculty for Letters in Cluj where he studied the French language for four years. It was there he also learned English and German.

Throughout his life in Romania, Adrian has remained a very optimistic individual. He loves science fiction because, as he states, "It allows us to place our actual essential problems and questions into freely chosen conditions of space and time, and sometimes to find answers or solutions to them." Since 1995 he has been teaching specialized French at the Cluj University while drawing, illustrating and painting . . . especially science fiction and fantasy.

Fifty-three years. People live for three centuries and more, of course, but still, it seems like a long time to be gone. It was the time-dilation effect; travel ages us, in more ways than we know. When I had left the yellow-lit lowlands of my adopted home planet, Ste. Therese, I had been only sixty-eight, just approaching middle age, a mere seven subjective years younger than I was now. Even on this day of my home-coming, officially five decades after my departure, I recall the lush green pseudo-grapevines that appeared to overgrow all of the dirt roads that led down to the spaceport, all under that diffuse amber light that always, on this planet, seems to equate autumn with spring.

The robot had, of course, stood first in that crowd that had seen me off on that long-distant (far more distant for the inhabitants of Ste. Therese, including the robot, I now realized) morning when I had set off on my personal grand tour, to Earth, to Ste. Marie and Ste. Anne, and to planets more distant.

I still recall his face looking up, as I saw it then, through the rearview screen of the departing orbit shuttle, as if it were a recent memory. Even at this moment, I see those features as I did during those nights when I designed them—all of the individual components, mathematically calculated, coming together to form the face of man.

As I saw the continents of Ste. Therese loom into view, I felt a growing uneasiness, as if I was returning to a problem from which I had run and which had remained unchanged; it was only upon recognizing this feeling that I realized that, *in all of my travels, I had never really understood quite why I had left. I had supposed that it had been a pilgrimage of sorts, or at least an escape to places distant. In any event, it had served to bring me away from my creation, something that, for reasons I could only vaguely discern, I seemed greatly to desire.*

There were changes, of course. When I had left, my chateau (so lovingly and precisely modeled on a seventeenth-century home in Provence, which I had admired as a child) had been surrounded by primary forest, virgin and untouched, consisting largely of great stands of tall, gingko-like trees and those strange pseudo-Metasequoias, which had once alarmed naturalists by their chance resemblance to the dawn redwoods of ancient China.

Now, all was different. The trees still stood, but only in ordered and manicured groves, surrounded by cultivated fields and well-tamed parkland. A few miles from my estate, where there were only one or two hardscrabble farms when I had left, there was now a village—no, a small town—complete with a church, a town hall, a square and a dusty lot to one side, which I knew from my experience on other worlds must be the plot laid aside for weekly market.

The biggest change, however, was the school. I had known that the Order of St. Aquin had put in a request to open an outland ecole on the portion of my property that I had tithed to the church. I had not expected the buildings and the grounds to be so imposing and so magnificent; more than anything, I had not expected, as I flew over the convent, to feel a pang of envy at the thought that the great stone mass of the church school might somehow rival my own temple, my mini-Versailles. On an impulse, I ordered the pilot to put down at the school's landing pad at once, rather than at my own estate. I felt an urgent need to speak with the presiding father.

Pere Regis Debray was as graciously conservative as his long-dead namesake had been radical. He offered me good coffee (very good indeed, I might add, grown in the richest *volcanic soil on Ste. Therese, roasted until black resin oozed out of every bean as if it were hashish, and ground by the aging father himself in my presence), a warm place by a large fire (made, I regret to say, from the limbs of my beloved dawn trees) in the school's high-timbered dining room and, that rarest of commodities from a priest, an honest assessment of things.*

My friend, *the father began,* or perhaps I should call you Monseigneur, since you have been to those of us here an absent feudal lord. I formally greet you on behalf of the Church of Rome and the Order of St. Aquin, and, more specifically, on behalf of the school established by said order for the moral, spiritual and intellectual instruction of young women. Have some coffee. Brandy may come later. One must keep a clear head at the beginning of things.

Yes, *he continued,* we have prospered here on this small world. I know that when you left you were the lord of a great tract of forest, and that now, as you return, you are surrounded on all sides by lands tamed by people who are themselves tamed, but, I beg of you, accept us. It is, I am afraid, only those who come first to a new land who are as truly wild as the land itself; those who come later are not wild groundbreakers, but builders.

The priest broke off abruptly, with an exaggerated sigh.

Well, *he went on with a wry smile,* that was the speech the town fathers cooked up to justify themselves. I think that you know how the rest of it will go. First I will try to justify our own conservatism, then I will try to defend each portion of the status quo as it has been laid down before me, and then I shall ask you, as our most honorable seigneur, to allow us to continue in our peasant ways, unmolested and uninfluenced by outside sophisticates, such as yourself.

I hope, *he said,* raising an eyebrow, that you will consider said speech to already have been made and spare me the embarrassment of continuing.

Illustrated by Adrian Barbu

I replied that I understood completely, and that he could tell his fellow settlers that I had no wish to bother them. On the contrary, I said, I was pleased at the thought of living near a quiet community filled with people as simple and as free from pretense as I wished that I could be. What I did not tell him was that to Earth, and to the other colonies, so wrapped up in their own affairs, I was no celebrity, let alone a great lord; I was merely an insignificant speck of matter who had spent too long traveling between the stars and now wanted to go home.

With our obligatory speeches finished, I had assumed that we were done with important matters. We would finish our coffee, Father Debray would break out some brandy, which we would sip while he filled me in on local gossip, and I would leave, knowing that I had been formally welcomed back into the community of Ste. Therese, a community that I had, in truth, never known.

After I had finished speaking, however, and our roles were, I assumed, played out, the old priest took a long sip from his coffee cup and looked at me over the rim, with eyes that seemed to measure me against, I thought uneasily, some alien standard. Presently, he set the cup down and spoke.

I must tell you immediately, *he said,* that it is the robot about whom I am the most concerned. No, no, don't get alarmed, he's not suffered any physical damage and I'm sure that he'll still perform all of the tasks you charged him with. It's just that, well, he has been with us a long time, and I have come to be concerned about his welfare. May I ask you some impertinent questions? Never mind consenting; I am an old man and a priest, so that gives me double license to be rude. Besides, these questions have bothered me for years.

First, why did you build a humanoid robot in the first place? The idea has been out of fashion for centuries and I can hardly imagine that you had some specialized need that required such a creature. Those

who want to create humans do so through genetics
and those who create intelligent machines design them
to fit their functions. Why such an exact duplicate of a
human being?

*I answered that it had been the challenge of the idea that
had prompted me. Before I had left Earth, I had designed
intelligent machines of the more conventional type. Indeed,
my last project had been for the Vatican, creating a large and
very powerful computer for solving the complicated questions of theology and ethics that always seemed to arise in
the face of new scientific discoveries and new technology.*

*When a cardinal had joked that I was creating an "arti-
ficial Jesuit" I laughed, but later I began to wonder just how
far I could go toward creating an artificial human purely
out of electronic components. I toyed with the idea during
spare moments, until, by the time I had finished my work at
the Vatican and was ready to move out to the colonies, I
had already had most of the design worked out. When I
had settled in here, I went ahead and constructed the thing.
I had always been taught that every machine should have a
purpose, so I gave the robot the task of keeping my house in
order.*

Tell me, *I asked*, is he . . . does he seem human to
you?

Very much so, *replied the priest*, very much so. I first
met him thirty-five years ago, when I came here to
supervise the construction of this school. I knew that
he was a robot, of course. The settlers nearby regarded
him as something of a local marvel with which to
impress visitors. But it was only because of that, only
because I had been forewarned, that I knew that he
was anything other than human.

At first, he just watched us as we cleared the
ground and began to lay foundations. After a while,
however, he volunteered to help us. I asked him
whether his other duties would allow him to spare the
time. He replied that his duties took no more than an

hour or two out of his day and that he would be grateful for the chance to do something useful and, he added after a moment's hesitation, to have a little human company.

He was an excellent worker, of course, strong, tireless, uncomplaining, fearless. His suggestions were always helpful and, at times, saved us a great deal of trouble. It was he who said that we should surround the school with a broad belt of St. Augustine grass to keep the vines from overgrowing everything. It was also he who told us which vines produced the grape-like fruit with which we make our wine, and who showed us the best method of fermentation. Although, *added the priest,* I was saddened to see that you did not see fit to equip him with the means by which he might enjoy the result.

When the school had been constructed and we were organizing our staff, the robot volunteered to be in charge of maintenance. Again, he insisted that he had more than enough free time and argued quite reasonably that, since you had designed him at least partly with such a job in mind, he would naturally be most suited for the position. I agreed and he has been, one might say, moonlighting with us ever since.

Here, look at this.

Father Debray reached into a nearby cabinet and pulled out a thick, venerable-looking picture album. He opened it to the first page and handed it to me.

This, *he continued,* is just the first of many scrap books. When the students look at these they do so with a sort of reverence that I can't help but find amusing. Then, each year, when the alumni return, they pore over these same scrapbooks and become tearful and nostalgic, and I am as moved by the wistfulness of the older women as I am delighted by the awe of the young girls. But look for yourself; I don't expect you to be impressed or moved or anything of the sort, since most of this will mean nothing to you, but notice the one thing that seems barely to change, even as the rest of us age.

I turned the pages slowly, dutifully studying the assortment of newspaper clippings, handbills, flat photographs and holograms. It seemed to be the usual sort of stuff that one would find in such a scrapbook: groundbreaking ceremonies, snapshots of different phases of the school's construction, opening day, a group picture of the first students, the first graduation ceremony.

I flipped over to the final page and found a very formal hologram of the school's fifth anniversary dinner. The oldest alumni, I noted, seemed barely older than the then-current students. How old would they be now, I wondered? Their early sixties? Almost young, by modern standards. I felt an irrational pang of regret that I had not stayed on Ste. Therese and perhaps become the lover, or even the husband, of one of these girls, although I knew in my heart that if I had remained here such a thing would not have come to pass.

Now look at this, *he said, handing me a much newer scrapbook.*

It was only partly filled, and the dates on the pictures and clippings were recent. The style of the girls' uniforms had changed somewhat, and many of them wore their hair and makeup in a manner fashionable on Earth shortly before I had visited that planet. By now it was probably a generation out of date. Here, however, it would still be new and a little daring.

In the pictures, the buildings and the grounds both looked older, and I saw that the saplings that had been planted by the first graduating class were now large trees.

I could see the one thing that remained the same, though. It was the robot. In the first volume, I had seen him holding a shovel as two girls cheerfully lowered a sapling into a hole that, I imagined, he had just dug. He was as unsmiling as an undertaker.

In the more recent picture, he stood under a tree, perhaps the same one grown tall, surrounded by a half-dozen smiling teenage girls. He was grinning. The caption read, "Senior Tree Committee and Friend." He was in several other photographs in both volumes. Other than his expression, he looked the same in all of them.

The robot's face has never changed, of course, *the priest went on,* but his range of facial expressions has. He was with us two years before I saw him smile. I had thought that he might be physically incapable of smiling, that you might not have given him that ability.

When I finally did see him smile, it was in response to a girl who was trying to flirt with him. That might have been out of politeness, though; it was not until much later that he began to smile with any frequency.

I do know that he was very troubled during those first years.

Father Debray paused, sipped his coffee and looked at me.

It was the day after the school's fifth anniversary banquet—you can see the robot in the hologram, sitting next to me at the main table; in fact, he was the guest of honor, and gave quite a wonderful speech—it was the day after that banquet that he first came to me in the confessional, so that I could hear his sins.

Oh, I was as surprised by it then as you are now. It wasn't merely the oddity of hearing confession from a robot; it was also the thought that this particular robot, the most blameless of all of the creatures that I knew, could sin.

At first I thought that it must be some kind of odd practical joke, perhaps some trick that you had programmed into him before you left, but I soon realized that he was serious.

Now, *Father Debray looked at me and folded his hands before him, almost as if he were about to pray.* Now I am going to do something that is not entirely according to the rules, perhaps; there are times, however, when a rule may no longer apply.

I am going to tell you what he confessed to me. Oh, it's not as bad as all that—he hadn't actually committed any sin and anyway, you are his creator.

First, of course, he told me that he had sinned. I then asked him what his sin was.

"I don't know," was his reply.

I chose my words carefully. "What leads you to believe that you have sinned?"

"I must have." He sounded firm and a little tired. "I couldn't feel this guilty if I hadn't sinned."

"That doesn't necessarily follow. You only have to *believe* that you have sinned in order to feel guilty."

He was adamant. "No, no, I've sinned . . . I've sinned badly. Only . . ."

"Yes?"

"How can I possibly not remember what I did? Or where? Or when? It must have been something horrible," the robot sounded like he was in real agony, "something so horrible that I've completely blocked it out of my memory."

By this time I was quite worried; I had never heard him sound like this.

"Please, please, let yourself relax a little bit," I admonished him, "and tell me how long you've felt this guilt."

He thought for a moment.

"It's been growing in me ever since . . . since some time after my creator left. At first, before the school was here and I was alone, it seemed almost small, like a little voice that was so quiet I could shut it out without much effort.

"But then, after I started working at the school, I began to be happy. That's when it really started growing. The happier I was, the more guilty I felt. And last night . . . last night at the banquet I was dancing with Jeannette and she was teasing me. You know how

Jeannette loves to tease me, all in play, of course."
Jeannette was the flirtatious girl who had first made him smile.

"She was teasing me by talking about how delicious the food had been, saying things like, 'Such a lovely banquet and the guest of honor doesn't even eat!' Then she suddenly stopped talking and looked at me and said something like 'It's not fair! It's not fair!' and hugged me and started crying.

"It didn't take me too long to cheer her up and by the time we finished the dance we were both laughing, but then later, when I was supervising the cleanup crew, it hit me."

"The guilt?"

"I looked around at the banquet room, at the decorations, the balloons and the banners, the empty champagne bottles, and I saw guilt everywhere I looked. My guilt. I felt guilty for being the guest of honor, I felt guilty for enjoying my job, I felt guilty because Jeannette loved me, and, most of all, I felt guilty because I couldn't eat the food or even taste it. That and one other thing."

"Yes?"

"I feel guilty because I don't have a name."

"Is that why you wouldn't take one? Guilt?" When I had first met him, I had urged him to take one, but he had refused, without giving any plausible explanation.

"I do not deserve to have a name," the robot said emphatically. "If I did, my maker would have given me one, but he didn't—not even a serial number. Even the lawn mower was given more of a name than I was.

"Look at how my maker treated me. He built me, he programmed me, he taught me, and then he left, without even giving me a name, let alone taking me with him. I must have done something awful, some unspeakable crime, something that drove him away. He was my only . . . my only friend, the only human being I had ever talked to. I owe my existence to him, everything that I am.

"And then . . . and then one day he just told me that he was leaving and that he'd be gone for fifty years and I should take care of the house until he came back. We were friends, and he just left without asking me to come with him and without even giving me a name. I must have done something very wrong to make him go away like that.

"And now," his voice was pleading, "I need to find out what I did, so I can confess and be forgiven—if it's a sin that *can* be forgiven."

"Don't worry," I reassured him. "If you've sinned and you confess, you'll be forgiven. The more you talk, though, the more it sounds like you haven't done anything wrong. You sound more like a lost child trying to understand why it's been abandoned by its parents. How long had you been in existence when he left?"

"Two years."

"You *were* a child, then. Even though he gave you the intelligence of an adult, you couldn't have had a chance to mature emotionally. You interpreted his leaving the way a child would have—with guilt and grief."

"Yes, but *why* did he leave? Why didn't he take me with him? And why didn't he give me a name? Don't you see? I must have done something wrong—people just don't treat each other . . . don't treat other . . . beings like that without a reason."

I told him to go home and to search his memory to see if there really was a sin that he had committed. I suggested that he come back to the confessional when he thought he knew something, but that I would be available for counseling if he needed help.

And now, at this point, *the priest said, looking up,* I must ask you the second of my rude questions. Why did you not give the robot a name?

I replied that I didn't really know. Before, when there

were only the two of us, it hadn't seemed necessary to use names. I rarely address other people by their names and it simply had not occurred to me to do so with him. When I had left, I had vaguely supposed that if an occasion arose in which he needed a name he would simply choose one for himself.

Father Debray raised an eyebrow.

Children, *he told me*, are rarely that simple. Particularly intelligent children.

The robot was no exception. From that day on, I was not merely his friend; I was also his confessor and psychiatrist. He eventually came to understand intellectually, if not emotionally, that he was not being punished by you for some great sin.

The guilt, however, would not be so easily exorcised. One day, a few years after that first incident in the confessional, he asked me, as we were concluding a long and rather draining counseling session, whether his abandonment, his namelessness and his guilt might be the result of Original Sin.

"I'd say no categorically to that one," I told him, "for two good reasons. First, if that were the case, we would all have been deserted by our parents while still unnamed. We were not, and there is no reason why you should be punished more severely than anyone else.

"As for your guilt, since you were not instructed in the teachings of the Church until you came to work at this school, you simply couldn't have been aware of the Sin enough to feel that guilty about it. Besides . . ."

"Yes?"

"Besides, you . . . uh . . . you just can't escape a psychological explanation for your condition," I concluded hastily.

"That's not what you were going to say, was it?"

"Well . . ."

"What you were going to say was that, besides, a robot's just a machine, and a machine can't know Original Sin, or feel guilt, or really feel anything else, for that matter. You were going to say that my creator probably abandoned me because I was just another household appliance, and appliances don't have any feelings, do they?

"Admit it, we've been tiptoeing around that issue for quite a while now, haven't we? Does the walking, talking lawn mower have a soul? Well, if you want the lawn mower's opinion, yes, I do have a soul.

"No, no, Regis, I apologize. I know that you are my friend and that you have always treated me as if I was a man, even though I am not. But now, I have to speak to you as a priest rather than a friend.

"I tell you that I know that I have a soul.

"How do I know this? It's simple. A soulless creature can feel no guilt. Wouldn't you agree?"

I agreed, of course.

"And we both know that I have felt great guilt."

"Yes, certainly."

"Therefore, we must conclude I have a soul. 'Ah, yes, but,' I can hear the little Jesuit in the back of your head saying, 'but what if he has only been programmed to appear to feel guilty?'

"Well, my creator put a little Jesuit in the back of my head, too. *That* Jesuit says that if I give every appearance of feeling guilty, or of feeling any emotion, or of being human at all, it is a much greater sin to deny me confession, or to deny me communion, than it would be to give a sacrament of the Church to an impostor. Agreed?"

"Agreed." I would have told him long ago what he was telling me now, if he had not needed to discover it for himself.

"And there's another thing," he added, "I know from my own experience that I feel guilt, which means that I have a soul. That subjective knowledge is just as real for me as your subjective knowledge of your humanity is for you."

"Your only other claim to a soul over me is that you are the descendant of a particular band of apes who had learned to pray, and that one of those apes created me in his image. But if an ape can have a soul, why can't a machine? Does it make sense that God should limit his soul dispensing to one species on one tiny planet?"

"No," I agreed, "it doesn't. But you know as well as I that the Church has long since accepted that fact. It's not me that you're arguing with. Who is it? Yourself?"

"Yes, as usual, and the questions are still the same. Why was I abandoned? Why didn't my maker take me with him? Why did he give me no name? And . . ."

"Yes?"

"This seems silly, but maybe it's as important as the other questions: If I was supposed to be a perfect replica of a human being, why was I not made able to enjoy the taste of food, or the feel of a glass of wine, or the pleasure of physical love? Father, I see the passion people have for these things, yet they're just ideas to me. Even sex is just an abstraction. Perhaps that's it; perhaps I'm just the *idea* of a human being without the sensations. Perhaps I'm just an abstraction."

I assured him that he was definitely much more than an abstraction, and that even if he did not know sex, he was far more capable of love than most people I knew, and soon he seemed more calm and went home.

But that encounter brings me to the third of my rude questions. Why did you not give him the ability to experience such simple pleasures? Even I, a priest, can appreciate a glass of wine or a good meal, and even I know what it's like to desire a woman.

Father Debray's question took me by surprise. I had to confess that I had never given the matter much thought; I am not a particularly sensual person, and when I had set out to design the robot, I had thought only to create a mental and emotional copy of a human being.

I said that I guessed that I had dismissed the question of how to duplicate physical sensations as too crude and simple a matter to pose any kind of challenge. I could not really remember.

The priest looked into his coffee cup and sat silently for a while.

Well, *he finally said*, in this, as in other matters, what the creator considers trivial can be very important indeed to his creation.

For all of his continued anxieties, though, the robot's condition was improving. He came less and less to discuss things in terms of his own guilt, and he began to read the works of philosophers and theologians. During the next few years, his attitude seemed to vacillate between skepticism and piety as he considered new doctrines, one after another, radical and conservative alike.

Eventually, he began to try out names. I had long suspected that something of the sort would happen, so I was not entirely surprised when, upon returning the school's copy of *The Consolation of Philosophy*, he announced that from now on he would not mind being addressed as "Theophilé."

Neither was I surprised a mere two months later, when, after reading Rousseau, he renounced the name "Theophilé" and swore only to answer to "Caliban." I informed him that he was hardly so simple a creature as to be a Noble Savage, but I humored him, knowing that this, too, would pass, as indeed it did.

After his Rousseau phase, he returned to namelessness for another year or so, until the day he came into my office carrying a copy of *The Wretched of the Earth*.

"Ah, Regis Debray, Regis Debray," he said to me wistfully, but not, I thought, without a certain good humor. "How is it that the best possible name for a Catholic Marxist such as myself has already been taken—and by such a reactionary old priest, too," he added, grinning and pointing an accusing finger at me. "What shall I call myself?"

"Well, whatever you do, don't pick anything as silly and obvious as 'Ché' or I'll never be able to address you with a straight face."

He looked at me with mock injury.

"Please, please, Father, even a robot has better judgment than that. No, no," he said, "I think 'Jean-Paul' conveys sufficient ambiguity."

"Is that after a pope or after the atheist?" I inquired.

"Both," he laughed, "both."

The nadir of his name-taking, though, came when I had to tell him that under no circumstances would I call him either "Alyosha" or "Myshkin," if for no other reason than to protect my health.

"I am an old man," I said, "and if I have to refer to you by either of those names, I'll probably have such a fit of laughter that I'll choke to death."

Eventually, the robot absorbed Dostoyevsky, and Marx, and the Church fathers, and Sartre, and the Sufis and Zen masters, and all the rest, taking what he found useful in each, and finally emerging from intellectual adolescence.

In the end, he chose to remain nameless.

It was during this time that he matured emotionally, too, I think. He seemed gradually to become aware that even if his creator didn't care about him, those who knew him did. It's true, too. The townspeople admire him, he has many friends on the staff of this school, and the girls adore him.

Father Debray smiled. I suspect that he's been the object of more than a few adolescent crushes over the years.

Which brings us, *continued the priest,* up to the present. It has been some years since your creation has shown much sign of his former troubles. There have been times when he has confronted me with an odd argument or an oblique complaint that seemed to reflect his old anxieties, but then he always has enjoyed a good theological debate.

And so, given this peaceful state of things, I was more than a little concerned with how he would take the news of your return. Would his guilt return? Would he fall into a depression or, worse yet, that rage that I had always feared would lie at the end of all of his questions?

It seemed, though, when I did tell him that you were coming back, that I had no cause for concern.

"Yes," he laughed, "my inventor has said that he would be gone about this long. He's a bit overdue, if anything."

"Well, Father," the robot continued after a pause, "it looks like I'll finally get answers to a few of my questions—although by now I've come to suspect that the most astonishing thing about them will be their banality."

That was all he said about the subject for some time after that. It was only three weeks ago, when the current term was about to end, that the matter surfaced again, and then, I regret to say, in a manner that I at first completely failed to recognize.

Here. *He picked up the latest volume of the school scrapbook, opened it to a page near the end, and handed it to me.* This is Marguerite.

I found myself looking at a snapshot of a couple sitting on a hillside with a picnic lunch (set for one, I saw). It was my robot, with a very pretty girl in her late teens. She was dressed in the school's uniform and had long, dark wavy hair. He had his arm around her and her head rested on his shoulder. She was looking up at him, I thought, with a bit too much adoration.

He is as close to her as he is to anyone I have ever seen. If he were a man, instead of being the imperfect imitation of a man, nature would have long since taken its time-honored course. Since he is what you have made him, however, there is naturally no chance of that.

Oh, *the priest waved his hand,* don't worry about any resentment on his part; when he tells me that he only wishes to be the best man at Marguerite's wedding, I believe him. The ancients might have said that he had a grave imbalance of humors: he is overflowing with *agape* and *caritas,* but *eros* does not exist in his world.

And do not, *Father Debray looked at me sharply,* do not think that, because I have chosen to be celibate, I see any virtue in your robot's enforced celibacy; virtue disappears when sin is not a possibility. It was for this reason that I was glad in spite of myself when the robot found it within himself to commit a sin.

Oh, no, don't worry; you haven't created a monster who goes around crushing little girls and throwing them down wells. The robot is by nature not prone to the kind of sins that are usually proscribed in the laws of God or man; he had to reach to find a sin, even a little one, if that's what it was.

This is how I became aware of it: One afternoon, when classes had let out for the day, but long before the evening meal, I was walking past a study room in the main building when I heard a sound like muffled weeping. I looked inside and saw Marguerite sitting at a group study table, staring at a piece of notepaper laying before her, a look of hurt and bewilderment on her face.

When I asked her what the problem was, she at first refused to talk; it was only after she realized that I would neither leave nor punish her for her silence that she began to tell me what was troubling her.

She began by showing me the piece of paper that she had been studying so intently when I first saw her. It appeared to be a list of wrongdoings, real or imagined, that she had committed, might have committed if given the chance, or had thought of committing during the previous month or so, with particular attention given to transgressions against the robot. Many of the peccadilloes (for that is what they all were) I knew to be entirely imaginary.

"Child," I said, taking her hand, "if you walked into the confessional with this list, the only sin for which I could prescribe a penance would be exaggeration. You're making up accusations against yourself. Why?"

She withdrew her hand and hugged her knees to her chest, curling up on the chair in a ball.

"Don't laugh at me, Father," she said in a voice that carried tones of resentment which I had never previously heard from her. "*I know* that I've done something wrong, even if you don't! I must have—otherwise . . . otherwise . . ."

She broke off in a sob.

"Yes?"

"He wouldn't . . . he wouldn't . . ." She caught her breath. "The robot was going to meet me two days ago, at noon, like he always does. We were going to sit in the big redwood grove and eat lunch—well, you know what I mean, I'd eat—and we were going to talk about my future, about what I might do after I graduated.

"Oh," she wailed, "I don't want to graduate now; I just want to die!"

"What did he do?" I was bewildered and a bit apprehensive.

"He . . . he . . . oh, I don't know . . . I must have made him mad in some way. He didn't show up at noon, and then, every time I've seen him since, he refuses to even *talk* to me. It's like I'm not even there. He always made me feel so good and now I feel like garbage! What happened? I just don't understand it!"

I talked with her for a long while after that and gave her what reassurances I could. Finally I suggested that she do what she could to put it out of her mind for the time being.

I said that I would discreetly find out about the robot's problem, emphasizing that it was *his* problem and not hers.

I didn't have long to wait. The next day, the robot came into the booth when I was hearing confession.

"Father," he said in a tight voice, "now I really have sinned."

"Go on," was all I said.

"The thought came to me a few days ago—I don't know why; it seems so crazy now—but it came, and it wouldn't go away.

"I realized that I actually didn't know what it was like to deliberately cause someone pain. Oh, I'd accidentally slighted people before, but I'd always made amends as soon as I found out about it. It had never occurred to me to be consciously cruel.

"And then," he paused, and went on, "another thought came. Perhaps there was some kind of power in cruelty. It seemed to me that, since the victim of cruelty feels so powerless, the power that's lost must go to the victimizer.

"Oh, I know that I'm not the first to imagine such a thing—I've read too much de Sade and too much history to delude myself about that—and I hardly desire the sort of power that cruelty might give me, but I wanted to know what sort of power that could be, how it would feel.

"It was a thought that wouldn't go away; it stayed with me, and it grew, until finally I came to wonder if this knowledge that I lacked might not be the key to answering the questions that had bothered me so many years ago. That's when I realized that I had already made up my mind to act.

"What could I do, though? I certainly wasn't going to kill, or even injure, anyone, which ruled out the most obvious ways of hurting someone. It was hard enough, I thought, to imagine snubbing a friend with no explanation.

"That reminded me of my lunch date with Marguerite and I knew what I had to do.

"I wouldn't show up to meet her and I wouldn't speak to her afterward. I would then continue to cut her off until I understood what power there was in cruelty, until I had some knowledge that might lead to an answer."

"I hear, my friend, that you've done an excellent job of holding to your vow." I tried to sound more droll than angry, and I think that I succeeded. "Have you found your clue yet, or must Marguerite continue to pay the price for your curiosity?"

"That's just it!" the robot cried. "I haven't found anything in this except pain! I feel like I'm hurting myself every time I see Marguerite and don't talk to her; I feel sick and awful when I walk away and I know that she's crying. If there's power, it must be . . . it must be . . . I don't know . . . overloading my circuits.

"That's it," he said in a quiet, tired voice. "I really am just a machine, and all of this nonsense about sins, and souls, and love, and the withholding of love really is nonsense; that alone, and nothing more. Tell me that that's it; tell me that I'm just a robot with a bad circuit, and then help me find my power switch and help me turn myself off so that I can have done with everything. Won't you, Father?"

That was too much. The solemnity of his request, the humanness of his pain and weariness, the very absurdity of his dilemma, the cruelty that he had inflicted on one whom he loved, all of these suddenly seemed to me to be some hysterical and tasteless joke.

I believe that that was the first time I have ever laughed out loud while hearing confession. I couldn't help it; he sounded so ridiculous and pathetic, and, yet, by the very nature of his emotional exhaustion and his remorse, he confirmed what I had already known— that he was truly human.

I spoke with him, and reassured him, and told him how many Hail Marys and Our Fathers he should say. Then I told him what he must do that would make a difference: he must go to Marguerite and tell her that he hadn't meant to use her or hurt her in any way. He must tell her that it had not been her fault and that (however he explained his behavior) he had never stopped loving her. If he told her that, and if she forgave him, it would be sufficient.

"You must, however," I admonished, "never think to do such a thing again. If there is a lesson to be learned from all of this, then you have learned it. If there is nothing to be learned, then that itself is a lesson. Now go and sin no more. I've had quite enough nonsense for one week."

I don't know what the robot said to Marguerite by way of explanation, but it appeared to work, because the next day I saw them talking and laughing together, lost in some private joke, utterly oblivious to the rest of creation.

They both gave every indication of being quite happy after that, and the incident seemed to be forgotten by the end of the term, when the robot gave her, as a graduation gift, a bracelet that he had made. It was of silver, inlaid with gold and niello, and I know that he had spent many hours just learning the technique and many more in making it. At the graduation ceremony, she wore it as proudly as a wedding band.

So, *said Father Debray abruptly,* that is the robot's story. Now I must ask you the last of my rude questions. Why did you leave and not take the robot with you? I think that most people would have been glad to have such an intelligent and agreeable traveling companion. Come on now, tell a nosy old priest what you can't tell those who know you better.

I told him that I made it a habit never to look too deeply into my own motives; I supposed, if pressed, that I would have to say that I had always felt uncomfortable living in close quarters with another person, and, I added, I had wanted some time away from the responsibility involved in guiding such a creature in its development. I really could give no other reasons, I told him.

That is it? *The priest shrugged and looked at me with an expression, I thought, almost of pity.*

That seemed to dismiss the whole matter. He then broke out the brandy, which we sipped as we exchanged gossip and discussed matters in the village and on Earth and more distant planets. By the time that I had bid him good night and the door to the church school closed behind me, I had put the odd discussion concerning the robot almost out of my mind.

Shortly, though, as I approached the brightly lighted grounds of my estate, I began to feel a vague, but growing, anxiety and a great tiredness.

I wanted to be going anywhere but home; I wanted to go to some place entirely private where I could just sleep and not have to speak with the robot or anyone else. I kept going because, finally, I knew that there was nowhere else to hide and that I must return to this, the place that I had built and called home.

It is here that I stand as the great front doors open and a figure like a man stands before me, bathed in light.

And now, facing my creation, I realize for the first time that I have no idea of what to say to the robot, none at all, and, fighting an urge to run and run and never stop running, I finally understand that this is his house more than it is mine, since he has spent all of his life here, and I only a few years; this is his planet more than mine, since he was made here, just as Marguerite and her schoolmates were born here.

This is his world and his life into which I am intruding, a life of friends and place and purpose, a life where he has been healed and redeemed, a world in which he is loved, and where I am little more than a myth, a cold and impossibly distant creator.

BEAUTIFUL SINGER

Written by
Steve Bein

Illustrated by
Lulkien

About the Author

Steve Bein lives in Honolulu, where he is completing his doctoral dissertation in comparative East-West philosophy. When he is not working on his dissertation, he spends his time rock climbing, scuba diving and practicing martial arts.

Steve has been fascinated with all things Japanese since the fourth grade and wrote "Beautiful Singer" while studying philosophy in Nagoya and Tokyo. He has been writing short stories for about as long as he can remember and has recently completed his first novel. "Beautiful Singer" is his first published piece of fiction.

About the Illustrator

Lulkien was born James C. Trujillo in Walnut Creek, California, and raised in Danville. He has been interested in art since grade school. During his junior and high school years, he received many honorable mentions for his artwork and was eventually awarded the title "most artistic student." This is the first contest he has won.

Lulkien is currently a student at California College of Arts and Crafts where he studies illustration with an emphasis on animation. At the beginning of the spring semester of 2003, he had his first gallery show with another artist and longtime friend, Bryce Shelton. He feels he has developed an eye for details in his artwork that demand extended viewing for a full appreciation.

Silence fell on the hillside. Orange and gold leaves of autumn drifted lazily to the ground, more of them below than still in the branches. One fell on the face of Lord Osamu Kanayama, his pallor contrasting sharply with the rich redness of the leaf. Most of his blood had already dyed the leaves on the ground in a uniform river of dark crimson. His body was gashed open across the spine, a deep cut from left shoulder to right hip, and his face still bore the crazed snarl he had worn in combat.

"I've never seen anything like it." Toshiro Saito stared down at his fallen commander, lungs still heaving, blood pounding an adrenaline-charged rhythm against his eardrums.

"Neither have I," said Minoru Nakadai, sheathing his katana at his hip. "Not at Kamakura, not at Higashiyama, never."

The two men were in many ways the opposite of each other. While Saito was lean and towering in his armor, Nakadai was fully a head shorter and almost as broad as he was tall. Saito had a face of leather, bronzed by the sun and hardened by years of combat. Nakadai had cheeks like red apples and deep, narrow, glinting slits for eyes, like two black marbles pressed into a ball of dough. Both wore the armor and topknot that marked them as samurai, as well as the twin swords, but standing next to each other, Nakadai looked almost like a bull, Saito a weathered tree.

"He fought like a madman," Saito said. "No, like a rabid dog. I don't understand it."

"Yes. By all rights we should be the ones lying here, not him. It's too bad; he deserved a better death than this."

Lord Kanayama had been, among other things, one of the most renowned swordsmen in the Owari territory. He had also been samurai, lord of the castle at Gifu, daimyo of the surrounding fief, and an ally and confidante to Lord Ashikaga-no-kami Jinzaemon, overlord of Owari. Up until a few days ago, Kanayama was one of Lord Ashikaga's generals and the commanding officer of both Toshiro Saito and Minoru Nakadai. In times of war, Lord Kanayama's counsel was always esteemed, and with a blade in his hands he was unrivaled within a hundred *ri*. But yesterday morning he was to have committed seppuku, his punishment ordered by Lord Ashikaga on charges of treason. And, that morning at dawn, Kanayama had instead taken his swords and his two fastest horses and fled across the Owari plains.

The first of these horses he rode into the ground. The second, stronger than the first, carried him all the way through the night until it broke a foreleg in his mad dash across the Kiso river. From there Kanayama had fled on foot, where it took some thirty hours for Saito, Nakadai and a dozen warriors to chase him down on Ashikaga's orders. And now, on this isolated hillside, he had doomed himself to suffer a dog's death at the hands of his own retainers.

"I cannot understand it," Saito said as he began to clean the blood from his blade. "If he had simply committed seppuku he could have died with honor. Instead, this! Fleeing like a common thief, hacking at us as if he'd never touched a sword. . . . By all gods, when he *kicked* you, I couldn't believe my eyes!"

That kick had sent Nakadai's girth tumbling

through a thorny bramble, breaking two ribs and slicing every exposed inch of skin a hundred times over. Nakadai was lucky; anyone who stepped within striking distance of Osamu Kanayama usually met with a swift death. The kick did more than dispatch Nakadai; it also off-balanced Kanayama and allowed Saito to sidestep his next crazed slash. Saito had taken a superficial cut to the forearm on that exchange, but in return Kanayama had exposed his back, and Saito spun and sliced him from shoulder to hip.

"It makes no sense," Nakadai nodded in agreement, looking at the body in disbelief. "I should be a headless corpse, and you should be bleeding to death from the stump of your sword arm, waiting for the lord to cut you down. There was no reason to his attacks, just madness. Perhaps what they say about his sword is true? . . ."

"Nonsense," Saito said immediately. "He was exhausted. He had been riding for days. He could have been injured when his horse fell at the river."

"That may be, but at Inuyama I saw him slay four men single-handedly, and that was after he took an arrow through the shoulder."

"I cannot explain it," Saito admitted. "Maybe he went mad. Nothing else would explain his turn against Lord Ashikaga."

"Nothing, except the sword."

Saito scoffed. "Put that out of your head. Are you a farmer's woman? Do you also believe goblins will take your children away in the night? It is an Inazuma blade! A sword without equal! Of course there will be legends attached to it."

"Not legends like these," said Nakadai.

"Get ahold of yourself! Legends were spoken of the lord himself. Do you truly believe he killed a hundred men at Kamakura? Neither do I, but that is what the villagers say of him. Choose, my friend, whether you

Illustrated by Lulkien

are peasant or samurai. Do you honestly believe spirits can control swords?"

Nakadai's head dropped for a moment. When it rose again, his fat cheeks were split in a smile. "You're right. Of course you're right. Our lord's death must be distracting me." He shook his head as if to throw off the last traces of a bad dream. "I'm sorry. Now, shall we fetch our retainers and return to Lord Ashikaga?"

Saito's eyes fell to the body once more. "You go ahead. Someone has to prepare the head and compose his death poem."

Nakadai nodded and Saito watched him amble up the hillside, on his way to find the dozen *bushi* who had accompanied them on the chase. Saito and Nakadai were the best horsemen among the group and had been able to navigate their mounts deeper through the forest than any of the others. Eventually they, too, were forced to dismount, the trees too dense to admit the passage of horses. The pursuit continued on foot, the horses staying obediently where they were left. Saito assumed that wherever Nakadai found the horses, he would also find their retainers.

That didn't leave much time. As soon as Nakadai's round figure plodded out of sight, Saito's gaze fell back on the body of his fallen master. It lay there, legs crossed over each other, the torso twisted in an impossible pose as the spine and rib cage no longer held it to a normal human shape. Kanayama's right hand still gripped the handle of his katana, which was so sharp that it sank two feet into the ground when its wielder fell.

Saito prayed it had not struck a rock when it dropped. He drew the Inazuma blade out of the earth, sighed when he saw that no stone had ground away the perfection of its edge. Inazuma, the creator of the sword, was a swordsmith the world would not see the likes of again for generations. Of course he had taken apprentices, but none of them had been able to replicate the genius of the master himself, and after his death, the Inazuma school dropped out of existence. That was four hundred years ago, and his legacy only remained in blades such as this, a treasure Saito never believed he would have the honor to wield in his lifetime.

Saito was quite a swordsman himself, even among samurai. Nothing along the lines of Lord Kanayama, but still he was more skilled than most. In addition to the fencing practice that all samurai made their purpose in life, Saito was also a longtime student of *iaidô*, the art of drawing the sword. He prided himself on the speed of his draw, on how fluidly it flowed into cuts and parries and counterstrikes. A master of *iaidô* could draw, cut and resheathe his blade before his enemy's corpse hit the ground. Saito was not there yet, but he was trying.

As it happened, this particular blade was forged by the master Inazuma especially for *iaidô*. It was named "Beautiful Singer" for the whistle of the katana's edge as it flashed out of its scabbard. An *iaidô* sword had to be lighter than most katanas for better speed on the draw; this one felt as if its mass was suspended by muscles of its own, an extension of his arm, weightless.

It was truly a masterpiece. The rumors surrounding it couldn't possibly be true. Saito laughed at the thought as he examined the blade in a beam of sunlight. He wiped the blade clean, admired the reflection it captured of the leaves above. It is an Inazuma blade, he thought. Of course there will be stories. Men would kill—men *have* killed—to possess a sword such as this. Where such treasures are concerned, the imagination is sure to wander.

He gave the sword a final polishing and, withdrawing his own katana, sheathed his late master's weapon in his own scabbard. It fit well enough; not perfectly, but not so loose as to rattle free. Then removing the masterful weapon and its sheath from his belt, he sat down and quickly unwound the cord wrappings from both swords' handles. Then he switched them, rebinding the Inazuma with the wrap from his own sword. He did the same with the braided cords wrapping the scabbards. Apprehension gnarled his brow as he eyed the handguards; switching those would take more time and tools than he had available. The illusion would not be complete. But then, it should not need to be. There would be no reason for anyone to examine the sword Saito wore on the trip home. If the others were loyal at all, their grief over the master's honorless death would overwhelm any other concerns.

Once the handle and scabbard of the Beautiful Singer were bound, he hastily rewrapped his own sword with the cord taken from Lord Kanayama. Both weapons disguised, he thrust Kanayama's magnificent prize through his own belt and returned his old sword to the late master. It was then that he heard voices approaching over the ridge. With one silent movement, Saito regained his feet and drew the Inazuma sword. The peerless blade glittered from its sheath and struck the head from Kanayama's body. The blood was minimal, most of it having already turned the ground to red mud, but Saito cleaned his new blade anyway. As he whipped it through the air to resheathe it, the blade truly sang, its song high-pitched, nearly inaudible, but nonetheless unforgettable. Though he could never explain how, Saito was immediately aware that this song had words, and in that moment he knew his fallen master's death poem:

> Glorious sun,
> coming to its zenith,
> shaded by a hand.

"That's perfect," Nakadai said later, when Saito recited the poem to him. "Yes, the lord himself could not have composed better. Too bad that it's all too true."

"What?" Saito looked up at his friend, distantly aware that Nakadai had spoken. The whistling song of the sword still clung to the air, washing over everything else.

"The master's life," Nakadai observed. "Surely you see it. He was the sun, shaded just as he was coming to the peak of his skills. Or have you written a poem better than you even knew yourself?"

"No . . . the poem wrote itself for me."

Nakadai laughed. "Well, then, perhaps you've attained a glimpse of enlightenment. Maybe you should shave that old topknot and join a monastery." Nakadai chuckled again, but Saito bristled at the thought of retiring his weapons and his station as samurai. He forced a laugh all the same.

They agreed to build a pyre for Kanayama's body just outside the woods, for it was possible that Lord Ashikaga would not allow a proper funeral if they carried the body home. Despite whatever demon had taken hold of the master in his final days, for most of his life, Kanayama had been an indomitable warrior and the object of unquestioned loyalty. At Saito's suggestion, Kanayama's swords were burned along with the body. The lord should die with at least that much honor, he argued. Besides, if Nakadai's ghost stories were true, they would be doing the world a favor by committing the Inazuma blade to the flames. No one seemed to notice the handguard on Lord Kanayama's sword, and no one mentioned the handguard of the late lord's weapon at Saito's hip.

•••

Lord Ashikaga-no-kami Jinzaemon was as fearsome as he was powerful. His reign over Owari was unquestioned; by now all his intelligent enemies had simply decided it was easier to wait until the old tyrant died, hoping the Ashikaga heir would not be blessed with the same demonic cunning as the father. The Owari territory was coveted land, to be sure, and every neighboring warlord deeply wished to wrest it from Ashikaga's control. Its long, narrow bay was protected by peninsulas on either side, making it a natural port with geological protection from the all-too-common threat of typhoons. Mountains to the north and west provided further protection against threats of a military nature. The Owari plains were rich, rice-yielding bounty, and to make the prize even more tempting, Ashikaga's armies were far smaller than the forces at his enemies' command. But with mountains and the sea protecting his flanks, Ashikaga could devote all his limited manpower to the protection of his eastern front, an easily defensible position for such a masterful general.

Once, long ago, two rival warlords attacked Owari simultaneously, one with naval power and one by land. Lord Ashikaga routed both of them, devoting only half his forces to each one. The first he flanked on both peninsulas as the boats stormed the port, enclosing the enemy in an ever-narrowing V of arrow fire. Flaming arrows did as much damage to ships as steel did to flesh, and the attack was broken off before the first sailor reached the shore. The land invaders were allowed to penetrate deep into the plains before the second half of Ashikaga's troops cut them off from behind and razed their supply lines. The enemy headed south, only to be cut off by archers returning from the sea battle. Turning west, the invaders encountered more archers returning from the opposite peninsula. Surrounded by troops on three sides and mountains on the fourth, the enemy was left to starve for a week in fertile crop land that was unfortunately three months away from the harvest. Both maneuvers were so surprising and so devastatingly fast that the opposing generals had no choice but to believe that

Ashikaga's entire army was deployed on the plains and on the sea coast at the same time, and that any general who could simultaneously deploy the same army in two separate places should be left to die in his own province unmolested, with the hopes that such inhuman skill would not be inherited by his successor.

For all his might and cleverness, Ashikaga was an ugly man. His face was like a skull with leather pulled taut across it, cheekbones cutting the sharp lines one might find in a prisoner's face after two weeks without food. On the left side a razor-straight line ran back from his mouth to a missing earlobe, its path a thick, white, hairless scar. His topknot and eyebrows were bushy gray, standing in sharp contrast to the ruddy skin permanently bronzed by years of harsh battlefield sun. His body bore the marks of combat as well, but by far the worst of his scars was the sickening twisted knot on his throat. In his youth, an archer had put an arrow through Ashikaga's gullet, and only by the grace of some buddha or demon did he survive. It was said he killed two more men that day before stopping to remove the shaft. Some said he even went back and hunted down the man who shot him. Eventually he recovered from the wound, but the healing had twisted the skin of his neck in an eddy of scar tissue, as cloth would twist around the haft of a spear. His vocal cords did not escape the damage. It was over a year before he could speak again or even turn his head, and ever since, his voice had been more of a growl, gravel under a wagon's wheels, the roll of distant thunder.

To Saito, it didn't matter whether the arrow had actually pierced the lord's throat or only grazed him, whether he really did stalk down that archer and get his revenge. If a man rose to such stature that people made up legends about him and recited them as if they were true, that was testament enough to his ability. Saito would always refer to the lord as Ashikaga-*sama* instead of the -*san* used for equals and would always honor him as a warrior and liege lord, regardless of what common foot soldiers whispered in the ranks.

Saito had been summoned to his general's audience chamber to offer his report on the death of Lord Kanayama. Ashikaga's guttural voice let out a sharp half-laugh when Saito recounted the kick that sent his companion through the bramble. "Do you expect me to believe Osamu Kanayama would *strike* a man when he had a sword in his hands?" The wolfish voice was bitter with disbelief. "Why did he not simply cut him down? What are you trying to hide from me?"

"Nothing, Ashikaga-sama. Nothing I have said so far would shield the late lord of any shame. You want the truth from me and that is what I have given you. I cannot explain his actions; he lost all semblance of control. I was loyal to him for many years, but Lord Kanayama died without honor and it was to spare him further dishonor that I took his head. If you still believe I am a liar, please allow me to commit seppuku to protest my innocence."

Ashikaga's black eyes turned down to the lacquered box at the foot of his dais. In the box was a heavy cloth bag, and in the bag was the severed head. "No, Saito-san," he brooded. "You will continue your story. Perhaps he was truly insane. Tell me the rest."

Saito related the end of the tale, from the death blow to the funeral pyre, describing everything in detail except the swords. He had no fear that Ashikaga would recognize the difference in his katana's new handguard, for no one entered the lord's audience chamber armed, save the bodyguards and Lord Ashikaga himself. The steward downstairs who had taken Saito's weapon was not of a position to recognize the difference in weapons, and so for the present Saito's secret would remain so. But it was with strong reluctance that he surrendered the blade at the door. Even as he thought of it now, the singing whistle he had heard in the forest echoed in the audience chamber, the tip of the sword crying out like a swooping steel falcon. How could the steward not know this was a sword above all others? Just the feel of it was divine, even still in its scabbard. Saito eased his tension in the knowledge that he would be rejoined with his side arm soon enough.

Ashikaga's rumbling tones brought Saito's attention back to the audience chamber. "You have been honest with me, Saito-san, even at the cost of your lord's honor and your own. You were correct to have burned the traitor's body; had you returned him here, I would not have allowed it. Your judgment is good, and both you and Nakadai-san have demonstrated your loyalty. You will not go as *rônin*."

Those words released the last uneasiness Saito had been holding, heavy in his gut since he arrived here. A samurai's life consisted of devotion to his master, and without a master that life became purposeless. It was Lord Ashikaga's prerogative to dismiss all of Kanayama's samurai and let them go as *rônin*, masterless warriors, to further dishonor the Kanayama name. Death would have been preferable; that much was obvious. Now Saito would not have to face such a fate, for Ashikaga chose to commandeer Kanayama's samurai and transfer their loyalty to him. The change would be an easy one for Saito; he already revered the old daimyo more than he could express. It had only been a matter of whether Ashikaga would accept such fealty, and now that worry had been swept away.

"Thank you, Ashikaga-sama," Saito said, bowing. "My life and my sword are yours."

"I am sending my third son to Kanayama's castle tomorrow. He will be the new lord there. You will accompany him and introduce him to his new home."

"Yes, Lord."

"How large is your current fief?"

"Five hundred *koku*, my lord."

"Now it is a thousand. When you arrive at Gifu with my son, he will select six of Kanayama's finest horses for you to take with you." Ashikaga noted Saito's puzzled look and added, "If you had returned my corpse to my enemy, my spirit would have haunted you for the rest of your life and slit your soul's throat when you died. You chose wisely, Saito-san."

Saito wondered what Nakadai had said when Ashikaga had summoned him to this room, whether he too received the same rewards. *Maybe it was my suggestion to build the pyre*, Saito thought. *No matter. The lord will increase or decrease my holdings as he sees fit, and a good vassal should pay it no mind one way or the other.*

All the same, when Saito returned home four days later with six new horses and a wide smile, his wife was pleased. Hisami was a beautiful woman, statuesque, not tiny and frail like the courtesans so many women tried to imitate. Of course, Saito was long-boned himself and so Hisami stood only to his shoulder. Among the other ladies, however, she held herself proud and tall like a hunting falcon on the wrist, sleek neck and gleaming eyes, knowing no fear. Today her kimono was pale orange with her under-robe showing the purest white. Her hair was, as ever, immaculate, wide-set with two long pins retaining her bun. Saito knew for a fact what anyone else might have guessed, that the pins were actually knives. For Hisami was samurai like her husband and equally prepared to take up arms and throw her life away at her master's command.

She was delighted to see the horses—the late lord's stables were excellent—and even happier at the expanded fief. One *koku* was the amount of rice it took to feed one family for a year, and five hundred additional *koku* would extend the Saito fief to annex the next town as part of its estate. It still wasn't much, comparatively.

Kanayama had been collecting perhaps twelve thousand *koku* worth of revenue before he died, and Ashikaga's domain was at least thirty times that, but a true samurai did not measure his wealth that way. Farmers and filthy merchants had to trouble themselves with such matters; monetary affairs were beneath Saito's notice. He would certainly make use of that wealth in equipping new retainers with swords and armor, but the details would be left to his housemaid. Finances were a concern for moneylenders and women.

As such, Hisami was delighted. "The lord must be very happy with you," she chirped, beaming as he handed over the horses and accompanied her to the tea room. "Doubling your fief and having you escort his son as well. As a bodyguard, no doubt. I'm sure that's why he sent you."

A mouse-faced maid entered noiselessly, set down a tray with tea and cups and vanished just as inaudibly as she had come in. "No," Saito said. "Lord Ashikaga needed someone who knew Kanayama's castle. That's why he sent me."

"That may be. But didn't Nakadai-san spend as much time there as you did? And yet you were chosen. Nakadai did not kill Lord Kanayama. Oh, don't look so surprised. The stories got here days ago. Lord Kanayama made a mistake, and it is a shame he had to die without face, but all the same, he was Osamu Kanayama. Ashikaga-sama sent over a dozen to kill him, yet you did it alone."

"I did it with Nakadai. And with regret." He sipped his tea. "Still, there is something to what you say."

Hisami bowed; better to thank her husband for being gracious enough to acknowledge her than to appear the insistent wife. "Our new master is very happy with you indeed. Why, he could have left us to rot as *rônin!* After all, that— Where is your sword?"

Saito's spine bristled tiny nails of ice. "What?"

"Your katana," she asked. "This one is different. The hilt and the handguard have foxes on them."

"Ah. Yes." His stomach twisted; a dull pain shot down into his testicles. Somehow he suppressed any change in his face or voice. "My katana was broken in the battle. I decided to leave it with the master's body when we put him on the pyre." Despite the nausea, the lie came smoothly enough. "It was an excellent blade. Even in dying, Kanayama exacts his price."

Hisami was silent for a pregnant moment, and Saito wondered whether his voice had been as even to her ears as it was to his. Finally she said, "Yes, that is a shame. It was a fine weapon, wasn't it?"

"I suppose this one will do. Lord Ashikaga gave it to me along with the rest."

"Hm. I hadn't heard that part of the story. Surely there is no shame in losing a blade to Kanayama, as good as he was. Strange to omit that part, *neh*? Hm."

Saito forced himself not to swallow. "You know how rumors are. By the time a story gets to the next village it is hardly recognizable. Surely the details were simply forgotten in the telling, somewhere along the way?"

"Yes, I suppose so. But have I seen those foxes before?"

The throbbing in his abdomen redoubled. This is what had worried him ever since he left the funeral pyre. Several years before, Lord Kanayama had visited Saito's home. It happened only once, just after he and Hisami were married. Saito and the lord sat together and Hisami poured tea. But it was the mark of a samurai to notice at all times the weapons carried by anyone nearby. A good wife had to have an eye for detail as well, in order to appropriately praise guests and to direct conversation when a lull or an unwelcome topic emerged. Hisami was both a good wife and a good samurai. She would surely have noticed the finely worked foxes resting at Kanayama's hip, and now everything depended on whether her memory had kept what her eye had caught. Saito cut off a curse and waited for the worst.

But today the gods were smiling on him. "I would swear I've seen them before," she said finally, "but I haven't got a clue where. Perhaps it was in another life. No matter. I suppose I've seen a thousand different swords coming through our village; why shouldn't this one look familiar, *neh?*"

Saito nodded, wanting to exhale all the stress in his chest but afraid to do it as long as she sat before him. "You can put these foxes out of your mind. Tomorrow I'm going to have the sword remounted with a new handguard. I think the crest of the house of Saito. Yes," he nodded, looking back at the foxes, "I think my father's crest would be excellent there."

"It certainly will. I'll send someone to the sword-smith immediately to make the arrangements."

•••

Hisami couldn't let her eyes rest on the new katana without rage welling up in her. How could those fools be so useless? Her husband had trekked across forty *ri* to get home, and over all that distance those ignorant, lowborn, misbegotten sons of peasants still didn't manage to take the time to tell her about the sword. Why on earth did she hire spies in the first place, if not to give her information? They told her about the money and the expanded fief; even the number of horses was correct. But the sword, a sword he would have ridden to the castle *without,* and which had been gifted to him before he ever received the horses. How could they have failed to notice it?

She was astonished that her husband remained as calm as he'd been, though for every minute their conversation lingered on the weapon he looked as if he were going to burst. He had a right to be upset; she should have had the alcove and sword stand already prepared before he ever entered the village. Now she was going to have to sneak a priest in here and have the alcove and stand blessed without Saito's noticing. No, she decided. Better yet, she would do it when he got the new crossguard fitted and tell him the blessing was for the sword now that it was truly his own. Yes, the family crest would be perfect for that. Certainly he would not be angry then.

In the meantime, she was going to have to set some of those newly-acquired *koku* aside for hiring more spies, and more competent ones at that. How was she to be a proper hostess if she didn't know who her unannounced guests would be well before they arrived? Drooling ill-bred mongrels! How she ever could have got by with such incompetents in her employ was beyond her understanding.

She was so mad at them, she almost forgot about her husband's tension. Riding usually took that out of him; he was so natural in the saddle. Today, though, he was decidedly on edge. Was it her failure with the sword stand? Somehow his unease didn't seem to be directed at her. Unless . . . yes, of course that was it. It was almost two weeks ago that he'd left, and before he departed she'd had her monthly bleeding and they hadn't been able to . . . yes, it was clear to her now. It had simply been too long for him.

An easy problem to solve, she thought, touching her hair. She'd fix it tonight.

•••

The singing of cicadas woke Saito from his sleep. A sheen of sweat cooled his chest as a breeze blew through the tiny gap in the sliding paper doors. Hisami lay next to him, naked, her skin lavender in the blue moonlight. She was still sound asleep, but then she could not hear the haunting sound.

Somehow the melody of the cicadas echoed the whistle of the Inazuma blade slicing through the air. It was as if the two sung in harmony, his memory of the sword's song a soprano to the alto of the chirping cicadas outside. He could not ignore their harmonizing. It seemed impossible, but as he recalled it, the sword's hum through the air was an uncanny match to the chirping in the garden. After a minute or two he found he could repress neither the cicadas' song nor the intrusion of his memories, so he got out of bed. His feet padded silently to the door. Sliding it aside, he stepped through to the next room and closed the door behind him. Hisami stirred slightly as the breeze swelled through the widened gap, but rolled back into her pillow as soon as he slid the door back home.

Beautiful Singer was sitting in the sword stand in the alcove. A moonbeam shone through one of the paper windows and cast a silky square of luminescence over the weapon. The song of the blade echoed in his mind. He walked over to the alcove and picked up the sword.

Its balance could not have been more perfect. Soundlessly he slid the sword from its ill-fitting sheath and spun it through the air. It was a thing of beauty. Inazuma truly was a master among masters; no other swordsmith could possibly duplicate the balance of lightness and strength Saito now held in his hand. Still naked, there was nowhere he could wear the scabbard, so he laid down the wooden case and reverently wrapped both hands around the sharkskin handle. Beautiful Singer floated in his grasp. He stepped forward and back with it in a ready stance, the Inazuma blade becoming one with him. A silent step off-line and he executed a mock parry and slash. The blade sang again as it fell, and indeed, somehow the cicadas were able to harmonize with it. It was as if Inazuma had taken the pulse of the heart of nature itself and crafted this sword with its rhythm. The gleam of the moon off the blade, the way it hummed in perfect harmony with the cicadas' song, the effect was unmistakable. Saito had never experienced a more perfect human creation in all his life.

Putting the sword back in that inferior scabbard would almost taint the weapon. Still, he could hardly leave its blade exposed in the sword stand. He glanced outside and saw the moon was still high in the sky. It would be hours before daybreak, hours before a new scabbard could be commissioned. Saito looked at the sheath on the floor indecisively. One of the horses stirred outside. Horses. Of course, he thought. Wasn't the city of Seki just half a day's ride away? And wasn't Seki home to the finest craftsmen in the country when it came to swords? The smiths, the polishers, the men who braided cords for the handles—Seki was home to all of them. The finest blades in the world were crafted in Seki, only six or seven hours from here. Saito picked up the scabbard and resheathed the katana. "I'm sorry," he whispered, "but for tonight the Beautiful Singer must wear a shoddy kimono." Then he dressed quietly and prepared for his ride.

•••

It was after noon when Hisami learned her husband was returning. A rider burst into the compound, enveloped in a cloud of dust from the road, and reported Saito was coming from the west and would arrive within the hour. She cursed the messenger for his lateness and ineptitude—a necessity, since thanking an informant would only make him lazy the next time—and sent another servant into town to fetch the swordsmith. She didn't have the first clue where her husband had been, nor why he slipped away in the middle of the night. The sword wasn't resting in the alcove when she awoke, but that meant nothing; a samurai was never without it. For a moment she was afraid she would find his body sprawled in the garden, slain by an assassin or a burglar last night. She knew it didn't make sense—why would anyone kill him and leave her alive?—but all the same she searched the grounds this morning and found no trace of him. Nor did she see any signs of a struggle, nor any evidence that a messenger from Lord Ashikaga had come to summon him. Though her network of servants and messengers stretched for twenty *ri* in every direction, not a single one of them could tell her of her husband's whereabouts. Several had heard a single horse galloping hard in the night, but none of the useless dung-eating cretins had identified the rider as Saito. Of course it was him, she thought. To think they did not even recognize their own lord! With the new wealth Lord Ashikaga had bestowed on the house of Saito she would hire night watchmen, instead of relying on imbecilic farmers and craftsmen to be her eyes and ears.

The only assumption she was left with was that Saito had gone to one of the pleasure houses. She could accept that, but it didn't explain why he'd been away so long. Perhaps last night didn't satisfy him. It pleased her well enough, but somehow he seemed distracted. It was only natural for a man to go to a pleasure house if his wife could not sate him, but why go to one so far from home? How was she supposed to settle the bill if she didn't know which brothel he went to?

She masked her frustration as well as she could when Saito finally rode up to the house. She could see the swordsmith coming down the road, shuffling in his deep blue robes, and she knew her husband would be happy to have his sword taken to be remounted. There was one problem, however: Saito wasn't wearing his sword.

"By all gods," Hisami exclaimed as he dismounted, "you gave me a fright. Where did you go last night?"

"What concern is it of a wife's where her husband

chooses to go?" His voice was gruff and she could see the sleeplessness under his eyes.

"I do not mean to pry. I was only worried—"

"Stop questioning me, woman! If you want to worry, worry about getting some tea and something to eat. I'm starving."

With an effort, she bottled her exasperation. Now she would have to find some excuse to send the sword-smith away. Getting him to come back again would be another feat; how could she explain that her samurai husband was without his sword? How could she explain to her husband that, to protect his honor, a respected artisan had to be curtly turned away? Before she could deal with any of that, however, she knew she had to dispel his anger. She sweetened her voice. "Of course. How thoughtless of me. Here, let me help you with your sandals. Haruko!" The name came from her mouth like the crack of a whip. Instantly a servant girl appeared. "Tea for the master! Can't you see he is exhausted from riding? And rice and fish! Can't you see he is hungry?"

•••

Hisami disappeared out the front door almost as quickly as the serving girl disappeared through the back, leaving Saito alone to wonder what had gotten into his wife. Usually she was properly obedient, but today she was salty. No, he corrected himself. Her tongue always carried an edge. That was one of the things that attracted him to her: she wasn't a meek little rabbit like so many other women. Still, there were times when such a tongue did not befit a woman, and it had already been a long day. The old saying held true: A samurai should only allow himself to be wedded to the sword.

It drove Saito mad to be without his Beautiful Singer. He always felt naked without a blade at his hip, and now that feeling was especially strong. The night ride to Seki was hard and very dangerous in the dark, but with his new weapon bouncing at his side he felt no fear. Naturally, he rode back in daylight, and though he was safe from the many dangers of riding by starlight, the trip home left him feeling far more vulnerable. In the dark, pushing a horse to its limit had its thrills: ducking the occasional low-hanging branch, wondering when or if his horse would falter, break a leg or throw him. Riding unarmed in broad daylight held no such excitement, only the ignominious possibility of being waylaid by bandits.

Saito shook his head and watched Haruko, the serving maid, quietly set tea before him on a lacquered tray. Wrinkles gnarled his cheeks as he pursed his lips in a self-reprobating frown. It was no band of highwaymen that left him feeling cold this morning. It was the sword, or rather the lack of it, and he knew it. Even without his katana, Saito wasn't completely unarmed. In his waistband he still wore his wakizashi, a short sword that no self-respecting samurai was ever without. As fine a sword as it was, a katana could break in battle. That was simple reality. A wakizashi was never to be used in combat except in the event that a warrior found himself without his primary weapon. The true purpose of the wakizashi was to be an ever-present reminder of the samurai's mortality. There were only two honorable ways for a true follower of *bushidô* to die: in battle or by his own hand in the act of seppuku. Both were the highest act of sacrifice in the service of one's lord. The wakizashi was the implement of seppuku, and since honor might demand a samurai's death at any time, he could never be without his short sword. No bandit could face Saito and his wakizashi and live. Saito knew that. Even though it was a shorter weapon, he was more than skilled enough to turn that disadvantage against an enemy. It was not the highway thieves that worried him on his ride back from Seki; it could only have been the sword.

What if something happened to it? The craftsmen of Seki were the best in the land, perhaps the best in the world, but still, none of them was on a level with the ancient master Inazuma. Would they show Beautiful Singer the respect she deserved? Saito grunted and sipped his tea. Of course they would. These were men who devoted their lives to the sword, just as Saito had, albeit in a different manner. They would have no choice but to honor her. How could anyone fail to recognize her beauty, her perfection?

And if they did fail? Saito wasn't sure how the question crept back into his thoughts. As he replaced the cup on its tray, a falcon keened outside. The cry swept over the house as the bird continued to circle and Saito heard a familiar note in it, the song of his Beautiful Singer. What if she were somehow damaged? The question was ineluctable, and with a moment's reflection he knew the answer: anyone who tarnished that sword would die.

It could be no other way. His response was only natural, he assured himself. Anybody who saw someone destroy a great work of art would be similarly moved. Could a person stand by and allow someone to tear the Tale of the Heike to shreds? Could one simply look on as a madman put the sculptures of Unkei to the torch? Never. None of the artisans at Seki would do any harm to his Beautiful Singer, but no one who damaged her could live.

Settled by his decision, Saito began eating his meal. A bowl of steaming rice and a small rectangular plate with slices of raw octopus were sitting on the table before him. Saito realized the serving girl had set them there without his noticing, and the realization shook him. Ordinarily it was impossible for someone to enter a room without him being immediately aware of how they stood, whether they were armed, what defenses

there were from where he was seated. That a mere
servant could walk in on him unawares was troubling
to say the least. "The ride," he said to himself, taking a
mouthful of rice from his chopsticks. It must have been
the ride that exhausted him so.

He nodded with satisfaction, and dipped a purple
and white slice of octopus in a shallow dish of soy
sauce and wasabi that Haruko had left him. Yes, it *was*
the ride. He'd been in the saddle for twelve of the past
fourteen hours, more than enough to wear on any man.
If it had been left to him, Saito would have stayed the
day in Seki, waited to retrieve his sword, and returned
home the following afternoon. But no samurai was his
own man. Saito was only an instrument of Lord
Ashikaga, and Ashikaga did not like his vassals
running about without his knowledge. Not even a
high-ranking samurai would leave his own village
without the lord's consent. Allowing one's warriors to
go where they pleased was the surest way to invite
insurrection and assassination. Saito was lucky that he
fell in the middle ranks among Ashikaga's legions,
high enough to wear the twin swords and topknot, but
low enough to escape scrutiny of his every move. Still,
it would not do for him to be absent from home should
the lord's messengers come to call. It would also be
imprudent to make another unauthorized voyage to
Seki; next time he would need permission.

The next time, he knew, would be soon. The
craftsmen he'd commissioned in Seki said if they
rushed, they could finish Saito's new handguard by
tomorrow. Saito knew they would have to keep their
forges burning day and night to do it; so much the
better, he thought. Weren't these tasks what the lower
castes were born for? The wooden scabbard he
requested would be ready by then as well, and wraps
for the handle and sheath were readily available. Very
well, he decided as he scooped the last of the rice into
his mouth. It would be tomorrow.

He sent for Haruko again and ordered her to tell the house's head messenger to prepare a carrier pigeon. Soon enough the messenger came to the porch and Saito dictated a request to make the trek to Seki. Satisfied, Saito went to the bath already prepared for him and drifted off to sleep.

• • •

The next morning a new pigeon was waiting in the coop of the Saito clan compound. A tiny cylinder of hollowed bone was tied to its leg, and the case found its way to Saito's breakfast table. He slid out the translucent scroll of paper from the little tube and read it silently.

Hisami's curiosity was obvious. "Lord Ashikaga sends word?"

"Yes," Saito replied. "He says the taxes are late in Iwatani. I am to go immediately to investigate." It was only a lie of omission. The tiny note did in fact say all of that. It also said that Saito's voyage to Seki was approved, but that in the future he would not be so vague in his requests of the lord. This last part was not stated directly, but rather by nuance. Not that Ashikaga himself had ever shied away from being blunt; quite the opposite, the man had no talent whatsoever as a diplomat. Subtlety was beyond him, perhaps even beneath him. But a pigeon could only bear so much weight in flight, and there was only so much room to write on such a tiny scroll. The note's actual text read, "Iwatani taxes late. Investigate and report. Seki approved; kill your pigeon keeper." Though unstated, the true message was clear. Saito's communiqué was deemed curt, presumptive and wholly improper for a vassal of his lowly status. He had committed an act of gross misjudgment in making his vacuous request to go to Seki without informing the lord of his purposes, but this time the lord would

choose to interpret this as the messenger's mistake.
Saito would have to find himself a new pigeon master,
a man of greater discretion. This essentially meant
Ashikaga would never grant Saito this sort of reprieve
again. One warning was more than the lord was wont
to give, and though the note made Saito's face redden,
he knew he was lucky.

Saito didn't bother to mention any of this to Hisami.
He barked to one of the house retainers to prepare his
horse. Hisami reached out and touched his hand. She
swallowed dryly before she spoke. "What's troubling
you?"

He grunted noncommittally. "Nothing. It's just that
Iwatani is so far from here. Our fief has expanded, but
it hardly stretches that far. This should be none of my
concern."

This was also a lie, but only partially. Iwatani was
his concern by way of sheer coincidence. The town lay
a mere thirty *ri* from Seki, on the periphery of Lord
Ashikaga's domain. Its nonstrategic location and small
population made it unworthy of a permanent garrison.
Thus if Saito rode to Seki, he would conveniently
become Ashikaga's closest samurai to the area. If Saito
hadn't sent his request, he wouldn't have been
dispatched to Iwatani. Saito wondered whether the
errand had been given as a minor form of punishment.

Again he chose not to voice any of this to his wife.
She would be suspicious enough of where he'd gone
the night before last, and all this time she'd been
holding her tongue about his sword. He knew she'd
noticed it was gone. She was samurai, after all. That she
hadn't made mention of its absence yet was only a
testament to her good sense. If she didn't ask, he
wouldn't have to answer, so he wouldn't have to lie,
and thus would not be caught in a lie. Her silence
preserved honor for both of them. Now if only he could
get out of the house and into his saddle before she
decided to say something.

"Don't worry so much," was her only advice. "The lord has already widened your fief, *neh*? Perhaps he has plans to extend it further. Perhaps he will grant you everything between here and Iwatani! That would be grand, wouldn't it?"

Saito smiled despite himself. "You are a good woman, Hisami. Buy yourself a new kimono while I'm gone."

She beamed. "Oh! Thank you! You're too good to me. Tell me when you'll be back so I can have it on for you when you return. And then I'll take it off for you, *neh*?"

He smiled again, but this time it was hollow. Somehow the thought of lying with her made his stomach turn. He was anxious to get on the road and return his Beautiful Singer to his side. "Yes. When I return."

"When will that be?"

He made some quick calculations in his head and said, "Tomorrow." On a map, Iwatani was farther than Seki, but the road to Seki followed the wide curves of a valley, making that journey the longer one. Getting from Seki to Iwatani involved backtracking along that valley, and he knew he couldn't retrieve his sword and finish his business in a single day. "There may be a great deal to settle in Iwatani," he said, stretching the truth again. "I can't promise I'll make it home tonight."

She nodded, smiled and helped him prepare for his journey. Saito only took a moment to locate the man in charge of his pigeon coops and tell him to start looking for his own replacement. Then he went back to readying himself for the journey to Iwatani. He packed only what he would require for the road, leaving behind everything he knew he might need should he be delayed in Seki and be forced to camp between there and Iwatani. A man only carried a bedroll if he planned to sleep on it, and as far as Hisami was concerned, Saito would spend tonight at home or at an Iwatani inn. Even as he chose to leave the bedroll stored where it was, he wondered why he was deceiving Hisami yet again this morning. In the seven years they had been married, he couldn't recall one instance of lying to her before yesterday.

●●●

"It is an exceptional blade, my lord," the swordsmith stammered. He wore the white robes of a Shintô priest, a black cap atop his head. All the smiths of Seki were priests as well, and their swords were fashioned with religious ritualism. It was their reverence and dedication that made them the best. "I have never seen the like."

"No, you have not." Saito expected relief to wash over him upon seeing his Beautiful Singer again, but instead his heart plunged into his bowels. The priest's nervous tone was enough to sicken him, and over the white-robed shoulder he saw his beloved sword lying stripped on the tatami mat behind the priest. The handle was removed from the weapon and the blade lay naked on a silk cloth. "What have you done to it?" he demanded.

The priest-smith's eyebrows raised momentarily at the accusation. "N-Nothing. The katana is fine; we simply have not remounted the handle yet."

"Why not?"

"The, um," the swordsmith faltered, "the inscription. You have seen it?"

"No, though you are an insolent one for asking." The smith may have been an ordained priest, but he still ranked below one of samurai lineage. "I know what it says. It is an Inazuma."

"More than Inazuma, Lord. It is the Beautiful Singer."

Saito's brow gnarled. "And?"

The priest-smith's eyebrows jumped again. "I dare not offend you, but it is best that you know: the blade is cursed."

"Is said to be cursed," Saito corrected him.

"But the legend—"

"Is nothing but a legend. I've faced scores of men on the battlefield; do you expect me to be afraid of mere words?"

The elderly priest swallowed. "Begging my lord's forgiveness, 'mere' is not a word I would use in connection with this blade."

"Quite to the point; it is anything but ordinary. I assume the work you have done for me is equally exceptional?"

The priest knew he had already overstepped his bounds and hastily turned to pick up the new hand-guard. "I sincerely hope it pleases you."

Saito took the metal disc in his hand. It was black-lacquered steel, with the Saito family crest gilded in the center. The crest was a double-diamond motif, one layered atop the other. A hole the shape of an elongated teardrop was cut to allow the katana's blade to be inserted right through the center of the diamonds. The double diamonds gleamed in gold against the black, and Saito inevitably thought of his deceased father. The Saito clan had long been samurai, but it was Saito's father who rode into battle under the flag of those diamonds and made them worthy of Ashikaga's notice. The house of Saito had been a minor one until then, but his father's victories pushed the family's star high into the sky, making Saito proud to bear his name. Saito hoped he could accomplish as much himself one day.

Next the priest offered Saito the new scabbard, while two other acolyte-smiths carefully fitted the Inazuma blade with its new handle and crossguard. The scabbard was oak, lacquered to a flawless black sheen with the Saito crest once again in gold leaf. The craftsmanship was unsurpassable, the final product a masterpiece, but Saito paid it no mind. His eyes glossed over the scabbard, but his thoughts remained locked on the sword itself. When the swordsmiths finally bowed and presented it to him, it was all he could do not to snatch it out of their hands and to thank them instead.

Once it was back in his grasp, he felt like a whole man again. Abruptly he realized his earlier haste and tried to cover it. "You have done well," he said, sheathing the sword. He bowed to the three smiths and they to him; then he was off to Iwatani.

●●●

The sight of a samurai on horseback was more than enough to terrify the average farmer. In the saddle, any warrior was fearsome—a thousand pounds of galloping muscle was threatening enough—but when that warrior wore the topknot of a samurai, his riding inspired fear and reverence in any commoner. So it was that Saito entered the village of Iwatani. Roads cleared for him and crowds hushed as he passed. By the time he reached the town square, all eyes were fixed on him.

"Who is your headman?" he bellowed.

A reed of a man scampered out from the encircling crowd and fell to his knees, dust rising around him. "I am, Lord." The village headman was old, nearing sixty, and one could see almost every bone and tendon in his body. Few commoners were overweight, but this man looked as if the skin had been pulled tight against his frame by some goblin sitting inside his chest. He was browned by long hours in the rice paddies and wore no more than a loincloth and straw sandals.

Saito looked down at the top of the man's head. "Your name?"

"You may call me Ojiya if it pleases you, Lord."

Saito urged his horse to retreat a few steps, then dismounted. "Rise, Ojiya. Look at me."

The frail little man obeyed. He met Saito's gaze with awe, as if staring at the very face of Buddha himself. Then, with the same reverence, he dropped his eyes again to Saito's chin. "My lord?"

"Taxes," Saito said, seeming to project his height over the man into his voice. It was no wonder the villagers were struck by him. A samurai ate fish and vegetables with every meal; these people were lucky to get more than a bowlful of rice gruel a day. They were also lucky to be drawing breath, Saito reminded himself. Without Ashikaga's protection, bandits or other warlords would steal even their gruel from them. That protection demanded a price. "Taxes," he intoned again.

"We have paid ten *koku*, my lord."

"The tax is forty."

Ojiya bowed again, trembling with nervousness. "My lord, we have paid what we can. You can see for yourself we have no more."

Saito's eyes roamed the surroundings. "I see perhaps a hundred of you standing here. Why are these people not in the fields?"

"My lord, it has not rained in twenty days. Lord Ashikaga must understand—"

"Lord Ashikaga understands what he wishes to understand; you are in no position to tell him what he *must* do." Saito's tone earned him a new fit of bowing, heads all around the square bobbing with renewed vigor. "Now then," he said after Ojiya returned to his feet, "you will tell me when the remaining thirty *koku* will be paid."

"Lord, we cannot—"

"You must have something stashed away. How else do all these people get food? I can see for myself they aren't farming it themselves."

"But the rain . . ."

"Rain does not concern me," Saito barked. "Lord Ashikaga protects you even through typhoons and earthquakes! If the elements cannot stop him, why should you allow them to stop you?"

Ojiya trembled where he stood. Those around the two could not pull themselves away. "My lord, if we pay even a bowlful of rice more, some of us will starve."

"I did not come for one bowlful. I came for thirty *koku*."

"We cannot do it," the headman stuttered. "Lord Ashikaga asks the impossible."

"The impossible?" Saito bellowed. "Do you call the lord an imbecile?"

"No!" Ojiya protested. "No, not at all!"

"But everyone knows the impossible cannot be done."

"Yes, but—"

"So only a true imbecile would demand something no one could possibly satisfy?"

"My lord, I only—"

"Then choose your crime, Headman! Have you called the lord a fool, or have you slandered him by telling me of an order he never gave?"

"My lord—"

It was too late. The Inazuma blade hung in the sky just long enough to catch the gleam of the sun, then fell like a diving hawk. The old man's head bounced next to his feet. A long moment later, his body dropped next to it.

Saito whirled the sword in a fast silvery arc that whipped most of the gore from the blade. Bringing it back around, he cleaned the remaining blood between his thumb and forefinger and resheathed the blade without ever looking down to find the scabbard.

"Now then," he said grimly to the crowd. "Who is your headman after Ojiya?"

•••

That night Saito lowered himself into a steaming cauldron of water, the bath heated by a volcanic vent. Minerals from deep in the earth scented the spring with flavors of copper and jasmine. Hot water turned his skin red and fragrant steam misted on the mirrored edge of Beautiful Singer. The steam would permeate the wood of her scabbard and warp it, so he brought her here naked, like himself. How beautiful she was, he thought. Even now she hummed to him.

How enchanting her voice was, never louder than when she sang through the headman's neck on the town square. It was as perfect a cut as Saito had ever delivered. Ordinarily an *iaidô* sword was not used to behead; such a thin blade was likely to lose its edge on hard bone. Better to slice the front half of the throat, cutting only the soft tissues. That was how Saito had intended to take Ojiya, but at the last moment some impulse made him extend his strike a hand's breadth further. It was almost as if Beautiful Singer wanted to prove herself to him—or perhaps he wanted to prove himself to her. In either case, they were a worthy pair. His draw was flawless, his cut precise, and the Inazuma blade severed the spinal cord without so much as a nick.

He could still feel her song, resonating through his hand as he tilted her steel to catch the dim light. He let his shoulders relax against the stone rim of the bath and sunk deeper into the water. The relaxation was well-deserved; he'd made a fine showing today. After Ojiya's execution, the villagers were prompt to produce a large golden Buddha worth almost a *koku* by itself. They promised another nine *koku* by the end of the harvest, thereby doubling the tax they'd already

paid. Saito said he would accept the statue and would
take their offer before the lord to determine their fate.
Every last one of them scattered afterward, save the
owner of the inn in which Saito now bathed. The
innkeeper was so anxious to avoid the samurai's wrath
that he charged nothing for the room and proffered a
meal such as no one in this village had seen in years. A
heavy meal and a hot bath normally made a man tired,
but Saito was feeling energized now that Beautiful
Singer was back at his side. His mind was on the
future, on the arrangements he would complete here
tomorrow, on what would come to pass after that.
Success here might warrant further rewards from Lord
Ashikaga. He decided not to go home and report to the
lord by messenger or pigeon. He would ride to the
castle himself.

•••

"Fool!" barked Ashikaga. "You killed him for that?"

"Of course," Saito said defensively. "He insulted
you."

"He did nothing of the kind. Of course I ask the
impossible! Ask these lazy peasants for three *koku* and
the most you can possibly hope for is one. But if I want
one *koku* and that is all I demand, I will never see half
of it. They never do the least bit of work unless you ask
the impossible. Making them strive hopelessly is the
only way to meet the least of your expectations."

Saito's face reddened under the barrage of
Ashikaga's words. He bowed his head, not out of defer-
ence but to hide his shame and rage. "My lord," he
stammered with all the control he could muster, "I—"

"Silence. You only harm yourself by speaking." It
was all Saito could do to stay in place on the floor.
Never before had he wished he were armed in the presence of his master. Now he yearned to hear the all too
familiar song ringing in this chamber.

"Look up," Ashikaga's bear-voice said. Saito swallowed his anger and looked the old warlord in the eye. "I am too harsh with you," Ashikaga rumbled. "You are no politician; it is not your place to understand such things as taxes."

Saito was astonished. An apology from Ashikaga was unheard of. Still, in this case, Saito thought, it was certainly warranted. "You did well in bringing this statue to me," Ashikaga went on. "As for the nine *koku*, I doubt they will produce more than two. Even then, I hope it does not kill too many of them to give it up. Dead farmers pay no taxes."

"No, Ashikaga-sama," Saito muttered, bristling at the insult, "they do not."

"I must educate my samurai better in the ways of politics. Or else I must send better-educated men to perform my errands."

This too made Saito grit his teeth. He said nothing in response. "I can see you wish to take your leave," the lord's gravelly voice intoned. "You are dismissed."

Saito bowed low, then stalked out of the room. Only when the door slid shut behind him did he release a growl of frustration. The audacity of that man! A samurai's existence was truly thankless, Saito thought. Even in apology, the lord found room to ridicule. He stormed down the stairs and into the weapon steward's chamber, where Beautiful Singer awaited him on a rack against the far wall. Six other katana were racked above her.

"Which one is yours, sir?" asked the sword steward, a boy of about twenty.

"Only the finest weapon in this room. How dare you place it below those others?"

The steward started at Saito's tone and dashed to retrieve his sword. "My apologies, sir, and please pardon me for not recognizing it as yours. It is a different blade from the one you last left with me, is it not?"

"Certainly not," Saito snapped, his hands hungry to hold her again. "And for one who does nothing but handle swords all day, you should remember quality of this caliber by feel alone!"

He snatched back the sword like a wild dog tearing meat.

"My apologies again," the steward faltered. "I only meant that the scabbard and the handguard, they are new, are they not? And quite beautiful if I may say so."

Saito's hackles rose. "New scabbard?" *Why should this boy notice something like that? He thinks I have something to hide,* Saito thought. *A new sheath means a new sword, and that means he knows about Beautiful Singer.* "Insolent cur! What makes you think I have something to hide?"

The steward's eyes went wide with bewilderment. "You wouldn't, sir! By all gods and buddhas, I never thought anything like that!"

Saito lunged into the room, kicking the table aside and sending the steward back on his heels. The boy tripped backward, tumbled to the ground, his head striking the sword rack.

"Do you dare to draw a weapon on me, boy?"

"No!"

"Then why move for the swords?" Saito took another menacing step forward and the steward scrambled from the room on all fours. He regained his footing and dashed for the hall, stumbled, landed face-first against the wall outside. He turned in terror as his aggressor emerged from the room. Saito wrapped his fingers around the Inazuma handle; he could already hear her song in the air.

"Stop!"

The command rumbled like thunder. Saito's eyes shot up the stairs and saw Ashikaga towering there livid. His scars and his glare were more fearsome than his sword, though that too now hung at his hip. "Explain yourself, Saito!"

"This boy insulted me," he said angrily. "He insulted me and my sword. I would reclaim my honor."

"Swords do not feel insults," the lord glowered, "and since you are my sword, neither should you."

"My lord, his impudence—"

"Stands. At my pleasure. He is a trusted man, and there are not many so trustworthy as to guard the weapons at my very door. Takagi!"

Takagi, the steward, was stunned to speechlessness, but he acknowledged his master's summons with a hasty bow. "Apologize to this man," Ashikaga growled, "for any offense you have paid him."

It took a moment for Takagi's tongue to function. "Ap-Apologies, sir. A thousand apologies."

"There," the old warlord said. "Does that satisfy your honor?"

It was not a question. "It will have to," Saito replied, his voice hollow. In equally hollow words he added, "A thousand apologies to you as well, Ashikaga-san, for the disturbance."

•••

At last these spies are doing me some good, Hisami told herself. Her new hires were working out better than anticipated. Of course she knew her husband was at Lord Ashikaga's stronghold; even the most incompetent of her informants could have told her that. What was new came from Seki. One of the informers she had just put on salary hailed from that region, and he was able to tell his mistress where her husband had gone on last week's midnight ride. What business the lord had in Seki, he couldn't say, but Hisami realized immediately what his only purpose there could be. He left with his sword and came back without it; he could only have paid a visit to the swordsmiths.

But why go in the dead of night? And why ride there and back at such a furious pace? Hisami was puzzled. Surely Lord Ashikaga would not have taken offense to such a simple errand had Saito only made the request. Strange indeed, she thought. What on earth could have been so urgent in Seki? There was only one way to find out. She called a stablehand to prepare her favorite horse. When she told him to pack her things for an overnight stay, the servant shot her a conspiratorial look; it was untoward behavior for a woman to leave the house without her husband, and downright scandalous for her to sleep elsewhere. No matter, she thought. Saito need not learn of it. It was one day's leisurely ride to Seki and a hard two days' ride to Ashikaga's castle. Even if her husband still had a mind to ride his horse into the ground, she should still be able to beat him home.

She pushed her steed harder than usual nonetheless, in order to reach Seki before sundown. Mountain roads were more dangerous for a lone woman than they were for a man, and while she knew she could handle any brigands foolish enough to cross a samurai's path, it was pointless to invite trouble.

The sun was just dipping below the treetops when her horse trotted through Seki's main gate. She presumed the priests would have left their forges by now, so she paid for a room at the inn and had a dinner there of tofu and abalone. The next morning, she set out to find a swordsmith.

"I am Hisami Saito," she told the black-robed youth who answered the door at the foundry. "I wish to speak to the man who met my husband."

The acolyte ran off and soon returned, accompanied by an old bald man wearing white robes and a black hat. "Saito-sama," the priest said nervously. "Please come in."

"Don't be afraid," she said, following him to a sitting room. "I do not come to express dissatisfaction with your work."

"Understood, madam, but I fear what you have come to talk about is far worse."

"Oh?" The two of them sat and the boy disappeared. The air was thick with the smell of steel and smoke and noticeably hotter than it should have been. The priest was sweating, though Hisami could not tell whether it was from nervousness or the heat from the forges.

"You are the wife of the Saito who came to have his handguard and scabbard replaced?"

"Yes."

"Then you know your husband carries an Inazuma blade."

"Hardly! He could never afford—" She stopped herself in midthought. Inazuma's works were priceless; not even by selling the entire Saito fief could she acquire one. Indeed, she'd only ever seen one in her life, and that one belonged to . . . Osamu Kanayama. Memory instantly resurfaced in her mind. The twin foxes! That was Kanayama's symbol and now it was on her husband's weapon. That was why he came here so quickly: to have the lord's crest removed before she could remember where she'd seen it. The shame of it was unbearable; her husband was a thief. There could be no other explanation. Kanayama could have bequeathed the blade to Saito before his death, but that would have been a thing of honor, not something to ride off in the dead of night to conceal.

"Thank you," she told the swordsmith-priest uneasily. "I believe I understand the situation now."

"I'm afraid you do not," he cautioned. "Whether or not the sword is your husband's, you must know the truth of it. It is cursed."

"Cursed? Rubbish!"

"It is true, my lady. Master Inazuma crafted that sword specially for Motoyori Hidetada, the famous warlord of Echizen. Motoyori was renowned for his swordsmanship and also for his passions. He never married, but he was known to have regular beds in pleasure houses throughout the north. One of his courtesans was a geisha whose beauty was said to be unmatched. Her voice was also without equal, and it is said she used to sing him to sleep.

"The story goes that this geisha fell in love with Motoyori and wanted to marry him. Of course a samurai of his station could never marry a woman of her profession, so instead she begged him to give up all other women but her."

"And did he?"

"A man cannot deny any request from such a beautiful woman. He said he would be hers alone, but as I said, he was a man of great passions. Inevitably he became unfaithful to her, and when she learned of it she tried to kill him. No mere geisha could best a swordsman of his caliber, of course, but she caught him unawares. Ordinarily he would have tried to restrain her, but he reacted unthinkingly to her surprise attack and killed her.

"Motoyori was so distraught by her death that he brought the blade that killed her back to Master Inazuma. He composed a death poem for his love, such as befits the passing of a samurai, not a lowly prostitute. Inazuma inscribed the poem on the tang of the blade. I have seen it myself:

> *Glorious sun,*
> *coming to its zenith,*
> *shaded by a hand.*

She was the sun, you see, glorious in her beauty and becoming ever more so until his hand put out her light. The sword became known as the Beautiful Singer thereafter."

Hisami's forehead furrowed. "A sad story to be sure, but hardly a curse."

"Motoyori only shaded the sun; he did not extinguish it forever. It is said her spirit followed the weapon, and when her death poem was inscribed, she entered the blade as well. Since his passions betrayed her, she would make them become his downfall as well. The sword performed better than ever after her death, a fact only to be explained by her spirit's strength guiding it. It is said to be lighter and faster than any other blade, and truly, madam, it is so. My own hands have held it. But her will exerts itself from within the sword. She drove Motoyori mad with rage and jealousy until finally he could no longer control himself. The urges within him took over and he died senselessly in a duel. He drunkenly accused another man of sleeping with one of his favorite prostitutes and was cut down in the street, too blind with jealousy for his sword to find its mark."

Hisami let out a long breath. It was evident in the priest's manner that he earnestly believed every word of his tale to be true. Indeed, he was so serious that Hisami was almost willing to believe him. She shook her head and better sense took over. "What does this have to do with my husband? He never knew this woman; she would have died hundreds of years ago."

"The sword remains possessed to this day, madam. All who have owned it have died. Some men fall quickly to its spell, others last longer, but every man succumbs. If I may ask, my lady, is your husband a passionate man or a temperate one?"

"Every samurai controls his emotions when needed," she said plainly. "Still," she mused, "in certain company he can be quick to laugh . . . and quick to anger."

"Then I fear the Beautiful Singer will make short work of him. You must get the sword from him and have her spirit exorcised."

"How am I supposed to do that? The sword's scarcely left his side since he brought it home."

"All the more evidence that it is still possessed, my lady."

The priest had a point, she thought. Why else would a man leave his bed, his wife, in the middle of the night for the sake of a sword? "Why didn't you exorcise it when you had it here?"

"We had no time," the smith-priest pleaded earnestly. "It was all we could do just to complete the work he'd commissioned in the time he allowed. We only knew the name of the sword when we removed the handle, and by that time he was already on his way here to retrieve it."

"And you told him what you told me?"

"Only that it was cursed, madam. He refused to listen to anything else."

Hisami considered the priest's tale. Possession? She thought only farmers scared each other with legends like that. Still, the story went a long way to explain her husband's behavior. He had always been "passionate," to use the priest's term, but never impulsive. Rashness was not a good quality in a samurai. The last five days were different, though. Riding off like that, then returning in a huff, leaving again the next morning—it wasn't normal.

Her mind turned to the late Lord Kanayama. That one was like a stone. Emotionally stoic, unflappable even in the midst of combat. Hisami never met him more than briefly, but in all her contacts with him she had never seen him laugh, never a frown or a grin. Yet he was wild as a tiger when he died. Could the sword have turned him? And if so, how much more quickly would it bewitch her husband?

She thanked the priest and took her leave. She would have to hurry now. Nothing about her husband was predictable anymore, and the consequences would be deadly if she were not home when he returned.

•••

Saito's mare galloped through the gate, dust billowing in her wake. She was breathing heavily, lungs pumping like bellows, and Saito was panting too. He'd ridden her hard, the wind from the ride cooling his sweaty brow. It was good to ride a horse like that from time to time. It spoke to the condition of the animal and also made it clear who the master was. He felt the need to assert his mastery this evening. Swinging off the saddle, he handed the reins to his stablehand and gave the horse a pat on her flank. On his way out he patted his wife's favorite horse as well, feeling energized from the ride. As he wiped the coarse brown hairs from his palm, his mood suddenly soured.

Hisami, dressed in gold and black, bowed deferentially as he slid open the door. "Welcome back," she said sweetly. "Allow me to take your sandals and put up your sword. I'll have the maid bring some tea."

"No."

"No tea?" she asked, proffering her hands for the sword.

"No," he said again, walking past her and taking his customary seat.

Hisami eyed the sword nervously. "Is something wrong?"

"No. Don't get so upset."

"Shouldn't a wife be upset when her husband goes armed in the house?"

"A wife should not be meddlesome," he grunted angrily. "Nor should she go out without her husband's permission."

She arched an eyebrow. "Go out?"

"Your horse is drinking deeply outside. It sweats."

"It is a hot day." She swallowed.

"No," he snapped. "It's been riding. Hard. Where did you go?"

Hisami struggled not to blush. "I did go riding earlier," she admitted hesitantly, "but only on business. To see that all our family affairs are in order." Her eyes fell to his weapon again.

"Meaning what?" he demanded.

"Meaning only that your behavior has been somewhat irregular for the past few days. I wanted to ensure that everything was well with you."

"I don't need a doctor," he grumbled.

"No, you don't."

His eyebrows knotted in a suspicious glare. "What do you mean, then?"

She blinked quickly and padded over to her cushion, across from his. "You know," she said, sitting, "I was thinking we still haven't had a priest come to have the house blessed. Why don't I summon one? Then we can have your father's emblem anointed as well, to bless your newly adorned sword."

"Again with the sword! Why can't you just let me be?"

"I'm not talking about the sword," she protested with a mask of false innocence. "A house-blessing is only natural. . . ."

"No priests! Our house is blessed enough."

His eyes transfixed hers with a murderous glare. "I went to Seki," she blurted out. "I know about your Beautiful Singer. And its curse."

"Nonsense!"

"It isn't nonsense. It's what killed Lord Kanayama. It's what brought you into ill favor with Lord Ashikaga as well."

"Meddlesome wench! You and your damned spies!"

Saito's face was red with fury. "It is a wife's duty to know the affairs of the house," Hisami retorted.

"It is also her duty not to let her ears stray in places they should not go!"

"Please," she implored, "let me summon a priest."

He jumped to his feet. "Never! This idiotic superstition is trying my patience. I won't hear another word of it."

"Then you won't hear another word from me."

Saito grunted, thinking the matter settled. It took another moment for her implication to set in. "What do you mean?"

Hisami worked up the courage to rise to her feet. "I cannot stay under the same roof as the spirit of that woman. It is obvious to me now that you are bewitched. Allow me to summon a priest for an exorcism or allow me to leave."

"What?!" The muscles in his arms tensed as if he were about to strike her. "This is ridiculous! Have you become some peasant now? What you speak of is pure fairy tale!"

"Then why does my husband scream and threaten me, armed, in his own house?"

"I scream because you've lost your mind!"

"Someone in this room has," she swore bitterly, her voice losing its implacable calm for the first time. "Let us find out who! Choose! Choose one of us, me or your spirit-whore, and let your choice speak for your sanity!"

Hisami's voice was an eagle's, piercing. Saito didn't hear it; his ears were filled with an all too familiar tune. The keening note sprang from his hip and trailed a silver arc through the air. The Beautiful Singer whirled and returned to its scabbard. Then the first drops of Hisami's blood hit the ground.

Pale, she raised a finger to her throat. Her trachea hung open, a crimson river flooding over her breast and dyeing her silken robes. It was a perfect cut, as long as a finger and half as deep. Her hand rose higher; she stumbled forward. Saito took a step back and watched her draw a hidden blade from her hairpin. She looked up at him, already dead on her feet, and made a final lunge. Then she fell to the floor.

Saito touched his cheek. Surprised, he rubbed blood between his fingertips. It was only a scratch, fine as a hair. A slash of red traced below his eye, as finely as an artist could paint one. A lake of the same red pooled on the floor. Saito looked down at his dead wife, at the spattered red flecks on her beautiful white cheek. Then he drew Beautiful Singer from her sheath and made sure she was clean of stains.

• • •

Saito fell to his knees under Lord Ashikaga's withering glare. He was ordered to Ashikaga's chambers the moment the news of Hisami's death reached the castle. Saito had never seen that gruesome face so angry. Rage flushed the skin, but the scars remained white, adorning the lord's scowl with strokes of war paint. "Explain yourself!" he roared.

"My lord, she stepped out of line...."

"No! You're the one who is out of line! How dare you kill one of my own without my permission?"

"She was only a woman."

"She was samurai!" Fury swelled in Ashikaga's face, even his scars turning red.

"But Lord, she was my wife. It is my prerogative to—"

"She was *my* samurai! And you dare speak to me of your prerogative?" Ashikaga rose to his feet, dark as a thundercloud. "You cut down one of my samurai without so much as consulting me? Without considering my honor? She questioned you on a matter that should well have been questioned, and you killed her for it. In this, she was more loyal than you."

"But Lord—!"

"Enough! You will commit seppuku, tomorrow at dawn. Get your affairs together and choose your second."

Ashikaga stormed off the dais and out of the room, the echoes of his words still vibrating in the air. The silence that followed was heavier still, leaving Saito alone in the emptiness to contemplate his fate.

•••

The first ray of morning crested the tree line and limned the paper walls with rose. The gathering was set. Ashikaga sat on a broad cushion, twenty armed samurai attending him. A platform lay before them, upon it a miniature table bearing a dagger folded in a sheet of paper. Minoru Nakadai stood on the left side of the stage, near the door. Outside the door, Saito was held firmly by the wrists, a pair of samurai watching over him. He was dressed head to toe in white, the color of death.

Beautiful Singer lay in the grasp of one of his guards. They would not let him touch her, lest he kill himself prematurely on her edge. He spent the previous night in a cell, denied any means whatsoever to bring about his death. The lord wanted him to die only on his orders.

Lying on the dark floor of his prison, Saito had a long time to contemplate his final two wishes. The first was for vengeance. Someone had betrayed him. It was not clear who at first, but after long consideration he concluded it could only have been Nakadai. Only Nakadai could have told Hisami of the Inazuma blade. He was obsessed with the curse. Nakadai could have seen his master's katana on Saito's hip and secretly reported it to Hisami. Saito underestimated him; he never would have thought the fat man could be so observant, so traitorous, so bold.

Yet Nakadai was the obvious choice to be Saito's second. In seppuku, the second was responsible for beheading the condemned after his self-disembowelment. For a samurai to die with honor, his second must also conduct himself with honor, and so it was a position of the greatest trust. Hisami herself could have been his second, were she still alive. Without her, it would either be Nakadai or Ashikaga's official executioner. The executioner was generally reserved for common criminals, not samurai, and up until Nakadai's treachery, the two of them had been lifelong friends. Besides, by choosing Nakadai, at least Saito could vocalize his hatred, even if he could not act on it.

Revenge being unrealizable, Saito's second dying wish was to hear Beautiful Singer's song one last time. Lamentably, that too would be impossible. The guard whose hands now sullied her sheath was under the strictest orders not to hand over the sword until Saito was kneeling before the sacrificial knife. It was customary for a samurai to die with his weapons, but many a man tried to hack his way out of a death sentence, and it seemed Ashikaga feared Saito would do the same. That Saito suffered the dishonor of being suspected of such cowardice would also please the lord. Saito wondered why he had become the object of such contempt. He also wondered whether, with Beautiful Singer in his hands, he could cut deep enough through the surrounding warriors to make a bid at Ashikaga's own neck. Perhaps that was why he was denied his sword. The possibility that Ashikaga feared him made Saito smile.

But such dreams were not to be. He would be without his weapon until he was seated with the knife in front of him and with Nakadai behind, ready to behead him once he committed the ultimate act of sacrifice. He would die with Beautiful Singer resting asleep in her scabbard, and he would never hear her enchanting voice again.

Saito smiled, and smiled triumphantly because suddenly he knew how to realize both of his wishes at once. When the door slid open in front of him, he felt no fear. When his guards shoved him forward, he walked confidently to the place where he would die. He saw Nakadai on the dais, his narrow eyes sorrowful. Saito bowed to him proudly and knelt before the knife.

"A request," he said serenely as he took his place. Nakadai stepped forward, his condemned friend's voice too low to understand. "Would you do me the honor," Saito asked, "of carrying out your duty with my sword?"

Nakadai looked down at the katana and Saito saw he did not recognize it. Then the big man looked up at Ashikaga and repeated Saito's last wish. The lord considered the request, conceded it with a gruff nod of the head. Saito took the sword by the sheath from one of his guards and carefully set it at his right side, where it could not easily be drawn. Still Nakadai approached it cautiously. The other samurai tensed, all of them expecting trickery. Saito watched as Nakadai crouched behind him, grasped the scabbard and lifted the sword. An *iaidô* master could have drawn and cut even with his sword in another man's hands, but Saito remained still. He closed his eyes and offered a prayer to Buddha.

Ashikaga nodded again, and with this permission, Saito took up the knife and ritualistically cleaned it with the paper. He stripped the white robes from his shoulders, baring himself to the waist. Then, with great resolve and immeasurable self-control, he picked up the blade and thrust it into his abdomen.

Sensation vanished in a wash of pain that left him in an icy shock. The room went white. His body was numb as the knife bit into him and then across. The last thing he heard was an ethereal song in the air, just before his head separated from his neck. His last thought was that his were not the only ears that heard it.

GOSSAMER

Written by
Ken Liu

Illustrated by
Nina Ollikainen

About the Author

Ken Liu was born in Lanzhou, a city at the bend in the Yellow River in north-western China. As a child he was obsessed with the literature of the fantastic. Besides the sixteenth-century fantasy, *Journey to the West*, and volumes of escapist and utopian essays by classical Daoist scholars, he devoured translations of H.G. Wells and novelizations of Hollywood science fiction epics.

Ken came to the United States at the age of eleven with this strong preference for reading science fiction and scribbling out story ideas on his computer. He opted to take creative writing in college. After three years as a programmer at a high-tech startup in Massachusetts, Ken is now enrolled as a law student and lives in Somerville, Massachusetts. He nevertheless dreams of someday making a living by writing fiction.

've never read a line of poetry that's beautiful," Peter said to me once, before I left him.

Laura thought he said it just to hurt me, which probably was true. Peter was like that. He never backed down in a fight and he gave no quarter. It was why I loved him.

I'm thinking back to the time, years ago, when Peter first stopped me in front of the library. "I disagree with you."

"That's okay," I said.

"There is an absolute standard for beauty. If you weren't so afraid of offending people you'd see it too."

I gave Laura a look. *Weirdo from another planet.*

She looked back (this was before she became blind). *He likes you.*

"Come with me to the Haidian exhibit, Emily," he said. "I'll show you why you are wrong."

We never got to the Haidian exhibit. That was the day the Gossamers landed.

•••

The piece I'm supposed to review is called "Momentum." The attendant, a young man from the city college, lets me in. It's February in San Jose, seventy degrees Fahrenheit.

I'm inside an old warehouse, the sort of place first

occupied by the garment sweatshops, then by the hardware sweatshops, then by the software sweatshops, and then acquired by the city college when the high-tech fever died. The air conditioning is very good; you can barely hear it.

There's nothing on the concrete floor or the wooden walls. In the middle of the warehouse they've built a square enclosure the size of an office cubicle with cinder blocks. It's dim because all the sunlight comes in from three windows along the side of the building.

The young man takes me around the enclosure, and now I see that the wall on the opposite side is made of glass. He hands me a flashlight and indicates that I should turn it on.

I move the bright circle of light around the darkness enclosed within. There are hundreds of Canadian geese inside the enclosure, their feet glued to the floor with epoxy. When the light moves over them they flap their wings desperately and stretch out their necks, trying to lift off with the floor attached to their feet. It's a confusing boiling sea of feathers and muscle strained beyond hope of recovery. I think the noise must be intolerable, but I don't hear anything; the insulation is very good.

I turn off the flashlight in a hurry. I imagine the geese will still flap their wings and stretch their necks uselessly for a few more minutes before the dim light will soothe them into quieter, slower pain.

"Good momentum, isn't it?" says the young man.

• • •

When I got up, Laura had already made breakfast. The kitchen was filled with smoke. Laura was a chainsmoker, which was beyond just unhealthy since she was a dancer. First thing she did in the morning before even opening her eyes was to paw the mess on her nightstand until she found her cigarettes. She pulled hard on her cigarettes, like a condemned woman. She said that was what she felt like, condemned to lung cancer and carbon monoxide poisoning. We had a hard time finding an apartment that would let her smoke. Except for San Francisco, the whole state had been declared smoke-free for years.

She handed me the paper. "Extraterrestrials Sighted Across the World," the headline read.

"Did you get this from across the street?" Laura sometimes liked to buy the tabloids there. We'd read them after we finished the comics or while we waited for a date to show up.

"It's the *Examiner*."

I looked again. So it was. "Oh my God."

The photographs showed indistinct silhouettes of cigar-shaped oblongs along the horizon. They had landed in small groups of three in 236 different locations across the world, distributed across the hemispheres, continents, urban and rural areas. Most of the landing locations were close, but not too close, to metropolitan centers.

The details were sketchy. No one had yet seen an alien. The ships were silent, immobile in the deserts, savannahs, abandoned airfields. All attempts at electronic communication had produced no results so far, but then again, it had only been less than thirty-six hours since the first landing.

Peter and I disagreed from the start about the ships. He called while Laura was doing the dishes.

"Have you seen?"

Peter and I were both second-year grad students. We were in a course on aesthetics together, which was too pretentious for me, but Peter loved it. I turned on the TV while answering him and remembered that he was supposed to take me to the Haidian exhibit.

"Nevermind that. Do you want to go see the ships? They are out by the airport, so beautiful."

Illustrated by Nina Ollikainen

I told him that I thought they were rather bland and unimaginative. Functional, like a pen. No, I didn't say that.

"Emily, you need to see them up close, in the sunlight and with the open space around them. We might even catch the aliens when they leave the ships!"

It was a date.

Laura thought it was a pretty cheesy move. "He doesn't have to spend anything. You are driving out to the airport for a first date?"

"Well, maybe I'll be able to write something up and sell it to the Sunday magazines."

"Hope you see some aliens then."

In retrospect, Laura was remarkably calm. Most people are when something happens that will change *everything*.

•••

The young man takes a picture of me as I turn off the flashlight. The Polaroid fades in to show me with my mouth twisted in a grim, determined look of dull surprise, as if I were trying not to throw up. He pastes the photo into an album of photographs of other visitors before me.

"This is the other part of the exhibit."

I look through the pictures. Most people have the same look of stupid surprise. A few have expressions of outrage or horror. A few are grinning. In one, a woman is trying to shield the eyes of her daughter from the geese, unsuccessfully, so you can see the curiosity on the child's face.

"The momentum goes from the observed to the observer. It's the conservation of energy." The young man hands me a pamphlet summarizing the piece.

"When will you be done?"

"Probably in a few weeks."

He's disappointed. That seems too long. But he's deferential toward me. I have a lot of power. The Gossamers trust my judgment. I finally realize that he's not just the attendant; he's the artist.

"So, did you like it?" he can't resist asking. He has to know. He probably holds an M.B.A. and there's a business plan behind the piece. The venture capitalists who gave the money for the geese (surely a fresh batch would be needed every few days), the warehouse, the publicity campaigns, the lunches and dinners with the editors at the *Review* to get me to come out here are probably breathing down his neck for some hope of return for their investment. He has to know.

"I don't know yet."

•••

We stretched our necks and stood on tiptoe, trying to look over the crowd around the airfield. A police line about a hundred meters from the airstrips stopped us. The crowd surged, held in check by that flimsy piece of plastic.

"That's a great deal of energy in reserve," Peter observed. We stood a little ways back on a small dirt mound.

The ships gave off a dark metallic blue sheen in the sun. They dwarfed the 747s beside them. There were three ships, all identical, with no external protrusions or indentations to mar the smooth cigar shape. I couldn't tell if there were any wheels or landing struts. I had the absurd wish that the ships would start rolling on their sides with the next breeze, frolicking in the sun like children in April.

"Perfect geometry," Peter said.

"Ummm."

"No one will ever write a poem with that kind of perfect geometry."

"Probably no one will," I answered, watching the ships not rolling away with the next breeze.

This was his way of courting me? I was a poet, or thought I was. I had had a few poems published in prestigious journals by then, and I was freelancing for the weekend journals to pay the bills. In the evenings I took classes that I thought would make me a better poet. I was twenty-five; what did I know?

The evening before we had argued in class about the purity of different forms of art.

"Music."

"Not pure. It's all based on the human auditory system, which is specialized for language."

Peter believed in absolute standards of art, which he thought would enthrall an amoeba as much as a man. He also believed that no human art so far approached those standards.

"Painting."

"Not pure. It's all based on the human eye, which is specialized for frequencies and intensities useful on the savannah."

"Sculpture."

And on and on. Poetry he denounced as the most human and therefore most relative of the arts. It couldn't even be translated from one human language to another. What good was it to an amoeba?

The whole class was up in arms against him. He defended himself with a glee that bordered on insanity.

And he had asked me out. Me, a scribbler of poems.

When it happened, we almost missed it. One minute there was nothing but the ships in the distance. The next, the air above the ships was filled with the shimmering rainbows of flickering wings.

They were about the size of a grown person's forearm. The bodies were divided into four segments; the second and third segments each had a pair of wings.

It wasn't obvious which end was the head at first, because as they flew, the bodies slowly rotated, parallel to the ground. They resembled helicopters with two rotors. Later on that impression would turn out to be more accurate than I had thought. They flew by rotating their four wings overhead, much as you and I would rotate our arms or legs to tread water. Like bumblebees, you wouldn't think they could fly, with their bulbous bodies. At the same time, they gave the impression of floating more than flying; graceful, like blimps.

The crowd was silent as they flew closer. There were darker patches at the extremes of the two terminal segments that were probably sensing organs. They hovered close overhead. Small, centipede-like legs, the only obviously biological parts of their anatomy, rhythmically moved down their bodies, beating the air. They were so light.

The news crews were running around like crazy, trying to get a good shot. Because we were on a mound and set back from the crowd, a reporter rushed in with her mike.

"What do you think?"

Peter didn't say anything. He was too absorbed.

"Gossamers," I said. It was the first thing that came into my mind. *For only Gossamer, my Gown—My Tippet—only Tulle—*

Peter gave me a startled look. "No! That's such a terracentric thing to say!"

"At least it isn't anthropomorphic."

• • •

I take the subway from the airport back to the commuter parking lot where I left my car. I like taking the subway because of the stations. When I was an undergraduate here with Laura, I sometimes managed to convince her to come with me on one of those "muse-hunting trips." We would take the subway from one end of the Green line to the other end of the Red line and then back to the other end of the Orange line.

The stations had such evocative names: Orient Heights, Alewife, Prudential, Symphony, Bowdoin, which I thought would inspire me to write good poetry (Laura said it was the only way she would ever get to see the rest of Boston, from underground). And the artwork. Every station had its own theme, executed down to the last tile on the wall. Some were obvious, like the photographs of ocean life at Aquarium and the black-and-white photographs of the school's history at MIT. Others were more fanciful. There were three-meter chimes that you could operate with an oversized handle on the wall while you waited for your train. One station had a seemingly interminable escalator on which, if you were going up, you would see clouds painted on a blue sky on the hanging vertical panels that formed the ceiling, but if you were going down, you would see a series of trains puffing steam painted on the other side.

My favorite was the large bronze hand that gave leaving trains a blessing, the middle and index fingers crossed over the tunnel. Once we spent a whole afternoon outside one station looking over every tile on which children had painted scenes of what they liked about life, and copied down those that struck us.

When we moved to California, that was the one thing I missed the most about the East: the subway stations. There is no real underground public transportation in California, the legacy of earthquakes and cars.

Years later, when I told Peter about the subway stations, I tried to make a point. Those stations to me were the height of art, better even than the Mona Lisa or *Pericles*. They had no institutional authority behind them, no volumes of criticism, no books of reproductions, no glass cases and armed guards. A few crazy college sophomores can come by and declare: That's art.

"That's not art, that's just decoration," Peter said.

"That's just semantics."

"No Gossamer would ever think so."

"Not until I review them." Resentment flickered between us. He was already jealous then, I think, of the power that I didn't ask for.

We argued; then we made love. Then we got coffee. I remember liking the way the cup was shaped, with its oversized handles and the picture of cows grazing on the side. We chatted quietly and civilly about the possibility for me to work from home so he could avoid the publicity that came with my public interpretations. We sat across the table from each other, avoiding silence.

Back in my house now, I take a moment to write down my impressions of "Momentum." I always write down what I remember about a piece only after I've gotten back from the airport. It allows time to filter away the inessential and leave behind those impressions that are strongest and most cohesive.

Feathers, pain, yearning, primitiveness, blood, concentration camp, objectification, death to bourgeois values, feathers, how will they clean it up, darkness, blindness, light, palpitations of the heart, feathers, heat, closeness of bodies, death, sound and fury, feathers.

They will like it because of the feathers, I think. The light, drifting snow of feathers in that souvenir glass box, the energy pent-up and released into useless blasts of air to keep the feathers floating, calmness above the fury below, these are the kind of things the Gossamers appreciate. The young man and his investors will be the next big thing and spawn thousands of imitators. If I were a goose, I'd go to another planet.

•••

Peter thought we got picked because he made calls every hour to the phone number of the committee, getting to know the receptionist, then Dr. Lester, then the coordinator. He was good at that sort of thing. It no doubt helped with his election campaign later. I thought it was luck.

In any case Lester, the chief scientific advisor for the contact team, was in our apartment on the Sunday a month later. He was appalled by Laura's cigarettes and ashtrays, refused my offer of coffee, and drove Peter and me downtown to the courthouse.

"So, Emily," he said to me across the metallic surface of the table in an interrogation room, "what do you do?"

"I'm a writer."

"A poet," Peter added.

"Can you see how you can be relevant to what I'm trying to do?"

I told him I couldn't, not unless the Gossamers expressed interest in poetry.

"Gossamers." He winced. That's the sort of thing he disliked. Playful names that were sentimental, had no scientific merit or the ring of hard, useful data. That sort of thing removed the wonder of the truly alien for an ignorant populace, Peter would say. I thought it made them understandable, familiar enough to be grasped and reasoned about. *They are so fragile.* In any case the press liked the name, and it had stuck.

"We've had very little luck with communication."

That much was true. Four weeks and the contact team had nothing to show on the fronts of mathematics, physics, astronomy, chemistry. Reels of data had been collected on the audio and visual output of the Gossamers and hundreds of linguists had pored over

them with no results. The Gossamers did not dance like
the bees or sing like the crickets. They appeared to
understand nothing that we had said or shown.

"We want to try something unusual, outside the
first-contact protocols." I wasn't aware there were any
first-contact protocols, but I supposed that was the sort
of thing you thought up when the public had watched
enough *X-Files* and expected you to have one. "We are
falling back on art."

"You want me to recite 'Ariel' to them?" Ridiculous.

"Maybe." He shrugged. "If that's what it takes.
Sing, dance, fingerpaint. You pretty much have free
rein to try whatever you want, as long as you manage
to elicit some kind of communication from them. Back-
and-forth, call-and-response, that sort of thing. We
need to know that they actually built those ships and
aren't just giant parasite wasps drifting through space
after all the sailors on the ships died of scurvy.
Otherwise we are just wasting time. And since you
named them," he shook his head again, "it's also good
PR either way."

I imagined the *Pinta* making landfall in the
Bahamas, Christopher and all his crew dead, the rats
rushing onshore to the astonished stares of the natives.
It wasn't as comical as I would have liked.

Peter and I were driven to the airport, which by
now was completely sealed off with barricades, fences,
and lines of soldiers. A few die-hard conspiracy-theory
nuts carried signs and shouted at the soldiers. Next to
the oblong Gossamer ships, a field of olive tents, like
mushrooms after a night's rain, flapped in the wind.

We walked into the tent which was filled with fluo-
rescent lights and bulky electronic equipment set on
flimsy foldout tables. Cables ran everywhere. Two
Gossamers hovered in a corner, surrounded by
cameras, microphones and linguists idly sitting by
with blank notebooks.

Lester came into the tent after us, carrying a box of Magic Markers, origami paper, glue sticks, finger-paint, chalk. "They are my daughter's," he said as he handed the box to me.

Peter was more of the visual artist than I (his focus was on sculpture), so I was surprised when he didn't go for anything in the box but took out a piccolo and went up to the Gossamers. I always thought a piccolo made a man look silly.

"We've tried everything from Bach to the Beatles; nothing elicits a response," one of the scientists said to him.

Peter ignored him and put the piccolo to his lips and began playing. I imagined it was some atonal piece from the late twentieth century, probably even something he wrote in college to prove his theories. I could make no melody, harmony, rhythm out of it. I wasn't even sure if there were any notes.

The two Gossamers hovered closer to Peter. The larger one, whom I had decided to call Schoenberg because one of its end segments was slightly larger than the other, making it look vaguely like a violin case, seemed to focus all the sensory organs at the larger end at Peter's face and hovered barely inches away from his nose. The other one, who had slight protuberances at both sensor ends that resembled the high noses of the German nobility, I decided to call Webern.

The scientists and linguists and Lester were excited. Evidently this was more reaction than they'd ever gotten. The cameras whirred and captured everything.

Peter stopped playing. Schoenberg and Webern hovered further back and began beating their wings faster. A high-pitched whine replaced the low-frequency buzz that was the usual background noise to their flight. The whine modulated itself in pitch and could be vaguely discerned as a repetition of what Peter had played. Everyone stood up in the tent, fascinated by the buzzing made by these giant insects. The total effect was far from pastoral, however, even though Dickinson thought that *to make a Prairie it takes a Clover and one Bee.*

"What was that piece?" Lester wanted to know.

Peter shrugged. "I don't know how to play the piccolo." He handed the piccolo to me.

What the heck. I took the piccolo and, because I didn't know what else to do, waved it around like a conductor's baton, vaguely in sync with the whining of the Gossamers. I self-consciously blushed, feeling even more ridiculous than Peter had looked.

The Gossamers began to fly around, describing the same arcs in the air as my baton. Their humming clarified and got louder. Schoenberg and Webern replayed Peter's random improvisation the whole afternoon. It was like listening to an enthusiastic child with no musical talent practicing the piano, doggedly repeating some random sequence of keys exactly over and over. No further attempts that afternoon produced any response. We could not get them to stop playing Peter's piece, even when I stopped waving the piccolo. When Peter and I got ready to go home that night, Lester informed us that reports were coming in from around the world indicating that Gossamers all over the globe have begun to reproduce Peter's music. We couldn't go home anymore, "for security reasons."

I told Peter, before we went to our respective tents, "I hope they stop buzzing like that tomorrow. It will drive me nuts."

"Beethoven isn't so universal, is he?" He had a large grin on his face.

"Neither is your randomness." *Or mine.*

"You'll come to like it. You'll see."

•••

At the terminal I duly compose my review for "Momentum," frustrated, as always, by the absurdity of pretending to understand what I don't really understand and the suspicion that I will again, despite my ignorance, be successful.

In ten years we have not made a single advance in communicating with the Gossamers qualitatively beyond the miracle that Peter and I created that day in the tent out at the airport. Their ships are hermetically sealed mysteries to us, and we dare not approach them until we can communicate with them meaningfully. The Gossamers live inside and about the ships, subsisting somehow with no visible intake of food, baffling all the biologists in the world. They won't leave the vicinities of the ships either, so we go to them, building elaborate networks of terminals and access chambers so we can bring our offerings to them, hoping for another sign, a breakthrough.

Once in a while a Gossamer will still hum Peter's song. The noise is produced by short bursts of air from the ends of the Gossamers' bodies, causing the bristles near the terminal orifices to vibrate. It's not exactly humming, but I don't know what else to call it. Peter's random sequence has a title now: "Miracle," of course. The London Symphony has made a recording of it. The Gossamers have also taken a fancy to a few other selected pieces of our new artistic endeavors. The competition to present a piece to the Gossamers is intense.

I wish we still made music like we used to, even the sort of thing I had scorned in college, the nubile teenage girls singing lyrics they barely understood written by overweight white men older than their fathers. I could at least dance to it and scan the mechanical meters. Peter was partly right; people have learned to like the kind of music the Gossamers liked. The radio stations don't play anything else and people have learned to dance to it. "It's universal," the music critics say.

I place my hands in the metallic mesh gloves next to the terminal, a faint red glow indicating that the machine is ready. The holographic projectors located around the world will bring my performance to the Gossamers in each location in real-time. The projection fields will surround the ships with their uncommunicative inhabitants. Thousands of cameras and people are watching my performance over the network, waiting to see if this will be a favorable or unfavorable review.

I have no methodology, despite all the interviews I've given to indicate otherwise. Lying is also part of a poet's art. Reviewing a piece for the Gossamers is a little like translating a poem; I never know how to start until I start.

So I wave my hands, watching as the virtual hands on the display mimic my movements. To represent the geese I fill the projection field with white triangles. A gentle swipe and the white triangles begin to circulate around the Gossamers and their ships. I turn my head to look at the other displays, showing what the Gossamers are experiencing from a few of the locations. The white triangles are gliding through them and their ships. Most of the Gossamers are motionless as the ghostly white images pass through them. I lower the lighting level so the entire projection field is gradually enveloped in purple darkness. I turn on the sound synthesizers so that the flapping of wings fills the air. From my tinny speakers they sound less like the wings of birds than the wings of bees. *Para criar uma pradaria basta um trevo e uma abelha,* I recall my attempts at rendering Dickinson into Italian.

"That's good momentum," I whisper to myself.

Then suddenly I change the whole scene. I force all the white triangles to the floor and turn up the volume on the flapping sound of the wings. I bathe the projection field with pure white brilliance, and as the human audience members looking in on the performance are

rubbing their eyes, the white triangles turn into real
geese, with feathers and death in the air above them. I
tell the cameras focused on the human audience to
freeze and compose all the faces into one collage. I
project the collage right away to the holographic field,
in the midst of the Gossamers. The human faces,
contorted in glee and boredom punctuated by sadistic
pleasure, lack shame.

I look at the other monitors, showing the reactions
of the Gossamers. Nothing. They seem to have
completely ignored the entire performance. The review
is a failure.

I sigh with relief for the geese, and with sorrow, for
the young entrepreneurial artist who'll have to find
another idea. But then the computer alerts me to the
screen showing the reaction of the Gossamers outside
of New York City.

One Gossamer comes into view. It has brought
several companions. They fly around their ship lazily,
in circles. Suddenly they land, clutching onto the
ground with their tiny legs, and begin to beat their
wings furiously.

Within moments my terminal is inundated with
congratulations for discovering yet another masterpiece of universal aesthetics. The young artist in San
Jose is now a celebrity. I think tomorrow we'll find that
the stocks for the geese farming industry will have
risen more in a single night than they have for the
previous fifty years.

I want to cry, so I leave the room.

•••

I told Laura about Peter's and my adventure when
I got back two weeks later. We had tried singing and
painting, dancing and reciting, and acted like wild
Bacchanalia participants. None of our outrageous
antics had worked.

"Did you know that I thought I would be an archaeologist when I was in high school?" She leaned back in her wicker chair, her dancer's legs bopping in the air.

"No, you never told me that."

"There was a theory, now discredited, that the Mayans fell because they tried to please the gods with everything they did, their art, government, sacrifices, dances, rituals. They could never figure out what the gods wanted though, so they went to more and more elaborate constructions, bigger temples, bloodier sacrifices, more grotesque body modifications, until they spent all their energy trying to please the unfathomable gods and collapsed overnight. You must try harder if you want to please the Gossamers."

Laura could keep a straight face when she said things like that. I could never tell if she was serious.

"You and Peter are just the beginning."

We giggled, while Dr. Lester announced to the world what Peter and I had done.

• • •

On my bottom shelf is a box of juvenilia, poems and stories written before I went to college. On the shelf in the middle is my thesis: a book of poems, one for each of the fifty states I traveled to the summer between my junior and senior years. On the top shelf is half a notebook of just-begun scribbles dated after graduation. Tarotological specimens of the faux-creative mind, Peter would have called them.

The *Review* hired me ostensibly to review art for their readers, but really because of my proven record of interpreting humanity to the Gossamers (if you can call a sample of one a record). I wrote about Picasso and Chagall, Schoenberg and Webern, Peter and me. I was quoted. I was invited to do more reviews and interpret more art for the Gossamers. I was quoted. I wrote about what I thought the Gossamers responded to and theorized about their aesthetic sense. I was quoted. I fretted, I worried, I rode on more airplanes and received more sophisticated equipment to convey my impressions of each piece to the Gossamers. I was quoted. I lectured, I taught, I defended, I published textbooks of art theory. I was quoted.

The momentum built until I believed in it. I taught others what I thought was the theory behind the Gossamers' artistic sense. There are other reviewers that the Gossamers seem to like, but we are a select club, and we guard our membership jealously.

I try to explain to myself, daily, why the Gossamers would accept Li Bai and reject Dante, or why they would accept dying geese, but not a burning woman. The momentum built, *but when I cannot make the Force / Nor mould it into word.*

•••

It's night by the time I wake up. My apartment is dark and quiet.

Amherst at night is the same as it has always been since that other Emily, whom I admire so much, had lived here, or so I'd like to think. The five colleges still generate the same seasonal and yearly migration patterns. And people still mind their own business.

I walk into the living room on my way to the kitchen to get a glass of water. A stray cat meows from the darkness, startling me. As it jumps out the window I notice that it had been playing with my terminal, which I had left on.

The computer alerts me to the Gossamers on one of the monitors. They are moving back and forth rhythmically, swaying in the glow of the holographic light around them. I am confused.

The editor at the *Review* has a high-priority message waiting for me. I open it before all the thousands of

other messages waiting for me in my inbox. It congratu-
lates me on discovering yet another piece of great art,
but is slightly peeved that I had done it without
consulting him initially. He wants to know the artist's
name.

I'm confused. Is he talking about the geese? I had
been sent there at his request. And the name of the
young artist in San Jose is well known by now.

I call up the logs and have the computer replay the
last holographic performance it had projected.

The field fills with neutral, gray darkness, and the
rhythmic sweeping back-and-forth of a single spot of
light, looking for all the world like a ball of yarn being
batted between the paws of a cat.

Then I remember the stray cat that had been
playing with my terminal and my heart skips a beat.
The cat must have been fascinated by that spot of light
and had been playing with it. The Gossamers had
liked what the cat did enough to have copied it.

All the careful structure of theory and practices that
I had built up over the years in my capacity as inter-
preter of the arts for the Gossamers is falling apart
around me like a house of cards. The Gossamers had
responded to a cat randomly chasing after a spot of
light.

• • •

When I finished packing my things, Laura and I
took off our shoes and rolled up the carpet (which was
mine) in the living room. We mopped the floor until it
was shiny and smooth, like ice. Laura wanted to play
a game. She told me to stand with my back to the east
wall while she stood opposite at the west wall.

"Run to me, gradually increase your speed until
you are running as fast as you can when you run into
me. Don't worry, I won't let you crash into the wall."

Laura was like that, crazier than a cat on a leash, as my father would say. I was already beginning to miss her. I crashed into her with a bone-jarring snap. We collapsed onto the floor, breathless.

"Do you know what shape you just made?" she asked when we sat up.

"A human pretzel."

"No, I mean when you were running toward me."

I told her that I didn't know.

"You made a logarithmic curve, a very small piece of a very long curve. Uniform linear acceleration and the constant rotation of the earth bent your straight line of motion into a spiral. Look."

She drew a curve with the tip of her left foot on the floor. It's like the curve of a snail shell, and I said so.

"Yes." She looked at me. "It's also the path a moth makes as it flies into a flame."

Then Peter came to pick me up. We were going to get married in Las Vegas, which was his concession to my conventional sensibilities.

By then "Miracle" was already beginning to be played on the air. Peter kept jumping from station to station the whole way, listening to that composition of his that he thought had turned two thousand years of music theory on its head. I wasn't going to correct him. He deserved a few days of triumph, I thought.

We climbed over the last hill, and the lights of Las Vegas spread out in the desert below us. The new mechanical, neon Gossamers, of all sizes, shapes, and colors, were everywhere in the city, covering all the buildings, fluttering their primary-colored wings at us. Peter stepped on the accelerator as we plunged toward the lights. I felt like shouting, *An Hour to rear supreme / His Continents of Light.*

I thought then, somewhat irrelevantly, that Laura was wrong. What I had made wasn't a perfect

logarithmic spiral after all, since gravity had kept my
feet on the ground and bent my path into a circle.
Laughing, I told Peter what I was thinking.

"Laura was never very good at math," I said.

• • •

It was pretty much over by the time they let me see
her. Laura had recovered enough to sit up in her bed,
sipping soup. She had lost all her hair and much of the
skin over her face in the fire, so her head was wrapped
up, like a mummy, with an opening for the mouth.

I sat down. "Hey."

"I loused up the math."

She had miscalculated the length of her cord so that
she had swung right into the fire instead of just outside
of it. She had intended to swing around and around
the fire, describing ever-closer arcs until she could cut
herself loose and dance gracefully into the lake on the
other side of the fire.

"How was the review?"

The Gossamers had not responded to it, whether
because of my distracted translation or because they
simply had no interest in her piece. I told her it went fine.

"You're lying." She turned her face toward mine.
"Remember that story about the Mayans I told you
about? I always thought about how I would have felt
if I had lived in those times, trying my hardest to
please the unknown and arbitrary gods."

I waited.

"I think I know now how I would have felt. I would
have felt free, utterly free."

Afterward Laura tried to teach dance. She died a
few years later when she fell from her sixtieth-floor
window. I pictured her falling as the tangent
momentum of Earth's rotation and the acceleration of
gravity pulled her toward the burning center of the

earth, falling faster and faster, describing the beginning of the opposite of a logarithmic spiral. I had a hard time imagining that curve. I was never any good at math either.

•••

It's not good to find out that you've been so good at lying that you've managed to deceive yourself.

I think of Peter, with his piccolo, and how he reviled my "translations"; how he stopped believing that the Gossamers are intelligent, and turned to giving impassioned speeches decrying the loss of art and culture; how he tried to get into politics, surely the most human of the arts. I think of myself, with my reams of translations and interpretations, my reputation built on them. I haven't written a poem in years. I wish I had painted even a single one of those tiles in the subway station. And I remember that day, when Peter and I realized that we were like two beetles at the opposite corners of a room, crawling toward each other in a spiral yet somehow never getting any closer, until we ended where the other had started.

On the display, the Gossamers are still swaying back and forth, like that imaginary mouse chased by the cat. In my mind, I see the rats from Columbus's ship on the shore of the New World, expressing wonder and boredom at everything, at nothing. The natives rush over, wondering at this new race of gods. For the Gossamers, how is art distinguished from noise? *And they will differ—if they do— / As Syllable from Sound—.*

The momentum is gone. I turn off the terminal. I feel free, free enough to write a poem.

Author's note: All quotations from Emily Dickinson are taken from her *Collected Poems.*

TEN YEARS AFTER

Written by
Sean Williams

About the Author

Sean Williams has been writing since 1990, working entirely from his home in Adelaide, South Australia. Prolific and diverse, he initially made a name for himself writing short stories, a number of which appeared in various "Year's Best" and other anthologies.

Sean now writes novels almost exclusively. His first, Metal Fatigue, was published in Australia in 1996 and appeared in hardcover in the U.K. three years later. The Resurrected Man followed in 1998. The Books of Change series, completed in 2002, are his most recent solo releases. A string of collaborations with fellow Adelaide writer and friend Shane Dix—including the Evergence and Orphan series—propelled him to popularity in the U.S. Their latest trilogy, set in the Star Wars extended universe, was a New York Times bestseller.

Sean has been Chair of the South Australian Writer's Center—the oldest such organization in Australia—and an occasional guest futurist for local media. In 2000, he received the prestigious South Australia Great Award for Literature.

When not writing, he enjoys deejaying and cooking curries.

A winner in the Writers of the Future Contest, his story "Ghosts of the Fall" appeared in Writers of the Future Volume IX in 1993.

It's been ten years since my story "Ghosts of the Fall" appeared in *Writers of the Future Volume IX*, and the question of how to begin remains as difficult to answer now as it was then. Aside from that, I'd like to think that I've learned a lot in the past decade. Being invited to write this piece for *Writers of the Future Volume XIX* is a powerful validation of that thought—just as winning a prize in 1992 was a powerful validation of my work to that point. Surely, I thought, I'd be able to knock out something that would stand as a public declaration of the debt I owe the Writers of the Future, and would give an army of new writers waiting in the trenches the motivation to charge.

The first port of call was obviously *Writers of the Future Volume IX*. It had been a long time since I'd walked down that particular memory lane. I was reminded of friends I hadn't spoken to for far too long. It begged the question: what happened to the other hopefuls who, like me, thought that the anthology would act as a springboard, propelling us on to a glittering career in publishing? Some, I know, are still hammering away at it; others have moved on to related fields. I skimmed through the stories, and marveled at all our raw creativity. There's hope in those pages. There's hunger. There's love. And there are also guidelines—signposts, if you will—to convert that creativity, those urgent passions, into a purposeful life in writing.

Unfortunately, there's also the content of the piece

I'd planned to write for this volume. A glance at the essays in Volume IX reveals just how much sound, writerly advice I'd had at hand, back then. I am startled by the way it had sunk in without me noticing, leaving me feeling like a plagiarist for wanting to issue advice that overlaps significantly with Octavia Butler's. ("Persist," she exhorted, and that's as true now as it ever was.) How could I even attempt to surpass Kevin J. Anderson's magnificent rant on the imaginary obstacles we put between ourselves and our writing? ("Put the butt in the chair and apply the fingertips to the keyboard." All I'd add is an exclamation mark.) Julius Schwartz's introduction to the world of comics contains Robert A. Heinlein's three rules of writing—and who could challenge them? (He also said: "Even the big names have to start somewhere. Don't let a little competition intimidate you.") And what could I have to add on the subject of story vitality that wasn't better said by L. Ron Hubbard, years before I first seriously put pen to page?

Where to from there? I'm a prolific writer and don't often suffer blocks, but this time—contemplating this article about the guiles, snares and consolations of the profession of writing about writing—I'll confess to being stuck. I let it simmer over the weekend, then came back to it. During the simmering process, one question recurred to me, as it has at many points during the last ten years: how do you teach someone to walk?

The way most people learned to walk was as toddlers, by repeatedly trying until they got it right. A balancing hand every now and again never went astray, and it was always good to have a shoulder to cry on during the inevitable frustration and after the odd bump. But would it have helped if our parents had sat us down and said, "Okay, here are the principles involved in knee-bending and heel placement. Go practice and we'll move on to advanced balance control tomorrow"?

Writing, like walking, I learned by doing, and I remain a big believer in that method. But it isn't everyone's first or best option. For the benefit of those people who prefer a more didactic technique I've provided a list of some of the other things I've learned, offered in the hope that you too might absorb them and then promptly forget where they came from.

I've learned that there is not one "correct" way to write, but that there is one correct way for me, right now, and that I need to stick to it with all the vicious tenacity of a crocodile, or else I become unproductive. I've learned that publishers want nothing more than to publish good books—but that everyone in the industry is constrained by the need to earn money, i.e., to eat, and that certain compromises must be made in order to ensure that. I've learned that writing a lot and accepting criticism where it's deserved is a sure-fire way to improve as a writer, but that poor criticism—or criticism poorly delivered—can kill a career. I've learned that you can be successful no matter where you're from, what age, class, race, income, religious beliefs, credit rating—none of this matters when it comes to the crunch. What does matter is whether your story is any good or not. I've learned that everyone has a book in them, but that this isn't anywhere near enough to be a full-time writer. Aspiring to be a career writer rather than to write just one book will increase your chances from almost zero to something a little bit higher. I've learned that being genuinely nice and open to all people is the best way to get what you want, in the long run. I've learned that maintaining a healthy social life is as important as anything I've said above, and that friends—in the field and out—are what keep us sane. I've learned that it's okay to say "sci-fi."

I've learned that the stereotypical writer is a fiction, that there are as many different types of writers as there are insurance clerks or gardeners. I happen to like meeting deadlines and writing in the morning; I write very badly when under the influence of caffeine or alcohol or other drugs; I write fifteen hundred words every day, whether the muse (or mood) is upon me or not. I like working with my editor. I don't think of my stories as children. I know for a fact that I'm not a genius, and neither do I think of myself as especially creative. I just use what I have to the best of my abilities.

I've learned that the perception of cliques and clubs in any field is mostly illusory, and that fan-voted awards are mostly popularity contests—as opposed to peer-voted awards like the Writers of the Future Contest. While it's nice to be among friends who are successful and productive—and to receive acknowledgement from readers and/or peers—that's not what will make or break your career. You are the person driving it, and you have to be in control at all times. I've been around long enough to see a few promising writers stall, their batteries flat from expecting to shine too bright, too soon.

I've learned that the motto I picked from one of the other Volume IX authors—"Write hard, die free"—is wrong. One should write hard in order to live free, otherwise what's the point?

I've learned that full-time writing, like any full-time job, has a lot to offer, but it also comes at a price. It demands communication skills of people who might feel more comfortable never leaving the house. It means interacting with a readership that is sometimes obsessive, intrusive and presumptive, but can be loyal, welcoming and extremely helpful too. And it occasionally demands that you sound off like an expert even though you know deep down that there are really no rules, that every writer must find their own way, and that you don't really know much more than anyone else about what that will take, ultimately, or what it will cost.

In glancing back at Volume IX, I did of course revisit my own story. "Ghosts of the Fall" is set in a post-apocalyptic version of my hometown, which has managed to become the last city left standing on Earth. The protagonist of the story, Hogarth asks himself: "Is it really worth it?" At the end of the story, the narrator, an older Hogarth, decides that if he had the opportunity he would go back and tell his younger self that it was indeed worth the effort. And so would I.

It's a long and winding road, but here I am: not at the end, but at least past a few of the milestones I had dreamed of seeing ten years ago. Writing full time was just a fantasy ten years ago; now it's a reality, and every bit as good as I'd hoped it would be. I will always be indebted to L. Ron Hubbard's Writers of the Future Contest for encouraging me, for giving me some new skills by which I could tackle my work, and for introducing me to a worldwide community of people who read, write and/or edit fiction. I can't emphasize enough just what all this meant to me then.

And what it means to me now. Writing is a hard course, and there are numerous obstacles in your path. Yet it is also true that everyone in this book has already reached a level of success many writers never achieve. It is hardly a revelation that it takes vast amounts of dedication and determination—and love of the craft— to stay the course. But the game is worth it.

I dare you to try. Perhaps you'll be one of the ones who survive, too.

WALKING RAIN

Written by
Ian Keane

Illustrated by
Daniel Willis

About the Author

Ian Keane was raised in Pennsylvania, the eldest of six children in an Irish-Catholic family. On leaving college, he drifted about the United States for a time, finally settling in the Southwest. He and his wife, Louise, have been married eighteen years. They spend their spare time hiking and backpacking in the mountains and canyons of the Southwest desert.

Ian is a professional environmental consultant on environmental hazards: chemical, biological, radiological and physical. He works for a firm based in Santa Fe, New Mexico, called CERL, Inc., environmental consultants, where he performs field services, laboratory analysis and maintains the company website. He notes this is the first time his ability to write has been recognized.

About the Illustrator

Daniel Willis was born into a military family, one that lived in Bavaria for seven years and traveled throughout Europe. After returning to the United States, he spent several years in New England, where he discovered the works of H.P. Lovecraft. His family eventually settled in Louisiana, where he graduated from high school.

After two years of college, Daniel spent five years moonlighting as a night auditor at a hotel and convenience store clerk, both of which afforded him ample opportunity to pursue his art. He then enlisted in the Air Force, which offered many new artistic venues in the form of murals, unit logos and commemorative military coin designs. He currently serves as a technician at Cape Canaveral Air Force Station.

At this late and early hour, the view outside the window of Tam Lum Kai's 24-Hour Coffee Emporium closely resembled a painting by Edward Hopper, except for the rain sweeping the streets. The surrounding buildings had the same stark angularity: dark, hollow spaces showing through the storefront windows, illuminated only by the harsh wedge of light cast from the coffeehouse. No vehicles were parked along the curbs or moved in the street, though that would change in an hour or so when trucks started making their early morning deliveries. There was Tam, sitting at the counter a few feet away, engrossed in a book that, if memory serves, was titled *Liberation Through Brain Respiration*, and me at a table, drinking joe and staring through the window at that miraculous rain. That was the first time I really noticed Death Girl.

She was standing on a corner across the street beneath a dim streetlight that did no more than pick out her silhouette against the night. I hadn't seen her arrive and had no idea how long she had been standing there in the rain. She stood for some minutes more, unmoving, while I observed her. I began to wonder if someone had placed a department store mannequin on the sidewalk while I wasn't looking. Then she stepped into the street, took a short hop to clear the water running along the curb, and headed for the coffeehouse.

"Customer coming, Tam," I said. He looked up,

glanced out the window, and grunted. He turned the opened book upside down on the counter, heaved himself to his feet and walked around behind the counter. Tam is Tibetan, short and on the pudgy side of stocky, looking like one of those Happy Buddha figurines you see sold in curio shops, but with dark, weathered skin. He has a ready grin and an infectious laugh, looks completely harmless, and was a resistance fighter back in his homeland before coming to the States to sell coffee. I'd had that story from his son one afternoon after we'd both had a few beers, and I had no reason to doubt him. I know dangerous people when I meet them and another pushed through the door of the coffeehouse at just that moment.

Her hair, plastered wetly against her cheeks, was as dark and coarse as Tam's, though her skin was paler. She appeared twenty-something, tall, and very pretty. She wore a khaki army-surplus field jacket, faded denim pants and tennis shoes, and she was soaked through. A dark blue canvas pack was slung over her shoulder on one strap. She offered Tam a small smile, ordered coffee, then headed straight back to the restrooms. Tam glanced at me, raised an eyebrow. I smiled and shook my head, and he arched the other brow skeptically. I shrugged and went back to staring out the window. That's mostly what passes for heavy conversation between Tam and me.

I watched the twin streams along the curb sides race each other down the street. I watched the light show in the sky palely and briefly fret the clouds, again and again. I filled my senses with the storm, but it didn't matter because my mind was all on Death Girl. I was instantly aware when she left the restroom and made her way to the counter. I heard her thank Tam as she picked up her coffee, heard too her steps on the hardwood floor, the sibilant scrape of her denim clad legs against each other as she approached along the counter. Staring through the window at the rain darkened street, I pretended not to notice the smell of wet hair and dampened skin when she stopped beside me, until she said, "May I share your table?"

The coffeehouse was full of empty chairs and tables. My mind screamed "Please don't." But I rose from my chair and looked down at her, motioned at the chair across the table and said, "Please be my guest." She hesitated, startled perhaps by my height—she wasn't likely used to being towered over—or perhaps it was because my manner did not match my appearance. I was wearing my traveling clothes: scuffed leathers and denim. My hair was long, fiery red and styled mostly by the freeway wind, and I was overdue for a shower. A scar pulled down the outside corner of my left eye. I looked like a big ugly weasel, according to a New Mexico sheriff who'd pulled me and my bike over on a helmet violation last year. But she smiled and took the chair on the adjoining side to my right, ignoring the one I'd indicated.

"I think I've seen you before," she said, and sipped at her coffee. Her voice had a low pitch with a flat accent I couldn't quite place. Easterner, I thought.

"Is that right?" I said, noncommittally.

"No, really. A couple of weeks ago up near Ouray. You were working on some kind of machine just off the highway."

I examined her with some curiosity; I had been in that area two weeks back, sampling airborne particulates. She'd toweled her hair in the restroom, so that it no longer clung, but hung about her face and neck in a rough mane. She wore a leather thong around her neck from which depended a small suede bag, in obvious imitation of a Navajo medicine bag. I had no doubt it contained a small piece of crystal and some corn pollen—medicine bags are all the rage among the New Age crowd in this town. "You have a good eye if you saw me from the highway. And a good memory for faces."

She leaned a little toward me offering her hand. "Name's Snowy," she said.

I hesitated a moment, took her hand and gave it a shake. "Rafe," I told her.

She smiled faintly as she retrieved her hand. "Well, Rafe, I wasn't sure you were the same man I saw, a hundred percent. But you do kinda stand out, and I have to admit I was curious about what you were doing."

"Ah," I said, sipping at my coffee while I thought that over. No reason not to tell her, of course, except that I was feeling unaccountably cautious. I couldn't seem to shake that impossible, irrational image that had settled into my mind when I first saw her, and wouldn't go away. Death Girl. I said, "I was chasing rain." Her face went as blank as still water for an instant, then she appeared puzzled.

"Chasing rain?" she echoed.

"I study rainfall," I explained. "I follow rainstorms around to obtain data."

She stared at me. "You're a *scientist?*"

"Believe it or not."

She shook her head slowly. She was silent a moment, then asked, "Are you, like, one of those guys who runs around after tornados?"

"I used to do that, but I gave it up a while ago."

"Why? Too risky?"

"No. I'm simply more interested in rain. There's more to it than rage and thunder, you know."

"Hm. So what were you working on at Ouray? It wasn't raining then."

"No, but it was about to. I collect air samples before and after the rains, and compare the results."

"What are you looking for?"

I shrugged. "It's a bit complicated to explain. Why were you in the area?"

She looked briefly annoyed at the change of subject, but said "I was there for the Shakespeare festival at Telluride."

"Hm," I said in my turn. She didn't seem the type, though I'm often mistaken in my appraisals. "I missed that, I'm afraid. What did they play?"

"*As You Like It* and *King Lear.*"

We discussed the plays for a while, of which she showed a layman's appreciation—that is, enthusiastic, but not overly profound. Which was fine, because that's about my speed, too. Somewhere in there Tam came by and refilled our cups. He had that completely bland expression on his face that he gets when he's grinning from ear to ear inside, but is too polite to show it, but still wants you to know that he's doing it. I threw him a covert sneer, but he did that trick with it a duck's back does with water.

"Snowy's an unusual name," I said later. "That short for something?"

She hesitated. "I shouldn't say."

"Why not?"

"You'll laugh."

I held out my hand. "Rafael Leviticus Kane, at your service," I said, completely straight-faced.

She stared a moment. "You're joking."

I grinned. She showed the ghost of a smile, took my hand and shook it exactly the way I had done hers earlier. "Niobe Snow," she said.

"Hmm."

"What?"

"That's not quite fair, you know. My name's much more hilarious than yours."

She nodded judiciously. "I'll allow that's true."

I sighed, shook my head sadly. "Suckered again."

For a while we drank our coffee in silence, watching the rain through the window. I'd been hoping it would let up, but if anything it was pouring down even harder. Snowy said, "So you're here to do more research?"

"No. Actually, I live about twenty miles south of the city. I'm heading homeward, or was before the storm hit. Looks like I'll have to drive my motorcycle through the rain." I looked at her. "And you? Why are you here?"

"I'm visiting my mother."

"She live nearby?"

"No," she said softly. Just that.

"I can give you a lift," I offered, "if you don't mind being exposed to the weather." Which wasn't likely from the way she had stood out in the rain earlier.

"Thanks," she said, her voice taut. "But I'm not staying with my mother."

"Oh."

Snowy sighed and in a resigned tone said, "She lives at the state mental hospital, Rafe. She's an inmate."

"Sorry."

She shrugged.

"Can I drop you anywhere else?"

She shook her head, watching me steadily. "I haven't found a place to stay yet."

A tense, uncertain feeling lodged beneath my sternum. Dreading "yes," dreading "no," I told her, "You could stay with me." She didn't answer. She just stood, slung her pack over her shoulder, and waited. When I got up and left, Death Girl followed me out.

• • •

The rain began to lessen, finally, as we passed south of the city limits through a region of hills sparsely forested by piñon and juniper. I drove a Brough Superior that I had reconditioned myself, the very model favored by T.E. Lawrence for speed and power, and which eventually ended up killing him. Almost killed me, too, for that matter, when someone shot out my rear tire on a mountain road last year. I had barely avoided taking a long dive into the Rio Grande gorge. People in rural areas around here can be very unfriendly toward anyone they suspect might be a government agent, which is why I endeavor to resemble a fed as little as possible. Didn't help that time, though.

My face, arms and upper thighs were chilled by the wind and rain, but my lower legs were warmed by the radiating heat from the rumbling engine, and I was warmed also where Death Girl nestled against my back, her arms clasped around my waist. Ahead of us the wild clouds flapped in slow motion, pale flames above the granite-buttressed mountains. As we rose through the hills, the desert opened up below us to the west, an airy region over which a half-dozen isolated thunderstorms floated, trailing dark, moist curtains from their skirts; what the locals call "walking rain."

I braked, drifting to a stop on the shoulder, letting the bike idle while I watched the scattered storms. The rain had tapered off to occasional needle-sized droplets. I looked back to the north, where it seemed that a murky fog had enveloped the city.

"Something wrong?" Snowy asked, looking back to see what held my attention.

I shook my head. "No. It's just been a while since I've seen a storm cell that extensive around here." From this vantage it was usually possible to see entire convection columns, all the way up to the anvil-shaped cloud formations that cap the thunderstorms soaring above the mountains that rose to the east of the city. It's one of the reasons I like living in this area. Not even the mountains themselves were visible now; just a charcoal colored mass of clouds, slanting streaks of rainfall beneath them. A washed-out yellow glow was barely visible behind the wall of rain, faint indication of the newly risen sun.

I started when Snowy nudged me in the ribs, hard. "What?"

"Sorry," she said, "but the rain's picking up."

More than that, I realized—we were now under a heavy drizzle and I had let the engine stall. I have a tendency to tune out when I'm focused on distant weather. The "walking rain" was strolling our way, pushed before a brisk north wind. I kicked the Brough back to life and pulled out onto the highway running southward before the storm.

• • •

A half-mile south of the village of Little Hills, I turned west onto an unpaved road. By this time the sky was a nearly solid gray, relieved only by barely visible contours where individual cloud masses over-lapped. Ahead I could see the tops of cottonwood trees that marked the line of an arroyo, their crowns tossing fretfully with heavy gusts from the north.

My house was situated above the arroyo within a cottonwood grove. I parked the bike in the breezeway between the frame and stucco structure that held my office and lab, and the old, flat-roofed adobe house in which I lived. When I cut the engine, I could hear water already running in the arroyo, mixing with the hushed roar of the wind in the trees.

Snowy slid off the back of the cycle and stretched, gazing about thoughtfully at the house, the yard, the trees. I opened one of the big panniers mounted on the back of the Brough, pulled out my duffel and handed Snowy her pack.

"Pretty spot," she commented, slinging the pack over her shoulder.

"Yes, it is," I said. "I was lucky to get it." I'd had it for a decent price from a retiring colleague who had moved to the coast to be near his family.

I let us into the house through the entry off of the breezeway that leads into the kitchen. The house smelled a little musty having been closed up for most of the last two months, so I blocked the door ajar for a bit of fresh air. There was a note on the painted tile counter near the sink, weighted down with my spare set of house keys. It had been left by Midori, my graduate assistant, who house-sits for me when I go on the road. The note said she'd restocked my refrigerator a couple of days ago and that Mr. Padilla had come by and fixed the leak in the well house.

I caught a movement from the corner of my eye, looked up to see Snowy lean back wearily against the stove. "C'mon," I said, smiling. "Let me show you where you can put your stuff." She responded with a half nod and a tired version of her usual small smile.

I led the way out of the kitchen, through the dining room, down a wide hallway that runs past the main entry foyer, to the rooms at the other end of the house. The long west wall of the hallway is made mostly of windows, with a double set of glass doors at its center leading out onto a wood deck. Pausing to look outside, I could see that the sky had dimmed to a twilight aspect, even though it was barely midmorning.

The hallway ends in a tee, with bedrooms to left and right and a bathroom in between. I led Snowy into the left, east bedroom, which I use as a library when I don't have guests, which is usually.

"The couch folds out into a bed," I told her, "and you can find linens and bath towels in this closet. Why don't you get yourself cleaned up while I see what I can put together for breakfast or whatever."

Snowy came and stood close to me. Her eyes, which I only then noticed were gray, seemed suddenly very large. "We could both use a shower, I think," she said. "And I was really hoping I wouldn't have to sleep alone, if that's all right with you."

"Yes," I said, my mouth dry. For this was, of course, what I had feared and hoped for from the moment she had entered the coffeehouse. "Yes, very much so." So we shared the bath, and then my bed, and later we slept in that warm place we had made together.

•••

I woke well past sunset, the air in the house very cool, Snowy's slow breathing warm against my shoulder. A freezing rain rattled against the windows, drummed upon the roof. I rose carefully so as not to disturb her rest, pulled on sweatpants and a T-shirt, and groped my way into the hallway. Once there I switched on the night-light, made my way to the kitchen, shut and latched the outer door. On the way back to the bedroom I goosed the thermostat, hoping to take some of the chill off of the house.

I stumbled going into the bathroom, muffling a curse as I stubbed my toe on something hard. When I closed the door and switched on the overhead light, I saw that I had tripped on Snowy's blue canvas pack. I sat down slowly on the tub surround, pulled the pack onto my lap and started going through it.

Almost immediately I found a hard, cold, familiar shape. When I drew my hand out, I was holding a Colt .45 service automatic. I reflected for a few moments before I turned out the light and returned to the kitchen, where I examined the weapon more closely. It looked clean and well cared for. I pressed the release and slid the clip into my hand. I worked the slide, noting that she didn't keep a round chambered. Sensible. I weighed the clip in my hand, then pushed each of the seven rounds out of it into a coffee mug I'd taken from the shelf above the sink. I put the mug back on the shelf, replaced the clip, and returned the weapon to Snowy's pack.

She stirred beneath the covers as I sat on the bed beside her, looked up quickly as I laid a hand on her shoulder, her eyes wide and startled for an instant. Then she relaxed, rolled onto her back, and gave me the warmest smile I'd yet seen from her—enough to give me a twinge of guilt over the bullets in the coffee mug. She looked like she wanted to be kissed just then, so I leaned over and did that, backed off before it could develop into something more involved.

"Hungry?" I asked. The smile widened.

"Ravenous," she answered.

"I'll start fixing something then."

"Anything I can do to help?"

"Nope. Take your time, come out when you want. Or go back to sleep and I'll call you when dinner's ready."

"All right," she said. As I started to get up she grabbed my hand. "Thanks, Rafe. I really appreciate your letting me stay here."

I squeezed her hand and let it go, got up from the bed. "I'm glad you're here," I said, thinking that I meant it more than I'd expected to. I gave her a smile of my own and left the room.

The rain was coming down harder now. Judging from the lag between lightning flashes and the sound of the thunder, the center of the storm was roughly three miles distant and getting closer. I tried to get a weather report first on the television, then on the radio, but the reception was too poor—one of the disadvantages to living in a remote area. I resolved to check my own instruments later, and maybe go online to get an area forecast.

As I started chopping onion in the kitchen, I heard a sound from the dining room. Snowy was wandering around, looking things over, familiarizing herself with the place. I hadn't switched on the overhead light in that room, only a couple of table lamps; she moved alternately from light to shadow as she went about the room. She was wearing one of my sweatshirts, which came down to midthigh on her, and little else that I could tell. The girl was sure making herself at home, though I had to admit she looked very good this way. I fumbled the knife I was holding and decided to keep my attention on the cutting board before I lost a finger. Eventually I got dinner far enough along that I could leave it for a while. I poured a couple of glasses of a dry California merlot I favor and joined her in the dining room.

Snowy was looking at a pair of framed posters I'd hung on the wall above the couch at the far end of the room. "Does all of your artwork feature rain?" she asked, taking the glass I proffered, while continuing to regard the posters.

"Pretty much," I said, looking at the landscapes.

"I can see the subject is the same," she said, "but they really don't go well together. The differences are . . . painful."

On the left and a little raised was a reproduction of a nineteenth-century woodblock print by Hiroshige, depicting a cloudburst on the Ohashi Bridge. The background is gray and muted, the river almost the color of the sky, the rain clouds mirroring the shadows beneath the bridge. Color is reserved for the bridge itself and the people crossing it. Most are huddled beneath parasols, another is protected by a wide bamboo hat, still another is crouched beneath a woven mat. Out on the river a lone figure poles a raft. Despite the rain lashing down from the skies and the evident discomfort of the travelers, the scene is soothing, almost peaceful.

To the right and lower I'd hung van Gogh's mad

interpretation of Hiroshige's print. All of the elements are the same, but the colors and accents are different. The sky is tinted a wild, ice blue; the river beneath is green, capped here and there with blue reflections from the sky. The bridge supports are oddly backlit from the right. The figures on the bridge seem more isolated and miserable, even the three that share the single parasol. Together, the prints symbolize to me all the paradoxical fascination I find in rain: the beauty of melancholy, the quiet pain, the violent serenity.

I said, "I like them together. And I have a fondness for rain."

Snowy said nothing to this, but she held my hand while we sauntered through my little gallery, rain sounds providing a gentle musical background. In one corner stood a folding silk screen, Mount Fuji painted on the silk, a dragon entwined within a rain cloud rising above and behind the mountain. In the opposite corner squatted a blocky stone carving of Tlaloc, the Aztec rain god, looking unamused at having to support my stereo system. On the wall between the big picture window and the hallway hung Mary Hoeksema's serigraph of walking rain in the Grand Canyon, painted in shades of charcoal and lurid red. On the floor below it was a Navajo rug, woven in the storm pattern design. Snowy became more and more relaxed as we toured my collection and drew closer to me, as though what we were seeing pleased her and made her pleased with me. This seemed very strange to me, since I could tell from her few questions and comments that she recognized little of what she was seeing.

We came around to the broad fireplace, centered in the long, north wall opposite the window, and my collection of Hopi kachina dolls on the mantel. "Yes, I know what they are," she said, when I started to explain what they symbolized. "They represent the spirits of gods descended to the earth, living with their people from the winter solstice to the summer, returning to their homes during the latter half of the year." She smiled up at me. "My father collects them. But I've forgotten a lot of the individual personalities," she said. "Tell me about them, please." So I did. I had eighteen spaced along the mantel, so I picked out some of the more interesting ones, those that had been well carved and whose garments and other accoutrements carried a lot of symbolism, and I told her their stories.

"What about this one?" she said, pointing to a figure at the end of the mantel. The doll was done mostly in browns and tans. Except for the rough mane of dark brown horsehair that framed the gray mask and the small feathers at the crown, the doll was carved entirely from cottonwood root. Rain symbols were painted below each eye. A dark green ruff was carved around the neck. The shoulders were draped by a sand-colored shawl and a dark brown skirt went round the waist. The hands carried a rasp and a resonator for making music.

I felt some disquiet as I was reminded of my initial impressions of Snowy, and thought again of the bullets in the coffee cup. "She is called *Masau'u Kachin' Mana*," I said. Something of my mood must have leaked into my voice, because she looked up at me curiously.

"A female kachina?" she asked. "What does her name mean?"

"It's usually translated 'Death Girl.'"

"Hm," she said, inspecting the figure. "Sounds ominous."

"It's not, really. Her name comes from the fact that she accompanies *Masau'u*, the god of the Underworld, during the spring plaza dances on the Hopi mesas."

"Oh. So she doesn't really have any important personal attributes?"

"Wouldn't say that. Heavy rains are supposed to follow her appearance." I paused, but Snowy remained silent. "That's generally a good thing from the Hopi perspective. Their whole religion is centered around trying to wring water from desert skies."

"I see," she said at last, very softly. "But I guess they wouldn't want her to hang around very long."

"Certainly not," I said. "Too much heavy rain would wash away the crops. It'd be quite easy for Death Girl to overstay her welcome."

Snowy looked very pensive. She raised a finger and stroked the doll's hair. I was about to ask what had saddened her, when white fire strobed through the room accompanied by a thunderous crack. I spun about reflexively as the lights flickered and went out. Colored after-images danced before my eyes and my ears rang.

"That was close," I heard Snowy calmly remark.

I began to grope my way toward the dining table on my way to the kitchen. After a couple of steps I stumbled and cursed. "Don't move."

"What is it?"

"I dropped my wine," I said, disgustedly. "There's broken glass all over the floor." I half expected her to ask me if I was all right, which I wasn't, and if I'd cut myself, which I had. I was more than half prepared with an irritated retort, but she surprised me by standing quietly and still. That calmed me down. I grasped hold of a chair within my reach, climbed onto it, and from there to the table. Lightning continued to illuminate the room in occasional, staccato flashes, accompanied by demonic kettledrums, though none came as close as that first strike. I picked a piece of glass out of my foot, climbed across the table, and stepped down to a clear section of the floor.

In the kitchen I wrapped a towel around my cut foot, fetched some storm lanterns from a storeroom in the hallway, and a broom and dustpan from the laundry. Snowy swept up the broken glass while I cleaned and bandaged my foot. I returned to the kitchen and finished up dinner, a quickie beef stroganoff that I reserve for occasions when I want to impress without much work. The rice was a little overdone, but we were both hungry enough not to care. We ate at the dining room table by the light of the storm lanterns. She was still wearing my sweatshirt, the sleeves pushed back past her elbows, though she had put on a pair of her jeans.

We sat at the table afterward, drinking wine and watching the storm. Rain drummed steadily on the roof, rattled against the windows, beyond which the black night was split from time to time with glowing cracks of intense white fire. Snowy wasn't as focused on the storm as I was; I noticed that her gaze shifted with increasing frequency to a point above and behind me. I looked over my shoulder to where the line of kachina dolls stood along the mantel, lit from below by the storm lanterns on the table. The odd play of shifting light and shadow made them appear to be engaged in a slow-motion dance. Except for Death Girl, who seemed to stand apart from the rest, wrapped in brooding shadows.

"You mentioned your father has a collection of these?" I asked, turning back to Snowy.

"Yes," she said, still watching the dolls. "He collected his first the night I was born."

"Which one was that?" I asked, thinking that I knew. As it turned out, I anticipated wrongly.

"Harvest Girl," she said.

"Ah. She's not really a kachina, actually. More of a tribal elder," I said. "I don't have that one; but then, my collection isn't all that extensive."

"Dad has dozens of them, all over his house."

"Where's that?"

"Sedona."

"I've been there. Kind of a 'New-Agey' town, as I recall."

Snowy smiled slightly. "That's an apt description of my father," she said.

"I'd taken you for an easterner somehow. Probably your accent."

She pulled her gaze away from the dolls and looked at me. "Mom and Dad both grew up in Maine; that's where the accent comes from. But I was born near Oraibi."

"Oraibi? On the Hopi mesas?"

"In back of a convenience store, on the first day of winter."

I sat back in my chair, staring at her. "C'mon!" I said. "Don't leave me hanging here; tell me the whole story."

Snowy shrugged. "There's not an awful lot to it. My parents were always traveling around to 'sacred places,' especially on Indian land, annoying the natives and sticking their noses in where they shouldn't." Her manner as she told the story became abstracted, her gaze focused on nothing in particular. "They probably shouldn't have been where they were, but Mom wasn't supposed to be due for another week or so. She was determined to obtain 'the Blessings of the Great Goddess' to sanctify my birth and decided that the Hopi mesas were the perfect place for it. Since Daddy's always been as loopy as Mom over things like that, he agreed."

Snowy sipped at her wine for a few moments, continued. "As my Dad tells the story, they got stranded on the highway by a heavy snowstorm and the proprietor's family let them warm up in their trailer home out in back. Mom went into labor, and I was born twelve hours later. Afterward, the store owner's wife tucked the doll into my blanket for luck."

"Interesting story," I commented.

"It's even more interesting when Mom tells it," Snowy said, her lips twitching slightly, whether toward a smile or a grimace I couldn't say. "According to her, she bore me at the top of a thousand-foot pillar of stone, on a night like this, while a hundred masked dancers circled us, chanting." She paused for another sip of wine. I couldn't think of anything to say that wouldn't sound pitying or callous, so I kept my mouth shut.

"Anyway, that's what started Dad collecting kachina dolls." She toyed with her empty wineglass, twisting it this way and that by the stem. I took the hint and topped us both. "So that's my story . . . What's yours?"

"Nothing so dramatic," I said. "I was born in a small town west of Lubbock and raised in a Baptist family. Ran away from home at sixteen. Joined the army at eighteen. Passed my high school equivalency in the service, won an army scholarship, graduated with a degree in meteorology from Penn State. Spent four years in the armored cavalry, made captain, and was immediately riffed."

"Riffed?"

"Reduction in force," I translated. "There was a big cut in the military budget and dropping personnel is the easiest way to balance the books. Especially officers."

"Why did you run away from home?"

I paused, caught off guard by the reversion. Like a fox she had doubled back along the trail. Finally, I shrugged and said, "It's a pretty mundane story. Nothing that doesn't go on every day in a million households. I didn't get on well with my old man is all."

She was silent, and I noticed she was watching me curiously. I became aware that I was running my forefinger along the ridge of scar tissue at the corner of my eye. I dropped the hand and picked up my wineglass, took a sip. "Anyway, I went back to college and earned a doctorate in climatology. Now I teach a college course in meteorology in the fall and winter and work on my research project the rest of the year."

"So you're properly to be known as Dr. Kane," she murmured, shaking her head.

"Is it that hard to believe?"

"You don't look much like an academic, even cleaned up and fed."

"You haven't seen me in tweeds."

"True. Something to look forward to, I'm sure."

"Ouch."

"Sorry. I'm a little prone to sarcasm."

"Really? I hadn't noticed."

She cocked her head slightly, licked a finger, sketched a tally mark in the air. "So what are you researching, Dr. Kane?"

I hesitated. "It's . . ."

". . . complicated to explain," she finished for me. "I know. You got somewhere to go? Or are you just trying to get me back into bed?"

"The thought had crossed my mind."

She flashed me a brief grin. "Tell."

I sighed. "Okay. But it'll be easier to show you. C'mon."

• • •

The breezeway was protected from the rain overhead, although the wind had blown sufficient moisture through the open ends to dampen the pavings. I led us to the door of my lab, lighting our way with the flashlight I keep in the kitchen. I got the door open, fumbled at the wall inside, flicked a switch; a dim glow illuminated the interior. Snowy turned back toward the house, which was still dark, then looked at me, an eyebrow raised.

"Emergency batteries," I said. "A power failure at the wrong time could cost me a good bit of work. Come inside."

Snowy looked around with as much evidence of interest as she had given to my artwork. The lab was as cluttered as these things can get, with equipment and parts on tables and shelves, in cabinets and bins. The walls were lined with charts and maps on which I kept track of observations that I preferred to view on a scale larger than could be displayed on my monitor.

My computers, one for work, the other for monitoring output from my instruments, were set up on a desk in one corner. I checked the latter, an older model laptop with a 486DX processor running under Linux. The system was up and functioning normally. I opened the log file, saw that Midori had been following the maintenance schedule, and had signed on every Thursday through my micro-network to back up the observation data files. I shut down the logs and looked around to find Snowy inspecting my charts.

"What am I looking at here?" she said, as I came up beside her. There were four charts, arranged in a box — two above, two below. Each chart displayed an outline map of four southwestern states: Utah, Colorado, Arizona and New Mexico. The base map held little detail: major cities, interstate highways and a faint dotted line that marked the center of the Continental Divide. Over each map I'd sketched a series of contour lines with colored highlighters. A legend indicated numerical ranges for each color. The chart on the upper left was labeled "Winter" at the top. The others were labeled "Spring," "Summer" and "Autumn."

"They show the average seasonal distribution of microscopic particles in the air," I told her.

"Huh. What does that have to do with rain?" she asked.

"More than you might think," I said, then paused. "I'll start by asking you to answer a question."

Snowy pulled up one of my folding chairs, turned it around and sat astride it, her arms propped on the backrest. "Shoot."

"What causes rain?"

Snowy frowned slightly as she ordered her thoughts. "Well," she said slowly, "water evaporates from lakes and oceans. The water vapor gathers in clouds. When too much vapor gathers, the clouds turn to rain."

I nodded. "It can certainly happen that way. You've heard weather reporters talk about relative humidity?"

"Of course."

"We usually relate humidity with comfort. When the percentage is high, the air feels wet, sometimes sticky. When the percentage is low, the air feels dry, and will irritate the nose and throat. The percentage is actually the amount of water vapor in the air 'relative' to the maximum amount of vapor the air can hold and remain stable. That varies a lot, especially with temperature; warm air can hold more vapor than cold air.

"When the relative humidity is at one hundred percent, the air is saturated. When it goes over one hundred percent, it is supersaturated. That's a very unstable situation; at that point, it only takes the barest nudge—a sudden shift of temperature or pressure—to make all of the vapor coalesce and fall out of the air."

Snowy tilted the chair backward, balancing it on its back legs. "You mean it rains," she said, dryly.

I grinned. "Well, sure, if you want to put it in crude inexact, layman's terms."

"Yes, by all means, and please."

"Okay, okay. It rains. And in a pretty vicious cloud burst that can cause a great deal of damage and mayhem." I said. "But rain usually occurs before the air supersaturates to that degree. Can you guess why?"

She rocked the chair back and forth a bit, looking up at the wall charts. "Particles?"

"Exactly. As water vapor approaches the saturation point, it starts to condense on airborne particles called 'nuclei.' These are fine particles of salt, silt and sand smoke from forest fires, terpenes from plants and trees, even pollution from automobiles and industry. Now, if there are too few nuclei available, the result can be the cloudburst I just mentioned. But what happens if there are too many?"

Snowy thought a moment, then nodded. "The vapor would be distributed over many nuclei, and none of them would get very large," she said.

"Outstanding. Since none of the droplets become very large, they can't form rain. Highly polluted air, whether of natural or man-made origin, has a difficult time clearing itself. So lack of rain can be the result of too little moisture, but can also be caused by too many airborne particles. Over land areas, a few hundred cloud nuclei per cubic centimeter of air, and a relative humidity of between 100% and 101%, are the very best conditions for rainfall.

"The charts," I said, turning toward them, "show seasonal concentrations of cloud nuclei." I began pointing out the various areas I'd shaded. "You can see that the metropolitan areas show the largest concentrations of nuclei, with the areas along the interstates showing the next highest. The wilderness areas show the least, and also the optimum rain-generating concentrations of nuclei. These data come from a variety of sources, but I've gone to some effort to confirm these concentrations myself."

"Why?"

"I need to be sure of the validity of the baselines, because I'm tracking a rather strange anomaly; one that I've had some trouble convincing my colleagues even exists."

"What anomaly?" Snowy asked, her voice strangely low. I turned away from the charts and looked at her, but her expression hadn't changed.

"A roving zone—I think of it as a 'bubble'—usually about a half-mile in diameter while in motion. When it is at rest, usually for no longer than two or three days, it can expand to roughly five miles. It follows a cyclic path through these four southwestern states," I said, tapping the map, "and moves at speeds of up to eight miles per hour. Within the bubble, conditions for rainfall, in terms of cloud nucleus density and relative humidity, are continuously optimized, independent of other local weather systems."

Snowy let the chair drop back to rest on all four legs. "How is that possible?"

I sighed. "I'm not at all sure, but I think it may be tied in with some sort of roving magnetic or electromagnetic field. In drier air, I've measured slightly higher concentrations of ozone within the bubble than exist outside of it; this is especially true when the bubble is moving at its top speed. The movement of the field through the dry air may be causing static discharges among the particles, which in turn produce minute quantities of ozone. This field may be the mechanism by which the excess particles are expelled from the bubble, though I haven't constructed a working model yet, as to how exactly that would work. On my next trip out I'll take a gaussmeter, and see if I can confirm the existence of the field."

"But it takes more than particles to cause rain, right? You also need moisture."

"True. However, air temperature within the bubble seems to be consistently 0.8° to 1.5° C higher than the surrounding air, depending on how fast it's moving. When the bubble is at rest, the temperature inside it climbs. That causes a low-pressure system that drags in surrounding moist air. I haven't figured that one out yet."

"What causes it?"

"I don't know that either, yet. I strongly suspect that it is a secondary effect of a combination of human activities, such as seasonal traffic patterns and the routing of power lines. I've found a few interesting correlations

Illustrated by Daniel Willis

but I'm going to need to do a lot more analysis to nail it down."

"Traffic patterns and power lines? What have they to do with each other?"

"Both follow highways, especially major roads like interstates." I pulled a map tube from a rack beside the table and extracted the sheet inside. I rolled it out on the table, pushing aside equipment that was in the way, and weighted down the edges with whatever was handy: an air pump, a cyclone particle separator, a couple of rotameters. I heard the chair scrape on the floor as Snowy rose and moved to my side.

The map covered the same four-state area as the charts, but showed the network of highways in much greater detail. I'd traced several of the highways with green and yellow highlighter. In some places the lines converged, while in others they split over roughly parallel routes before merging again. "These are the routes I traced last year, and my observations for this year follow them closely. The cycle takes about fourteen days to complete, give or take a day or two."

While I spoke, Snowy studied the map intently. She put her finger down on the map near Albuquerque, traced the route up the interstate to Denver, over to Grand Junction, and down along local roads to Durango. From there it moved west to Shiprock, southwest through Navajo land, and south past the Grand Canyon to Flagstaff. From Flagstaff the route headed southwest through Sedona, cut suddenly eastward from Prescott to Winslow. From there it led straight back to Albuquerque along the interstate, a loop of roughly sixteen hundred miles. There were small variations in the route, but they did not amount to much.

When she completed the loop, she withdrew her finger and looked at me. "As it happens, you traced the actual direction of the cycle. I first noticed the pattern here," I said, tapping the line of the highway between

Albuquerque and Denver with my finger, "as a progression of thunderstorms that recurred every two weeks. At first I thought it might be a feature of the annual monsoon, but . . ." I broke off as Snowy's expression finally dawned on me. Several years ago I'd found a stray cat that had gotten itself trapped at the top of a utility pole. Snowy had something of that cat's look on her face: frightened, cornered, willing to fight. "Are you okay?"

She closed her eyes, shuddered slightly. "Sorry," she murmured. When she opened her eyes again, her face looked calmer, though tired. "Got a little dizzy there for a moment. I might've had a little too much wine. Can we go back inside?"

"Of course," I said. "My fault, I guess. I'm tired myself, but I tend to get a bit focused when I'm discussing my work."

We returned to the house. Snowy helped me clean up after dinner, after which we headed back to the bedroom. I figured we were both pretty tired, but Snowy started getting amorous as soon as we settled in beneath the blankets. I was feeling a nagging guilt that I might be taking advantage of her; that she felt she owed me this, as the price of my letting her stay with me. So I put my hand over one of hers and said in a low voice, "We don't have to do this if you'd rather rest." She didn't say anything in response, but neither did she stop, and it wasn't long before I didn't want her to.

•••

It was an odd rhythmic sound that woke me. *Snick-click*. Pause. *Snick-click*. Repeated over and over, barely audible above the still-heavy rainfall. I put my hand out to the side, realized that Snowy was gone. There was a glimmer of light to my left and I looked that way. Through my bedroom window, across the wet expanse of the deck, faint illumination was gleaming from the dining room window. I realized then that the power had come back on sometime during the night; I was seeing the glow of the small table lamps I had never bothered to switch off.

Snick-click. Pause. *Snick-click.* The sound was coming from beyond the foot of the bed. I reached for the table lamp to my left and fumbled it on. Snowy was sitting in an armchair tucked into a corner of the bedroom. She hadn't dressed and she had one foot drawn up on the cushion, her knee folded against her chest. Her other foot was on the floor. She was leaning forward in the chair, her arms crossed over her upraised knee. She held her .45 in one hand. With her thumb she was sliding the safety back and forth. *Snick-click.* Pause. *Snick-click.* Her expression was remote and a little pensive.

"Snowy?" I called to her softly. No reaction. I repeated her name, raising my voice a little. Her expression did not change, but she began to speak, quietly, musingly, as though she were thinking aloud.

"The rains began when I was very young," she said. "Only a little at first, and not all of the time. But they got harder, until we had to move. Wherever we went, sooner or later the rains would come. By the time I turned twelve, they were following me constantly.

"My parents were badly upset by this, especially my mom. She tried to drown me in my bath one evening, at a place not far away from here. But Daddy heard the noise and came and dragged her off of me. After that Mom became increasingly irrational and random in her actions, except when she was near me. At those times she was quite single-minded. But I survived those episodes as well, and one day Mom went to live at the sanitarium."

Snowy grew quiet for a space. She stopped clicking the safety on the gun. The sound of the rain, half forgotten while she spoke, rushed back to fill the silence. I didn't like the fact that she had the .45 in her hand or what that might imply about her intentions, but I wasn't very worried. I'd searched her pack and clothes well, and I knew there were no bullets for the weapon, other than those hidden in the kitchen. What I'd heard so far was heartbreaking enough, but Snowy hadn't finished.

"After that Dad and I traveled alone in a battered blue station wagon that the two of us were always having to fix. I actually got to be a pretty decent mechanic during that time. He tried to keep up my schooling while we were on the road, making me read while he drove, and making up complicated math problems for me to work out in my head. But he was getting desperate, I could tell. Because we were always on the move, he couldn't work at any normal job, and we were running out of money.

"When I was fifteen he took us to the Mohave Desert, hoping that the lack of moisture would stop the rain from following us. It seemed to work, but I got very sick and weak. I would've died, I think, if I hadn't somehow managed to return here. Years later Daddy told me that I had slipped out of the hospital, had stolen a car in Barstow, and abandoned it near Gallup. All I remember is that the rains came back, and I recovered."

Tears trembled in Snowy's eyes, spilled gleaming trails down her cheeks, but at the same time her expression of calm abstraction never wavered. "I've been on my own ever since. I eat at soup kitchens or scavenge from restaurant dumpsters. I sleep at shelters, or under highway overpasses, or in abandoned houses. If I go far enough away from here, from my center, the rains do not follow. But I weaken, until I must return, or die. I can take no job that lasts more than a couple of days, for soon the rains catch up, and floods, if I wait too long, and fires from the lightning strikes. I do what I must to survive...." Snowy's voice faltered a moment. I moved to the edge of the bed and sat facing her. She glanced at me as I settled, looked away. I wanted to touch her, to somehow offer comfort, but there was a remoteness in her expression that held me away, even as something deep within me broke and wept.

"I live in fear," she said calmly, but with tears still falling. "I don't know what would happen if powerful people found out about me, but I'm certain it wouldn't be good. At the very least, it would mean the loss of what small freedom I have. Sometimes I dream that I am tied down on a table under bright lights and masked surgeons are leaning over me with glittering knives. Or that I'm trapped in a coffin, paralyzed but aware, fed and voided through tubes, while faceless men move me around like a chess piece, for reasons I can never know. I was discovered once. By someone who seemed as close to me as a sister." Snowy's voice descended to a barely audible murmur. "That was very bad," she said, lifting the gun and bending her wrist to view it from the side. She looked at it for a moment, then let it fall to its original position. "Very bad," she repeated.

"Snowy?" I said gently after she had been silent for a while.

"Yes, Rafe?" she answered, surprising me.

"Please look at me." She did. "Snowy, I don't want to see you hurt. You're not well. Can't you see I want to help you?"

Snowy closed her eyes and nodded, tears leaking from the corners. "Yes, Rafe. I know you mean me no harm. Once I thought differently, but now I know better."

"What do you mean, 'you once thought differently'?" I asked uncertainly.

She opened her eyes, and her expression became

intense, almost feral. "You kept showing up! Wherever I went, there you were, right behind me. I did not know why you were following me, or for whom. I only knew that you were trouble."

"Snowy, I've never seen you before yesterday!"

Snowy spread a hand over her face, made a sound that was half a laugh, half a sob. She slid her fingers back over her scalp, pushing her hair back, shaking her head. "You've seen me all right," she said. "You've just never *noticed* me. You were chasing your damn rain!"

I stared, numbed by her vehemence.

"I punched holes in your gas tank in Gallup," she said. "In Denver I slashed your tires." Random vandalism, I had thought at the time. "You didn't take the hint," she went on, "so I ambushed you up near Taos. The angle was bad and the bullet punctured your tire." I felt as breathless as if I'd just been nailed in the gut. "When you didn't go over the guardrail I almost took another shot, but decided to see if you'd back off. But you just kept right on chasing me."

I couldn't believe what I was hearing. Movie stars and politicians get stalkers, not scruffy climatologists. This was insane!

"I decided to finish things, finally. I confronted you last night at the coffeehouse and learned nothing but confusion. You didn't act like you were chasing me. You just seemed a nice fellow who would have been content to admire me from a distance and let me drink my coffee in peace. When I sat down with you, you seemed wary at first, but soon became friendly enough. Then you trotted out that ridiculous story about chasing rain and I wasn't sure what to think." She shook her head. "Look at you! Even now you don't believe the truth; you just think I'm a dangerous lunatic!"

I decided it was time to put an end to this. I'd have to restrain her somehow, until I could get the sheriff to pick her up. "C'mon, Snowy," I said, rising slowly. "I think you'd better . . ." She pointed the gun at me and pulled back the slide. When she released it, the slide sprang forward into place. I froze. With this model, I knew, the slide should have locked back if the gun were empty. "Sit down," Snowy said. I sat.

"The weight is noticeably different when the clip is empty," she said. She reached with her left hand, picked up something from a small, round table beside the chair. Her medicine bag dangled from her fingers by its leather thongs. It looked flat and empty now. "So relax." She leaned back in the chair, let the gun fall off center.

"What are you going to do?" I asked quietly. This was very bad trouble—people with paranoid delusions and a willingness to use violence are among the most dangerous of psychotics. And that was what she was, I thought. No mistake.

Snowy shook her head, looking miserable. "I've been asking myself that all night," she said. "I like you, Rafe. A lot. I wish we could be together. For a while, I thought everything would turn out all right. I'd just stay out of your way while you were out sampling and measuring, and eventually you'd quit and move on to something else." She laughed briefly, sadly through her tears. "I even had a weird fantasy that I would come by and visit you sometimes. You would always be glad to see me, and would never ask questions when I had to leave. Then you took me into that lab of yours and showed you my damn maps. I know you mean me no harm, Rafe, but you are more dangerous to me than any street freak looking for a little rape and robbery. You know how to track me and you can show others how to do it, too. And you won't stop, because you don't really believe that you should. So what should I do?" She looked out the window at the rain. "As miserable and lonely as my life has been, I want to keep it."

I lunged forward while her attention was diverted, but she reacted with incredible speed. A violent shiver seemed to flow through her body as she dropped the pistol and seized my extended arm. Quick as she'd reacted, she could've shot me. Why hadn't she? I didn't know, but I felt relief when I heard the gun thump on the carpet. Then she squeezed, and I sagged back in shock as I felt both bones in my forearm snap. She dropped my arm, leaned forward, seized my neck with bruising force.

I staggered backward, pulling her out of the chair by the grip she had on my throat. She may have had a psychotic's strength, but she weighed considerably less than I did. I fell back onto the bed, drawing up my legs, planting both feet solidly in her midriff. That loosened her grip a little. I used our combined momentum to roll backward and heaved with my legs. She went up and over. For a moment she seemed suspended, as though she were performing a one-armed handstand on my neck. Then she lost her grip as she passed over my head and crashed through the bedroom window.

I struggled to my feet, gasping through my bruised throat, cradling my throbbing arm. Rain and wind were whipping into the room through the broken pane. Out on the wooden deck I could see that Snowy was already rising. I jumped for the doorway, gritting my teeth as I banged my arm on the jamb, and pounded down the hallway. I glanced over my shoulder, saw her turning toward the big glass doors that separated us. Her face seemed even more feral in the blue white flash of the lightning that flared across the sky at that moment.

I jerked open the door of the hallway closet and managed to tap out a three-digit code on an illuminated keypad just inside, left handed. An indicator light went from red to green, and I yanked my pistol-grip shotgun

out of its cradle as I heard the crash of glass behind me.
I turned and fired at the figure flinging itself toward me.
The recoil spun me to my knees and bruised my wrist.
The shotgun dropped from my awkward left-handed
grip, but the force of the blast caught Snowy full in the
chest, throwing her backward through the broken glass.
I picked up the shotgun from where it had fallen, held it
between my knees and pumped another round into the
chamber with my left hand. Then I stood and faced the
deck.

I stopped as though I'd hit a wall. Snowy was
climbing to her feet, dripping blood. She stood,
stooped slightly forward, looking at me. Then she
dived to the side as I raised the shotgun and triggered
another blast. I spent an awkward few seconds getting
another round chambered, then moved cautiously to
the door and out onto the deck. The rain was a cold
lash on my naked skin, and I realized I was standing on
broken glass in my bare feet for the second time
tonight. I couldn't worry about that now, though. She
was nowhere in sight. To my left, curtains flapped out
of the bedroom window. To my right, light shone
through the dining room window, still intact. I looked
up and around the roof line. Nothing.

I hobbled forward, wincing with each step. The deck
extended beyond the walls of the house for another ten
feet, coming almost to the edge of the arroyo, and was
four feet above ground level at the farthest end. I moved
forward, shotgun aimed at the edge of the deck in case
she was hiding just below the edge. Nothing. She might
be hiding underneath, though. I moved carefully along
the edge toward the stairs that led to the ground.

The deck erupted beneath me. Wooden planks tore
aside like tissue from up-thrusting hands that clawed
at my legs. I was thrown from the edge of the deck, and
hit the sodden ground rolling. I had a brief glimpse of
a dark shape beneath the deck lunging toward me
before my momentum spun me over the edge of the

arroyo and into the swirling current. I struggled to keep my head above the surging water as I was swept helplessly downstream. On the bank above I saw Death Girl pursuing me like Fate, her sprinting form silhouetted by lightning flares, rain symbols tattooed over cheekbones, gusts lashing her hair wildly about her face. I heard drums beating in that moment, and voices chanting, before the world flared one more time and went away.

• • •

I smelled rain on the freshening breeze and paused to look for the front. Midori and the two undergrads continued to sort out the parachute shrouds, which had gotten tangled in a stand of cane cholla when the radiosonde landed. Freeing them undamaged from the cactus was a ticklish job requiring time and patience.

The tall cumulus towers to the south had been displaying violent internal activity for over an hour, and the tops were now showing signs of glaciation. The bases had darkened considerably, and shadowy streaks were visible below. I estimated we had about ten minutes before the walking rain reached us. Heaving a sigh of resignation, I directed the kids to load the instrument package and radar target into the pickup, while I cut the canopy free and folded it up. I felt a fugitive twinge or two as I bent to my task, remnant aches from the injuries I had sustained last year.

I handed the canopy up to the undergrads in the back of the pickup truck, then climbed in behind the wheel and started the engine. Midori rode with me in the cab, while the students wedged themselves into corners in the bed of the truck, bracing themselves with indifferent success against the occasional jolts that bounced them around whenever one of the tires dropped into a prairie dog burrow. The ride went more smoothly once we reached the jeep trail and I breathed a sigh of relief when we made it past the dry wash that crosses the road leading back to the college. I was less worried about getting wet than I was about being trapped behind a flash flood. I now had firsthand experience of how bad that can be.

The flood had battered me around pretty badly; I'd ended up with a broken leg, two fractured ribs and a concussion to go along with my broken arm, bruised throat and cut feet. I woke up in the hospital several days later, my physician assuring me that I was a very lucky man in that faintly weary, disapproving tone that says, "I don't know why I bother fixing you up when you do stupid things like this." As if I'd gone skinny-dipping in a flash flood on purpose. Of course, I hadn't told anyone what had really happened that night, and my sleepwalking story sounded pretty thin.

The rain caught up with us as we reached the college. I pulled up behind the Sandow Environmental Sciences Building and we hastily unloaded the pickup. I had Midori return the truck to the motor pool while the kids and I brought the equipment up to the lab. It was already almost 7:00 p.m., so I let the kids go and started packing things away. Midori came in while I was stripping down the instrument package on the radiosonde and helped me get it squared away. She's been my graduate assistant for two years and would be going on to my old alma mater, Penn State, to complete her doctorate at the end of the semester.

"Want to go get some coffee at Tam's?" Midori asked me as we finished up.

"Mind if I take a rain check?" I said, not really feeling up to it.

"If you do, it'll be the fourth one this month."

"Has it been that many?" We had started getting together for coffee regularly about six months after she became my graduate assistant, strictly on a friendly basis.

"More, really. We haven't gone since you got out of the hospital. I don't want to impose, though, if you still aren't feeling well." I became uneasily aware that she wasn't the only one of my friends I'd been neglecting.

"No, you're right. It might be a good idea after all. Meet you in half an hour?"

"I'll be there."

The rain had lightened a bit by the time I drove the Brough out of the SES parking lot. I was happy to have the cycle back; the Colfax County sheriff had found it abandoned up near Cimarron last year. I was still in the hospital at that time and hadn't even known it was missing. It took a while to clear all the red tape, but I'd finally been able to check it out of police impoundment last month, apparently none the worse for the wear.

The coffeehouse was doing a fair amount of business when I arrived. Tam was occupied with a customer when I walked in, but noticed me as I passed the counter, smiled and waved. I took a table near the front window and a waitress brought me a cup of Sumatran, without my having to ask for it. Midori came in a little later and we talked for a while, discussing various topics: her doctoral project, which involved a fairly inspired algorithm she'd developed for climate modeling, questions for the midterm exams, and some of the more promising undergraduate students in the program this year.

"Where are you with your research paper?" she asked after a while.

"On hold, for the moment."

"Problems?"

"A few."

"Anything I can help with?"

"Not really. It's just that the data from the last trip aren't confirming my results from the first year. I may have to can the project."

"Huh? When you called in last year, just before you got back, you were fairly crowing over how well things were coming together. You couldn't wait to get into print! What gives?"

I shrugged. "I was wrong, that's all."

She stared at me, frowning slightly. "You've found something special that you're keeping secret," she said flatly. "Do you think I'll talk about it? Is that it?"

"Of course not! Where'd you get an idea like that?"

"There's nothing wrong with your data from the first year, Rafe. I've been over it and it's solid. If the variance on last year's observations had been that extreme, you'd have known about it right away."

I leaned back and sighed. "Yes, I've discovered something, but it is something that disqualifies all of my observations as data relevant to atmospheric sciences. And yes, I'm keeping it secret, because it is not anything anyone needs to know. I'm not trying to make sure that my findings remain quiet until I publish, Midori. I have no intention of publishing any of my research on this project. Not now. Not ever."

She sat silently for a time, digesting what I said. Midori is not the type who blurts things out impulsively. She considers well before she speaks—a trait I often value, though it can be occasionally disconcerting. Unfortunately, this was one of the latter times. "I've put a lot of work in on this project, Rafe," she said. "I realize I'm just a grad assistant and that this kind of stuff is my job, but I like to think the work I do counts for something. If it's all got to be for nothing, I think I deserve some sort of explanation."

"I really can't discuss it. I'm sorry."

"This is beginning to sound like some kind of deep, dark conspiracy."

"If so, it's a very small one."

"Does any of this have anything to do with your accident last year?"

I raised an eyebrow at her. "How in the world do you manage to make a connection like that?"

"Does it?"

"No."

She took a sip of her coffee. "Who was the woman?"

"What are you talking about?"

"That rancher who found you. What was his name . . . Emilio Roybal? He said there was a naked woman standing on the side of the road where he found you."

"He said he got a glimpse of a woman as he drove by, and that she was gone when he stopped and got out of his truck. It was dark and raining heavily."

"But he found you lying where he saw her standing, a hundred yards from the arroyo."

I shrugged. "I don't remember a lot that happened after I fell into the flood. . . . "

"Sleepwalking," she said dryly.

"Yes. Sleepwalking. Maybe after the current threw me on the bank, I managed to stagger to the road before I fell. Or, maybe I was thrown that far—freakier things have happened. He saw me out of the corner of his eye and his imagination did the rest."

"Your leg was broken."

"People in shock have been known to stand, even walk, on broken limbs."

"Rafe, *please*."

"Midori . . ." I started getting angry, but I knew she didn't deserve that. I sighed and leaned back in my chair, staring out the window. "You won't believe it."

"Does that mean you'll tell me?" When I didn't answer, she said, "Rafe, I promise even if I don't believe you, I'll keep secret everything you say."

"All right," I said. "All right. But I'm going to sit here and watch the rain while I tell the story, so I won't have to see the expression on your face." I paused, watching the raindrops trace lightninglike lines along the window pane. "It started the night I returned from my trip, right here at this table. That was the first time I really noticed Death Girl."

• • •

The hour was late. The streetlights cast wavering yellow trails that slid like snakes along the wet pavement. A large puddle between the window and the street showed a protean, spiky topology as raindrops pierced its surface; it looked almost alive enough to slide out of its low-lying nest and crawl off down the street.

The place was empty except for Midori and me. And Tam, who had locked the front door sometime in the last couple of hours and come to sit with us, bringing a full pot of coffee with him. I don't know how much he understood as he sat there and listened; his English is somewhat broken. But he sat quietly and said nothing, and somehow I hadn't felt inclined to stop talking or to ask him to leave.

We sat quietly for a while, and when I finally dared to look, I saw a troubled expression on Midori's face, which I more or less expected. Tam was wearing a reflective smile, which I found astonishing. I was intensely curious to know why, but I knew from experience he'd say nothing substantive until he was ready.

I looked back to the window and said, "Okay, Midori. Out with it."

"Why didn't you tell anybody about this woman, Rafe?" she said.

"You mean like the police?"

"Especially the police. The woman is an obvious lunatic!"

"I don't think so."

"You don't?" She stopped, speechless.

I looked at her. "Lunatics can't tear through solid,

two-by-six wooden boards with their bare hands. Or survive point-blank blasts from a twelve-gauge shotgun."

Midori shook her head. "You were hurt. You must have missed her with the shotgun. And the deck was probably rotted out in that section."

"No. I've surveyed the damage and, apart from being ripped in half, the wood is sound. And if I missed my shot, I've no way to explain where all the blood came from," I said. "So okay—she's probably a little messed up; who wouldn't be with her background?"

Midori looked at me in slack-jawed amazement. "You believe her story?" she asked, wonderingly.

"Yes."

She shook her head. "Okay. Say, for argument's sake, her story is true. Say that rainstorms really *do* follow her around. She's still too dangerous to run around loose. Can you really be so lost in your sexual tunnel vision that you can't see that?"

I shrugged, but the remark stung, perhaps too much. "Is that your experience of me?" I said, keeping my voice mild. "That I would allow lust to overrule my sense?" I looked back out the window. "Or did you really think I hadn't noticed all these years how pretty you are, or what good company you are to have around?"

Tam chuckled.

After a few seconds, Midori said quietly, "How would I know about that? You've never given me any sign."

"Of course not. I'm your teacher. It wouldn't have been right," I said gruffly, already regretting letting her goad me like that. Again she was silent. Midori was second generation American, but her parents were still old country enough to give her a Japanese first name. And to impart to her a sense of the responsibilities of a teacher toward a student.

"All right," she said at last. "Why *haven't* you told the police about her?"

"I don't want her harmed."

"Pity she doesn't feel the same way about you."

"I'm not so sure. She might not have gone as far as she did if I hadn't jumped her. And I think she must have fished me out of the arroyo. Remember where I was found, and what Mr. Roybal saw."

"So you don't think she's dangerous?"

"On the contrary, I think she can be very dangerous. Gods and goddesses can be that way."

"Gods and goddesses . . . You're making me wonder about your sanity now."

I smiled. "Well, perhaps she's not a deity. But she's the closest thing to one that I've ever met. A real live rain spirit. I don't know the nature of her bond with the rains, but I know it's real and unique. How could I possibly wish her harmed, or penned, or restricted?"

"I've never thought of you as being particularly religious," Midori said. "Just the opposite, in fact. Now you sound like my grandfather telling Shinto fairy tales."

"She is a Devi," Tam put in.

I looked at him, raising an eyebrow. "You would say an angel. Or a demon. Some of each," Tam amplified.

"How can she be both?" Midori demanded.

Tam made a circling gesture with his hand. "The wheel turns. There is time for everything. Especially for a Devi."

I nodded. "I gave up on religion long ago. I can't believe in gods, or eternal life, or divine justice, simply because I might wish these things to be true. Many can, of course. I have no problem with that. From time to time I envy it.

"Rain has been my refuge since I was a child. It has been the natural, impersonal force that has ruled my life. Now I've encountered rain's avatar, the living personification of that element."

Tam squeezed my shoulder. "You have been blessed, my friend."

"How can you say that?" said Midori. "Rafe was nearly killed!"

"We all die," Tam told her. "Most of us without seeing the divine in this world." He looked back at me and nodded emphatically. "You have been blessed."

Midori retreated into one of her reflective moments. "Do you care about her, Rafe?" she asked in a low voice. "As a person, I mean?"

"Yes."

"Do you think you'll ever see her again?"

"Yes."

She looked up at me. "You sound very sure."

I nodded at the window. "She's out there right now."

Midori turned, gasped.

"A Devi," Tam whispered. He began chanting a prayer in a low voice. In the dim illumination of the streetlight stood Death Girl, looking exactly as she had a year ago.

"How long has she been out there?" whispered Midori.

"About fifteen minutes, more or less," I said, rising to my feet.

"Rafe?" Midori said, turning and raising her hand as if to stay me. I caught it and gave it a squeeze.

"I'll see you later," I said.

"Where are you going?"

I gave her a quick smile, turned and left.

Outside I kicked the Brough to life, already soaked halfway through. I drove down the driveway to the street and around to where Snowy stood waiting. She slipped onto the saddle behind me and put her arms around my waist. I glanced aside as I pulled out into the street, looking through the window to where Midori and Tam sat, watching us. I hoped that I would see them again.

BLOOD AND HORSES

Written by
Myke Cole

Illustrated by
Britt Spencer

About the Author

There are some who say that the pen is mightier than the sword, but in the life of Myke Cole, both have equal measure. When he's not writing, Myke can be found plying his blade in a kendo dojo or on a Society for Creative Anachronism tournament field.

Myke would like to think of himself as a full-time writer/swordsman, but he'd be lying if he said he didn't have to work a day job.

About the Illustrator

Britt Spencer is from Lexington, Kentucky. He has been enrolled in an art school since the fourth grade, however he finds it impossible to accurately state any time in his life when he officially started artistic maturation.

Britt is currently attending the Savannah (Georgia) College of Art and Design, studying the field of commercial illustration. Although more accustomed to the fine arts, he is equally fascinated with the design elements that graphic design employs.

The subject matter of Britt's artwork is generally very conceptual and alludes constantly to science, anatomy, psychology, ideology, politics and sociology. His personal website portfolio is located at www.brittspencer.com.

he three horses are beautiful beyond belief. They tear up the Xianjiang plain with supernatural speed. My bullets are faster.

The desperate riders won't fare any better than their steeds. They'll die long before they can obtain a drop of the oil they seek to steal. It is still safely shut away in the pipeline beside them.

They can't outrun me. They race along the massive stretch of pipe rushing barrel after barrel of the precious black fluid out to Bombay and the Arabian Sea. But neither the oil in the pipeline nor the horses are faster than the turbines in my exoskeleton.

The distance between horses and exo shrinks with each passing second.

The exo's smartsystems allow me to focus on dialing in my coordinates as it keeps me a steady distance above them.

I catch my breath just looking at those horses. The Chinese historical annals I used to teach called the horses "heavenly," and they were as right today as they were two millennia ago. The dignity that Han emperors used to pay so dearly for is still obvious in the flowing manes and flaring nostrils. The horses make the brush strokes of the ancient Chinese painters come to life.

Ask me about that and I can tell you. I used to teach history.

The riders wear dirty caftans and turbans. They

strike a horrible contradiction with the animals they ride. They're probably Kyrgyz, or maybe Kazaks, like me.

Except they're not anything like me. Maybe they're like my grandfather. He was old enough to remember when our people knew hunger, before we turned our back on our past. I know exactly who they are.

They're starving, desperate nomads looking to stave off hunger with a little pilfered oil. I'm a history professor trapped in a machine capable of leveling a small city, wondering how I can bring myself to hurt them.

Pipe-2's voice crackles over the commlink. Almaty Pipeline Authority just assigned her to me yesterday. I can't remember her name. "Efim, wake up." A pause, then, "Pipe-1, wake up."

The horses' flanks reflect the rays of the setting Xianjiang sun. How can the tappers look so filthy and their steeds look like they're cast of bronze? I sigh and flick my jaw to trigger the commlink. "Pipe-1. Yes, I'm on them." It comes out flat. What should I say? *I'm a history professor. I don't like playing soldier. Leave me alone.*

Pipe-2 says, "I got it." Insubordination. I should correct her, but I don't bother. She's only doing what we're both here to do, what our families and Kazakhstan have demanded of us. Command isn't exactly my strong suit. I run the pipe out of duty. By choice, I teach history. Ask me about Nazarbayev and his political machine, sit down over coffee and biscuits and we can chat about the Virgin Lands Campaign or maybe even the Kalmyk-Russian alliance. That's what I'm good at, thinking and teaching, not commanding and killing. Not defending pipelines.

I'm not right for the job, but Kazakhstan feels differently. The oil in that pipe has transformed us from a Kazakhstan of starving beggars, the likes of the nomads coursing beneath me, to a Kazakhstan so wealthy that they will never have to work. Kazakhstan puts their best and brightest up to protect that oil.

One hundred years ago, their best were the old-world soldiers of tawny muscle and steely eye. Today we kill with machines so complex that intellect has finally replaced muscle as the currency of battle.

The same genius that earned me professorial tenure chained me to the exo's controls. That's the law.

We all do our seven-year duty to Allah and Kazakhstan. But very, very few of us score well enough on the aptitude examination to qualify for the pipe-run. Lucky me.

Six of my required seven years of pipe duty have passed. One more and I can trade my bullets for books and live again.

"Breaking to attack," Pipe-2 reports.

Now I can see her. She folds up her spoilers and drops like a bronze beetle toward the fleeing tappers. Good. Let her do the killing this time. She drops close enough to the ground that her backtrail kicks up huge clouds of pollen, steppe shale and dried grass, whirling and then raking across the earth. The ordnance arms on her exo unlock and extend to an attack position.

The riders split up, like they always do. It's not a problem for us. I don't know about Pipe-2, but I'm short, one year to discharge. To a veteran like me, there aren't a lot of new tricks in the tapper bag.

Pipe-2 does it by the book. Without breaking course, she locks on the third rider, already galloping toward the hills away from the pipeline and lets fly a howling fusillade of smartrounds.

I'm still marveling at the horse as the ammunition flies its magazine. The smartrounds scream as their engines kick in and they begin to adjust, tracking their target. The horse's hindquarters bunch and stretch, hooves pounding the terrain, *eating* the ground. I can see what those ancient Chinese emperors sought in these heavenly horses. The bright equine eyes are eager with the passion of speed and power that was the closest thing to flight in a world that lacked the technology to reach the sky. All this was before Islam, oil and self-guided bullets became daily fare in Xianjiang. The current Chinese emirs of Xianjiang don't care about anything save the oil and their next meal. One depends on the other.

The horse defies nature with its speed, pawing up desperate clouds of dust, eddies that are split by the smartrounds' supersonic windtrails, which part them as precisely as a micron wire through a tender throat. The billowing dust blossoms to swallow rider, bullets and windtrails whole.

I glimpse the rider coax the horse into leaning impossibly low, the animal a vision of dexterity as they disappear behind a boulder, the smartrounds hounding them into their graves.

The remaining two riders race ahead. Pipe-2 continues by the book, covering one flank and blocking escape. I have no choice but to cover the other.

The rider closest to the pipe leaps a small tap, perhaps of his own making. We rocket over the tendril of crudely soldered copper, duct tape and plastic, unsuccessfully concealed by a pile of dirt and brush.

We gain on the ancient might of the heavenly horses. One of the riders reaches into his caftan. Allah, those horses are beautiful.

We rocket past the tap. Only Allah knows where that stolen crude is being piped, most likely to a drum beneath the ground for later retrieval.

The thousands of barrels rushing through the main-line are hardly diminished by such a tiny leak. But my grandfather used to run this pipe just as I do now, and he made the party line abundantly clear: One tap is nothing, but when you let one slide, from sympathy or carelessness, it becomes a thousand. He didn't need to

Illustrated by Britt Spencer

remind me what it had been like to live like these tappers beneath me. I know their history. Years of pipe-runs haven't made me forget it. Better them than us.

A divet is rising up along the trail of the chase, a deep cleft over which the pipe is supported by broad steel crossbeams. The riders will have to go around, but show no sign of slowing. Pipe-2's ordnance arms rotate. She's switching to explosive BAMs. The clustering action should give her enough range to kill both of the riders without damaging the mainline's outer piping. Then we can go back for the tap.

The innermost rider leaps upright onto his saddle, then off the horse and onto the pipe itself, pulling a rifle from beneath his caftan.

I've seen these acrobatics a hundred times before and it always makes me catch my breath. Pipe-2 has seen it too, but is less impressed. "Eyes on, Pipe-1, that fool is armed."

Fool to fight, but a fool every bit as magnificent as the horses themselves. The horse, brilliant as it is beautiful, breaks right and veers for the hills. I am relieved to see it go. It, at least, will survive.

The tapper raises his weapon to his shoulder. He reminds me of my grandfather. Definitely a Kazak. Did my great-grandfather look like that? Did he have the same sunken eyes? The same desperate ferocity? Of course he did. We all did. Once.

I can see the words forming on the tapper's lips as he aims his weapon. *Allah ho Akhbar*. The Chinese- and Kazak-speaking tappers spout Arabic they don't begin to understand. We Kazaks were true believers once, but that was three generations ago when we were newly rich. My father called those the "ugly jewelry" days. Now we're a nation of lip-service Muslims who might occasionally stop drinking for a holy night if we thought our elders would bother us about it. The tappers of Xianjiang never drank. Religion aside, they couldn't afford it.

The fool tapper's well-placed shot clips one of Pipe-2's folded spoilers. Pipe-2 goes spinning. The commlink blazes in my ear, "I'm hit!" Damn. Now I have to get in the fight.

The tapper's antiquated PPC is not a real threat to Pipe-2's exo, but she's definitely shaken as she recovers to her original flight path. Her panic is evident. She drops her BAMs in a scattered arc, mostly on the pipe.

The clustered explosions are too weak to damage the triple hull of the pipe. The fleeing horse, however, gets to enjoy the full effect. There isn't anything left of it bigger than a shoebox. Pipe-2, stone you. There are a few things that all the oil in the world can't replace.

The tapper who shot Pipe-2 is gone. I spare myself a second to look at the broken remains of the horse. It often feels as if my real life is lived in the precious quiet moments between the screaming explosions of fire power, those scant seconds when Chinese-Kazak nomads are my cousins and not walking-dead oil thieves.

The BAMs kick up a cloud of dust so big that I have to fly on instruments. It is a relief. I'd rather not see the tappers' faces.

My heads-up lights an alarm. It's showing tappers in the scores coming from the east. This is a lot more than I've ever seen in one place before.

Pipe-2 comes into view through the dust. I flick the commlink to tell her to drop back, but then I see the problem. Her right spoiler is a nub of melted metal and plastic where the particle beam hit it. She's losing control. She cries out to me, "Efim! What the hell is going on here? I can't get the exo to stabilize!"

"I see it. That PPC had eater agents, you're losing a spoiler. Set her down."

"Merciful Allah . . ." Now Pipe-2 sounds frightened, and she should be. Eater agents are not old technology, and Pipe-2 is looking at the possibility of losing her exo. There's no way to tell how much she got on there, but the agents will slowly decompose all of the metal alloys they come in contact with until they spend themselves. Pipe-2 knows exactly what will happen to her if the tappers catch her on the ground unarmored.

Pipe-2 extends the exo's legs and hits the ground with a running jolt. The exo jogs along uneasily from the momentum.

"Hostiles incoming!" I cry into the commlink.

"I've got them," Pipe-2 replies. "Must be a camp nearby."

I grab the controls; the exo folds up and dives low. I've got to hit them while they're all still clustered together. Give them time to disperse and I could spend the rest of my life running them down one by one.

And I've got to get them *all*. Because it's them or us, and it's better to teach about them in history survey classes and dream about them and see your grandparents in their sunken, angry eyes than to be them. But I want to be them, if only long enough to cut through the air on the back of one of those magnificent horses.

My grandfather strung himself along the same miles I was running now, and all so that I would never have to bed down in a dirty yurt, empty-bellied and praying desperately to *Allah ho Akhbar* to let me see another sunrise. Better not to risk a few barrels or a few million. They were history. I taught about them once. Soon, I'll teach about them again. Until my discharge, I slaughter them.

The autofeed is reporting our actions to Almaty Pipeline Authority, detailing every bullet fired. They've probably already dispatched backup, but it will take them at least an hour to reach our position from Almaty.

That will mean more dead. *Far* more than I'm about to bring about now. The pipeline authority won't waste the manpower on the nomad community; they'll just put the squeeze on some of the local Chinese emirs, trusting that those thugs know which side their bread is buttered on. I've written papers on the atrocities the emirs have committed; they put heads on spikes, rape children, poison wells.

Leaving only the ordnance arms extended, I fold up the foils and legs and drop down, easing up to full speed. As the exo reaches the bottom of the dust plumes kicked up by the BAMs, I can make out the plain beneath it. It is oddly peaceful, weeds waving, flowers radiant with color. The plains of Xianjiang have always been two-faced. They reach up to strike us pipe-runners down, favoring the nomads with their great dusty hands, and then—realizing they are beaten—they pretend not to know what all the fuss is about.

The mass of tappers surge forward toward Pipe-2's grounded exo. It's not often they have a pipe-runner in their grasp. Behind them is probably the most impressive piece of their entire arsenal, an old mainline hulk, its treads still shaking off rust from the Great Jihad that brought Islam to power in western China thirty years ago.

Recent history, but history just the same. My grandfather had told me that the hulk looked like a vulture, but I can't see it. It looks more like a squat, grinning bullfrog. The turrets whirl and squeal, puffing outward like an ochre dewlap. And around it, a sea of those magnificent horses. The contrast is almost offensive.

What's more offensive is the result when I open fire. The barrels sweep left and right like a lethal push broom, and the tappers go out like sand from a yurt threshold. I see one tapper throw his arms up, dropping an antique rifle and billowing outward as his caftan explodes into shades of red and a sickening gray that can only be his internal organs. Another man is thrown as his horse catches a round through its neck, spinning the beast up in the air and landing it directly on top of its rider, undoubtedly crushing him. They all fall like this, dozens, scores. Each one is wearing the face of my grandfather, the waiter who served me my drink just yesterday, my tennis partner. Each one is my whole nation just a few short generations ago.

Allah ho Akhbar, indeed. *I'm a history professor. Better them than us?*

The remaining tappers take cover. A few dive behind the hulk, others lay behind rocks or mounds of earth in the idiot assumption that something like that can actually stop a 20mm round. Stupid and desperate; this isn't about oil to them or even ugly jewelry. They want to live. The tappers die in droves, but the hulk shambles on.

I can hear Pipe-2 shudder through the commlink. I can't remember the last time we lost a pipe-runner to a lucky tapper. Eater agents have been banned by a Geneva Convention amendment, but desperate people don't follow our rules.

My commlink crackles. It's a distant signal. "Pipe-1, this is Interceptor-6. Relief Lance is inbound to your position. ETA twenty minutes." I acknowledge and look back to Pipe-2. Backup is coming much faster than I expected, and I hadn't expected Interceptors. They'll finish this fight, hulk or no, in moments. But twenty minutes is still a long way off.

The remaining tappers outrun the hulk easily, the heavenly horses moving with a speed that pushes nature's envelope. I strain to see a touch of reality, their hooves touching the ground, but I can only glimpse a blur of muscular legs and puffs of sand. Their pulsing bodies are the strokes of some long dead painter's brush. The exo's gun barrels track them eagerly. The dirty riders, crouched like wicked parasites in the saddles, whip their steeds for all they are worth, desperate to reach Pipe-2 before I can rescue her. It's not often they have a chance to grab hold of a pipe-runner and make her pay.

The hulk zeroes in on her. She's in real trouble. The turrets have given up chasing me and now lock solidly on Pipe-2, who has stopped, firing her remaining smartrounds. Idiot. They're called smartrounds for a reason; the screaming bullets don't even bother with the hulk, its damp heat signature indicating armor they can't pierce. Instead, the rounds hunt the charging tappers, who pose the lesser threat. They are torn from their saddles by the agile fire, their screams overwhelmed by the howl of the bullets.

The hulk fires, main and supporting turrets supplying a grouped pattern which neatly blows off one of Pipe-2's exoskeletal legs.

The woman is dead. There is no way I can get to her in time. Not now. Pipe-2 collapses backward. She should be screaming into the commlink, but I think she's past that by now. It simply doesn't occur to the average pipe-runner that they might actually fall victim to a ragtag tapper band, no matter how big. We're safe, locked inside powered armor, an unmatched arsenal at our fingertips. All they have are horses whose ancient grandeur cannot help them escape their animal reality. Beauty, presence, magnificence, no matter how great, is no match for a bullet.

Those same bullets have lifted us above these filthy oil thieves with their religious fanaticism and their desperate grasping for life. We believe that, we hold it dear. And here is Pipe-2, about to be overrun, about to lose to them. Heavenly horses and desperation may be enough this time.

The hulk thunders toward her. I rocket around for another pass and fire on the hulk. I know the armor, old as it is, will certainly stop the bullets, but maybe at least I can distract the pilots while I switch over to heavier ordnance. The hulk barrels onward. Pipe-2 hasn't popped her canopy. She's waiting for me to save her.

I've already delayed too long. I switch to hellfires,

sight down the back left tread of the hulk and let fly.
The red whoosh of fire turns much of the sand behind
the hulk to glass. The scattering flames driving the
tappers away, howling human torches. I have bought
Pipe-2 a bit more time. But the hulk continues forward.
I didn't hit the mark.

Which is ridiculous. I'm a better shot than that. This
is Pipe-2's life here. I can't just let her die because I'm
nostalgic about a bunch of scavengers who won't come
out of the middle ages. No, that's not right; they *can't*
come out, we won't let them. I've taught this very
point in a hundred history classes. My grandfather
would be furious with me. Why the indecision? The
choice is clear. Destroy them or be them. The world is
a competitive place. It's competitive for blades of grass
and bunny rabbits. It's competitive for starving
nomads, pipe-runners in crippled exos and idiots who
hesitate to save their own comrades. Another point
I've taught time and again.

The mounted tappers surround Pipe-2. They wheel
their horses as they fire shot after ineffectual shot into
Pipe-2's exo. Particle beams and bullets alike dance
across the exo's armored surface. One of the tappers
has even drawn a long sword and is slashing at it.

I can't see how much work the eater agents have
done. If I don't give her some cover fire, and right now,
they'll break through.

The horses strain, each beautiful neck a waiting
target. I try to tell myself that the fire might accidentally
hurt Pipe-2, but I know that's a stupid argument; not
firing will hurt her more. I steel myself to do my job.

My exo jerks sharply. I'm hit. Preliminaries from
the heads-up show no real damage, but it's enough to
get me to overshoot the hulk and bank sharply to get
my bearings.

I see the shooter. It's a lone tapper howling Allah's
name from atop a small boulder. He's holding an old

shoulder-mounted LOSAT missile tube. I finish him. There's no horse to slow me down this time.

But the sound of my own fire is almost drowned out by the sound of cracking metal and a scream of static over the commlink. I turn to watch the hulk roll over Pipe-2, crushing her to pieces. The exo is finished and so is she.

You waited too long and now she's dead. One of yours. She's history. You're a history professor, you know all about dead people.

That hit from the tapper didn't make a difference; I could still could have gotten to her in time, if I had wanted to. An ice pick lances my gut and scalp.

My next hellfire finds the hulk neatly between main turret and body and transforms it into a ball of splintering flame. The tappers are still cheering. I don't think any of them have even grown up with the legend of a pipe-runner downed by their own. This one will go down in their songs.

They may wear my grandfather's face, but I carry it in my mind. It scowls at me now, chiding me for letting this happen, for letting all that we have fought for be crushed by these mirrors we struggle not to look into. It isn't just my grandfather either, it's thousands of others back in Kazakhstan, each one with a right not to have to live like these people now celebrating around the exo's corpse and their own shattered hulk.

Does it have to be them or us? Old men aren't always smart. My grandfather could have been wrong. History teaches us this. I know, I teach history. My discharge is around the corner.

A few more bullets send the remaining tappers scattering. Somewhere underneath the flaming remains of that hulk, Pipe-2 is becoming one with the superheated molten glass that my missile has made of the sand.

Them or us. You read history, or you become it.

The tapper's victory over Pipe-2, grounded and confused, had been easy. Their euphoria evaporates as I swing back and low, releasing another hellfire in their midst. The flames catch something in the hulk, possibly the magazine, that triples the force of the explosion. The tappers go flying, burning and screaming. No. Those aren't screams. They're shrieks, neighs and whinnies, horses burning.

It's what is best. I grip the exo's controls so tightly I fear I will break them. Them or us. My grandfather would not have worked for nothing.

Another hellfire, two. Several riders scrabble out of the fire, making a mad dash away from the pipe. I bring the exo in high, no hesitation this time, and switch over to guns. The fleeing tappers are too small to distinguish between horse and rider and I'm not bothering anyway. The bullets reach out and pluck them from the ground, one by one, casting them head-long into the dust beside their own entrails.

I spin the exo once, twice, looking for survivors. The heads-up confirms that the scene is barren. They're dead, all of them.

I give one more quick scan, and then extend the legs and set the exo down as close as I can to Pipe-2. The scene is an inferno, so that my exo cracks the sand-turned-to-glass even at the distance where I set down.

The fire eats flesh and metal alike; there won't be much left when it burns down. I can still make out the forms of the horses, burning orange, blue and white.

The painter's brush strokes are gone, streaking color replaced by harsh charcoal. Two thousand years of beauty and grace reduced to crackling fuel.

I should be mourning Pipe-2, I know I should. My grandfather would have, and the nation certainly will when they find out she was lost.

The commlink crackles. "Pipe-1, this is Relief Lance. We're showing a lot of fire here and no vital signs from your fire teammate. We'll be on site in roughly five minutes. What's your status?"

What can I say? I succeeded? Failed? I stand and watch the horses burn. My stomach dives as it occurs to me that their corpses might actually be melting together with Pipe-2's.

The commlink again, "Pipe-1, this is Relief Lance. What is your status?"

I toggle the link. "I . . . Pipe-2 is dead." My voice breaks. They think it's Pipe-2 I'm choked up over.

"Got that. Are you under fire?"

"Negative. Area is secure, all hostiles are neutralized."

"Acknowledged. Any stragglers? Should we send out additional intercepts?"

Why bother? Pipe-2 is dead. The horses are dead. I couldn't save either.

In a few minutes, the sky will darken and churn as the relief lance arrives to mop up. But no mop-up is necessary; I did the job just fine myself.

"Helluva firefight for a guy about to get out, Pipe-1. I'm so sorry." He's trying to be sympathetic. I suppose I should appreciate it.

Around me, the corpses continue to burn. The exo, the horses, the hulk, the motley band of tappers, all history. Xianjiang alone remains unchanged, settling down into its own rhythm, breezes from the fire gently ruffling the grass.

All history. I know about history. I'm a history professor. I teach about the past.

The future whines its way over the horizon, trailing in the wake of the approaching exos of the relief lance.

INTO THE GARDENS OF SWEET NIGHT

Written by
Jay Lake

Illustrated by
Asuka Komai

About the Author

Jay Lake was born in Taiwan, the same year the Beatles first appeared on The Ed Sullivan Show. *Life has since taken him from Mt. Kilimanjaro to Point Barrow to Ulaan Baatar, and on to Portland, Oregon, where he makes his living in the information technology industry and resides in a Queen Anne Victorian with his family and their books. Jay won the Amateur Short Story Contest at the 1997 WorldCon, while his first published story went on to win the Best of Soft Science Fiction Contest in 2002.*

Jay—prior to winning the Writers of the Future Contest—had been a frequent and fervent entrant over many quarters, doing well but never quite reaching one of the top three spots in quarterly competition. This story succeeded in his very last quarter of eligibility. Jay notes he "continues to craft speculative fiction at a feverish pace."

About the Illustrator

Asuka Komai was born in Tokyo, Japan. She's been drawing since she was very little and believed she would be a cartoonist. In her early teens, she took an interest in writing stories. As a result of her intense curiosity in many things, she found it almost impossible to pick one profession and started designing sets for TV studios, musical stages and festival venues. Two years later she gave it up and, at the age of twenty, started learning English.

At the age of twenty-eight, Asuka came to the United States to study art. During the first year, she was an intern for an art gallery in Manhattan, but found she couldn't live without creating something. Now, as a student at the Fashion Institute of Technology (one of the State Universities of New York), she has been pursuing her dream: writing her stories in English and illustrating them. Why not in Japanese? Because she feels English is the language in which she can express herself . . . all over the world.

Chance Meeting by Road

"Penny for your thoughts, stranger."

Elroy glanced around. His mind had wandered as he followed his footsteps down the ancient metal highway. No one was in sight.

He felt a tug on the leg of his trousers.

"Down here, stranger. Fancy a Justiciary penny?" The voice was high, almost squeaky.

Elroy looked down. A tan pug dog with a black face and ears trotted on its foot paws next to him, one thumbed paw loosely caught in the muslin of his trousers at the level of his right knee. The pug wore a green-flowered waistcoat.

At two meters in height, Elroy towered far over the Animal. "A Justy penny? Truly?"

"Spend 'em anywhere," said the pug with pride. The dog's brown eyes darted back and forth, while a long tongue licked its nose. Its curly little tail wagged quickly.

Considering the unmodified muzzle, Elroy thought the pug had a remarkably clear voice. It offered him the promised penny in its right thumbed paw. Without breaking his stride, Elroy leaned down and grasped the coin. He slipped it into his belt pouch. Justies spent anywhere, not like the various city scrips backed only by faithless reputations and threat of local violence.

Elroy was returning from a year-long spirit quest among the Little Brothers of High Impact in the Glass Mountains of Oklahoma. He was headed home to his family's little treetop cabin in the rain forest around Pilot Knob. Elroy wanted to climb lianas, gather bananas in the clearings and hunt tamarin monkeys in the high forest canopy. He wanted to court a familiar girl, wed the old-fashioned way and raise a family up in the trees as Texans always had, which required funds, something he had in small supply after a year in a monastery. And he was still five hundred kilometers from home, a long, lonely walk down the decrepit highway.

The pug tugged again at his trousers. "Well?"

"Animals." Elroy shot a sidelong glance at the pug. "I am thinking about Animals."

The pug sidestepped away, disappointment flashed in his canine eyes. His tail drooped. "I did not pay for an insult, friend."

"You neither bought my friendship with a Justiciary penny, stranger," snapped Elroy. "But I won't insult you. I said 'Animals,' not beasts."

"Your thoughts, then?" The pug growled and narrowed its eyes.

Elroy could see the pug's hackles rise above the collar of its waistcoat. He sighed, regretful for having mishandled the situation so quickly. "What is servant to a mounted man, peer to a footed man and master to a legless man?"

The pug's hackles dropped back below its flowered collar. "A poor riddle, as you already gave me the answer. Scarcely worthy of my investment."

Elroy slowed, stepping to the roadside next to a weathered sign that read "New Dallas 82 km, Fresh Fruit Next Left."

"My deepest apologies, gentle pug." Elroy recalled his school days and the whippings he routinely received from Master Stenslaw for inattention to the finer points of law and social custom. "I am rarely approached under the terms of the Mutual Contract and am unversed. I intended no offense."

"None taken, I'm sure," muttered the pug.

"Enough, then." Elroy smiled. "I stop to dine. It's poor fare I have, but I offer it freely."

The pug laughed, a strangled bark. Its tail flickered again. "I like generosity in the young. They are usually too callow to comprehend the value of a gift freely given. Let us instead repair to the fruit vendor ahead. In recognition of your kind offer to share your food, I will stand us a pair of kumquats or whatever else they might have that suits."

A Dinner of Fruit in the Rainforests of Texas

"Well, you're a couple of likely lads." The old woman at the fruit stand smiled a gap-toothed smile.

"I am hardly a lad, good woman. Do not mistake my size for youth." The pug drummed its claws on the edge of the old woman's table. "We will have two kumquats and a liter of wine fit for consumption."

"No kumquats today; guavas three for a New Dallas dollar. I'm out of wine, but you can have sweet plum jack, two NewDees a liter," she recited in a bored voice.

"Two Justies for the guavas and the plum jack," the pug countered.

"Three."

They bargained in a desultory manner, settling on two Justiciary pennies and a New Dallas dollar, which the pug handed over from the pocket of its waistcoat.

"Thank you, my good woman." The pug stepped back from the table. "Get our supper, my boy."

Elroy considered arguing that he was not, in any sense, the pug's boy. The smell of the guavas changed his mind, being far more appetizing than the stale bread crusts he had planned to eat. He took the three guavas and the liter of plum jack, served with the loan of a translucent tube with white volumetric markings on the side, and followed the pug away from the fruit stand.

• • •

They ate in the shadow of the glossy green leaves of a blooming mango tree. Elroy was grateful for the two guavas the pug had generously given him. They passed the plum jack back and forth swig for swig, although Elroy drank considerably more than the pug at each pass. The mango tree sat on a bluff above the highway, giving them an excellent view of several kilometers of the road. In the distance, a land train puffed dark smoke and light steam into the sky, while the heavy scent of the mango blossoms and the drone of insects lulled Elroy toward sleep.

"*Magnifera indica.*" The pug waved at the tree above them. "In Vedic tradition, this tree symbolizes abundance and divine sweetness." The pug grasped the tube of plum jack in both thumbed paws and gulped. "Alcohol is dangerous for small dogs," the pug continued, panting. "Slows down their breathing, interferes with the central nervous system."

The conversation worried Elroy. Animals were not beasts, and for the pug to refer to its base canine ancestry so casually violated a widespread taboo. The great projects of the Viridian Republic had long since vanished from history, save for Animals, who now labored in many of the occupations of the world. They carefully fashioned their succeeding generations in their own images and were equally jealous of their heritage and the secrets of their kind. Elroy held his tongue, choosing silence over potential insult.

"Well," the pug continued after a long pause, "a man who knows when to hold his thoughts." It passed the plum jack to Elroy.

"I am a traveler far from home. It is trouble enough for me to know my own thoughts, let alone mind those of others."

"A worthy attitude. Would that all were as wisely discreet."

Elroy opted for tact. "Discretion is the better part of a man."

The pug studied Elroy closely, licking its nose repeatedly as brown canine eyes scanned his face. "Are you heading home or setting out?"

It was a question not asked in polite conversation. Elroy recognized the seriousness of the pug's request and gave consideration to its openhandedness with the guavas and the plum jack.

"Returning, sir pug, from a long course of spiritual study and physical pursuits."

"Were you successful?"

Elroy shifted, uncomfortable but trapped by the pug's hospitality and the opening created by his own honest answer. One boy in every generation from his town of Pilot Knob was set out on the road to the Little Brothers. Some returned, some did not. Many who did became village hetmans in their time. Elroy felt no ambition to rule, but he had found balance, strength and a small measure of wisdom among the Little Brothers—qualities he recognized as desirable in a future leader. "Yes, I succeeded."

"So your duties to faith and family have been fully discharged?"

"Yes. I am free and bound for home."

"Then I would offer you a post of service with me, for a time." The Animal smoothed the front of its flowered waistcoat, showing more than reflexive nervousness. "My terms are generous, especially if we meet with success in my ventures."

Elroy did not want to take service with the pug, to be distracted from home and finding a bride. On the other hand, starting a family took money, or at least resources. The pug's Justiciary penny had already doubled his savings, and having left the monastery, he was no longer a mendicant.

"What service, what terms and what is the mark of success?"

The pug licked its nose. "I need a person of discretion and physical skill to assist me as a traveling companion and bodyguard. I offer expenses, board and a Justiciary penny per day, plus substantial bonuses upon success of my own mission." The pug paused, plucked at its waistcoat as it stared forlornly at its foot paws. Its curled tail drooped. "I was a gardener, but have been lost to my work. I need help to find my way back into the Gardens of Sweet Night."

Elroy laughed in spite of himself, spraying plum jack on his crossed legs and the grass in front of him.

"A child's bedtime tale," he said, coughing up more plum jack, "and one with which to frighten bullies and cowards. A thousand pardons, but your jest is in poor taste."

The pug drew itself to its full seventy centimeters. "I do not jest. I know the way back to the Gardens, but it is not a road that I can travel alone. I can see I have wasted my time here. Good day, sir man."

"Wait, wait." Elroy stretched a hand toward the pug, palm outward. "I can see that you are serious about this fable. How is it that you plan to return?"

"Well," the pug sniffed, "it is an arduous journey, hence my need for a traveling companion. I have offered you a position of trust to travel at my side, if you will trust me to know where I am going."

Elroy nodded. "Your funds will stand me good stead when I return home. It is not my ambition to be a servant, but I will accept your wage. I am a human man called Elroy, and I will take your service."

"Friend Elroy, I accept your offer of service under the terms discussed. I am an Animal called Wiggles."

Elroy was profoundly glad he had no more plum jack in his mouth as he swallowed another laugh.

Somewhat is Learned Concerning the Gardens

They walked toward New Dallas the balance of that day before settling down to rest under a baobab tree on a sparsely vegetated plateau. "*Adansonia digitata*," Wiggles identified the tree. "The South African baobab. They grow in rain shadows and drylands, since they do not favor too much water. The tree is not native to the Western Hemisphere. We are lucky it is not in fruit—they are notoriously rank."

The trunk of the tree was broad, like a wooden silo ramified with exposed roots, spreading to a great crown high above their heads. "I've never seen one," said Elroy. Baobabs did not grow around Pilot Knob.

"They can store one hundred tons of water. In their native ecosystems they serve as reservoirs that anchor dryland ecosystems. There is one in Babylon much larger, but that is the nature of things there."

Elroy waited politely for the pug to continue.

Wiggles sighed. "Babylon, one of the Gardens of Sweet Night." He scratched in the loam at their feet, drawing seven long ovals like sausages laid end to end. He pointed to them in turn.

"Heligan, Babylon, Suzhou, Eden, Daisenin, Gethsemane and Tuileries." His voice was sadness itself. "The green wealth of our Earth, captured and multiplied by the guiding genius of man and Animal."

"And you came from there?"

Wiggles nodded, a very manlike gesture. "Born and raised in Heligan."

"Why did you leave?"

The pug stared at Elroy, licking his own black face. "There was a misunderstanding. I was cast out for eating the apples of our lord."

"Your lord?"

"Liasis, High Commissioner of the Cis-Lunar Justiciary and Lord of Implementation for the Atlantic Maritime Territories."

Elroy had never heard of such a person. "Who is he?"

"The man who owns the world."

● ● ●

They watched the stars rise over the eastern horizon, the two of them stretched out together under the edge of the baobab's scattered branches. Venus came first, then Yurigrad, brightest of the thousand satellite stars, on its fast course through the sky.

"The stars shine like diamonds cold and hard in the skies that surround the Gardens," said Wiggles in a sleepy voice.

"This Liasis . . ." Elroy struggled with the name. "How does he own the world?"

The pug's tail thumped against the ground. "Do you pay taxes at home?"

"Me, no, but the village of Pilot Knob tithes every third moon."

Wiggles sat up, began grooming himself, tongue lapping through his fur. He stopped for a moment. "To whom does your village tithe?"

"The Travis Caldes."

Wiggles burrowed briefly into his groin. "And to whom do they in turn pay taxes?"

Elroy recalled his lessons in civics and economics. "I suppose they must pay them to the Republician government in Waco."

Another pause for air. "And to whom do the Republicians tithe?"

"I never imagined that they tithe anyone, sir pug. I did not know who might stand above them."

"Everybody tithes, in one fashion or another. And it all flows upward, friend Elroy. Only the Lord Liasis does not tithe. He and a few of his brethren."

"How can it be," wondered Elroy, "that if I am a free man, everything is owed to someone of higher station?"

"What does freedom mean?" Wiggles turned around several times and went to sleep.

● ● ●

The warmth of the new day washed over them. The baobab lay some kilometers behind. Elroy considered his bread crusts with longing as Wiggles spoke.

"I believe I can find a maglev station to speed us on our way to New Dallas. We will have far to go from there."

Old tutelage in archaeoscience tumbled through Elroy's memory. "Maglev. Magnetic levitation, yes? An ancient mode of rapid transport."

"Correct." Wiggles smiled while licking his nose. "Normally subterranean. This system was originally developed near the end of the First North American Ascendancy. As I recall, the La Grangians reconditioned it."

"I had no idea it was still active."

"Many things move above your head and beneath your feet of which you have never dreamed."

The discussion of last night still weighed on Elroy's mind. "How free am I?"

Wiggles laughed again. "You breathe of your own choosing, yes?"

"Yes, I suppose that I am free to breathe."

"Some people dwell in places where that is a right, licensed and paid for every turning of the moon. Yet they consider themselves free."

Elroy was shocked. "Free? When they must pay for the very air they breathe?"

"Some claim there is absolute freedom in holding responsibility for every aspect of their lives, including the air they breathe. Every day they live or die by the consequences of their actions."

Behind them, a shrill blast from a steam whistle warned of an oncoming land train. Elroy and Wiggles left the road to stand in the twinned shadows of a honeysuckle that struggled over slow years to overwhelm a banyan tree.

"*Ficus benghalensis.*" Wiggles tapped a thick aerial root with a thumbed paw. "A relative of the mulberry, mistakenly thought by the ancients to be a fig tree. Another colonizer of these American shores. Traditionally, this tree represents shelter given by the gods, a symbol of their benevolence toward man."

The clanking, screeching land train overtook them, all brass piping, bright paintwork and great iron wheels. Elroy did not feel particularly sheltered.

Beset by Wolves, Any Man May Be a Hero

The land train groaned to a shuddering stop before their banyan tree. The sixth and final car halted directly in front of Elroy and Wiggles. Three security wolves jumped over the red and yellow ironwork sides, surprising them. One slammed Elroy back against the banyan tree using a rough arm across his chest while another knocked Wiggles down to pin him under a foot paw.

The lead security wolf leaned one forearm against the banyan tree while tapping Elroy on the chest with his staff. The wolf was definitely male, as were his gray and tan fellows. They all wore black armored vests. He growled through a toothy smile. "You two pups are in our crimebase, freshmeat." The odor of his breath gagged Elroy.

Elroy was frightened, not for his life, but certainly
for his safety, and that of Wiggles. Gathering his calm,
he protested, "You don't even know our names. We
have rights under the Mutual Contract."

"Rights." The lead wolf laughed, a very human
sound. "I've heard of those." He leaned closer, the
lolling tongue nearly swiping Elroy's nose.

"This little dog is a dangerous character, friend
man. You'd do well to avoid his type." The wolf
glanced down at Wiggles, squirming and whining on
his back. "Breeding error, you know."

Elroy sized up the three wolves. Each stood taller
than he, armed with iron-shod staves and stun guns.
One was occupied standing on Wiggles, while the
other two cornered Elroy against the aerial roots of the
banyan. Bad odds, from a poor position, but he would
not allow either fear or tactics to keep him from his
responsibilities. His vows with the Little Brothers
forbade attack, but defense was another matter entirely.
Elroy centered himself as he had been taught, then
drew a steady breath.

"Sir pug is my employer, and I owe him loyalty."

"Freshmeat, you don't listen well. . . ." the security
wolf began. Elroy spun a left snap-kick that landed on
the wolf's scrotum. Spinning through the kick, Elroy
grabbed the staff as it tumbled from the shocked wolf's
thumbed paw, following on to catch the next security
wolf across the forearm.

The second wolf screamed as its ulna shattered.
Elroy shoved the iron tip of the staff into the second
wolf's chest, pushing it back into the banyan, before
whacking the groaning first wolf alongside the head to
keep it down. He turned to help Wiggles, only to see
the pug with his jaws locked on the inner thigh of the

third security wolf. That wolf shook Wiggles free and leapt on the pug, just as Elroy brought the staff down with a resounding thwack on the back of the wolf's head, pulling his blow so as not to kill.

Panting with adrenalin and relief, Elroy used the staff to lever the unconscious wolf off Wiggles.

"Sir pug, are you well?" he gasped.

"That son of a beast smashed my phalanges," screeched Wiggles. "I fear I cannot walk, and more wolves are certain to come from the fore of the train."

It was terribly rare for a human to handle an Animal so, but Elroy scooped up the pug as his own breathing settled to a manageable rhythm. "Then this would be a fine time to remember where a maglev station might be."

He fled into the jungle, carrying the iron-shod staff in one hand and Wiggles in the other. Elroy mumbled a prayer of thanks that he had not maimed or killed the security wolves.

•••

They crouched in an understory deadfall on the jungle floor, listening for sounds of pursuit. The old rotted trunk was surrounded by large, flat leaves fallen from above, each the size of a serving platter. The leaves decayed with a gentle sugary smell.

Elroy's fear had been replaced by a rising sense of anger—at the situation, at the wolves, at Wiggles. "By the Cattle of the King, what was that ambush? My masters took my vow not to strike in anger and already I am in default. I am paying dearly for your wage, sir pug."

"A moment, please," said Wiggles. "Allow me to

collect my thoughts. You do fight very well for a peasant boy from the Texas jungles."

Elroy folded his hands and made a constrained bow within their sheltering greenery. "My spiritual masters practice an aggressively strenuous form of ethics. Now tell me, what brought the security wolves down on us?"

"Flaming Sword," said Wiggles. "The ones who cast me out. They guard the secrets of the Gardens of Sweet Night."

"The constabulary of your Lord Liasis?"

The pug drew himself to his feet with a groan. "The secret police, perhaps. Ancient tradition holds that a flaming sword bars the gates of the Garden of Eden, namesake of one of the Gardens of Sweet Night."

Elroy examined the staff. "I would expect the secret police to carry the fiercest of weapons."

"Not here, on the surface. It is forbidden by both common sense and the Mutual Contract. They expect no sharp resistance here. They will not make that mistake with us twice."

In the distance they heard the scream of the land train's steam whistle, long blasts in groups of three. Wiggles growled, his ears laid back flat. "They launch the search, as if we were dangerous brigands. Damned canids."

Elroy examined the jungle around them. His mind and body were calm again. "Well, then we must find your maglev station quickly. I presume it is hidden underground or I would have heard of such a thing before." Elroy paused, working through his line of reasoning. "A maglev must use a lot of energy, and something that old would not be well shielded. Do you have a means of locating that kind of energy leakage?"

Wiggles looked surprised. "Excellent thinking, friend Elroy. You have been better tutored than I had hoped. I do have something like that, but to my embarrassment, against all propriety, you must again carry me. My foot paw pains me sorely."

Elroy scooped up the pug. "Show me the way." He trotted through the green-shadowed depths of the jungle floor, harboring regrets.

•••

"Ware tigers, friend Elroy." Wiggles's voice was muffled against Elroy's shoulder.

"Surely you mean wolves?"

"No, I scent felids. Large beasts, not Animals. I understand that *Panthera tigris sumatrae* have become naturalized here in Texas."

"A wonder to behold, I am sure," Elroy replied, wondering how Wiggles could scent the difference between a beast and an Animal, "but I am ill-equipped to stand off something larger and less foolish than your flaming wolves."

"If a tiger appears, I am confident you will think of something."

This stretch of jungle floor looked much like any other to Elroy, with dangling lianas and scattered deadfalls. Butterflies strayed down from the high canopy, drifting through isolated shafts of green-tinted sunlight.

After a time, Elroy voiced his thoughts. "Between the tigers and the wolves, I worry if we will emerge from this jungle intact."

"Regretful you took my pay?"

"No." Elroy surprised himself. "The wolves attacked

without warning and offered no legal authority. Further, your money earns my way toward starting a family."

"Surely a thought worth a Justiciary penny." Wiggles gave another of his odd laughs. "Put me down here, please." He began snuffling around on all fours in a spiraled circle in the loam, limping to favor his left foot paw.

"Here." Wiggles's voice carried from behind another banyan tree. "Bring that stick you have been carrying."

Elroy stepped around the tree to see Wiggles digging into the loam, scattering leaf mold and dirt behind him. He could hear Wiggles's thumbed paws scrape on something solid. The pug backed out of the hole, then stared up at Elroy. Elroy noticed the flowered waistcoat was as clean as it had been when he first met Wiggles—a sign of smart matter, although Elroy had never actually encountered the stuff.

"Open it," suggested Wiggles.

Elroy peered into the hole. A metal hatch cover lay exposed about eight inches below the jungle floor, a large handle inset within a rounded recess. Elroy reached down with the iron-shod staff, levering it against the handle. He leaned with all his strength.

The handle did not budge.

"Harder," snapped Wiggles. Elroy noticed the pug's hackles were rising. He thought he could hear the distant echo of the steam whistle.

Elroy leaned against the staff, pulling with his entire weight, until his feet almost left the ground as the staff bent back.

The roar of a tiger startled him greatly.

The hatch handle screeched as it slid across the rounded recess. Elroy and the staff collapsed on Wiggles's dirt pile as Wiggles bounded to the sprung hatch and tugged at it with his thumbed paws.

The tiger roared again.

Elroy grabbed the hatch, pulling it wide open as Wiggles dove down the hole. Elroy tossed the staff after Wiggles and swung himself into the hole to the sound of a startled yelp from below. As he pulled the hatch cover closed, he saw the green eyes and tufted face of a Sumatran tiger peering in at him.

Wiggles's encouraging words echoed up from the darkness below. "Don't worry. It's the smallest species of tiger in the world."

A Magnetic Journey of Conscience to Flower Mound

They stood in a dimly lit hall, high-ceilinged and quite large. The echoes of Elroy's feet scuffling on cracked tile carried some distance. The whole area had a musty, oily smell, overlaid with the cool damp common to subterranean spaces. Vague reddish light from hidden sources obscured much more than it revealed.

Wiggles thumped his tail. "Excellent."

"Yes?"

"This was the Denton station. It is long out of commission since there is no town here anymore. The line still runs through it straight to our destination, however. I have already summoned a service car for a trip to Flower Mound, which you call New Dallas."

"So this is the maglev," whispered Elroy.

"Well, the station anyway. You will see the train soon enough."

They waited on a concrete bench in the silent dimness. Wiggles whimpered periodically from the pain in his paw. After a while, Elroy realized their mistake.

"What will happen when the wolves discover the hatch?"

"First they will discover the tiger, I suspect." The pug snorted. "But in any case the dirt will have taken care of things by now. It isn't very bright, but it knows its job."

"The dirt?" Elroy realized Wiggles was an absolute oracle of lost technology. "Was it nanotechnology?"

"Exactly. Moderately intelligent nanodirt. It is self-restoring. That's what I looked for. We use it in the Gardens of Sweet Night. I have a detector sensitive to its signature."

When the maglev service car finally arrived, its running lights brightened the station. Elroy saw tall vaulted arches, cracked murals on the wall and a row of long-shuttered shops. Tiny pairs of eyes gleamed in the shadows by the tunnel mouth.

The service car itself was an almost featureless polished wedge, much different from the steam-driven iron trains that Elroy had seen all his life, and quiet as a stone. Elroy added disappointment to that day's catalog of emotions.

●●●

"Flower Mound." Wiggles stretched, shaking out his fur while licking his nose. "The lotus is a flower of great significance, symbolizing purity and divinity. These days people call this place New Dallas, but it is built on a most spiritual foundation."

"It is only New Dallas, sir pug, not the Vatican Aresian."

They stood in the Flower Mound maglev station. Similar in design to the abandoned Denton station, it was well lit, dressed-stone walls bearing sculpted metal light fixtures. A tile mosaic floor supported scattered travelers seated on concrete benches or reading wall posters. The shops here were long-shuttered, too.

Elroy had left the iron-shod staff in the service car, since it seemed too conspicuous to carry through the station. He grumbled, "I walked all the way to the Glass Mountains while this world beneath could have carried me in comfort."

"But you were free every step of the way, yes?"

More free then than he was now, Elroy realized. "Are we much closer to the Gardens?"

"We are until the Flaming Sword picks up our trail," said Wiggles darkly. "Those wolves had no reason to carry nanosensors out there, but it won't take them long to reason out where we went. We must move onward and upward. Support me by clasping my thumbed paw, please. It would be a scandal for me to be seen riding in your arms."

Elroy extended a downward hand. "First, I suppose, we must find a way out of this station. Surely they do not employ a secret ladder here?"

●●●

"I am embarrassed to say that I feel enslaved by your wages." Elroy clutched the two Justies the pug had just given him, filled with a sense that he had surrendered control of his fate.

Wiggles smiled. "Freedom. An ideal of some

concern to you. Consider that the meanest felon digging a ditch in restitution to his lord is a free man. He may place his mattock thusly or so at his own choice, bend or stand as he wishes."

Elroy leapt to the flaw in Wiggles's proposition. "Yet he is in chains, undeniably bound, his actions constrained."

"Those chains are of his choosing," said Wiggles. "The felon chose his crime, with the ditch as consequence. When I offered you service, you chose to join me. The Justiciary pennies in your hand and the pangs in your conscience are consequences. You are, of course, at liberty to resume your original journey."

They sat on a bench in the Gamelan Garden, a park in the center of New Dallas, just off Simmons Road. Wiggles had demanded rest in a cultivated park. He had declared Gamelan with its orchids and fleshy vines and vast bromeliads the palest imitation of the Gardens of Sweet Night, but still balm for his injured soul.

Elroy shook his head, studying the coins in his hand. "I will stay." He did not want to admit it, but Elroy was becoming fond of Wiggles.

"Caring is a surrender of freedom. You may see that I am trapped by my love of the Gardens, that this lovely *Odontoglossum hortensiae* so reminds me of." The pug sniffed at a pale, fleshy flower, his tail wagging. "Flowers are the mothers of insects, you know."

"Did they name it 'Flower Mound' for the orchids that grew here?"

"Goodness, no." Wiggles laughed, his tail slapping the bench. "In those bygone days, what grew here were dryland plants such as prairie grasses, pecans and mesquite."

At Elroy's puzzled look, Wiggles added, "You know. *Prosopis glandulosa*. A nitrogen-fixer that anchored the boundaries of prairie." The pug rubbed his left foot paw with a thumbed paw. "My foot is sore hurt, friend Elroy."

Speaking the Language of the Sky

They stood in a line at the base of the mooring mast that towered above them, a slender blade of white metalloceramic stabbing into the sky toward the great bulk of the airship *Child of Crisis*. Elroy had seen dirigibles cruising above the trees all his life, since the usual airway from New Dallas to Monterey ran above Pilot Knob. He had never been close to one.

Elroy craned his neck to study the gondola at the bottom of the airship. It was doubtless quite large, but still appeared miniscule against the bulk of the gasbag. "I've never ridden the air before."

"To do so down here is of no comparison to the Gardens of Sweet Night."

"My experiences pale next to yours, sir pug," Elroy snapped, "but leave me the joy of what little I have to call my own."

"Peace, friend Elroy." Wiggles squeezed Elroy's hand, his small thumbed paw dry and stiff. "I did not mean to offend."

"Next load! Group six!" A red-faced young woman, her skin much paler than Elroy's woody brown complexion, shouted from the boarding doors at the base of the mast.

Wiggles checked his chits. "Let's go." The two of them shuffled through the hatch onto a small elevator with a number of other passengers. Behind them, Elroy saw the line of waiting people and Animals through the closing hatch.

The elevator hummed almost below audibility. Wiggles had warned Elroy about the sensation of being pushed down while the little car climbed the inside of the mooring mast. "I wish there were windows," Elroy whispered.

The car suddenly lurched, shaking in its rise. From the conductor's shocked gasp, Elroy gathered this was not part of the usual ride. They stopped for a moment, then began moving up again.

A bulging man with a thick, burred Mississippian accent sounded panicky. "And what would that have been?"

The conductor picked up a small handset from her control panel and listened. The car shuddered upward, much less smooth in its motion than before. Elroy could hear a deep groaning through the walls of the elevator.

They staggered to a stop and the doors hissed open to reveal a tiled floor about waist high to Elroy. The conductor dropped her handset. "There is a problem down below. The airship is casting off for its own protection. Please remain calm and stay in the elevator car."

"Flaming Sword," whispered Elroy. If they stayed in the elevator, the wolves would come for them, endangering the other passengers. He had to get away, to protect himself and everyone else. Elroy scooped Wiggles up in his arms like a beast and pushed toward the open doors.

"Here there, boy." The man with the Mississippian accent grabbed Elroy's arm. Elroy spun, swinging his elbow into the Mississippian's chest with a prayer for forgiveness. He had no time to reason with the man. Elroy miscalculated his blow and felt ribs crack.

"Moment of Inertia," Elroy wept through clenched teeth. "May the Little Brothers forgive me." He hopped one hip up onto the ledge that was the floor outside, and rolled out of the jammed elevator. The conductor plucked at his heel, but he ignored her.

The massive bulk of the *Child of Crisis* filled the sky above Elroy. Ahead of him, it stretched into the distance, the shimmering metallic bulge of the airship's gasbag dropping below his view. The boarding platform at the top of the mast was about four meters square, while a slender spire arched up above him to meet a set of lines depending from the airship's nose. A narrow gangway about three meters long led to the open hatch of the gondola underslung along the forward curve of the airship.

Two sailors in crisp blue uniforms were unfastening the gangway from the open door, preparing to drop it loose. Wiggles whimpered as a series of explosions echoed up from the ground below. The platform swayed beneath Elroy's feet. There was no time for thought. He sprinted toward the gangway, screaming, "Wait, wait for us!"

One sailor looked up, the gangway's release chain slack in her hand. The other yanked his chain, causing the right side of the gangway to drop away from the hatch while the chains on the left took its full weight.

Elroy raced over the edge of the boarding platform onto the sagging gangway as the other sailor belatedly released her chain. Elroy pushed off as the gangway fell away, straining into the jump with Wiggles tucked firmly under his left arm. As he fell, Elroy reached forward with his right hand. It was like running the trees in his home jungle, only far more deadly.

The gangway tumbled away beneath his feet to swing from the boarding platform, revealing perhaps a hundred meters of empty air between Elroy and the flagged paving stones of the airfield. His fingers missed the hatch coaming, then grasped at the swinging chain as the second sailor hauled it in. Elroy caught the chain, but his body swung forward with the momentum of his jump and smashed against the gondola wall. Wiggles yelped, muffled by his arm.

As Elroy swung back on the chain, spinning over the airfield, he saw the boarding platform falling away from him. He realized the dirigible had cast off and now rose into the sky. People from the elevator were helping the bulky Mississippian onto the platform, while the conductor waved her fist at Elroy. Far below, he could see a fire at the base of the mooring mast, with figures struggling around it.

"Need a bit of help there, lad?" The female sailor peered down at him. Elroy spun slowly on the chain, grateful of the support wrapped around his forearm, even as the pressure of his weight threatened to crush his wrist within the chain's tightening grip. The two sailors peered from the open hatch above him.

"If you please," gasped Elroy. He wondered what the warm, acrid smell was, then realized he had pissed his pants.

"We'd need to see a boarding chit." The two of them grinned like monkeys sharing an armload of rotten papayas.

"A thousand pardons." Elroy shuddered. "I am somewhat constrained at the moment." He slipped two links down the chain, the length circling his wrist binding tighter. He could feel bones grind against one another. Elroy hissed with pain.

The woman pulled a serious face, rubbing her chin. "A right problem there, lad. Rules say we have to see the chit afore you can pass the hatch."

"Ancient law, that is," the second sailor added. "Protects everyone's rights, that does."

They both laughed.

Wiggles squirmed beneath his arm. "Money. Offer them money."

Elroy's hand slipped, and he felt an astonishing pain as his elbow threatened to come loose in its socket, counterpoint to the grinding in his wrist.

He clenched his teeth. "Perhaps a gratuity would be in order."

"Now you're speaking the language of the sky, lad." The two sailors hauled in their chain.

• • •

"Despite the irregularities of your embarkation, your boarding chits seem to be in order."

Elroy's wrist throbbed so severely that he had trouble focusing on the purser's words. They stood in the officer's abbreviated workspace in a forward cabin of the airship.

The purser was an aging golden retriever wearing a blue jacket with epaulettes. Its fur was braided in tight cornrows, each one clasped by a clip decorated with an ancient copper coin. It stared at Elroy and Wiggles as if they were unpleasantly spoiled cargo loaded by some error. "It seems I am stuck with you for now. What transpired back there at New Dallas?"

Wiggles glanced sidelong at Elroy, who took that as a hint.

"Sir purser," Elroy began. He was not sure what he should say, but he had brought them aboard the ship. He felt the way he had when summoned before the abbot for some infraction. "I am in service to this noble pug. We were chased by brigands. We thought to escape by boarding the *Child of Crisis,* but they were closer than we realized. My most humble apologies for bringing risk upon your vessel."

"Brigands," said the purser flatly. It stared at Elroy, its large brown eyes sweeping up and down his grimy beaded vest and torn muslin trousers. It then turned its gaze on Wiggles, whose green-flowered waistcoat was, as always, immaculate.

"I may be a foolish old Animal who has spent his life among the free folk of the air, but I know brigands when I don't see them. Those were security wolves, firing indiscriminately down there with heavy weapons." It glanced at their boarding chits. "You two are fully paid and bound for Odessa Port. I've a mind to have you both tossed from the hatch to save me further trouble, but it's a fact that the Air Charter protects *Child of Crisis* and all her passengers and crew from precisely this harassment. Now tell me what you're really about."

Wiggles scratched his ear, then licked his nose. His tail stayed tight to his body as he spoke. "My servant and I are pursuing a quest."

"And that quest would be?"

Wiggles spoke with a quiet, proud strength. "Through error, I have been cast out of the Gardens of Sweet Night. I now make my way home."

The purser studied them a moment. "In their

common room up against the belly of the gasbag, air sailors tell stories of those who die in the wide arms of the sky. Every man and Animal longs for a peaceful death in the air, followed by a sky burial. What we—they—say is that the bodies rise up singing into the heavens, until they come to the Gardens of Sweet Night. That is where they find their reward." It laughed, a stuttering bark deeper and richer than Wiggles's wheezing moments of humor. "Somehow you do not seem like one who has returned from the dark clouds of death."

"It is but truth, friend purser. My story is as real as the Gardens themselves, for all that they may be myth to some."

"I do know more than the simple sailors."

"If you know the world," said Elroy unexpectedly, "you know injustice." He surprised himself with his words. "We have been pursued with a vengeance out of all proportion to any offense. You have your Air Charter. We have only our wits and our luck. I beseech your help in surpassing this wicked pursuit and gaining entrance to the Gardens."

"You speak well for a servant," said the purser. "As it happens, I have conceived of a way to lend a hand, spite the security wolves and keep the *Child* from multiplying her current difficulties, all in one stroke. If I can persuade the captain to spite those who trespass on our ancient rights, we may throw you from the hatch after all. Would you care to experience a sky burial of your very own?"

Rise Up Singing

The crew common room was low and dark, with a

convex ceiling following the swell of the gasbag. Elroy, at two meters of height, could stand only along the slant-walled sides where the ceiling reached up to about the top of his head. Long and narrow, with no windows and poor lighting, it felt to Elroy like the sarcophagus of some giant from prehistoric America.

"You effected our rescue quite well," said Wiggles.

Elroy snorted. "I assaulted an innocent man, then leapt into empty air, to be saved by dumb luck and a long chain."

"You saw what needed doing and did it."

"Perhaps. But not now. What *are* we doing here?"

Wiggles rested in the hammock with Elroy, curled up against his side. One of the sailors had cleaned and bandaged his wounded foot paw, but the pain clearly bothered the pug.

"Hiding from passengers who will certainly be questioned at Odessa Port by the Flaming Sword. For the same reason the captain, too, cannot afford to see our faces."

"I know. I wondered about the sky burial. I am afraid of being tossed from the hatch."

"They will cast us out in a sort of flyer that is used to send out the dead. We will not plummet to the ground, but rather be rescued by secret friends."

Elroy still did not trust what was to come, but he had trouble imagining such an elaborate effort would be expended just to kill him. It couldn't be any worse than his leap onto the airship.

• • •

Elroy kept a wary distance from his rescuers, Nero and Mycroft, in the little storeroom where they were supposedly preparing his body. "You are *not* tying me to those splints. That's no flyer."

"Here, there," Nero said. "Your funeral is in ten minutes. You don't want to be late for it."

"Elroy," snapped Wiggles, "we do not have time for this."

"Look." Nero displayed a small bone-handled knife. "For later. To cut your way out. Trust us, you'll feel like a new man after your funeral."

Elroy stepped over to the splints. They were body length, cross-braced to a large capsule of a dull-colored matte plastic. Nero had given him a blue uniform jacket, without epaulettes, while Mycroft stood by with a winding sheet for the "corpse."

"Wiggles . . ." Elroy began. Control of his situation kept slipping further away from him.

The Animal licked his own nose, then grasped Elroy's hand with a thumbed paw. "We must, friend Elroy. This will work."

Elroy lay down with the greatest reluctance and allowed Nero to bind him to the splints. The straps came across his upper arms, leaving his forearms free from the elbow down—not restraints, exactly. Nero slipped the bone-handled knife into Elroy's right hand. Wiggles crawled between Elroy's legs, where he was enclosed in the winding sheet that Mycroft wrapped from Elroy's feet to his waist. The sheet was some sandpapery weave of sackcloth cheaply printed with block patterns of birds soaring among blazing stars.

"Oh, are you in for a treat. While we're in the cargo hold, try to remember you're dead," Mycroft whispered in Elroy's ear. "Don't breathe where the passengers might see you."

Nero and Mycroft hoisted the splint ends and
carried Elroy as if on a stretcher into the aft cargo hold
of the *Child of Crisis*. Eyes slitted open, Elroy could see
through his lashes an honor guard of four sailors to one
side of the great double doors of the aft cargo hatch.
Two of them played a fast-paced dirge on an electric
sackbut and an out-of-tune finger harp. The musical
effect was unique in Elroy's experience.

The purser stood in front of the hatch doors with a
small book in its hand. Nero and Mycroft lowered
Elroy onto the deck, the capsule beneath the splints
taking his weight. Elroy could hear a rustle of people
behind his head, presumably passengers and crew in
attendance of his funeral rites.

"Crew, passengers, the ship, our mother," intoned the
purser. "I beseech all to draw near and take comfort." It
made vague motions with the book in its thumbed paws.

"In accordance with the rules of the Air Charter first
granted us by the counselors of La Segunda Republica
Norteamericana in years of lost history, and further in
accordance with the timeless rites of the Brotherhood of
the Sky, we gather today to commit to a sky burial the
mortal remains of able airman third class Vulpen, born
of the airship *Fortune's Enemy* and in service on the
Child of Crisis since his seventh year. As our customs
dictate, the remains of airman Vulpen will be cast out
into the air for a sky burial, that his soul might guide
him upward to the Gardens of Sweet Night where he
may find his eternal reward."

Elroy moaned, very quietly. He was supposed to cut
the bonds with the knife in his hand, but where was the
promised flyer? Elroy began to sweat.

The purser continued. "The captain has taken us up
above the clouds so that airman Vulpen's soul may rise

up singing into the glorious light of the day star, bearing his mortal remains to that which awaits him. As I open the hatch doors, I ask everyone to bow their heads in respect for the dead."

"You're on," Mycroft stage-whispered. Through his slitted lids, Elroy watched two of the honor guard crank open the hatch doors while the other two wheezed and tootled their way through some airmen's paean. A sharp draft of very cold air swirled in as Mycroft added, "Don't cut too soon, friend."

Mycroft and Nero ran forward, dragging Elroy with them. The purser's smiling face flashed by with a wink and a pained squeal from the electronic sackbut, then Elroy launched into the air.

He described a long arc down from the airship, screaming with every gram of his strength as the rumpled clouds below him grew larger and larger.

In the Belly of the Orange Balloon

A crack like the snapping of a mighty tree trunk interrupted Elroy's prolonged terror. Within the winding sheet, Wiggles nipped at his calves.

Their free fall pulled abruptly short, slamming Elroy into the straps that held his body. The one across his shoulders slipped to his neck, nearly strangling him as it bruised his larynx. Improbably, he still held on to the knife.

His fall turned into a gentle trembling flight above the clouds. Elroy lay face down, pulled against the straps by his own weight. Wiggles struggled against the winding sheet, threatening to break through and resume his own independent fall.

Elroy found his voice well enough to snap at Wiggles. "Stop moving, sir pug." To his surprise, he was no longer screaming.

Elroy craned his neck, trying to look over his shoulder. Above him to each side was a large, orange fabric wing with jointed skeletal ribs, like the wings of the flying foxes of his home forest in Pilot Knob. Elroy heard a steady hissing noise distinct from the flapping of the air across the fabric wings.

"Something is happening."

"What?" demanded Wiggles, who had wrapped all four paws around Elroy's left leg.

"We are no longer falling and something is hissing above us, between our new wings."

"This is the whole point of a sky burial." Wiggles's voice was muffled by Elroy's legs and the winding sheet. "We're in an orbital drop-up pod."

"This is the flyer?"

"Yes. It flies to orbit. We're heading back to the Gardens."

Elroy watched as a great balloon slowly spun itself into being around them.

•••

They sat on the floor of the balloon, propping the splints across its inner curve for something to lean against. Opaque, about five meters in diameter, the balloon enveloped them in a diffuse orange light leached from the sunny sky outside.

Elroy had used the knife to cut them away from the splints. He then carefully tucked it in the pocket of his uniform jacket. His wrist, strained from their embarkation of the dirigible, caused him excruciating pain

Seeking something else on which to focus, Elroy noticed that the inside of the balloon carried a sharp chemical odor, redolent of freshly milled plastic with a metal undertone.

Wiggles watched Elroy sniff. "Nanotrace is what you smell. You know, that knife won't harm this balloon."

"Neither will it harm me, now that I have put it away, sir pug." Elroy hugged his legs. He was cold, shivering, and he felt very lost.

"You have lost your nerve. You suffer from shock, I think." Wiggles scooted next to Elroy, curled his small body against Elroy's side.

"Nerve?" Elroy tried to laugh, succeeding only in producing a dry cough. "I will never have nerve again. The Green Man help me if I ever so much as hop from a log. I want to go home."

"You are going home. We're going back to the Gardens. They are the true home of every person, balm for the soul and liniment for the body."

"A plague on your gardens." Elroy stifled a sob. "I nearly fell to both our deaths in New Dallas, then again just now. We are floating through the sky in an orange bubble, I am hungry but my stomach threatens never to take food again, and I have to pee somewhere in this empty ball. I miss my quiet treehouse in Pilot Knob. I have had enough of your quest."

Wiggles was silent for a while, his tail thumping gently against the fabric of the balloon. Elroy heaved and choked through tearless sobs, burying his face in his knees. After a time he stopped, only to stare at his orange-tinted hands.

"You're going to the sky, Elroy," Wiggles finally

said. "You will walk in the Gardens of Sweet Night and learn the true meaning of wonder."

"I'd *like* to learn the true meaning of a hole to pee in."

"Just urinate on the fabric of the balloon. It's very smart. It will carry the urine away and break it down for raw materials."

●●●

"Why does the waist of the balloon sometimes flatten widely, then contract to a ball again?" Elroy had been watching the orange walls for quite some time.

"I believe it makes more, then less, of an airfoil."

"Airfoil . . ." Elroy mused. "That means wing, right?"

"Yes, friend Elroy. A lifting body." They were again curled together at the bottom of the balloon. The purser, or perhaps the sailors, had thoughtfully included a package of supplies at the back of the stretcher. Elroy ate sparingly of a waxed packet of airship flat bread. He had no great desire to see what the skin of the balloon might do with his excrement. The urine processing had been sufficiently alarming.

"The balloon," the pug continued, "rides air currents and thermals to the highest altitude it can reach in that manner. It is a very clever machine, in its limited way. Once it decides it will profit no further from soaring the middle atmosphere, it will commence a steady low-power jet burn fueled by conversion of atmospheric gases. We will feel that as a slow push downward. At some point, when it has gained sufficient altitude from that procedure, somewhere in the upper atmosphere, the final motor, a flat fission device, will boost us into low orbit. The process can take several days, but it is quite efficient, and therefore cheap. Especially as the balloon is reusable."

Elroy shook his head, straining to believe. "Orbit. In space around our Earth."

"Yes. In the high places, where the Gardens of Sweet Night sweep forever about the mother world."

●●●

Wiggles made Elroy don the flimsy silver suit he found in the purser's package. There was a smaller suit, more of a bag with a head at one end, for Wiggles. The pug explained. "Survival suits. Simple spacesuits, really, although quite dumb for space equipment. Now that we are boosting toward orbit, the balloon cannot protect us from the extreme cold."

"They cannot possibly bury their dead in the air this way," said Elroy. "This technology is costly and complex."

"Senior officers are sent off this way. Crewmen such as the late airman Vulpen are normally sent out the hatch with a small sounding balloon, enough to keep them in the air for a few days."

"I have never found a dead airman on the ground."

"How many airmen die each day? How big is the ground? I also would imagine the Brotherhood of the Sky is considerate of where they perform their rites."

Elroy mused on the Brotherhood of the Sky. "Now, *they* were free."

"Free because they travel about?"

"Yes." He imagined life on an airship, seeing the great cities of the world from high above, immune to wars, to floods and fires, avoiding famines and pestilence.

"It is unlikely Nero or Mycroft have ever set foot on soil. Remember how high the mooring mast was in New Dallas?"

"I assumed it was a safety measure."

Wiggles shook his head, licking his nose. "The Air Charter was written to cover aerial operations of ground-based organizations. Now, the airships are in perpetual flight. If they were to land, and the Justiciary could catch them on the ground, the crews would forfeit property and freedom. Born in the air, they are citizens of nowhere and tithe no one. They have no rights at all on the ground."

"So they are free, but not to walk the forests or swim the rivers."

"Free within their domain, but absolutely restricted to it."

Elroy thought about the massive bulk of the *Child of Crisis*. "If the airships never touch the ground, where are they built?"

"In orbit, where different laws and regulations apply. The airships are built in space and lowered with massive orbital drop-down pods, analogous to orbital drop-up pods like this one."

"So they pay for their ships by smuggling goods or funds back to space in these orbital drop-up pods."

Wiggles barked his short, odd laugh. "I appreciate a young man with a keen grasp of economics."

"They must bury a lot of officers. Some of them many times over."

"I am given to understand their death rate is uncommonly high at times," Wiggles said in his most serious voice.

Nighttime in the Light of the Day Star

The heavier thrust finally eased. Elroy felt himself floating off of the floor of the balloon. He and Wiggles both wore the thin silver suits, enclosing even their heads, the hoods having transparent panels across the face. Elroy tried to move, but instead began to spin. His head began to spin with the roiling in his gut.

Wiggles's voice echoed tinny and thin within Elroy's silver hood. "Have a care, friend Elroy. We are in microgravity, often called weightlessness. It can be dangerous and distressing to a newcomer."

Elroy grabbed for a splint, but succeeded only in knocking it into a spin as well. He needed to talk, to focus his mind on something other than the distress of his body. "We have been in this balloon for two or three days, sir pug. I am very tired of the view, no offense. What happens now?"

Wiggles wagged his short tail, visible by the rippling in his silver spacesuit. "Friends of the purser will come for us soon."

"Does it ever happen that the Flaming Sword or other agents of the Lord Liasis find these drop-up pods?"

"Yes."

•••

Elroy had been thinking about Wiggles, about the wages he took and the choices that had been forced upon him. The balloon shuddered, and he found himself pressed against the fabric of the balloon. Elroy realized that the pain in his wrist had subsided quite a bit.

Wiggles kicked off, sailing in his silver suit to be next to Elroy. "We have been taken in tow. Let us hope for friends."

"How will we know?"

"Friends will stow the balloon gently for future use. Enemies most likely will force their way in."

"Wiggles," said Elroy, "when we are released, by friend or foe, I will stand with you, but I will be your servant no longer."

Wiggles gave Elroy a long, thoughtful look. "Why?"

"I am not made for service. I do not need the funds so badly as to surrender myself. Since we boarded the airship, every choice has been taken from my hands. I will stand beside you and help you get back to the Gardens, not for payment, but for friendship."

"Thank you, Elroy. I hope you can leave your regrets behind as we continue."

Pressed against the fabric with Wiggles, Elroy watched for signs of civilized entry.

They came soon enough. The balloon suddenly stopped. Elroy and Wiggles collapsed to the new floor that had been the wall at their back, drawn down again as if they were back on the ground. The orange fabric rapidly lost tension as it settled around them. With a gentle sussing noise it began to tighten in on itself.

One of the fabric panels split open above them, the rangy brindled face of a badger peering in. It wore a canvas work vest. "Ho, new friends. Is there cargo to be recovered?"

Wiggles unsealed his silver hood, motioning Elroy to do the same. As his hood opened, Wiggles spoke. "We are a special shipment, sir badger, courtesy of the *Child of Crisis*."

"Always looking out for us up here in the high places, that Renton. A great purser and a better person, but can't resist sending us little surprises from time to time." The badger pushed and nudged at the collapsing fabric of the balloon to open an exit for them.

"I am Wiggles, a gardener from the high places, and this is my friend Elroy of Pilot Knob, Earth."

The badger nodded gravely at Elroy. "Pilot Knob is a place I've never heard of, but coming in this pod you've visitor's rights. Be welcome. And you, Sir Wiggles. Are you truly just a simple gardener?"

"With respect, I decline the question pending further discussion, sir badger."

"Which says enough about the special shipment. You may call me Horace. We must go now. By virtue of the method of your arrival, you have been summoned to a Concilium meeting."

They stepped out of the shrinking balloon into a large bay reminiscent of the rear cargo bay of the *Child of Crisis*, except everything here was ceramic, plastic or metal. Elroy was fascinated by the profusion of colored pipes, thick cables and cabinets, with small doors and cunning hatches everywhere.

Horace led them to a hatch two meters tall, obviously intended for human foot traffic. Elroy paused to look at a small glass panel at the left of the door. He stared at the tiny lights that crawled across the panel until the great blue arc of the earth swung into his view.

"Welcome to space," said Wiggles.

Elroy reached out to touch the panel. It was cold. He felt his sense of wonder unfolding like flowers in the spring. "Why does the man who owns the world live up here high above?"

Wiggles barked a soft laugh. "Where else would you find such a view?"

The badger tugged at Elroy's silver sleeve, urging him along.

•••

They passed through several short, winding corridors, lined with the same riot of pipes, cables, and access hatches as the cargo bay. To Elroy's nose the place smelled painfully clean. It had an aseptic, neutral scent impossible to achieve in an organic environment. Horace stopped them outside a double hatch emblazoned with a stylized paw print.

"Here is the Concilium. I counsel respectful attention, and the best kind of honesty in answering their questions."

The doors hissed open before them. At a gentle push from Horace, Elroy and Wiggles stepped into the room.

Elroy gasped. For a panicked moment, he thought he had stepped into open space. The Concilial chamber was roofed with a transparent dome, eight meters in diameter and open to half the sky. The great blue and white arc of the planet Earth was nowhere to be seen, but the room was flooded with the light of the sun, the day star. All around his head, Elroy could see stars great and small, many of them in motion, like Yurigrad seen from Earth.

He pulled his gaze from the sky to the Concilium. Variously seated and standing about a low, round table almost three meters across, eight Animals stared at him. There were no human people in the room except for Elroy. He saw four dogs of varying breeds, including another pug, as well as a raccoon, two coyotes and a puma that bulked large along one arc of the room. As with every Animal, all wore a single item of clothing to symbolize their work or rank. Every vest or jacket or waistcoat was as unnaturally clean as the one Wiggles wore.

The Concilium pug leaned forward, drumming its claws on the metal tabletop. "Wiggles."

"Clement," Wiggles acknowledged. Elroy glanced down to see Wiggles sag his shoulders, tail drooping.

"A gardener, indeed." Clement's voice oozed reproach. "Who had you hoped to deceive?"

"I *am* a gardener, Clement."

"And a great deal more besides. In light of your misdeeds, our Lord Liasis is much inflamed with hope of hearing news of you."

"You are free Animals here." Wiggles turned his head, staring from one Conciliator to another. "Liasis is not lord of places such as this. The Mutual Contract does not hold sway above the soil of Earth."

The puma rumbled a low growl. Elroy had never seen such a large Animal. It was greater in size and apparent ferocity than even the security wolves. "Clement misspoke. Liasis is not our lord, but he is yours, Sir Wiggles. We are good neighbors and seek to satisfy his reasonable requirements."

Wiggles nodded. "In return for reasonable rewards, perhaps, friend puma?"

The puma licked a thumbed paw. "It is the way of things, little dog. Your sun now sets."

Clement stared up at Elroy. "You, friend Elroy, are free to go. Horace will escort you to the airlock."

Wiggles waved Elroy back with a small gesture of

one thumbed paw. Elroy reached out to touch Wiggles, thinking perhaps to pull him along. The badger grabbed Elroy's hand, whispering, "Come quickly, man, while they still allow."

The doors of the Concilial chamber began to hiss shut upon Elroy's view of Wiggles's green-clad back. Beyond his friend the pug, Elroy saw the puma rising and turning to come toward Wiggles. Wiggles's head was bowed, his tail almost slack in its unkinked dejection, as the paw print doors closed.

●●●

Horace led Elroy rapidly through a series of cluttered corridors. Elroy stalked behind the badger, angry and confused.

"By the Moment of Inertia, what was that business? I will not allow a friend to be so betrayed!"

"Peace, friend Elroy. The Concilium is constrained."

"But that—Clement, Clement *knew* Wiggles. It said a few choice words, and Wiggles just stood there. After all we went through to come this far."

The badger stopped, turned to face Elroy, staring up at his human height. "Clement and Wiggles are littermates. Each chose a different path in life. Wiggles has deviated from his path, and Clement seeks to right perceived wrongs."

Littermates? "This is about the apples in the Gardens then? A touch of brotherly jealousy?"

"You know nothing of what happens here in the high places, man from Earth, let alone the Gardens of Sweet Night. Wiggles was chancellor to Lord Liasis—a high official of the Justiciary in his own right."

Chancellor? Elroy leaned back against the corridor

wall, pipes pressing into him. His worldview shifted underneath him like the falling gangway above New Dallas. He had no conception of what he should do next.

Horace tapped a claw upward into Elroy's chest, emphasizing his next words. "The Concilium was threatened, challenged for orbital rights and various alleged violations of law and charter. Wiggles worked secretly to defend Clement's interests, tried to make things smooth. In doing so, he betrayed the trust of his Lord Liasis. Fear of Liasis was stronger than loyalty to his brother, so Clement reported Wiggles to the Flaming Sword. From this came his fall."

"For brother to betray brother . . ."

"You have an appointment with the airlock. The Concilium has declared you free to go."

Stepping Into the Sunlit Dark

Horace led Elroy to a man-sized hatch set in a wide spot in a corridor. Another window stood next to it, showing the lights of the stars, both moving and still.

"Here is the airlock you should use, friend Elroy."

Elroy stared out the window. "What is out there?"

"Space."

"I mean, where am I going?"

"Space."

Elroy sputtered. "That's ridiculous. I would die."

The badger pushed a button, causing the hatch to open. "Then it is a lucky thing that you seem to be wearing a spacesuit. I should seal my hood, were I you."

Elroy considered fighting the badger, rebelling against the order, but to what point? It was the Concilium's home, they certainly had security to deal with him. He would only harm Horace, who had been kind. With a sigh, Elroy stepped into the small room behind the airlock, pulling the silver hood back over his head.

"This is it? I am just to step out into the sun-drenched dark to die? I have come all this distance to meet my end? This is senseless."

Horace gave him a long look that seemed almost sympathetic. "There is a deeper game in play here. Trust that you will be alone, but not friendless."

Elroy watched the hatch slide closed as he sealed his hood. The soft silver suit crinkled around him, expanding and tightening in different places at the same time as a hissing sound began, first as almost a roar before trailing off to nothing. The floor released its hold on him, and Elroy drifted slightly away from it. He felt the same absence of direction they had felt in the drop-up pod.

Weightless, Elroy kicked his way out of the other end of the open airlock, into the depths of orbital space. It seemed expected of him.

•••

I have finally found true freedom, thought Elroy. I am free of everything. Free of weight, free of responsibility, free of action of any kind.

Elroy's experiences in the orange balloon helped him keep his stomach and his mind anchored in place as he spun gently away from the rambling assemblage of the Concilium's high place in the sky.

He had never asked what their charter was, whose council they were. Perhaps they spoke for all the Animals. He wondered what Horace had meant by deeper games. The business in the Concilium chamber had seemed almost rehearsed, a play perhaps. Who was being fooled? Wiggles? Elroy himself?

Earth rolled by his vision, transiting like a drunken giant. He noticed two kinds of stars; the sharp, far ones that didn't move except as he did, and the blobby, bright ones that moved at many speeds in many directions. The moving group must be the satellite stars, places such as Yurigrad. Perhaps they were other high places or other adventurers like himself. Elroy felt his pulse echo in his ear. He was very, very far from Pilot Knob. The sunlit face of Earth showed the far side of the planet, so he could not even find his home.

"I suppose I shall die here," he said aloud as he began again to pray for the harm he had done, to the security wolves and the unfortunate Mississippian. He prayed for the family he would never have and prayed for Wiggles.

Horace's voice echoed in his ears, from inside the silver hood, "Not if you listen to what I tell you."

Suit radio, Elroy realized. "You have interrupted me at prayer, sir badger. Are we playing your deeper game now?"

"There is little time," snapped the badger. "Many things are not right at the moment and you would do well to listen. I can help you help Wiggles. That great oaf Alcindor, the puma, even now sets out to return friend pug to his angry master. Can you see our station?"

Elroy waited with a smile for the Conciliatory home to spin into view.

"Yes, I see it now."

"Watch for a departure. Alcindor is about to set out in a maintenance sled with Wiggles. I have gained control of his autolaunch processes. I will direct the sled to pass very close to you. It will trail a line. You must grasp that line and secure yourself to the sled."

Elroy's smile broadened as the station rolled away from his view. The importance of everything diminished like a rock down a well. "Perhaps I shall grasp a shooting star as it trails by, friend Horace. I thank you for your kindness."

He yawned, a great gape that threatened to enclose his nearly dreaming mind.

"Sparks and fire," swore the badger. "Your oxygen is running low. Listen, friend Elroy, attend quickly. This is a maintenance sled. There are consumable service points at the base of the sled body. If you warp yourself in along the line, you may be able to steal air from its service reserves. I can intercept his telemetry and feed false data to keep Alcindor from wondering about the wallow from your added mass. Find the sled, steal air and ride it in pursuit."

Elroy hummed, then sang, "I shall steal thunder from the storm and fly with the lightning."

In his ears, Horace sounded sad. "Goodbye, friend man. I have tried. Luck to you."

Elroy watched the blue Earth spin slowly by, thrilled by the patterns of the clouds.

• • •

"Now, Elroy, now!"

He couldn't remember the voice, couldn't see anyone, but as Elroy blinked he saw a silver line swinging toward him. Like swinging down the lianas of his jungle home, he thought, although he could see no green. His ears told him that he was falling, so he grabbed the silver liana to stop himself.

Black spots moved before Elroy's eyes, obscuring his view of the dark beyond. The silver vine yanked at his wrist, renewing an old, forgotten pain, but it restored his sense of upwardness. He looked at his feet, seeing a great house of metal far below, impossibly shaped and larger than any estate had a right to be.

The Concilium.

Elroy remembered a dog named Wiggles, a friend and boon companion. Wiggles was in trouble, needed Elroy's help.

Elroy climbed the silver vine, noting that it lacked leaves. He wondered why he was surrounded by the night, above, behind and below him. After a while the vine ended in an irregular wall of metal. There seemed to be an inordinate number of small cubes, pipes and metal balls. Elroy grabbed a sturdy pipe, releasing his silver vine.

In front him, Elroy found a row of taps, little serrated cones topped with colored handles. Each colored handle was labeled: "N_2H_4" was red, "H_2" was orange. A blue tap handle read "H_2O."

He needed air. H_2O was water. H_2 was hydrogen. His vision began to black out as Elroy found a white tap handle labeled "O_2." Air, or at least oxygen.

He turned the white tap handle. Pale fog jetted out of the tip below the handle, disappearing almost immediately into a crystal spray, which then vanished. Air, apparently, but how was he to breathe it?

Elroy's stomach felt tight, as dark and uninterested as his mind was becoming, but he fingered the closure of the silver hood. Elroy could imagine the effects of vacuum on his skin and eyes. So first he tried to kiss the tap through his silver hood. To his surprise, the hood slipped onto the tap, pulling his face right up to the maintenance sled.

He turned the tap, feeling the jet of gas swelling his hood and pushing into his mouth with a sensation like drinking from a well-shaken bottle of ale. The black spots in his vision went away and Elroy began to giggle. His ears thrummed.

Elroy felt very alive, very fine, sliding among the tiny stars.

Into the Gardens of Sweet Night

"Wake up, boy."

The smell was natural, like real air. Elroy knew that he wasn't in the Concilium's high place anymore. He could smell soil, plants, open water. And close by, the musky scent of large canids.

Elroy opened his eyes. A tall, lanky human, with skin as pale as a jungle puffball, leaned over him. Two security wolves flanked the man, clad in armored vests and carrying matte black energy pistols gleaming with tiny colored status lights. One of the wolves leaned over to stare into Elroy's face. "Will he survive?"

"There may be some residual effects from the oxygen overdose." The pale man stood up, favoring Elroy with a sad smile as he turned to leave the room.

"Won't matter much longer." Both wolves laughed full human sounding laughs through their long tooth jaws. "Come on, boy, it's time for your confession."

They pulled Elroy to his feet, almost dropping him to the floor as he slid off the exam table. Elroy stumbled with them, a thumbed paw gripping each of his arms far too tightly.

"Where are we?"

"Heligan," the wolf to his left snickered. "Some of us will live to enjoy it."

Heligan. One of the Gardens of Sweet Night. Elroy looked around as the wolves yanked him into a corridor. The hallway was carpeted and paneled with dark hardwoods, resembling the public halls of the monastery of the Little Brothers of High Impact. Nothing at all like the metal burrows of the Concilium.

"Where are the plants?" He stared at the wooden walls with brass hand grabs punctuating them.

The security wolves laughed again, both relaxing their grip as they walked. The left one, the apparent spokesman, flexed the claws of his thumbed paw into Elroy's arm, puncturing skin even through the silver suit. Elroy could feel blood welling inside his sleeve.

"You'll be seeing them from inside the soil soon enough. Our Lord Liasis likes the freshest fertilizer."

The time had come for defense, Elroy realized. The vows he had taken, then broken in Wiggles's service, would never require him to go meekly to his death.

The knife was still in his jacket pocket, unreachable beneath the silver spacesuit. Elroy found his center, as he had learned in the Glass Mountains of Oklahoma. His perception of time stretched, each footfall on the carpeted floor like the slowest of drumbeats.

If he accepted a ragged wound in his right arm from the clawed grasp of his captor, he could bring that arm at full swing across the chest of the wolf to his left, while moving his left hand still inside the other wolf's grip to close both hands in the rib-smashing technique the Little Brothers called "Kitten and Ball." He had learned at the land train that security wolves could be fought like men.

The Little Brothers taught that plan was thought, thought was action, action was deed. Elroy slumped to the left, then spun on that heel into the grip of the lead wolf. He pulled his right arm against the loose set of the right-hand wolf's claws, gaining the painful ragged wound he expected, joining its pain to that of his bruised bones.

Increasing his spin, Elroy brought his right arm across the chest of the wolf, twisting his body so the flat of his left hand could provide counterpressure to the coming blow. With a crunch of collapsing ribs, the surprised wolf faltered in his step, allowing Elroy to break free on that side and spin around.

As the injured wolf fell, his partner swung the black energy pistol up to fire it at Elroy. Elroy finished his spin, slipping into a snap-kick that threw the energy pistol upward in the grip of the second wolf. Shoulder first, Elroy slammed into the second wolf's chest as a violet bolt of light struck the wooden ceiling of the hall. The wood above him charred as Elroy drove the wolf back into the wall. Elroy grabbed the wolf's armored vest at the left lapel, using it to slam the wolf against the wall.

The vest slipped off the wolf's torso and down its arm as the Animal spun. Elroy fell away, surprised, clutching the vest so that it was ripped entirely off the security wolf. His momentum carried him to carpeted floor, next to the weakly kicking foot paws of the first wolf. As fire alarms screamed above his head, Elroy tensed for a counterstrike from the second wolf.

It slumped against the wall, whining and whimpering. Elroy saw a braided silver strand dangling down its back, emerging from the fur at a point several vertebrae below the joining of neck and shoulder. He flipped the vest over in his hand.

Torn silver filaments on the inner side of the vest matched the strand. The wolf muttered, dropped to all fours and began to stagger away, gun, vest and Elroy forgotten.

Elroy shrugged on the vest, which fit him loosely, then grabbed one of the energy pistols. The first wolf rolled to look up at him as Elroy aimed the pistol at its head.

"You will never escape my Lord Liasis," the security wolf grinned through pained gasps. Elroy could barely hear him over the din of the alarms.

"I don't plan to." Unwilling to pull the trigger, to kill a weakened enemy, Elroy reversed the energy pistol. He smashed the butt into the side of the wolf's head. It slumped onto the carpet, still breathing.

Elroy left the other security wolf's vest alone. He walked down the hall past the wolf's creeping, whining fellow, humming a battle hymn from the Little Brothers in counterpoint to the whooping fire alarms.

He wondered how to find Wiggles.

●●●

Elroy ducked through several hatches until he found a maintenance closet in which to rest. He had begun to tremble in the aftermath of the fight. The whooping fire alarms were an increasingly distant wail, and Elroy had the cold sweats.

He laid his energy pistol against one of the lockers in the closet, rested his hands on his knees and took a deep, shuddering breath. He had trained with the Little Brothers to acquire focus and strength, not to render Animals into beasts.

"Detachments moving within fifty meters," whispered a flat voice from his collar.

Elroy jumped, slamming his head against a locker. He twisted around, seeing the bunched silver hood of his suit overlaying the paneled black of the armor vest.

"Do you wish to evade?" It was the voice inside his hood again.

"Horace? Wiggles?"

"Status unknown." There was a brief crackling noise. "Tactical interface feed is being conducted through your suit communications."

Elroy felt a sharp prickle of fear. "Are you the vest?"

"Cognitive prosthetic, canid, combat, model one seventeen bis."

Robust technology, thought Elroy. It made sense. Every Animal he had ever seen wore a single item of clothing on their upper body. Elroy had always thought it was to emphasize their differentiation from beasts. With the size of most of their brain cases, Animals must store portions of their consciousness in these things.

"I want to find Liasis," he said. Where Liasis was, he would find Wiggles as well.

The vest whispered, "Exit this locker, proceed twelve meters to your left and pause. I will direct you from there."

Elroy grabbed his pistol, stepped out of the hatch and proceeded twelve meters to his left.

• • •

The vest guided him down corridors and through access tubes that climbed up and down. As the vest tracked the location of wandering security wolves, it told Elroy to make sudden pauses, and sometimes changed instructions even as he moved.

Elroy thought to ask it if he was visible to other vests.

"This unit has a tracer function."

How strange that the other security wolves had not yet used it to track him. Elroy was beginning to feel very set up. "Can you turn it off?"

"Disable tracer is a priority four order. Do you have priority four authority?"

Wiggles. Wiggles was supposedly Chancellor, or had been. "Chancellor Wiggles ordered me to help him."

"Tracer disabled."

Wiggles, it seemed, still had a name to conjure with.

"What else can you do?"

"Level one help is available. Options are: armor characteristics, biometrics, canid interface, cognitive extension, external communications, maintenance, memory and storage, miscellaneous settings, product specifications, shielding, smart matter, stealth, tactical support, weapons interfacing, user preferences. Please specify your desired path."

Elroy sighed. It was far more complex a technology menu than he had time to deal with. "Nevermind. Just keep telling me how to find Liasis."

"Wait thirty-five seconds, then open the hatch to your right and proceed downward two levels."

Elroy counted to thirty-five, then opened the hatch.

•••

The vest whispered through his open hood, "Once you exit this service tunnel, proceed left thirty meters and you will be before Liasis's audience chamber. Enter the chamber and you will be free to proceed to target."

Elroy was moved by an impulse he couldn't define, rooted in a vague belief that anything that spoke must have desires of its own. "I don't need to take you in there."

"Where else would I go?"

"I could take you off, leave you here. You would be safe, free." Even as he said it, Elroy felt foolish.

The vest made the static noise again, several times in a row. Elroy wondered if that was its thinking noise or its laughing noise.

"I am a cognitive combat prosthetic. I am an item of clothing for an Animal. What does freedom mean to me?"

"You know enough to ask that question," Elroy pointed out.

More static, then silence. Elroy waited, listening for noises behind the door. He heard none.

"There are four security wolves in front of Liasis's chamber," the vest finally whispered. "If you are prepared, you can overwhelm them with your energy pistol."

"And you?"

"I will come. If you win free again, I will still be with you."

"I'm not going to make it, am I?"

"In order to avoid panic dysfunction I have disabled my risk assessment functions. However, it is obvious that you should commence operations immediately."

More wolves, wolves he would certainly have to kill. Elroy already had too much blood on his hands for the sake of Wiggles. Having come this far, he could see little point in turning back. Elroy said a brief prayer for those about to die. He checked the charge on the energy pistol, placed his finger on the firing stud and palmed open the service hatch.

Welcome Into the Presence of the Lord

Elroy stood before a great pair of double doors. They were carved each from a single brass-bound slab of teak four meters tall, decorated with complex motifs of twining leaves. The grand hall where he stood was littered with the burnt corpses of four security wolves. Part of the carpet was on fire. He mildly regretted the flash burns on the glorious doors. Three different kinds of alarms wailed in the distance.

Elroy raised a spacesuit-clad foot and kicked open the right hand door.

Like the chamber of the Animal's Concilium, the audience chamber of Lord Liasis was transparently roofed. Elroy stepped forward then stopped, his eyes drawn up by a green glare.

There were no stars, no depths of space above him. Instead, a network of greenery rose, curving out in two directions to meet in the sky high over his head, extending unguessably far in its long axis. It had to be

Illustrated by Asuka Komai

at least two or three kilometers to the far side of the green sky. Adrenaline rush of combat forgotten, Elroy stared into the infinite life of plants.

He was accustomed to the riot of the green jungles of Texas: lianas and giant ferns and glossy dark-leaved orchids in the lower reaches punctuating the echoing silences of the deep forest, while high above in the middle layers and the canopy, a violent profusion of epiphytic and parasitic plants hosted butterflies, monkeys, insects, birds and animals of all descriptions. His home tree in Pilot Knob stood amid a roaring chaos of viridian life, changeless in its endless cycle of destruction and renewal.

The Heligan Garden was a different order of nature altogether. Elroy's energy pistol dropped to point toward the carpet as he stared up at roses, ivy, yew, boxwood and a thousand plants for which he had no name. In all their shades and color they grew in glorious array, relieved by paths and walls and smooth rolled meadows, interspersed with pleasances and statuary and cunning ponds whose banks had clearly been laid stone by stone at the direction of generations of master craftsmen.

An overpowering scent of green, tame and orderly but powerful, swept through him. Elroy realized Lord Liasis's audience chamber roof was not transparent. It was absent. The room was open to kilometers of the most cultivated garden in existence.

"Just one of my seven gardens. Admittedly, perhaps the finest."

Elroy picked up his pistol, turned to look at Lord Liasis. The High Commissioner of the Cis-Lunar Justiciary and Lord of Implementation for the Atlantic Maritime Territories was a thin man, slightly shorter than Elroy's two meters, with flowing white hair. His eyes were a piercing shade of green, and his smile had a natural bonhomie. Clad in a blue morning suit, he carried a glass of wine in his right hand.

Wiggles stood next to Lord Liasis, looking down at his feet and smoothing his flowered green waistcoat with his thumbed paws. Elroy thought Wiggles's tail wagged.

Behind them, the audience chamber stretched for several hundred meters, unroofed in glorious green and carpeted in burgundy and gold. There was no furniture save a wooden throne against the distant wall.

"What of the apples of your lord?" Elroy asked in a soft voice.

"My gardens have many trees." Liasis's smile stretched to a toothsome grin. "Some bear strange fruit."

"And your tale, sir pug?"

Wiggles looked up at Elroy. "True, as far as it went. Not the entire truth."

Elroy stroked the trigger of the energy pistol. The vest whispered risks and priorities in his ear, but he ignored it. "What would be the entire truth?"

Liasis's smile dropped away as he spoke, his voice mild and his tone almost bemused. "One legacy of the La Grangian restoration is a strong prohibition against hereditary power. The Secretaries-General taught them that lesson. When a man ascends to a position of great responsibilities, there is a certain, ah, physical price that must be paid."

"Some do cheat," Wiggles added, "but it is frowned upon. There are no children, normally."

"I have need of a young man, a human, of compassion and strength, wit and ruthlessness. I have a strong preference that he not spring from the Great Families of the high places, so as to be free of our politics and alliances. Lord Deimos offered a younger nephew, but the eventual price would have been far too high."

"My home is in a tree in the jungles of Texas, with the family I hope to establish. I have no wish to meddle in the business of the Lords of the High Places."

Liasis gestured with the wineglass. "Would you care for some? From Scandinavia's finest vineyards. Orbital wine is never quite the same, you know."

"Elroy." Wiggles's voice was earnest. "Let me be plain. I was sent to travel among the people of Earth, to find and test a worthy successor from outside the circles of the ruling classes. I required a young man who would bring no untoward ambition with him into the Gardens of Sweet Night. You are the one success I encountered: capable, thoughtful, ethical and strong. At my recommendation, and on the strength of your journey here, Lord Liasis now seeks you for his heir, to train and mentor that you might someday become a lord of space."

Elroy shook his head. "What a strange way to choose an heir. Had you asked me to come here and be a gardener, I might have rejoiced." He laid the pistol down on the carpet, careful to point it away from the Lord Liasis and his chancellor.

"Had you brought me here and shown me the curve of the blue Earth and your wondrous Gardens, offering me dominion in exchange for loyalty freely given, I might have rejoiced. Instead, at your behest, I have beaten, wounded and killed, staining my soul with blood. I made an Animal into a beast. Four wolves lie dead outside your very door, other men and Animals maimed and wounded along the way. My vows are broken, lives have been ruined or taken, all for your little game." Elroy dropped the vest to the carpet.

Lord Liasis's voice was gentle. "No. Not for a game. For dominion over the kingdoms of the earth and the high places. A small price to pay for proof of your fitness to succeed me. We test those outside the pale because it is the only true way to find new blood."

Elroy began to strip off the silver spacesuit. "Lord, in taking service with Chancellor Wiggles, I sold my freedom and made choices to do things I regret. Acting on my own, I would not so much as kill a man to take an apple from him. Why would I kill for something as foolish as dominion over the kingdoms of the earth? All I ever wanted was to start a family—the very thing you would deny me even with all your proffered riches."

Elroy dropped the spacesuit, then tossed the purser's coat onto the carpet, followed by Nero's knife and his carefully hoarded pay. He turned to walk away, stopping before the door to look back at Liasis and Wiggles once more.

"The world, Elroy," whispered Liasis, spreading an open hand. "I can give you the world and these Gardens in the sky. What greater gift is there?"

"Lord Liasis, dominion is a hard sentence to serve. My greater gift to myself is that I choose to remain free. I leave your service as I entered it."

"Many wolves wait outside," said Wiggles. The pug's tone was both hopeful and sad.

"I know." Elroy looked up one last time at the Heligan Garden, breathed in the peaceful scent of green, then opened the door to walk out free and unafraid.

THE YEAR IN THE CONTESTS

Written by
Algis Budrys

About the Author

Algis Budrys was born in Königsberg, East Prussia, on January 9, 1931. East Prussia (now the republic of Belarus) was at that time a part of Germany, but Budrys is a Lithuanian from birth, because his father, the Consul General of Lithuania, was merely stationed in East Prussia at the time. The family came to America in 1936.

Budrys became interested in science fiction at the age of six, when a landlady slipped him a copy of the New York Journal-American Sunday funnies. The paper was immediately confiscated by his parents, as being low-class trash, but it was too late. Shortly thereafter, Budrys entered PS 87 in New York. There, he was given a monthly publication called Young America, which featured stories by Carl H. Claudy, a now-forgotten juvenile science fiction author, and such serials as "At the Earth's Core" by Edgar Rice Burroughs. He was hopelessly lost, and by the age of nine was writing his own stories.

At the age of twenty-one, living in Great Neck, Long Island, he began selling steadily to the top magazine markets.

He sold his first novel in 1953, and eventually produced eight more novels, including Who?, Rogue Moon, Michaelmas *and* Hard Landing, *and three short-story collections. He has always done a number of things besides writing, most but not all of them related to science fiction. Notable among them was a long stretch as a critic.*

He has been, over the years, the Editor in Chief of Regency Books, Playboy Press, all the titles at Woodall's Trailer Travel publications, and L. Ron Hubbard's Writers of the Future, where he works now. He has also been a PR man for various clients, including Peter Pan Peanut Butter, Pickle Packers International and International Trucks. His favorite client was Pickle Packers International, for which he participated in a broad variety of stunts; but his most challenging client was International Trucks, for which he crisscrossed the country for four years, from the Bridgehampton Race Track on Long Island to the sin palaces of Long Beach.

In 1954, he married Edna F. Duna, and is still married to her, an arrangement that suits both of them. They have four sons, now scattered over America and the world. Life is good.

he year 2002 was rich in the length of its winning stories and in their variety of styles and themes. Something similar acted on the winning illustrators, as you have seen (or will see) in leafing through this volume, which is, as you surely know, volume nineteen in the series.

The judges in this year are named on the cover of this book. They are amazingly prestigious and knowledgeable contributors to L. Ron Hubbard's original (and still growing) vision. This has been true from the very beginning, though some names are, sadly, no longer with us and others, happily, have stepped forward to take their place.

We are pleased to welcome new judge Brian Herbert to our stellar panel of judges for the L. Ron Hubbard Writers of the Future Contest. Brian Herbert is co-author of *The Butlerian Jihad*, a recent New York Times bestseller, and has co-authored three other *Dune* prequel novels with author and Writers of the Future Contest judge Kevin J. Anderson. Among Herbert's own published works are the novels *Sidney's Comet; Sudanna, Sudanna;* and *The Race for God.* He co-wrote *Man of Two Worlds* with his late father and former Writers of the Future Contest judge, Frank Herbert. His recent releases include his biography of Frank Herbert entitled *Dreamer of Dune* and *Forgotten Heroes,* about the U.S. Merchant Marine.

The enterprise goes ever forward, and the authors and illustrators in this volume will, in due course, take their firm place in the history of speculative arts. For the 2002 year, these are:

L. Ron Hubbard's Writers of the Future Contest winners:

First Quarter
1. Matthew Candelaria
   Trust is a Child
2. Brandon Butler
   A Few Days North of Vienna
3. Myke Cole
   Blood and Horses

Second Quarter
1. Ian Keane
   Walking Rain
2. Joel Best
   Numbers
3. Robert J Defendi
   A Silky Touch to No Man

Third Quarter
1. Carl Frederick
   A Boy and His Bicycle
2. Steve Savile
   Bury My Heart at the Garrick
3. Michael Churchman
   From All the Work Which He Had Made . . .

Fourth Quarter
1. Jay Lake
   Into the Gardens of Sweet Night
2. Steve Bein
   Beautiful Singer
3. Geoffrey Girard
   Dark Harvest

Published Finalists

Luc Reid   Ken Liu
A Ship That Bends   *Gossamer*

L. Ron Hubbard's Illustrators of the Future Contest winners:

Jared Barber   Adrian Barbu
Staci Goddard   Vance Kelly
Asuka Komai   Mike Lawrence
Lulkien   Britt Spencer
Nina Ollikainen   Youa Vang
                    Daniel Willis

Our heartiest congratulations to them all! May we see much more of their work in the future.

NEW WRITERS!

L. Ron Hubbard's
Writers of the Future Contest

OPPORTUNITY FOR
NEW AND AMATEUR WRITERS OF
NEW SHORT STORIES OR NOVELETTES OF
SCIENCE FICTION OR FANTASY

No entry fee is required.
Entrants retain all publication rights.

ALL AWARDS ARE ADJUDICATED BY
PROFESSIONAL WRITERS ONLY

PRIZES EVERY THREE MONTHS: $1,000, $750, $500.
ANNUAL GRAND PRIZE: $4,000 ADDITIONAL!

Don't Delay! Send Your Entry to
L. Ron Hubbard's
Writers of the Future Contest
P.O. Box 1630
Los Angeles, CA 90078

CONTEST RULES

1. No entry fee is required and all rights in the story remain the property of the author. All types of science fiction, fantasy and horror with fantastic elements are welcome.

2. All entries must be original works, in English. Plagiarism, which includes the use of third-party poetry, song lyrics, characters or another person's universe, without written permission, will result in disqualification. Excessive violence or sex, determined by the judges, will result in disqualification. Entries may not have been previously published in professional media.

3. To be eligible, entries must be works of prose, up to 17,000 words in length. We regret we cannot consider poetry or works intended for children.

4. The Contest is open only to those who have not had professionally published a novel or short novel, or more than one novelette, or more than three short stories, in any medium. Professional publication is deemed to be payment, and at least 5,000 copies or 5,000 hits.

5. Entries must be typewritten or a computer printout in black ink on white paper, double spaced, with numbered pages. All other formats will be disqualified. Each entry must have a cover page with the title of the work, the author's name, address and telephone number, an approximate word count and e-mail address if available. Every subsequent page must carry the title and a page number, but the author's name must be deleted to facilitate fair judging.

6. Manuscripts will be returned after judging if the author has provided return postage and a self-addressed envelope. If the author does not wish return of the manuscript, a business-size self-addressed, stamped envelope (or valid email address) must be included with the entry in order to receive judging results.

7. We accept only an entry for which no delivery signature is required by us to receive it.

8. There shall be three cash prizes in each quarter: a First Prize of $1,000, a Second Prize of $750 and a Third Prize of $500, in U.S. dollars or the recipient's local equivalent amount. In addition, at the end of the year the four First Prize winners will have their entries rejudged, and a Grand Prize winner shall be determined and will receive an additional $4,000. All winners will also receive trophies or certificates.

9. The Contest has four quarters, beginning on October 1, January 1, April 1 and July 1. The year will end on September 30. To be eligible for judging in its quarter, an entry must be postmarked no later than midnight on the last day of the quarter.

10. Each entrant may submit only one manuscript per quarter. Winners are ineligible to make further entries in the Contest.

11. All entries for each quarter are final. No revisions are accepted.

12. Entries will be judged by professional authors. The decisions of the judges are entirely their own, and are final.

13. Winners in each quarter will be individually notified of the results by mail.

14. This Contest is void where prohibited by law.

NEW ILLUSTRATORS!

^{TM}

L. Ron Hubbard's
Illustrators of the Future Contest

OPEN TO NEW SCIENCE FICTION
AND FANTASY ARTISTS WORLDWIDE

No entry fee is required.
Entrants retain all publication rights.

ALL JUDGING BY
PROFESSIONAL ARTISTS ONLY

$1,500 IN PRIZES EACH QUARTER
QUARTERLY WINNERS COMPETE FOR
$4,000 ADDITIONAL ANNUAL PRIZE

Don't Delay! Send Your Entry to
L. Ron Hubbard's
Illustrators of the Future Contest
P.O. Box 3190
Los Angeles, CA 90078

CONTEST RULES

1. The Contest is open to entrants from all nations. (However, entrants should provide themselves with some means for written communication in English.) All themes of science fiction and fantasy illustrations are welcome: every entry is judged on its own merits only. No entry fee is required, and all rights in the entries remain the property of the artists.

2. By submitting work to the Contest, the entrant agrees to abide by all Contest rules.

3. The Contest is open to those who have not previously published more than three black-and-white story illustrations, or more than one process-color painting, in media distributed nationally to the general public, such as magazines or books sold at newsstands, or books sold in stores merchandising to the general public. The submitted entry shall not have been previously published in professional media as exampled above.

If you are not sure of your eligibility, write to the Contest address with details, enclosing a business-size self-addressed envelope with return postage. The Contest Administration will reply with a determination.

Winners in previous quarters are not eligible to make further entries.

4. Only one entry per quarter is permitted. The entry must be original to the entrant. Plagiarism, infringement of the rights of others, or other violations of the contest rules will result in disqualification.

5. An entry shall consist of three illustrations done by the entrant in a black-and-white medium. Each must represent a theme different from the other two.

6. ENTRIES SHOULD NOT BE THE ORIGINAL DRAWINGS, but should be large black-and-white photocopies of a quality satisfactory to the entrant. Entries must be submitted unfolded and flat, in an envelope no larger than 9 inches by 12 inches.

All entries must be accompanied by a self-addressed return envelope of the appropriate size, with correct U.S. postage affixed. (Non-U.S. entrants should enclose international postal reply coupons.) If the entrant does not want the photocopies returned, the entry should be clearly marked DISPOSABLE COPIES: DO NOT RETURN.

A business-size self-addressed envelope with correct postage (or valid email address) should be included so that judging results can be returned to the entrant.

We accept only an entry for which no delivery signature is required by us to receive it.

7. To facilitate anonymous judging, each of the three photocopies must be accompanied by a removable cover sheet bearing the artist's name, address, telephone number, and an identifying title for that work as well as an email address if available. The photocopy of the work should carry the same identifying title, and the artist's signature should be deleted from the photocopy.

The Contest Administration will remove and file the cover sheets, and forward only the anonymous entry to the judges.

8. To be eligible for a quarterly judging, an entry must be postmarked no later than the last day of the quarter.

Late entries will be included in the following quarter, and the Contest Administration will so notify the entrant.

9. There will be three co-winners in each quarter. Each winner will receive an outright cash grant of U.S. $500, and a certificate of merit. Such winners also receive eligibility to compete for the annual Grand Prize of an additional outright cash grant of $4,000 together with the annual Grand Prize trophy.

10. Competition for the Grand Prize is designed to acquaint the entrant with customary practices in the field of professional illustrating. It will be conducted in the following manner:

Each winner in each quarter will be furnished a specification sheet giving details on the size and kind of black-and-white illustration work required for the Grand Prize competition. Requirements will be of the sort customarily stated by professional publishing companies.

These specifications will be furnished to the entrant by the Contest Administration, using Return Receipt Requested mail or its equivalent.

Also furnished will be a copy of a science fiction or fantasy story, to be illustrated by the entrant. This story will have been selected for that purpose by the Coordinating Judge of the Contest. Thereafter, the entrant will work toward completing the assigned illustration.

In order to retain eligibility for the Grand Prize, each entrant shall, within thirty (30) days of receipt of the said story assignment, send to the Contest address the entrant's black-and-white page illustration of the assigned story in accordance with the specification sheet.

The entrant's finished illustration shall be in the form of camera-ready art prepared in accordance with the specification sheet and securely packed, shipped at the entrant's own risk. The Contest will exercise due care in handling all submissions as received.

The said illustration will then be judged in competition for the Grand Prize on the following basis only:

Each Grand Prize judge's personal opinion on the extent to which it makes the judge want to read the story it illustrates.

11. The Contest shall contain four quarters each year, beginning on October 1 and going on to January 1, April 1 and July 1, with the year ending at midnight on September 30. Entrants in each quarter will be individually notified of the quarter's judging results by mail. The winning entrants' participation in the Contest shall continue until the results of the Grand Prize judging have been announced.

12. The Grand Prize winner shall be announced at the L. Ron Hubbard Awards Event to be held in the year subsequent to the year of the particular Contest.

13. Entries will be judged by professional artists only. Each quarterly judging and the Grand Prize judging may have different panels of judges. The decisions of the judges are entirely their own and are final.

14. This Contest is void where prohibited by law.

ENTER THE COMPELLING AND IMAGINATIVE UNIVERSE OF
WWW.BATTLEFIELDEARTH.COM

Discover the exciting and expansive universe of *Battlefield Earth*, which has an arsenal of features, plenty of content and free downloads. Here are a few highlights of what's in store for you:

- UNIVERSE—Find out about the different characters, places, races, crafts, weapons and artifacts that make up the universe of *Battlefield Earth*. Also discover the major events that led up to the discovery of Earth by the Psychlos, and the technology that they have used for hundreds of thousands of years to terrorize the galaxies and crush their enemies.

- COMMUNITY—As a member of the *Battlefield Earth*® community you have access to free downloads, including screensavers and desktop wallpaper.

- TRIVIA—Do you know:
How the Psychlos discovered Earth?
What element is lethal to Psychlos?
Where the Brigantes originate from?

**NEXT TIME YOU'RE ON-LINE
ENTER THE <u>BATTLEFIELD EARTH</u> SITE—
WHERE L. RON HUBBARD'S MASTERPIECE
OF FICTION COMES ALIVE!**

Mission Earth
BY
L. RON HUBBARD
The ten-volume action-packed intergalactic spy adventure

"A superbly imaginative, intricately
plotted invasion of Earth."
—*Chicago Tribune*

An entertaining narrative told from the eyes of alien invaders, *Mission Earth* is packed with captivating suspense and adventure.

Heller, a Royal Combat Engineer, has been sent on a desperate mission to halt the self-destruction of Earth—wholly unaware that a secret branch of his own government (the Coordinated Information Apparatus) has dispatched its own agent, whose sole purpose is to sabotage him at all costs, as part of its clandestine operation.

With a cast of dynamic characters, biting satire and plenty of twists, action and emotion, Heller is pitted against incredible odds in this intergalactic game where the future of Earth hangs in the balance.

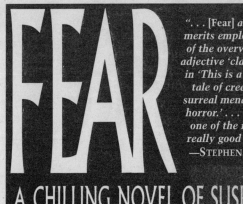

FEAR

A CHILLING NOVEL OF SUSPENSE

"... [Fear] actually merits employment of the overworked adjective 'classic,' as in 'This is a classic tale of creeping, surreal menace and horror.' ... This is one of the really, really good ones."
—STEPHEN KING

Professor James Lowry doesn't believe in spirits, or witches, or demons. Not until one gentle spring evening when his hat disappears, along with four hours of his life. Now the quiet university town of Atworthy is changing—just slightly at first, then faster and more frighteningly each time he tries to remember. Lowry is pursued by a dark, secret evil that is turning his whole world against him while it whispers a warning from the shadows:

If you find your hat you'll find your four hours. If you find your four hours then you will die. ...

L. Ron Hubbard has carved out a masterful tale filled with biting twists and chilling turns that will make your heart beat faster as the tension mounts through each line of the story— while he takes a very ordinary man, in a very ordinary circumstance and descends him into a completely plausible and terrifyingly real hell.

Why is *Fear* so powerful? Because it really could happen.

Paperback: U. S. $6.99, CAN $9.99
Audio: U. S. $15.95, CAN $18.95 (2 cassettes, 3 hours)
Narrated by Roddy McDowall
Call toll free: 1-877-8GALAXY or visit www.galaxypress.com

Mail your order to:

Galaxy Press, L.L.C.
7051 Hollywood Blvd., Suite 200, Hollywood, CA 90028